CALL OF TITAN

A FANTASY ADVENTURE

PAUL MOUCHET

PAUL MOUCHET PUBLISHING

CONTENTS

Dedication   VI

1. Raiders in the Night   1

2. The Rite of the Way   12

3. The Call of Titan   25

4. To the City of Aarall   32

5. The Temple of the Fist   45

6. Sister Nevara   51

7. Combat Training   59

8. Brother Rime   66

9. Sister Miyuki   70

10. Theology Class   74

11. Sister Gale   79

12. Fall From Grace   92

13. The Rite of Abandonment   99

14. The Mountain   106

15. The First Day   110

16. Tracks in the Night   115

17. The Final Day   119

18. The Aftermath   128

19.	Amilta, the Lost Daughter	135
20.	A Hopeless Quest	144
21.	The Wolf in the Girl	149
22.	An Unwelcome Return	156
23.	The Captain of the Guard	163
24.	The Cheeserie	168
25.	Sammuel F. Larder	173
26.	Karim	177
27.	The Blue Yeti	181
28.	On the Scent	189
29.	A Deeper Problem	195
30.	No Rest for the Weary	200
31.	Brother Powder	204
32.	The Village by the Sea	208
33.	The Long Trek Home	214
34.	Through Berrat Eyes	219
35.	Mangy Wolf Hunt	226
36.	Indigo Willowbrook	231
37.	Trapped	235
38.	The Wolf Spirit	243
39.	The Hut in the Woods	252
40.	Resonance	260
41.	Betrayal	265
42.	Where There is Life	269
43.	Hunter Hunt	275
44.	Instinct and Courage	278

45.	From the Beyond	284
46.	Jaycob and the Wolves	290
47.	Return to the Hut in the Woods	297
48.	The Reunion	303
49.	The Return to Aarall	309
50.	Reporting to the Captain	316
51.	The Captain and the Wolf	320
52.	Homecoming	328
53.	Reporting to the High Priest	333
The Story Continues...		338
Amaruq – The Wolf Spirit		339
Afterword		364

To my wife, who believes in me, even when I struggle to believe in myself.
Without her support and infinite patience, I would have never realized my
dream of becoming an author.
And, to my big sister Louise, thank you for helping me bring my stories to life.

Chapter One

Raiders in the Night

"Out of my way, human," the Berrat boy of fourteen years said as he pushed Kit from behind, knocking the nine-year-old girl to the ground, sending her face-first into a pile of leaf litter. "You don't belong here."

Kit set her jaw and looked up at the boy. The light of the bonfire danced across his face, giving him a menacing appearance. "It's my village, too, Coltyr. I wasn't bothering anybody."

"Your being here bothers us," Alyn said, stepping in beside his friend. Both boys were bare chested, wearing leather trousers decorated with colorful beads and small shells. "Run into the forest. If the wolves don't get you, the slavers will. Either way, we'll be rid of you."

Kit's gut twisted as the pair hovered over her. Since her arrival as a baby, she had never done anything to harm anyone, and yet, the villagers refused to accept her as a member of the community. Children and adults alike looked at her with disdain, just because she wasn't Berrat. It wasn't her fault she was a human. She had done nothing to warrant their hatred. All Kit ever did was try to fit in.

"I'll tell Old Sky Eyes," she said, thrusting her chin out at the pair. "I'll tell him what you did and you'll both be punished."

"Leave, both of you," Kit's mother, Riva, said as she neared, putting herself between the child and her tormentors. The tiny woman's bone-white braids reflected the flames of the bonfire, making them stand out against her deep bronze skin. Riva pinned her pointy ears back as she bared her teeth at the boys and hissed. "I don't care who your parents are. I swear by the great spirits, if you continue to torment my daughter, I will deal with you myself."

"You don't scare us, witch," Alyn said, stepping towards the woman. "My father says you both should have been run out of the village. Her, for being a human and you, for bringing her here. I'd likely earn a feather if I was the one who finally got rid of you."

"We both would," Coltyr said. "Take your abomination and leave."

Kit picked herself up off the ground and moved in beside her mother. Riva, a Berrat woman in her early thirties, wrapped her arm around the child. In spite of Kit's young age, she was already significantly taller than her mother and the two boys tormenting her.

"Leave her alone," Riva growled. The deep rumble in her voice startled Kit. Her mother had always been there for her, to watch over her, to protect her, but she'd never heard her make that noise before. "Bother her again and I'll make you wish you'd never been born. Do you understand me?"

The boys withered under the woman's glare, each of them taking a slow step back. "Your mother won't always be there to protect you, human," Alyn grumbled. "And my father will hear of your threats, witch. You'll be sorry."

As the woman and child made their way through the gathered villagers, Riva pulled Kit close. "You need to stay away from those boys. They're nothing but trouble." And with that, they took their place on the ground before the nightly bonfire, its warmth a welcome respite from the chill night air. Those that were seated nearby picked themselves up, glowered at the pair, and moved away.

Kit's chest heaved as she fought back tears. She didn't understand why the villagers were so cruel to her. The little girl shivered as she clutched her fists against her body. "Ananak," she said, a term of endearment Berrat children used when speaking to their mother or grandmother, "I'm cold."

"Come closer, Kitten," Riva said, holding out her arms for the young girl. Her pointy ears twitched as her adopted daughter climbed onto her, snuggling against her for warmth. "You're getting much too big to make a nest on my lap," she said with a loud grunt, feigning that the child was crushing her.

Kit's huge brown eyes immediately welled up as her mother brushed an errant strand of ebony hair from her face. The girl pulled her knees up to her chest and wrapped her skinny arms around them, trying to make herself as small as possible.

"But I'm only nine," Kit said as she batted away her tears. When her child tried to climb off, Riva wrapped her arms around the little girl, holding the small human tightly to her tiny Berrat body, tickling Kit until she screeched out in delight.

"Nine years? Are you really that old, Kitten?" Riva asked, trying to catch her breath after laughing for so long. "I remember when I found you, you were barely bigger than a peanut."

Kit reached down to pick up the toy she had dropped. She stroked the long black hair that adorned her tiny doll's head. "Why is my hair black instead of white like yours and everyone else's?"

"Why do you ask me this question over and over? Your hair is black because you are Nomad. I am your mother, but you are not my child. A Nomad woman is your birthmother."

"Is that why everyone teases me? Because I don't belong here?"

"You do belong here," Riva replied as she fought back her own tears. "They tease you because they think you're different. Their parents should teach them better."

Kit's jaw tensed as she gave her mother her best frown. "I'll show them, Ananak. I'll show them I'm part of the community. I'll show them I belong here."

Riva hushed her daughter as Elder Achak, Alyn's grandfather, took his place before the community. The man's gray hair had many shoulder-length braids, with eagle and hawk feathers interwoven throughout. Like the other warriors, he was wearing a tanned leather vest and breeches with brightly colored dried berries and shell decorations. His heavily weathered skin resembled well-aged hide, telling the story of many years spent in their harsh northern climate.

"It has been nearly two moons since the last slaver attack," Achak called out, the roaring blaze of the nightly bonfire at his back. The dancing flames jumped high into the night sky, creating an ominous lighting effect, making the village elder appear wreathed in fire. "Our vigilance has paid off, and I believe it's time to relax the rules and return to our old ways," he bellowed, eliciting cheers from the younger members of the community. Kit's stomach tightened as a smug smile crossed his face. She imagined that Alyn would look just like his grandfather when he was older.

"We. Are. Berrat!" Achak shouted, running his fingertips over his long, pointed ears. "We are small of stature, but we are a force of nature. No other race on Orth can spirit bind with the northern animals, making us the most fearsome of all the northern peoples." Again, the younger villagers cheered at the elder's words.

Old Sky Eyes, often considered the wisest elder in northern Berrathia, held up his hands, calling for silence. Like Achak, he was old and weathered, and he wore similar light leathers, but he had only one single braid of steel-gray hair that went well past the middle of his back. He wore no adornments of any kind. Though he was quite short and bone thin, the old man had a quiet confidence about him. Most Berrat had eyes of green or gray, but his were brilliant blue, reminiscent of a clear summer's day sky.

"Achak is quite right," the elder intoned in his calm, soothing voice. "Our vigilance has paid off." Shouts of anger and distrust from the youth quickly drowned him out. It was Old Sky Eyes who had forced this nightly bonfire ritual upon the villagers, and to hear him say that he agreed with Achak made Kit want to vomit. She couldn't understand how he could side with the man. Sky Eyes paused, patiently waiting for silence.

"Each night, the community gathers before the great fire. It lights our village. It brings us together. It helps to keep us safe. It has been two moons since our last attack, but until the slavers have been stopped, we cannot become lax in our ways." The older villagers nodded in assent, while the young shook their heads and quietly cursed the village's leader.

With a deep sigh, Sky Eyes moved his hands rapidly in front of himself, forming intricate patterns with his fingers. As he did, tiny wisps of white smoke formed in the air in front of him.

"Behold," he called out with dramatic force. As he spread out his arms, a vision of Orth appeared above him, slowly rotating, the illusion catching reflections of the fire behind him, making it look like the world was ablaze.

"We are a miniscule village in a vast kingdom." As he said the words, the kingdom of Berrathia lit up with a bright red marker and showed their location next to the great North Sea.

"We live in harmony with the land, but there are those who would do us harm. They seek to remove us from our homes for reasons we cannot fathom."

"We are small, but we are mighty," a young man yelled from the assembly. "We have the great spirits to protect us."

With a wave of Sky Eyes' hands, the illusion disappeared. The elder closed his eyes for a moment before he spoke further.

"We can be fierce, especially those of us who have taken a warrior spirit, like that of a great bear, a wolverine, or a wolf." Sky Eyes paused for a moment, as even the young were agreeing with him now. "We are Berrat and our connection with the animals of the north makes it possible for us to spirit bind with them, and to take their form at will."

Cheers from young and old alike met the old man's words. Again, the elder waited patiently for the community to become silent.

"But who among us has done that? Raise your hand and stand before us." There were a few villagers who seemed as though they wanted to raise their hand, but in the end, nobody came forward. After a few minutes, Old Sky Eyes addressed the community again.

"We are losing our ability to bind with the animals; to shift into their form, and that is why we must remain vigilant. We Berrat can escape from danger and survive; it is what we do best. It has allowed us to endure the countless times the gods have ravaged our lands. We survive by avoiding conflict, but to avoid the slaver raids, we need to know they are coming."

"Your magic will protect us," one of the women called out. She was clutching an infant to her breast and her eyes shone with adoration for the elder.

Sky Eyes smiled and bowed his head slightly. "Gaia has blessed me with powerful magic, but I am just one man, and I am old and tired. I cannot protect you like I could when my back was straight and my bones didn't ache with each step I took."

"You have led us for too long!" a Berrat warrior exclaimed, stepping forward to challenge the elder's words. "I am Ahiga. I and mine will defend our village, like we always have."

Kit growled at the sound of the man's voice. Ahiga was Alyn's father, and the leader of the village warriors. Riva shushed her daughter, stroking her hair.

"How many of your warriors did you lose in the last raid?" Sky Eyes asked him, his voice calm with a touch of steel to it. "How many of the community were stolen from us?"

Ahiga's face hardened as he tried to find a suitable retort. In Kit's eyes, the man suddenly appeared small. Several of the other warriors taunted him to speak up. Instead, he lowered his eyes.

"None of us doubt your bravery, Ahiga, but the slavers don't come straight at us. They sneak in under the cover of darkness. They spirit away the young without anybody knowing. If you can't see them, you can't fight them," Old Sky Eyes explained.

"You are an old coward, Sky Eyes!" shouted Elder Achak. "You would have us cower and hide while the rest of Orth lives on! You..."

Before Achak could finish, two arrows struck the elder in the chest, cutting his words short. Ahiga turned to see from where the arrows had come, and was struck by two arrows of his own, one in the chest and one in the throat. Blood poured out from the wounds, turning his bronze skin scarlet.

"Take cover!" Sky Eyes yelled. He scanned the trees, looking for the attackers. As he did, three arrows sailed just over his head, missing their mark and landing in the bonfire behind him.

Kit's head swiveled about as she searched for the attackers. She fought against her mother's hold on her, desperately seeking out the raiders.

"Polar fire," Sky Eyes yelled. Immediately, his body glowed with a pale blue aura, and an exquisitely crafted short bow appeared from nowhere in his left hand. As he drew back the bowstring with his right, an ice-tipped arrow materialized. He released the arrow at an unseen target in the treetops. A moment later, a human dressed in black linens fell to the ground, the elder's arrow embedded in his heart.

In the mayhem, people were screaming and children were crying. Raiders came crashing out of the trees in groups of four, their dark clothing helping them blend into the shadows. While the slavers attacked and killed the Berrat men, others were snatching up the women and children, grabbing them by the hair, dragging them off into the night.

One raider, a tall, lanky man, his face covered in scars, had captured five children, pulling them by their long white braids. The children were squealing and clawing at their captor, but he was undaunted by their attacks. As he was about to pull them into the cover of the forest, Kit caught sight of them. Pulling herself away from Riva, she raced to the bonfire and grabbed a flaming branch as thick as her arm.

With Riva behind her, yelling for her to return, Kit unleashed a war-cry as she raced towards the abductor, swinging her flaming branch wildly. The man laughed at her as she barrelled towards him. Showing no signs of fear, Kit leapt through the air and brought the flaming branch down onto the side of the man's head, lighting his greasy, dirty blonde hair on fire.

The raider quickly relinquished his grip on the children to squelch the flames, allowing his captives to escape. Meanwhile, Kit readied herself for another attack.

The children stood motionless, staring at their rescuer with their mouths agape. Kit waved her arms and screeched at them at the top of her lungs. "Run! Run and hide. I won't let him near you!"

The raider bore down on Kit as she swung her flaming stick in front of herself, desperately trying to keep him at bay. "You'll fetch a handsome reward at auction," he said, a foul grin on his face. With an open hand, the man struck the small girl in the cheek, sending her sprawling, her flaming branch tumbling out of reach.

As her attacker moved closer, his arm outstretched, hatred burned within Kit's chest, blurring her vision, igniting a fury unlike any other. He grasped the child by the hair, dragging her to her feet. "We'll beat the spirit out of you, child. If we can't, you can fight in the pits."

The tiny protector felt no fear, only rage. The slavers were a menace. They tore people from their families. They killed any who fought back. She didn't care if they ended her life, she would not go quietly. The young girl kicked wildly, while dragging her nails over the man's wrist. With a cry of pain, the slaver released his grip, but his prey didn't run. She only took a few steps back and balled up her tiny fists, preparing herself for another attack.

"You can't have me," she bellowed. "I'll stop you. I'll stop you all."

"The pits it is," the man said with a sadistic grin as he closed the distance between them. "I'm going to enjoy watching you being gutted."

Three arrows struck him in the stomach, chest, and face in rapid succession, cutting off his words. The raider garbled something incomprehensible before he fell face-first in the dirt at Kit's feet. She spun around to see Sky Eyes duck between two of the huts, likely in pursuit of other raiders.

Riva snatched Kit by the wrist and dragged her off towards the village's main lodge. The child swung her fists at her mother several times before realizing who had her.

"I freed them," Kit yelled as tears flowed down her cheeks, creating streaks over her dust-covered, deeply tanned skin. "He was going to take them, but I stopped him."

"I know, Kitten. I know," Riva said as she hurried for cover. She was about to rush through the entrance of the community lodge when two village elders blocked their way.

"She is not welcome here, Riva," the elder growled, practically spitting each word into the woman's face.

Riva pushed Kit behind her, shielding her from the man's words.

"You should have left with that *thing* many years ago. The humans are a curse to us, stealing our family, destroying our way of life. Look what they've done. She is one of them."

The elder held a bone-dirk in his hand. As he drew it back, his mouth fell into a hate-filled sneer and the corded muscles in his arm twitched.

"Anoki!" Sky Eyes bellowed. His magical bow disappeared, instantly replaced by a wicked-looking dagger. "You would dare threaten our own?"

"She is not of our blood. That child is an abomination!" Anoki's eyes were wild, spittle flying from his mouth as he shrieked at Sky Eyes.

"That abomination, as you call her, just saved five younglings, including your granddaughter!" Old Sky Eyes had seen well over seventy summers, but he still moved like a great cat, with power and grace in each stride he took. Though Anoki stood nearly a head taller, the elder bore down on him with a look of deadly intent.

"I didn't know," Anoki stammered as he dropped his dirk to the ground. "She's not of our blood."

Kit buried her face in her mother's neck and cried uncontrollably. "There, there, my sweetness," Riva said, trying to soothe the child and calm her fears.

Sky Eyes gave Anoki one last look of admonishment before he magically replaced his dagger with a short bow and disappeared back into the night.

As Riva led her child into the great lodge, Kit cringed while the eyes of the villagers fell on her with hatred and distrust. Some of the people whispered as they walked past, while others openly hurled insults at the Berrat woman and her Nomad child.

Kit ground her teeth together as fury raged in her belly. No matter what she said or did, they would always hate her. It wasn't fair.

"Ignore them," Riva said as she led Kit to the rear of the lodge, positioning herself and her daughter safely between two thick wooden pillars.

From behind her mother, Kit peered out, finding the venomous gaze of those who stood nearby, their expressions filled with malice. "Why do they hate us?" she asked, barely getting the words out through her sobs.

"Because they are fearful," her mother replied, struggling to keep her voice calm. "You are not Berrat, and I brought you into the village. Many people fear what they don't understand."

Riva cupped the back of her daughter's head and drew her in close to herself. For an hour, they stood in silence, wondering when the raid would come to an end. As the rest of the community continued to gawk and murmur amongst themselves, Kit's anxiety continued to build. What lengths would she need to go to before her village would accept her?

"We have driven off the intruders," a village warrior decreed as he entered the lodge, holding the severed head of a human raider in his hand. "They will regret their decision to attack."

The community met the words with cheers and adulation. Several other blood-splattered warriors joined the first, pumping their fists into the air, celebrating the moment.

"There is nothing to cheer about," Sky Eyes interjected as he pushed through the crowd. "They have taken at least seven of the community, and many more were killed."

Silence immediately fell on the group. Sky Eyes spotted Riva and Kit at the back of the lodge. He motioned for them to join him as he worked his way to the center of the room. At first, Riva held her position, but she eventually brought her child to meet the leader. Sky Eyes held out his hand, beckoning Kit to stand beside him.

"If we are to celebrate anything," Sky Eyes declared, "we should celebrate what our community member, Kit, has done this night."

The assembled Berrat responded with hate-filled murmurs and jeers at the elder's words. Nobody was willing to speak out directly against Old Sky Eyes, but they made no effort to hide their objections.

"This child, all by herself, rescued five other children. She had no one to help her, no one to protect her, and..." the old man's eyes drifted over each and every villager, "no one to support her, beyond her mother. In the face of overwhelming danger, she put aside her fears and came to the younglings' defense."

The people seemed unsure of themselves. Their murmurs continued, but their objections appeared to be lessening.

"From this day, she will be forever known as Kit Standing Bear, for she is the embodiment of our most revered warrior spirit, The Great Bear!" Sky Eyes declared.

"Only the greatest of warriors are bestowed such an honor," Elder Anoki spat out. "You have gone too far, Sky Eyes."

Anoki, along with the elder who had tried to block Riva's entrance, stormed out of the lodge, drawing the warriors and a good number of other villagers along with them. Sky Eyes shook his head in disbelief before he turned back to the few remaining villagers in the lodge.

"Thank you," he said, lightly bowing his head to each member. "Go now, comfort those who have lost a loved one this night. Be there for one another."

Chapter Two

THE RITE OF THE WAY

~ One Year Later ~

As Kit lay on her back and gazed up at the stars, she saw above her The Hunter, The Healer, The Wise One, and The Warrior. For the Berrat, it was the night called the Rite of the Way, a time of spirit guides and pathfinding.

This was the night when all children ten years of age are accompanied by their fathers to a place special to their family; in the mountains, the forest, or the meadows. After having fasted for a full day, each child is taken to this sacred location and left alone, with their father watching from a safe distance. Through the night, each child waits for the Great Spirits to reveal which path in life they are to follow.

"Ananak, why do I have no father?" Kit had asked her mother this many times, but she never received an answer to the question. "All the other children have fathers with them."

Riva looked down at Kit, her eyes filled with sadness. "I have not wanted to share my secrets with anybody," her mother said slowly, carefully choosing each word before she spoke. "But on this night, your Rite of the Way, I will answer all your questions."

Her mother's lower lip started to quake, and her fingers fidgeted while she tried to find the words. With a hitch in her voice, she said, "Not long before you came into my life, our village was raided by slavers. They killed many of us and took many more into captivity. I was one of those who were taken."

Kit's heart ached as the pain of recalling the memory took hold of Riva. "Ananak, if the memories cause you pain, I don't need to hear them."

"They are painful," she responded, taking a deep breath to help steady herself, "but you do need to hear this." Casting her eyes up to the heavens, she continued the story.

"While in captivity, one of the vampire guards had found me attractive. Rather than let me be sold off, he decided to turn me and take me as his mate. Sweet Gaia, he was so strong. He easily overpowered me, sinking his teeth into my neck. At first, it hurt. A lot. But a moment later, the excruciating pain passed and in its place was a profound sense of peace and belonging. I thought that's what happened when a vampire turned somebody, but when the guard pulled himself away from me, my blood dripping down his chin, he looked terrified. His eyes were wide, and he babbled nonsense at me. A moment later, he rushed from my cage, leaving the door wide open. I bolted from my cell, along with every other person in there with me. We were immediately set upon by guards, but I managed to escape. I was too afraid to look back. I didn't want to see what was happening to the others. I just ran as fast as my feet would take me."

"Ananak, are you... a vampire?" Like so many other times in Kit's life, the words came tumbling out of her mouth before she had a chance to consider what harm they might cause. But, in that instance, her mother just smiled and let out a thin, nervous laugh.

"A vampire? No, I was not turned that night. I don't know why, but I wasn't." Riva ran her hands over her pant-legs, as though trying to remove invisible wrinkles. "When I made it home, I told my tale, exactly as it happened, to the village elders. They sent me to the shaman to be inspected. She took me into a sweat tent, where we stayed for what felt like hours. I told her the tale, and while I did, she prayed and called to Gaia to protect me. Just before we were done, she told me that my experience had left me barren, but before the moon was full, I would have a child."

Kit was only ten years old, but she understood the significance of the shaman's words. "How could you have a child if you are barren?" she asked. Her mother had never spoken so openly to her, and she was afraid to break the spell, but again, the words were out before she could stop them.

"I didn't understand either," Riva laughed. This time her laugh was genuine. "But, as predicted by the shaman, it happened." Before continuing, Kit's mother closed her eyes. "It was a moonless night. I was laying in my cot when I heard the cries of a baby outside the door to my hut. I opened it to see what was happening. There was nobody there. Again, I heard the cries, but they were further away. I walked between the huts, following the wails as they continued to move away from me. Panicked, believing a child was being abducted, I ran through the darkness. Before I knew it, I was a good distance away from the village, at the edge of the forest."

Riva's eyes were still shut, but her expression changed to that of pure joy. Kit could swear that she could actually feel what her mother was feeling.

"When I entered into the forest," she continued, "I saw a light. It was warm and inviting. It drew me to itself. As I got closer, the light became brighter. I was filled with peace, tranquility and, most of all, love. A voice so sweet and caring said to me, 'On this night, I entrust unto you, my child. Where I must go, and what I must do, she cannot come. But know this, good Riva, she will change the world, for Gaia has foreseen it.'"

Kit could barely breathe. Gaia, the earth god, the great spirit, had spoken of her to her birthmother? "Ananak, what happened next? What did my birthmother look like? Did she actually speak with Gaia?"

"I don't know what your mother looked like. She was bathed in a brilliant white light, making it impossible for me to see her. I can't say for certain if she spoke with Gaia, but she told me that she had." Riva was looking up at the sky as she finished the tale. She turned her gaze back on Kit. "The next thing I remember, I was walking into the village with a bawling baby in my arms." She smiled warmly at Kit. "That would be you, Kitten."

"What happened next? Did you take me to see the shaman?"

Riva's face went dark. "No, Kitten, I didn't. I didn't get a chance to. By the time I had returned, many of the villagers were awake. You were making enough noise to raise the dead." She laughed lightly at her comment. "When the elders saw me, they took you away from me, stripped you of your clothing, and examined you from head to toe. Because you were not Berrat, they did not want you in the village. And..."

"What, Ananak? What?"

"They claimed you were an abomination. You had 'growths' between your shoulder blades, thin, nearly imperceptible ridges. They were about to take you away when the shaman came out from her lodge. She insisted you be returned to me at once. There was a heated discussion, but in the end, I got you back. Reluctantly, they allowed us to stay in the village."

"Oh, I see," Kit replied. Her heart was breaking. She could hardly breathe. "That's why everyone hates me?"

"No, my sweetness, my Kitten. They do not hate you... they fear you."

"But I'm just a girl! Why would they fear me?" Kit practically shouted at her mother, her blood boiling with rage.

"Hush now, my Kitten," Riva took her child's hands into her own. "Almost everyone fears the unknown. The circumstances of your arrival were, well, unprecedented." Riva abruptly ended the story. "It's time to end the questions. I must leave you now so that you may continue with the rite."

"Ananak, please don't leave me. I'm... afraid."

Riva reached into the small satchel that she carried over her shoulder. She produced an ulu, a wolf-bone utility knife, commonly used within the tribe. "Here," she said as she offered it to her daughter. "Keep this with you. It will keep you safe."

Kit held the knife in her small hands. Surprisingly, it fit perfectly. She examined it closely, turning the small blade to look at each side. It was old, incredibly old, indeed. "Thank you, mother. Was this your knife when you were young?"

"It is the very knife I held when I went through the night of my own Rite of the Way," she said. There was a tinge of, something, in her voice.

"Tell me about your rite, mother." Riva shook her head in reply. "But you said I could ask you anything this night and that you would answer me."

"After. After you have completed your Rite, I will tell you."

"Now! Tell me now, please, Ananak. You promised."

"Okay, I'll tell you, but only because I promised..." Riva took a deep breath, and tears welled in her eyes. "My experience was, difficult." Her eyes were practically pleading Kit not to ask for more information. When Kit didn't stop her, Riva reluctantly continued. "During my Rite, I, too, was frightened, and my father gave me an ulu to hold onto, the very same ulu I just gave you. I took the ulu and clutched it close to myself while my father moved away, watching me from afar. I waited and waited for my spirit guide to come. I waited for so long that I fell asleep. The sound of a bleating sheep woke me from my deep slumber. It startled me, and when I jerked to sit up, I cut myself on my ulu. I grasped my hand, trying to staunch the bleeding. When I raised my eyes, the sheep was standing before me, its face only inches away from my own. I took her face in my hands, accidentally smearing my blood all over it. The pain in my hand vanished immediately. The cut was gone and so was the sheep."

At this point, Riva was deep into her story. Her eyes had practically glazed over as she continued. "My father came running to my side, his eyes wild. 'A blood covered sheep!' he yelled. 'You were visited by a blood covered sheep!' I tried to explain what had happened, but my hand was healed. The cut was gone. When we returned to the village, he forced me to tell the elders. I tried to tell them what had happened, but my father interrupted, continuing to present the story as he had witnessed it."

When she looked at Kit again, there was fire in her eyes. Hate. "My father. My own father would not believe me. The elders would not believe me. My father's version spoke of an omen, an ill omen, and that my life would be forfeit. I was to be slaughtered, and with me, many of my family and tribespeople."

"But why? Ananak, why wouldn't they listen?"

Riva dropped her chin to her chest. She had resigned herself to the fate that they had decreed. "We are a superstitious people, Kitten. We believe in many things. Some are true, and some are the ravings of lunatics."

Kit wrapped her small arms around her mother's neck, taking her in a warm embrace. "I'm glad Old Sky Eyes let you come with me tonight."

"You have no father," her mother said. "If he didn't let me come, you'd have missed out." She pulled away from Kit's embrace, lightly brushing the hair away from her eyes. "Old Sky Eyes, he is the wisest elder in our village, perhaps the wisest in generations. He sees what others do not. He sees you, Kitten. The others did not want you to partake of the ritual, but he overrode them all, for you."

Riva stood up and smiled. "Enough stories. The night is nearly over. Dawn will be upon us soon and you have not yet begun the ritual. Little piece of my soul, my little Kitten, when in doubt, listen to your heart. It will always speak the truth, even if it isn't what you want to hear. Now, may your path be revealed unto you, and may it lie straight and level before you." She pressed a small stone into Kit's hand. "Last night, I dreamed that I gave you this stone." She gave her a quick kiss and ran to a location far enough away for Kit to be alone, but close enough that she could keep an eye on her.

⸎⸎⸎◈⸎⸎⸎

Kit waited while her mother took up her position. She could barely see her in the distance. Knowing that Riva was watching over her, Kit thought of all that had been said that night. What path did she want to take? Would it be one of the Great Four, or would it be one of the many paths in-between? Kit was drawn to the path of The Warrior, and yet part of her yearned to help, like The Healer. With a deep breath, she put her worries aside. She calmed her breathing and quietly listened to her heartbeat as it mingled with the quiet of the cool midsummer's night.

It was not clear how much time had passed before the full moon emerged from behind the clouds and bathed the clearing in a soft, golden glow. The beating of strong wings drew Kit's attention to a tree limb high above. From the lofty perch an eagle peered down. A slight rustle to her right revealed a white-tailed hare eating from a small bush of bearberries. Hares were never active at night. It was far too dangerous for them. A shiver ran down her spine. There was a soft scraping of leaves and bark far in front of her, and as she turned to see what was making it, Kit caught a glimpse of a sizable black shadow moving in the shrubs to her left.

A fisher, a large weasel-like creature, launched towards the rabbit.

Without a second thought, Kit threw the stone in her hand at the hare, who, startled at the sound, ran off and vanished just before the fisher landed on the now empty space. It swiveled its head towards Kit and hissed.

A chorus of shrill cries from a nearby bush startled the fisher. Its head swiveled between Kit and the bush. The animal was being forced to choose between protecting its babies and exacting revenge on the girl who had spoiled its hunt. The fisher hissed again before dashing towards its bawling kits, its long body and thick tail working in harmony as it wove its way towards the brush.

The sudden appearance of a wolverine cut its escape short. The encounter was brief and vicious, with the wolverine opening up the underbelly of the fisher with a single swipe of its wickedly clawed paw. Without thinking, Kit jumped onto the larger animal. Using her ulu, she slashed open its throat. The wolverine was dead within seconds. Kit was about to pick up the wounded and unconscious fisher when the eagle screeched out a warning and launched itself from its perch. The heavy beat of its wings heralded its imminent arrival. Kit paused for barely more than a breath when the voice of Riva came through to her. "Listen to your heart."

"No!" Kit roared. "You can't have him!"

Kit threw herself over the fisher, shielding it from the eagle's attack. Pain blossomed in her left arm as the eagle's claws found purchase. Kit had come between an eagle and its meal. She waited for the raptor to turn its attack on her, but it never came.

With her heart thundering in her chest, Kit slowly raised her head and faced the bird. The eagle, with its bright yellow beak and pale golden eyes, stared back at her intently, intelligently. The clouds obscured the moon for a moment and the eagle shimmered. It became translucent. As the moon reappeared, the bird's form became opaque.

"Are you my spirit guide?"

The eagle continued to stare down at Kit, its head turning slightly. It adjusted its grip on Kit, causing a new, intense pain to rip through her arm.

What does one say to a Spirit Eagle?

"This fisher has hungry children. I do not want them to be without a mother, without someone to care for them. They'll die otherwise."

The eagle cocked its head slightly.

"I would have died without a mother, without anyone to take care of me." Kit wasn't sure if that was the right thing to say, but the eagle continued to stare at her, so she continued. "I don't know if the wolverine also had hungry children, and if it did, I'm deeply sorry. But the fisher's babies are here, and it would have eaten them, too. If you are hungry, there is the wolverine." She moved her head towards the dead animal.

To Kit's surprise, the eagle flew over to the wolverine's carcass and slowly fed, all the while keeping its eyes trained on Kit.

The fisher stirred beneath the small girl. The creature had been gravely wounded. Kit had no herbs, no poultice, and she knew no spells. She went to the bearberry bush, hoping to feed the baby fishers a berry mash, but the bush was covered with moths. Bear moths, by the dozens! They swarmed past Kit as she approached and then covered the dying fisher. They stopped its bleeding, vanishing into the wound. For a few moments, the fisher appeared to float above the ground, and then it awoke, standing on its four legs.

The fisher paused, its eyes darting between Kit and the eagle. It stood motionless, as though holding its breath, waiting.

The hare appeared before Kit, holding her polished stone in its mouth. It stood before her, staring at her with its beady, black eyes. With a flick of its head, it tossed the stone at Kit's feet. For several seconds, it stood motionless, staring at the young girl. The rabbit twitched its nose and bowed to Kit before crossing over to the fisher. The fisher immediately killed it and shred it into small pieces. With deliberate care, it carried the pieces to its babies to eat.

Kit dropped to her knees, filled with a sense that a great lesson had unfolded before her. Even if she could only understand a small part of it, she was confident that one day its meaning would become clear to her.

The spirit animals vanished, one by one, until only the eagle remained. It hopped across the ground until it stood directly in front of the young girl. It slowly reached out and picked up the stone with its great yellow beak. It made a strange piping sound and tossed the small, smooth stone into the air. As it hung in the air, a swarm of bear moths enveloped it, their tiny beating wings fluttered briefly around the stone before it fell into Kit's hand. The eagle and the bear moths vanished in a blinding flash of moonlight.

Kit turned to find Riva behind her, shaking badly.

⁂

"Ananak!" Kit's eyes were wide with wonder. "Did you see that?"

Her mother grabbed Kit firmly by the wrist and gave her a shake. "I saw nothing. You saw nothing. You will not speak of this. Do you hear me? Do you? You will not speak of this."

Kit yanked her arm out from her mother's grasp.

"I will NOT be silent," she stated, challenging her mother. "The Blessed Four, all of them, came to me! All of them! I deserve to know what this means!"

Riva cast her gaze to the ground, her reaction crushing Kit's heart.

"Don't you want to know what it means, Ananak?"

"I know what it means, child. You think the gods have blessed you. That's what you think, but you're wrong. They haven't blessed you; they've cursed you! I have seen so many futures for you, Kitten, and there is blood and death awaiting you in so many of them. Let others give themselves to the gods to play with! You will say that nothing happened, do you hear me? Nothing happened!" Riva shook with fear, sorrow, and anger.

A strange chill ran through Kit, blowing upon her heart, and awakening her own cold anger. Old hurts surfaced. Slights that she had suffered from childhood acquaintances and neighbors. "I can't ever be the Berrat child you wanted me to be! You took me in. You gave me your love, and for that I will be eternally grateful! But this tribe hates us both! Do you think my experience is going to make it worse? Do you want me to lie to protect myself, or to protect you?"

Riva slapped Kit so hard that she staggered backwards, lost her balance, and fell awkwardly to the ground. Tears streamed down the girl's face. She put her hand to her cheek, her fingers lightly brushing her stinging skin. Her lower lip trembled. It was as if her mother had stabbed her in the heart with her ulu.

Kit cringed. It occurred to her that, in a way, her own words were sharper than any knife could ever be, and it was too late to take them back. In that moment, she wished that she could.

Where did that anger come from?

"You…" wailed Riva, "are not of my womb, but you are my heart and my soul, even if you hate me. I cannot stop you from telling the truth. For your own sake, leave. It may keep the tribe, and you, safe. Go! Being god-chosen does not mean your every step is blessed, or that your path will be painless. I will tell the elders that I fell asleep, and that when I awoke, you were gone."

Kit sat motionless as her mother walked away. She was torn. She didn't know what to say or do. Her words tasted like ash in her mouth. After several minutes, Kit chased her mother down the mountainside, wailing for her to stop and wait.

In the distance, fathers and children were walking back towards the elders' camp. Their torches flickered like tiny bobbing fireflies in the darkness.

She continued racing hard to catch up with the Berrat woman. Regardless of how Kit felt, Riva was her mother. She had saved her, raised her, and nurtured her. Kit would do anything for her.

When she finally caught up to Riva, she took her hand in her own. "I'm sorry, mother. I love you. I will do as you say. I will remain silent." She stared up at her mother and waited for a reaction. She looked for a signal, something, anything, that said that everything was alright. Riva kept her eyes forward.

Kit's heart was breaking, the pain stabbing at her chest, but she knew that she was only getting a small piece of what she deserved. The two walked in silence while Kit clutched her mother's hand.

When they reached the elders' camp it was still night, with the Blessed Four still shining in the sky. The elders sat in a row, Old Sky Eyes in the center, and two others on either side of him. The fathers and children were seated in front of the elders. They all stared at Kit and Riva, who were the last to arrive.

Sky Eyes called each child by name. In turn, they presented themselves to the elders. Their fathers walked with them and stood behind them. Sky Eyes asked each child about what they had experienced. Their fathers were there to verify their stories.

The spirits had chosen a few of the children to be gatherers, several to work in crafting, a couple to teach and one to be a storyteller. Three of the children were chosen to be hunters, and finally, one to be a warrior, a warrior who was apparently needed elsewhere.

The warrior's father limped slowly forward, tearfully reporting that the Bear Spirit had taken his son that night. He had watched as they ascended to the stars. Old Sky Eyes looked with pity upon the man, feeling the pain he was enduring.

"The Bear is the most powerful of the warrior spirits," Sky Eyes said with reverence. "If he needed a sacrifice, your son, then he took him with cause. Something is coming. There is no other reason for this. Your son's life is the price for the Bear's protection over us. We thank you for the great service your son has provided to our community this night."

The rest of the elders echoed the sentiment.

At last, it was Kit's turn. Old Sky Eyes motioned her forward. She wasted no time taking her place before him, getting down on one knee. Kit bowed to each of the elders, and finally to Old Sky Eyes himself. Her body relaxed at the warm, reassuring hand of her mother on her shoulder. Without a single word, she offered Kit her love and support.

Finally, Old Sky Eyes spoke. "Kit Standing Bear. You have been raised as one of our own, yet you are not Berrat by birth. I would be lying if I didn't say there were some who did not think you worthy of taking part in the Rite of the Way, but I overruled them. All of them." He chuckled as he eyed the other elders. "So, tell us, child. What happened tonight? What path has been opened to you?"

Kit lifted her head to speak but paused when her mother cleared her throat.

"She is ashamed to speak, Oh Wise One, so I will speak for her." Riva paused and took a slow, deep breath and shook her head. "Nothing happened. Nothing at all."

A murmur rippled through the assembled Berrathians. The other elders grinned smugly.

"Quiet!" shouted Old Sky Eyes. His steely gaze fell upon the young girl. Kit could have sworn his eyes held a glint of laughter. "Is this true, Kit?"

This moment marked one of the few times in Kit's life that her brain overrode her mouth. She considered the elder's words carefully. If Kit said yes, then she would have lied, and it would insult the spirits that manifested to her. If she said no, she was disobeying her mother, potentially causing undue pain and suffering to the person she loved more than anything. With no answer seeming to be the right answer, Kit chose to say nothing at all, clamping her mouth shut before words, unbidden words, came spilling out of her mouth. She was about to stand and walk away when the heavy beat of wings made her pause.

An eagle made of moonlight landed on Kit's knee. She was soon joined by the hare, the fisher, and the wolverine. Hovering above Kit's head was a cloud of bear moths. Behind, Riva sunk to her knees, sobbing quietly.

A warm wind blew, taking the moonlight spirits with it. Those assembled were quiet, except for Old Skye Eyes, who clapped his hands and rose from his place on the ground, wrapping his arms around Kit.

"Anyone who still thinks this child here is no true Berrat can leave right now."

The assembled people remained silent, motionless.

"What does it mean, Wise One?" Kit asked.

Old Sky Eyes considered the question as he let his gaze fall upon the other elders, and the gathered community. "Never have I heard of a child being chosen by The Healer, The Wise One, The Hunter, The Warrior, and The Great Spirit herself. What does it mean? It means that all paths are open before you, Kit Standing Bear. Your path is your own to choose, and you are not bound to any."

Sky Eyes took Kit gently by the chin, tilting her head up so that he could look into her deep brown eyes. "They show a remarkable faith in you, young Kit."

"She will leave us. I have seen it." Riva's voice was hoarse. She turned away, unable to bear the meaning of her own words.

Sky Eyes rubbed his chin and frowned slightly. "Maybe she will, maybe she won't. The choice is not mine, nor yours, nor the spirits'. It is hers and hers alone."

Riva nodded slightly.

"Riva," asked Sky Eyes, "are you still having the same visions?"

"They have never stopped."

"Visit me tomorrow," he said with a slight bow. "We can speak of it at length."

Kit rose and wandered among the other children. They all kept their distance from her. "Spirit-touched," some of them murmured, making the sign against evil.

That was the night when Kit's life changed, everything bringing her here, to this moment, under the signs of the Blessed Four.

CHAPTER THREE

THE CALL OF TITAN

Over the next two years, life only got harder for the little human. The villagers, young and old alike, openly taunted Kit, calling her names, insisting she was unworthy of the title 'Standing Bear.' While Riva did her best to shelter her child from the onslaught, Kit met it head on, refusing to back down, refusing to cower.

The young nomad had just celebrated the anniversary of her eleventh year with her mother. She was at the outskirts of the forest, just beyond her village's compound, playing with the small doll Riva had made for her. In the toy's tiny hands, it held a battle hammer in its right and a shield in its left.

"Stand back," Kit yelled at a nasty looking weed, pretending it was a vicious monster for her doll to fight.

"I am Kit Standing Bear, and by Gaia's hand, I will smite thee." Kit giggled wildly as she thrashed the tall, spindly weed with her doll's miniature battle hammer.

"Enemies are easy to defeat when they're make believe," Alyn said with a hate-filled sneer. He was now a young man of sixteen years. He was bare-chested and well muscled with various adornments, including an eagle feather woven into his white braids, marking him as a warrior. The whites of his eyes stood out in stark contrast to the black stripe that ran across his face.

"I wonder how tough you are now that there's no one here to protect you," Coltyr added. He was shorter than Alyn, with long white hair tied over his head in a top knot. Like his friend, he was also bare-chested, but he wore no adornments nor markings on his face.

Kit stole a quick glance past the young men to the outermost huts. They had cut off any chance of her running home. Straightening her back, she stepped towards the shorter of the two aggressors, looking him square in the eye. "I must be tough enough that you felt the need to bring a warrior along. Is he here to protect you? Are you too afraid to face me on your own?"

The young man's gaze darted over to Alyn. When Coltyr swallowed hard, a tiny grin pulled at the corner of Kit's mouth. With a scoff, she held out her toy, waving the doll in his face.

"Maybe you'd like to fight against my dolly instead? Or maybe your friend here is going to fight for you?" The words came tumbling out before she considered the impact they might have. Kit knew better than to provoke these two, but in times of stress, her mouth was rarely attached to her brain.

With surprising speed, Coltyr snatched the doll from her hand.

"Look who needs a baby doll," he taunted, his voice mimicking the whiny tone of a child as he dangled the doll just beyond Kit's reach. "Whatcha' going to do, baby? Are you going to cry now?"

With equally surprising speed, Kit kicked Coltyr solidly in his crotch, making him drop her doll. He made a sad gurgling noise as he grasped onto his private parts before buckling to his knees.

Kit's head snapped to the side when Alyn struck her across the face with his fist. The young girl stumbled a few steps before she spun around to confront him. She wiped away a long streak of blood from the side of her lip, which was already beginning to swell.

Alyn picked up the doll and gripped its torso in one hand, its legs in the other. With a sneer and a twist of his wrists, he ripped the tiny figure in half and threw the pieces in her face.

Kit's heart sank as she looked down in dismay. It wasn't just a toy; it was a gift her mother had hand crafted for her. Kit slowly raised her chin, stopping when her gaze locked onto the smug-faced warrior. By Gaia, she hated him. He was the embodiment of every member of the community and the unrelenting cruelness they showed her. Her eyes narrowed. Her body trembled. Her lower lip quivered, but her nerve never wavered.

"Is li'l baby *Kitten* going to cry?" Alyn asked, pushing his hooked nose up to Kit's. "Is that what you're going to do, li'l baby *Kitten*?"

She tried to kick the young man, but he swiftly lifted his leg to block her attack. With his left hand, he struck Kit across the cheek. Red welts immediately rose up from where his fingers had made contact.

With a quick step to her side, Kit brought her right fist around in a swinging arc, and caught Alyn in the side of his head, causing him to stagger slightly.

"Don't you ever call me *Kitten*," she said as she moved in closer and rained down a flurry of punches, hitting the boy repeatedly in his face and shoulders.

A hard kick to her back knocked Kit to the ground, her face scraping across the damp, leaf-covered soil. She rolled over, finding Coltyr staring down at her with dead-looking eyes. The boy stood motionless, seemingly unsure of what to do next. Suddenly, his mouth twisted into a hate-filled sneer. With a grunt, he reared back and kicked the girl in the ribs with all his might.

Kit cried out, clutching at her side.

"C'mon Coltyr," Alyn said. "She's had enough. We need to leave before her mother hears her screams."

"She got what she deserved," he said, spitting on the girl. "Be thankful we didn't kill you, human."

Alyn grabbed Coltyr by the shoulder and dragged him away. With a laugh, the pair bolted back towards the center of the village, leaving Kit squirming in the dirt.

With the retreat of the two boys, the young girl crawled to her knees, her hands still pressed hard against her aching ribs. She scooped up the two halves of her doll from the ground and cradled them in her arms. Her fingers gently stroked the torn leather.

"I wish I could heal you."

Several tears dropped onto the lifeless body of her broken toy before Kit lost control of her emotions and she started to bawl. The young girl took off towards the forest, running aimlessly through the trees until she came upon a massive pine. After a quick look around to ensure nobody was following, she dropped to her knees and scampered under its expansive bows.

Clutching the broken toy to her chest, she cried herself to sleep.

⎯⎯⎯◇⎯⎯⎯

"Who's there?" Kit asked, standing at the edge of a steep cliff overlooking the Northern Sea. Her eyes were drawn to the horizon, across the vastness of the sparkling surface of the frigid waters.

She peered over the edge of the cliff. The sight of the rugged shore hundreds of feet below caused her head to spin. A brisk wind kicked up from across the ocean, pelting her face and hands with tiny shards of ice crystals.

"I am not afraid," Kit called out, standing a bit straighter. "Who are you?"

"I am your destiny," a deep, sonorous voice called back, echoing in Kit's mind. The hairs on the back of her neck suddenly stood at attention.

"I will make my own destiny," she called back, the words falling from her lips before her brain had a chance to consider them. The water beneath the cliff roiled and churned as a giant ice statue came bursting through the surface, growing until its face was even with Kit's. The statue was of a bare-chested man with frost-blue skin, and white, short-cropped hair and beard. Though intricately detailed, his eyes lacked any trace of life, imparting an eerie stillness. On his head rested a crown made of ice, carved to look like a ring of horns or perhaps great teeth. The deep scowl which cut into his granite-like features barely lasted a moment before his expression softened.

"It is time, little angel, for you to travel to the kingdom of Arnnor and pledge your loyalty to me," the statue declared, his mouth unmoving, his eyes unblinking.

"Why would I do that?" Kit asked, crossing her arms over her chest, thrusting out her chin.

The statue paused, as though considering what answer might best suit the defiant child who stood before him.

"If you will pledge your loyalty to me, pledge that you will free me from my icy prison, I will bestow upon you life everlasting."

"Nobody wants to live forever," Kit said, scoffing at the offer.

"If you can free me, what would you have me bestow upon you?" the statue asked.

She considered the question for a short while before a smile crossed her face.

"I know what I want," Kit declared, unfolding her arms and placing her hands on her hips. "I want the people of my village to stop hating me. I want to fit in."

"That is all you would ask in return for freeing a god?"

"I didn't know you were a god," she said, looking down at her bare feet as she wiggled her toes. "What's your name?"

"I am Titan, The Traveler," the statue boomed, causing Kit to stumble backwards as the face of the cliff sheared off and fell to the ocean below.

"I've never heard of you," she said, raising her eyebrows at the statue. "Gaia is the only one who watches over us. You are a liar and a false god."

"You are an impudent child," the statue said, perhaps with a hint of a laugh in his voice. "You will serve me well. Free me and everything you want will be yours. Awake now, little angel. Your journey is about to begin."

⌘

"Thank Gaia. You're safe." Kit's eyes fluttered open to find her mother, Riva, kneeling at her side. The woman's eyes were glassy as she looked down on her child. "We've been searching the entire village for you."

"I had the strangest dream. I dreamt a statue talked to me. He said his name was Titan, the Traveler."

Riva shook her head and drew her mouth into a deep frown. "No," she said, her voice cracking. "No. He can't have you. Not yet. It's too soon."

Kit didn't understand her mother's reaction. It was just a dream.

Old Sky Eyes took a knee beside the Berrat woman and placed his hand on her shoulder, gently stroking it.

"You knew this day would come, my dear Riva. You foresaw it in crystal clear detail."

"What did you see?" Kit asked as she sat up from the deep pile of pine needles on which she had fallen asleep. There were branches and twigs clinging to her clothing and her tangled mass of black hair.

"That it is time for you to leave," Riva said as she hung her head, the words becoming stuck in her throat.

"To leave?" Kit asked. She waited expectantly for a reply, but all Riva could manage was to nod her head.

"Where will we go?" Kit asked.

"You are to travel to the city of Aarall, in the kingdom of Arnnor," Riva replied. She seemed to be struggling to maintain control over her emotions. "You will seek out the Temple of the Fist, but I cannot come with you. This is something you must do without me."

"I won't leave you behind," Kit said, her brow furrowed. "I... I need you."

"Oh, sweetness," Riva sighed as she squeezed her daughter's hands in her own. She stared at the young girl as though trying to burn her image into her mind. "I need you, too. You've made my life complete. You've given me joy beyond anything I could have imagined, but this is what *has* to happen if you ever want to fit in."

Fit in? This was what she asked the statue for. More than anything else in the world, this is what she wanted. She hated being apart, despised and ridiculed just for being herself. But as she looked into her mother's tear-filled eyes, her desire faltered.

"I choose to stay with you." Kit looked at Sky Eyes. "Gaia said my path was my own to choose. That's what you told me. I don't want to leave my mother."

The elder smiled down at Kit. There was a profound sadness in his eyes. "You can choose to ignore the call of Titan if you wish, but the path laid before you will give you everything you want. A chance like this may never come along again."

"Little piece of my soul," Riva said. "I want nothing more than to spend all my days with you at my side, but I would ask you to trust me. Aarall holds the key to your destiny."

Destiny. That's also what the statue had said to her. Had her mother shared the same dream? How else could she have known this? Kit's gaze locked onto Riva's.

"You need to do this, Kitten," the Berrat woman said, tears pouring down her cheeks. "It breaks my heart, but I know it is the path you must take. You may not understand it now, but you *need* this."

As Riva spoke, it was as though a shutter had been drawn back and Kit suddenly saw the light. There was truth in her mother's words. She didn't understand how, or why, but she knew in her soul that this was the path she should take.

"What will I do there?" Kit asked, her eyes brightening. The idea of getting away and going on an adventure made her spirits soar, fueled with the hope that she may find a place where she would not be an abomination, where she would fit in and be welcomed.

"You are to become a Priest of Titan," Sky Eyes answered. Kit cocked an eyebrow at the elder, her mouth drawn up into a tiny grimace. Her reaction made the old Berrat laugh. "Priests are leaders who do great deeds in the name of their god."

"Great deeds?" The words inspired Kit. "What sort of great deeds am I to do?"

"You will..." Riva started, unsure of how to finish the sentence. She furrowed her brows as she considered the question. Averting her eyes, she finally responded. "You will discover that when you're older."

"Okay," Kit said with a shrug. "I will go. I trust you."

Kit, Riva, and Sky Eyes crawled out from under the bows. As they emerged, Kit held up the pieces of her toy as sadness shone in her large, brown eyes.

"They broke my dolly." Her voice cracked as she spoke the words. "I tried to save her, but they were too strong for me."

Old Sky Eyes caressed the back of Kit's head. "You will find that you cannot save everyone, Kit. It's a hard lesson to learn, especially for one so young. Prepare for your journey, your time is at hand."

Chapter Four

To the City of Aarall

Kit said her goodbyes to her mother and Old Sky Eyes. Riva had wanted to accompany her daughter on the trip, but Sky Eyes intervened. The elder had assigned an experienced guide named Jeger to accompany her to the border of Arnnor, insisting that, for Kit, the journey was as important as her destination.

"Look, the little baby is running away," Alyn said. "Running away to hide with her people."

"You're a coward," Coltyr added.

Perhaps this was exactly what Sky Eyes meant when he told her she'd face trials on her journey, and those encounters would help her to grow, making her better prepared for her quest to free Titan. If dealing with these two bullies was the worst of her challenges, she felt she had little to be worried about.

"You're going to die," Alyn said, stepping closer. "You likely won't even make it out of the forest."

"And then you'll be sorry," Coltyr said, joining his friend, doing his best to appear intimidating.

"I'll be sorry I'm dead?" Kit asked. "Passing to the Beyond would be a small price to pay to never have to listen to you two ever again." The young girl looked to her guide, Jeger, for some support, but the man wouldn't even look her way. "While I'm away, I guess you'll have to find somebody else to torment. Maybe my mother can make you another dolly to rip in half."

"I'll kill you if you ever come back," Alyn said, narrowing his eyes. "I swear to Gaia, I will slit your throat and watch the life bleed from your eyes."

"If you want me to leave, maybe you and your shadow can get out of my way. Or maybe you two cowards would like to gang up on me one last time before I'm gone."

"Enough," Jeger said, stepping in front of the pair. "You've had your fun and I want to get this journey over with."

And with that, the guide pushed the two bullies out of the way and headed off, not bothering to check if his charge was following. Kit offered Alyn and Coltyr once last sneer before she followed, fully expecting one last attack from the boys. To her surprise, they simply turned and walked away.

The mountain range that surrounded the city of Lilloet extended south for many miles, rearing up on either side of the valley like great white-haired sentinels. The mountain's gray foreboding rock face stood in stark contrast to the vibrant emerald-green grasslands and the deep sage-green hills covered in majestic northern pines.

"Is Owl's Dell a big city?" Kit asked as she bent down to pick a delicate blue and yellow wildflower, almost losing her balance under the weight of the knapsack she was carrying. "I've never been to a city before. Are they beautiful?"

"We won't get close enough to see the city," Jeger replied dismissively. "It's out of the way and I don't want to spend one minute longer with you than absolutely necessary."

Ignoring her guide's surly demeanor, something she had a lifetime of practice doing, Kit scampered through the waist-high flowers, letting her hands drag along their tops. She squealed quietly to herself and squatted next to a patch of vivid yellow blossoms. They had tall, slender stalks and bright green leaves. "These flowers smell like honey," she said, burying her face in the thick mass of blooms.

Jeger turned back and scowled. The deep bronze skin of his face and bare chest glistened with sweat. The hunter wore his braids so tightly that they pulled his face back and made his eyes appear perpetually narrowed. Though he bore none of the painted markings of a warrior, he did wear the bones of a beast around his neck, an honor typically reserved for warriors.

"If you can't move faster, I'm going to leave you here for the wolves," Jeger called back to Kit, his bone necklace clacking against his bare chest. "With such long legs, you should be faster."

"I'd be faster if you weren't making me carry this pack," Kit yelled back as she tried to get her tangled mess of black hair out of her face. "It weighs as much as I do."

"Sky Eyes insisted I prepare you for the journey," the young hunter yelled as he broke into a run. "I am to accompany you to the port city of Cormorant, at the kingdom's border. By the time we get there, you will be strong enough to finish the rest of the journey on your own."

For several more hours, Kit followed the hunter as he wended his way through the countryside. Though Kit could hardly catch her breath, Jeger appeared as though he could run forever. After nearly two more hours of running, with her lungs burning so intensely that Kit feared she might pass out, the Berrat man finally slowed to a walk as they approached a small copse of birch trees with a fast-flowing stream running through it.

"We'll stop here for the night," Jeger said, cupping a handful of the ice-cold water from the stream. It was just one of many that they had crossed on their journey from Lilloet to Owl's Dell.

"Prepare our camp and I'll hunt for food," Jeger said as he wiped his hands on his leather pants.

"Why not let me hunt?" Kit asked as she let the heavily laden pack drop from her shoulders.

"I've seen you try to use a bow," Jeger replied, shaking his head. "We would starve if I left the hunting up to you."

"If I can't hunt, how will I feed myself when I travel from Cormorant to Aarall?" she asked, her hands placed firmly on her hips.

"Fine," Kit's guide said, throwing his hands up in exasperation. "String your bow and let's move."

Despite the amount of noise Kit made, and her dreadful aim with her bow, they managed to take a small feral pig.

"Eat your fill," Jeger said as he sliced a hind leg away from the heavily charred carcass that roasted over their campfire. "We can't keep any of this meat with us while we sleep, otherwise we'll have every scavenger within five miles on us."

The pig was quite small, but there was more food than they could stomach. After an hour of gorging, Jeger threw a large pile of small sticks onto the fire, causing it to erupt into flames, consuming the remainder of the meat.

"Don't let the gizmos get you," Jeger sniggered with a mean-spirited laugh as he closed his eyes, the light of the fire casting him in a ruddy, golden glow.

Kit had never seen a gizmo, but the adults spoke of them like they were animal-demons, ready to snatch up disobedient children in the night. Supposedly, the gizmos were some sort of Berrat-animal hybrid. They walked on two legs like a Berrat, but, in every other way, they resembled their animal half –wolverines, white foxes, or gray wolves– and they were all mindless beasts that killed indiscriminately.

As Kit lay her head down on the cold, makeshift bedroll, she clutched the razor-sharp blade of her ulu, the bone knife her mother had lovingly given her for protection. The weight of loneliness pressed upon her heart like an insurmountable burden, and tears welled up in her eyes as memories of her mother's warm embrace flooded her mind.

She could almost feel Riva's soft touch, hear the gentle lullabies she used to sing, and smell the comforting scent of her mother's hair. The realization that those tender moments might be gone forever tore at Kit's soul, leaving her feeling small and vulnerable in the vastness of the world.

In the silence of the night, Kit's prayers to Gaia were desperate and heartfelt. "Please, Gaia, watch over me. Guide me through this darkness and protect me from the shadows that haunt my dreams."

The tiny weapon in her hand served as a tangible reminder of her mother's love and strength. It was both a source of comfort and a painful reminder of the separation they now endured.

As exhaustion overtook her, Kit's eyes grew heavy with unshed tears. She clung tightly to the ulu, finding solace in its familiarity, as she allowed herself to succumb to the depths of sleep. In her dreams, she sought her mother's embrace, desperately longing for the warmth of her love to fill the void in her heart.

⌘

It took Kit and Jeger the better part of a moon to travel from Lilloet to Owl's Dell. There were no roads between the two cities and the broken terrain made for slow travel. Each night, Jeger gave Kit lessons on how to use her bow, but she barely showed any sign of improvement, at least, that's the way she felt with the way her guide constantly berated her efforts.

The next stretch of their journey would take them to the kingdom's capital city of Taseko, which had been under slaver control for many years now.

"If you cannot use your bow to hunt, I'll have to teach you how to forage," Jeger said, his frustration with Kit coming through loud and clear.

Over the next moon, while they traveled along a well-established set of dirt roads between Owl's Dell and Taseko, the pair covered ground at a much faster pace. Jeger continued to hunt for his food, while Kit foraged wild roots, plants, and berries for herself. Several times along the way, the pair had to quickly duck for cover when they spotted bands of human slavers carting their Berrat prisoners to the market.

"Why don't we free them?" Kit asked as she peered out from the tall summer grasses. "There are only four slavers with weapons."

"I am no warrior," Jeger said, slowly shaking his head. "I may be able to bring down one or two, but it's not worth the risk. They are not of our tribe."

"What does it matter which tribe they belong to?" Kit growled. "They are people, like us. If you walk away, you're no better than the slavers. If you're not going to try to save them, I'll do it myself."

When she pulled out her ulu, the hunter groaned.

"You can't attack four grown humans with just your ulu. Give me your bow," Jeger demanded as he pulled the arrows from his quiver. He jabbed each one into the soft ground in front of him before silently stringing Kit's bow.

"We will probably die," he said as he handed Kit her weapon. "I have a family and I'm going to die trying to help strangers."

"The strangers have families, too," Kit said, her eyes fierce. "Is yours more important than theirs? How can you face your family knowing you let these people be taken like this?"

Jeger's eyes became dark as he stared at the young girl next to him. With deliberate effort, the hunter nocked an arrow as he ground his teeth.

"You aim for the two slavers on the left," he said, looking through the tall blades of grass. "I will take the ones on the right. Don't wait to watch your arrows. Shoot, nock, and shoot again. Don't stop until you've exhausted your arrows or until they are all dead."

Kit nodded as she nocked her first arrow and drew it back. Her hands trembled as she raised the arrow tip towards the slavers. She had never tried to kill someone before. These were people too, even if what they were doing was evil.

"Three... two... one," Jeger whispered. When he finished his countdown, they both released their arrows. As instructed, Kit didn't bother watching to see if she had hit her target. She quickly snatched up another arrow, nocked it, and took aim. The two men she was to shoot at were both running full speed towards them with long blades in their hands. She stood and released another arrow, then quickly reached for another. She raised her arrow tip to aim again. There was only one man running at her now. Kit released her arrow, grabbed another, and nocked it. She raised her bow again, ready to shoot, but there was no one there. Had she shot them both?

"We need to make sure they're dead," Jeger said, drawing his ulu as he bolted from their place in the willowy grasses. With remarkable speed, the man raced ahead of Kit, disappearing for a moment in the grass, and reappearing again seconds later. By the time Kit had her blade drawn, Jeger was at the wagon.

Kit's heart was beating so hard that she feared her chest might explode at any moment. She took long, deep breaths to try to calm her shaking hands.

"You did surprisingly well, Kit," Jeger said as she arrived at the wagon. Her face reddened at the compliment. It didn't take her guide long to free the Berrat prisoners, three young men, two women and four children. Unlike the people of Kit's tribe, these Berrat had mousy-brown and black hair, and even though they were speaking Berrat, she had difficulty understanding what they were saying.

After several minutes of broken conversation, one of the captives, a woman of perhaps thirty years, began speaking in *Sprak*, a common hand language shared among all tribes. The woman's gestures were changing so quickly that Kit could only make out a few of her words. Jeger seemed able to understand, although his own gestures were much slower and less precise. The freed slaves appeared to be explaining the safest route home, and how to avoid the slaver patrols.

After expressing their gratitude, the Berrat captives were off, returning to their homes. Jeger returned to the fallen slavers, retrieving the spent arrows.

As the pair resumed their journey to Cormorant, Jeger was quieter than usual. He appeared lost in thought while he walked along side the young girl. Finally, after an hour or so of silence, the hunter spoke up.

"Watching you today," Jeger said, his brow furrowed. "You are the bravest child I have ever seen. You deserve the title of Standing Bear. I did not believe Sky Eyes' words. I did not believe that you had saved the children. Today, I know it to be true."

That tiny bit of recognition settled warm in Kit's chest, and for the first time since she'd left her village, she didn't feel quite so alone.

⟪⟫

While passing through a small forest, the pair spied a family of brown bears, a mother and two young cubs. "Gather branches," he said, gesturing to the towering trees surrounding them. "We need to start making more noise as we move through these woods. If there is one bear family here, there will be more." When Kit gave him a questioning look, her Berrat guide shook his head. "These bears don't want anything to do with us. If they know we're coming through, they'll give us space."

"What about wolves or... gizmos? Don't we want to stay quiet, so they don't find us?"

"Well," Jeger said with a laugh, "then you'll have weapons at the ready. Either way, we'll be better off."

Eager to impress her guide, Kit scouted the area and soon found a thick, sturdy branch. She tugged at it with determination, finally wrenching it free from the tree's grasp. Proudly, she presented it to Jeger, her eyes shining with anticipation.

Jeger examined the branch, nodding appreciatively. "A fine choice, Kit," he commended, before swiftly snapping it in two with a controlled motion. Kit's eyes widened in surprise, and she watched as he handed her the two pieces.

"Now, listen closely," Jeger began, his voice filled with both wisdom and excitement. "These two parts can be clacked together to create a loud noise, scaring away any bears that may cross our path. But they can also serve another purpose."

Intrigued, Kit leaned in, her curiosity piqued. Jeger continued, "These broken halves can be wielded as weapons, like the kali sticks of old. With proper technique, they can aid in defending ourselves against any foe who may threaten us."

With patient guidance, Jeger demonstrated the basics of fighting with the kali sticks, showing Kit how to hold them, how to strike, and how to defend. Kit listened intently, her eyes gleaming with fascination, even if her movements were somewhat clumsy.

As they practiced, Kit's laughter filled the air, mingling with the sound of clacking sticks. Her swings were wild and unrefined, but the child's enthusiasm was boundless.

When the lesson concluded, Kit was breathing heavily, a mix of exhaustion and excitement coursing through her veins. She gazed at her teacher, her eyes shining with gratitude. "Thank you, Jeger," she said, her voice sincere. "Even if I'm not very good at it yet, I appreciate the lesson. I feel safer."

For the first time, Jeger smiled warmly at the girl, his rugged face softening. "You're welcome, Kit," he replied, his voice brimming with affection. "Remember, it's not just about skill. It's about the courage to face the unknown and the willingness to learn. You have shown me both today."

With renewed energy, Jeger and Kit continued their journey. The clacking of the kali sticks accompanied their every step, a symbol of their shared experience and the growing bond between the guide and his young charge.

⁂

The rest of the journey from Taseko to Cormorant went without incident, despite it taking them well over a moon to get there. The Berrat slaves they freed had given them valuable information on how to avoid the raiders who patrolled the area. They had also told them of game trails that would keep them off the main roads and take them on a shorter path to the port city of Cormorant.

"May Gaia watch over you and see you safely to your destination," Jeger said as they reached the northern border between Berrathia and Arnnor. "My instructions were to bring you to the border, which is what I've done. But if you ask me to, I will stay with you until you reach Aarall."

"Thank you, Jeger," Kit said with a shy smile, an unexpected warmth spreading through her chest. Nobody outside of her mother and Old Sky Eyes had ever treated with her with such respect. "With what you've taught me, I'll be okay."

"Head south from here, until you reach the stone road. Follow it south all the way to Aarall. Be wary of those you see along the way. Not all humans are as honorable as you."

The last compliment was more than Kit could bear. She quickly turned and trotted off through the grass, hiding her tears from Jeger. After she had a chance to clear her eyes, she turned back and waved.

"Thank you," she called out again before she sprinted off.

⁂

After two weeks of heading south along Arnnor's north road, Kit spied an enormous statue carved into the side of a great mountain that overlooked a massive city to its west. The statue was nearly identical to the visage of Titan from her dream. He was a bare-chested man with pale blue skin. The top of his head was snow-covered, with a crown of large icy horns protruding from it.

She smiled to herself. Her journey was nearing its end. It was midday, but if she hurried, she could arrive before nightfall. Picking up her pace, the young girl charged along the road, only slowing when the human city came into view. The closer she got, the more Kit's heart raced. She took a deep breath, wiped her hands on her legs, and pressed forward.

Bright, colorful tents lined the road as Kit approached. People of all races were trading in goods, with payment often being made in the form of small metal disks. She spied one man who appeared to be packing foods into large, woven baskets. He was a Southerner, with skin so dark that he could have been carved from a block of ebony. His bright brown eyes spoke of someone who was both kind and intelligent.

He rubbed his short, curly black hair and gave Kit a sad smile as she approached him. The man may have been significantly overweight, but beneath his ample rolls, he was extremely well muscled. His bright blue linen shirt was bursting at the clasps, straining to keep his body covered.

"Are you hungry, little girl?" he asked, holding out a small loaf of bread. "Please, take it," he said as he pushed it towards her. "No charge." The man's eyebrows rose high as he motioned yet again for Kit to accept his gift.

"You're very brown," Kit said as she took the loaf.

"And you're very dirty," the man replied, flashing his pearly white teeth.

Kit's eyes lit up when she bit into the fresh roll. It may well have been one of the tastiest things she had ever eaten. Famished, she stuffed the bread into her mouth faster than she could swallow it.

"Easy there," the man said. "No need to rush. I have more if you're hungry."

Kit smiled at the man so broadly that her cheeks extended out past her ears.

"My name is Comden," the kind man said as he pulled out another loaf of bread. "What is your name?"

"I am Kit Standing Bear," she replied, swallowing hard to push the large chunk of bread down her throat.

"I am to be a Priest of Titan," she continued, accepting the second loaf with a broad grin.

"A Priest of Titan? Oh, you best be hurrying along then. The Temple will be closing its doors soon." Comden advised.

Kit gave the man another bright smile before she scampered off towards the city entrance, stuffing the bread in her mouth as she ran along.

When she arrived at the gates of Arnnor, she was exhausted beyond comprehension, and so filthy she could have easily been mistaken for a walking pile of muddy rags. At least the loaves of bread had sated her hunger.

The twelve City Watch guards manning the city's main gate harassed Kit as she tried to enter.

"State your business, street rat!" one of them bellowed at her. "Aarall is no place for beggars!" The man towered over Kit. He was wearing brown leather armor, trimmed in white. On his left breast was a white patch emblazoned with a red castle-tower. With his tanned skin, long black hair, and dark brown eyes, Kit may have considered him handsome, but his behavior marked him as heinous to the core. Without missing a beat, Kit straightened herself, and jutted her chin at him in defiance.

"I am Kit Standing Bear, and I am here to serve my god, Titan!" she declared, speaking in the common tongue, something her mother had been teaching her since she was four years old. This was yet another reason for the villagers to hate Riva. The common tongue was the language of humans, who forced everyone else to learn if they were to do business with them. One of the guards roared with laughter at her declaration.

"You wish to seek asylum at the Temple, street rat?" he asked with a guffaw. "Off with you now before I crush you under my boot." And with that, the surly guard unleashed another bout of raucous laughter.

While the obnoxious guard was in the midst of his hysterics, a mountain of a man came stalking out of the guardhouse. He, too, had tanned skin, brown eyes, and long black hair. The colossal man stepped away from his post and bore down on the guard tormenting her.

"That will be quite enough out of you, Corporal Karr," the huge man growled. "We are here to serve the citizens and protect this city. The captain does not pay us to intimidate children." The big man motioned to a woman struggling to keep her four children under control while she pushed a small cart filled with winter wheat. "Help get her supplies to wherever it is she's going. I will teach you to respect the citizens if it's the last thing I do."

As the corporal skulked over to the woman and her misbehaved children, Kit's protector gave her a warm smile. It seemed that, even in this wondrous place, people were cruel and mean-spirited. She had hoped, now that she was with humans like herself, she would be treated kinder and with more respect. It seemed that would not be the case. If she was going to free Titan, she'd be doing it on her own.

"I am Lieutenant Harding of the City Watch. Is it your wish to visit the Temple of the Fist?" Kit stared up at the man and nodded. "If you would like, I can guide you there. The city streets are not a safe place for a young girl such as yourself to be wandering aimlessly about."

Kit doubted the kindness the man was showing her. He was dressed like the other guard, and though he had just stood up for her, she paused. Just as she was about to refuse his help, the lieutenant cocked an eyebrow at her.

"I am certain that you can make the journey on your own," he said, rubbing his stubbled chin thoughtfully, "but it will take us the better part of an hour to walk there, and I know the shortest route. The Temple locks its doors at sundown. If you lose your way, you'll be spending the night on the street."

Though his stern expression was hard like granite, there was also a glimmer of softness to the man. More importantly, his words rang true in her ears. Kit felt no deception, no ulterior motive. Whether it was instinct, or her desperate need for help, she couldn't be certain, but beneath the guard's imposing exterior, she sensed a heart she could trust.

"Thank you," Kit said. "Lieutenant is a funny name," she added when the man offered to take her by the hand.

"That is not my name. Lieutenant is my rank in the City Watch. Did I hear correctly? Your name is Kit Standing Bear?"

Kit stared blankly at the giant while she considered him, her head bobbing slightly in response to his question. The big man took a knee beside her making him appear less threatening. "Where are you from?"

"I am from Lilloet," Kit said proudly. "I am Berrat."

The lieutenant sucked in a breath at the girl's declaration. Had she misspoken? Was it a mistake that she spoke of her home, declaring herself to be a foreigner? He stared at her for several seconds, shaking his head before a deep sadness crossed his face.

"I see," he said, finally. "If you're from Berrathia, I'm guessing you have never been to a human city. Is that correct?"

"What is the City Watch?" Kit asked, ignoring his question. She wanted to know more about her new guide and her new home.

"The City Watch and the Temple work together to keep this city safe," he said. "I am a soldier. Something you might refer to as – a warrior."

The man was big and imposing, but he was not dressed like the warriors from back home. He had no face paint, nor did he wear any feathers or strung teeth. She would have a lot to learn in this city. It was not like her home.

"I want to be a warrior, too," Kit said, her eyes wide as she saw the man in a new light. "I am going to free Titan."

"I hope you do," Lieutenant Harding said as he stood and offered his hand. "But if you're going to do that, I first need to get you to the Temple."

Chapter Five

The Temple of the Fist

Kit barely said a word for most of the trip through the city, her mind racing, trying to comprehend what she was experiencing. She had never seen buildings made of stone and wood before. Some of the structures looked like they held more people than her entire village.

Most of the roads were made of stone, and the hooves of horses and the wheels of carts made loud staccato noises as they traveled along. Wolf-like creatures, called dogs, of different shapes and sizes roamed wild through the streets, waiting for people to give them scraps of food.

Kit wrinkled her nose and covered her mouth with her hand as they passed through Old Town.

"What is that horrible smell?" Kit asked, her voice muffled beneath her fingers.

"Tanners," Harding said, wrinkling his own nose at the stench. "They are curing leather to make it stronger. That other smell is from the Smelters, who boil down metals to be used for tools and weapons."

Kit didn't really understand much, if anything, of what the man was telling her, but she listened closely while her eyes continued to soak up as much of the city as they could.

From Old Town, they emerged into a much more pleasant place where the houses were not so densely packed together and there were even a few trees. As they continued along the roadway, they turned into the city square. Kit's eyes were immediately drawn to a massive staircase leading up to an austere building of white stone that was reflecting the oranges and reds of the day's dying light.

"The Temple of the Fist," Harding said with a hint of satisfaction in his voice. "This is the largest temple to Titan in all of Arnnor, possibly in all of Orth. Is this where you want to go?"

Kit stood in dumbfounded awe as she stared up at the massive building. She let go of the lieutenant's hand and walked silently up to the staircase. Expert craftsmen had carved the steps from single enormous blocks of stone, each one practically coming up to her thigh.

"This part of the journey is yours to make on your own," Lieutenant Harding said as he moved in beside her. "You will receive no assistance while you make your ascent. To do so would cheapen the experience."

"Thank you for your kindness," Kit said with a deep sigh as she adjusted the pack on her back. "One last mountain to climb before I rest."

"You won't find much rest while you're at the Temple," her guide said with something of a laugh. "But I trust you will find your way to Titan within those walls."

Without another word, Kit climbed up the first step, and then the next, and then the next. As she ascended, the wind became stronger, colder. The stairs felt as though they were turning into ice, biting at her hands and feet as she clambered her way to the top. As she finally crested the last stair, the monolithic Temple loomed over her. She wasn't sure if her knees were shaking from the climb, or if she was simply terrified. The wind continued to whip around her, its unrelenting cold chilling Kit to the bone. Her teeth were now uncontrollably chattering but the elements could not dampen her resolve, not with Titan's words from her dream ringing in her ears. Undeterred, she simply lowered her head and pressed forward.

There was still a good distance to cover, from the top of the staircase to the front doors of the Temple. The top landing, constructed of huge, flat stones, stretched out for hundreds of feet until it reached another smaller, broader set of stairs leading up to the Temple doors. As the dying sun caught tiny flecks in the stonework, it reminded Kit of her dream when she looked out over the North Sea.

The wind intensified as Kit walked across the stone expanse. With each step, the wind bit deeper at the small girl, seeking out every seam in her clothing. With each breath, Kit's lungs began to sting, forcing her to cover her mouth with her sleeve.

When Kit made it to the final few steps that led to the entrance, she paused before the highly polished black-oak doors, flanked on either side by two imposing statues.

On the left was an enormous white wolf with markings on its fur that resembled the tribal symbols she'd seen the Berrat warriors paint on their skin. The long ruff of its neck had multiple braids in it, adorned with small colorful beads. Across its shoulders was a golden yoke, as one might see on the back of an ox.

On the right was an even more imposing statue of a bald, cerulean-blue Frost Giant. His hair and beard looked to be carved from ice, and within his fist was a bone trident that stood even taller than the man holding it. Upon his shoulders were two massive, spiked pauldrons, tied together by golden chains. Thick golden bracers covered in runes adorned his wrists and ankles.

Pulling herself from her revelry, Kit's eyes scanned back to the black-oak doors. She hoped that she was not too late and that they had not yet been locked. The young girl shuddered at the thought. She didn't think she had enough strength to climb back down the stairs to find a place to sleep.

Before she had a chance to think further, one of the doors opened soundlessly and an ancient-looking man stepped out. His skin was dark brown and covered in thick, heavy wrinkles. His blue eyes, though quite bright, were set back deep into his skull. The wind whipped his white and silver robes about him, while his flowing gray ponytail and wispy chin whiskers flapped like pendants in a hurricane.

"Peace unto you, Kitten. I am Father Hoarfrost, the High Priest of this Temple. I've been expecting you."

"You were... expecting me?" Kit's eyes widened. "How? How do you know my name?"

"You are not the only person our god speaks to." The ancient man gave the young girl a toothy smile that soothed her soul. He took Kit's hand and guided her inside. The venerable man's hands were gnarled and old, but she could feel true power in them. A sudden warmth passed through her entire body, removing the chill that had settled deep in her bones.

"Old Sky Eyes would like you," Kit said as she allowed the man to show her into the building. "You both have the same-colored eyes."

Upon entering the Nave, Kit's footsteps echoed off the walls. Far above, in the darkness, Kit could hear wings beating, likely from birds that had found their way into the Temple but could not find their way out. The High Priest spread out his arms in a display meant to draw her attention to the grand size of the room. With a powerful, booming voice, the old priest declared, "Welcome to the Fist of Titan. May Titan's grace be upon you."

The people in the Nave stopped what they were doing, made a cross with their arms over their chests, and replied, "His peace unto you."

The old priest briskly moved Kit deeper into the Temple. Compared to the outside, the interior was dimly lit, and it took several minutes for her eyes to adjust to the change. All around were braziers casting a ruddy red glow which barely illuminated the area.

In the middle of the great chamber was a white marble statue of Titan. At well over forty feet tall, it was an impressive work of art, but it was barely a shadow of the great statue that overlooked the city. The carving depicted the same powerful man from Kit's dream, except for the manacles around the god's wrists, connected to the floor in thick iron chains. The expression on the face of the statue depicted unbridled rage, making it look like it was glowering at anyone who may have walked through the Temple's entrance.

Dozens of worshipers knelt before it, muttering muffled prayers. Some were young while others were hunched and worn with time. All were draped in off-white sackcloth robes that covered their bodies from neck to boot.

"What do the people pray for?" Kit asked. Her voice sounded extra small inside the grand room.

"They each have their own reasons," the High Priest responded. "Most hope to gain Titan's favor, but the truly devout ask for nothing. Instead, they offer their prayers for Titan, hoping he might someday be freed from his icy prison, deep in the North Sea."

Kit shivered at the thought of being stuck in a cage, deep beneath the surface of the freezing cold waters. Outside of her dream, she had never seen the North Sea, but she had felt the cruel bite of the wind that came down from it.

"Father?" Kit asked as she considered the old man's words. "Who trapped Titan? Why would someone do such a thing?"

"Those are questions that many wise people argue about daily, child," the old priest replied. "They are some of our faith's greatest mysteries."

Kit gave the old priest a sour look. "How are we to free him? Will he tell us where to find him?"

"The way to Titan is not easy, but it is clear. Work hard and listen even harder," Father Hoarfrost told the child. "The words of Titan are often no more than a whisper, and you must strain to hear them. But, as his servants, if we are just and true, and we have earned his favor, he does speak to us."

Kit had considered telling the old man that she had already heard Titan's voice, when a severe looking priest of perhaps fifty years came pacing towards them, interrupting her train of thought. The woman's back was badly hunched, and she had long black hair pulled back in a tight knot behind her head. She had the same dark skin as the other Nomads, but her nose was so crooked that Kit couldn't help but giggle at it.

"So, you are the new *recruit*," the woman said, looking at Kit from head to toe as she crinkled her nose.

"Kit," Father Hoarfrost said in a gentle tone, "this is Sister Nevara. She will be your teacher until..."

"Until I say otherwise, Father," Sister Nevara said with a scolding tone. "But before we do anything, this child needs to be scrubbed clean and shown to the children's communal dorm room. I want her fresh of skin and of mind when we begin our lessons."

As Sister Nevara led Kit away, Father Hoarfrost called out, "May Titan's grace be with you."

"May Gaia keep you safe," Kit called back, her eyes filled with concern.

"What did you say, young lady?" Sister Nevara said, giving Kit a shake in the process. "This is a Temple of Titan. We do not speak of false gods."

Kit was about to protest when the sister gave her another good shaking, dragging her off towards a stone stairwell at the back of the Temple.

"May the earth god watch over you, too," Father Hoarfrost said with a bit of a chuckle.

Chapter Six

Sister Nevara

In spite of Kit having her eyes shut tight, she could see the morning light streaming through a window. She shivered a bit and pulled her thin woolen blanket up to her chin. She could still smell the harsh soap that Sister Nevara had used to scrub her from head to toe. Her straw mattress reminded her of the bedding she had in Berrathia, but she was not enjoying the scratchy cloth that covered it.

A small noise from beside her bed roused the young girl. She opened her eyes and gave a tiny yelp.

Hovering over her bed were four of the strangest looking people that Kit had ever laid eyes on.

"I wonder why Sister Nevara brought a human to sleep with us *outcasts*?" a boy, who appeared to be Kit's age, asked. He was wearing the same sort of off-white sackcloth worn by the people she had seen in the Nave when she arrived. He appeared to be somewhat taller than Kit, with shoulder-length brown hair, pale skin that had a greenish tinge to it, and short pointed ears.

"We are not outcasts," replied an extremely tall girl, also dressed in the same sackcloth robes. The girl had to be twice Kit's height and her voice was deeper than the men of her tribe.

"In a city of Nomads, we are just that," said a short, thick-armed boy with a shadow of an orange beard.

"Give the poor girl some room," said a Berrat boy with a honeyed baritone voice. He was perhaps a year or two older than Kit. She furrowed her brow as she stared up at him. The boy had unnaturally bright red hair.

"Hello?" Kit said, blinking up at the small crowd gathered around her cot.

"Oh, look," someone said, calling out from behind the others. "The man-thing can talk."

Kit's eyes bugged out of her head when she peered out beyond those standing in front of her. Sitting on the bed next to her was a girl of some sort, with brown and white fur covering her body. Short, stubby spiral horns protruded from the top of her head. If Kit didn't know better, she would have thought this girl was a Berrat, mid-transformation into a goat.

"What sort of creature are you?" Kit asked, throwing her legs over the side of her cot.

The hairy girl became livid, making crazed bleating noises. She stood and pawed at the stone floor with her hooved feet and yelled, "I am not a *creature*! I am Tahr!"

Dropping her head, she charged at Kit, butted her in the stomach, and sent her crashing into the empty cot beside her.

"Iba, that's enough," the red-headed Berrat said as he grabbed the girl by the arm and wrestled her down onto Kit's bed. "I'm sure she didn't mean to insult you. She just got here."

Kit picked herself up off the rough stone floor and rubbed her ribs where the girl had head-butted her. "I'm sorry, Tahr, but you startled me."

Iba was thrashing under the Berrat's grip, bleating out words that sounded an awful lot like curses.

"Don't call her Tahr," the pointy-eared boy said. "That is her race name and to refer to her that way is rude. Her name is Iba."

"It's still better than calling her a mountain gizmo like most people do," the giant-sized girl said, making Iba struggle harder.

"I'm sorry, Iba," Kit corrected herself, wincing badly when she touched a particularly sore rib. "My name is Kit Standing Bear."

The red-headed Berrat's eyes widen. "You?" he said, shaking his head. "You call yourself *Standing Bear*?"

"It's a name given to me by my village elder," Kit said, suddenly feeling defensive.

"Where are you from?" the boy asked, his eyebrow cocked, giving him an irresistibly charming look.

"I am from a small village south of Lilloet," Kit said. "Where are you from? I've never seen a Berrat with red hair before."

"I," the boy said, giving Kit a broad grin, "am Dannith Fox-Dancing of Taseko. My friends call me Danny, but you can call me Foxy."

Danny ran his fingers through his impeccably styled flaming red hair. "I am one of several red-haired Berrat who live in my village."

"Taseko?" Kit asked, her face becoming somewhat ashen. "That city is run by slavers."

"Ya, I know," Danny replied. "That's why I was sent here when I was a babe. To keep me from being captured."

"You're still a babe," the giant girl said, blushing heavily.

"I am Silverleaf, a half elf," the pointy-eared boy said. "My tall friend here is Amara. She's a Gigas."

"And I am Slate," the stocky boy said, holding his calloused hand out to Kit. "I am a dwarf from under the Mithril Mountains."

"So, what did you do to be brought here when you're so old?" Iba asked.

"What did I do?" Kit asked, furrowing her brow. "I did nothing."

"What she means is," Silverleaf interjected, "why are you here? Children come to the Temple because nobody wants them or because their parents are trying to hide them from some danger."

Kit shrugged. "I was told by Titan to come here so that I could free him."

The entire group howled with laughter at her assertion.

"Called by Titan," Iba said, slapping her fur-covered hands on her thighs. "Sure."

"Enough," Danny growled. "You'd think you'd all know better than to torment a new arrival. What is this, payback for all the times people scorned you? You should be ashamed of yourselves."

A deep blue frost coalesced around Iba's furry hands. A strange look crossed the girl's face before she launched a bolt of ice. The impact knocked Kit on to her back, drawing the ire of the other children.

"If this girl thinks she's going to free Titan," Iba said as she stormed for the door, "she's going to need to get a lot tougher. I just gave the girl her first lesson." The Tahr slammed into Sister Nevara, who had just entered the room.

"Where do you think you're going, Acolyte?" The woman glared down at Iba, who completely ignored her and scooted past the priest, quickly exiting the room. "You are all late for breakfast. Come now, gather up and we'll head to the dining hall together."

Danny reached out a hand, offering to help Kit off the ground.

"What was that?" Kit asked, rubbing her chest where the ice bolt had struck her. She didn't like the confused expression the red-headed boy was giving her. "How did she do what she did?"

"Battle spell," Danny said as he pulled Kit up to her feet. The boy scrubbed his forehead. "If you don't know what that is, you've got a lot of catching up to do."

"I don't know what this ruckus was all about, young acolytes, but you'll fall in line and follow me to breakfast immediately, if you know what's good for you." The woman spun on her heel and retreated out the door.

"She treats us like we're five years old," Danny said, taking his place in line beside Kit. "She'll probably still treat us like that when we're full priests. Don't let that gruff exterior fool you, she's one of the kindest people on the face of Orth. Just make sure you have your takeaway work finished on time."

"Takeaway work?"

"Ya," Danny said with a grin. "It's what she gives us at the end of class to takeaway and do before the next class."

"This is all so strange to me." Kit swallowed hard, wondering if coming here was a mistake.

"Don't worry," Danny offered. "I'll teach you what you need to know to get caught up."

As Kit and the group of other acolytes followed Sister Nevara into the dining hall, Kit could not help but think they looked like ducklings following a mother duck.

Kit's eyes grew wide as her head swiveled about. The space was enormous, much larger than the community hut at the center of her village. There were tall, skinny windows on either side of the room, illuminating the eight long rows of tables stretching from the entrance to the back of the hall.

Seated at the outer tables were young children of maybe five or six years. There were alcoves between the windows. From within the recesses, fires burned brightly, giving the room a sharp, smoky aroma. Sister Nevara led them between the rows until they were near the front of the dining hall, where there were a good number of adults seated at tables on a raised dais.

"Why is Kit sitting with us acolytes?" Iba bleated out. "She should be seated with the other novices."

"That will be quite enough," Sister Nevara scolded, bearing down on the goat-girl.

"Well, we worked hard to earn our place here," Iba continued, the small beard on the bottom of her goat-face twitching.

"When you are High Priest," Sister Nevara said, shaking her head, "you can decide who sits where. For now, Acolyte, you keep your mouth shut and your ears open, unless you'd like another moon of kitchen duty with Sister Miyuki."

Iba's mouth slammed shut. As she climbed over the bench to take her seat at the table, she glared at Kit and made a hard, raspy noise, deep within her throat.

As the group took their places, a group of older children, perhaps thirteen or fourteen years of age, came into the dining hall past the table of adults, carrying trays of food. At their lead was an extremely fat woman wearing white and silver robes, covered by a heavily food-stained apron.

"And you must be our new arrival," the fat woman with honey-colored skin said as she lifted a large plate of food from her tray and slid it in front of Kit. She carefully wiped an errant strand of her blue-black hair off her sweaty face.

"I am Kit Standing Bear," Kit said, bowing her head slightly to the woman. "Thank you for this food. It looks delicious. May Gaia bless you and your family."

The fat woman's face went bright red as her head swiveled about, wondering who might have heard.

"Oh, sweetness," the woman whispered to Kit. "We don't speak of any other gods in Titan's temple. Some of the other priests... oh dear, they will whip you badly if they hear you."

"Are you a priest?" Kit asked, her face burning at what the woman had just told her.

"I am Sister Miyuki," the woman replied, her almond-shaped, bright green eyes twinkling with joy. "I am the Temple cook and it is my pleasure to serve you today. Please, you should eat right away while it's still hot. All of you, start eating. The class bell will ring any minute now."

Sister Miyuki turned and waddled off, waving for the acolytes to come join her.

The rest of the children dug into their food-laden plates. With a smile, Kit joined in, shoveling the food into her mouth with abandon. Within seconds, she was making small groaning noises, her eyes practically rolling back into her head.

"I know," Danny said as he pushed a sweet roll into his mouth. "Sister Miyuki's cooking is the best in all of Arnnor."

Kit had just finished mopping up the last of her food with a fluffy white roll when a series of bells rung out. The varied tones of the bells' peals reminded her of a tiny songbird from back home, which gave her a terrible pang of homesickness. She wondered what her mother was doing.

"Let's get moving," Sister Nevara called out as she rapidly clapped her hands together. "Brother Powder isn't going to wait all day for you to make it to his classroom."

Not wasting a moment, the ducklings followed their leader, up the stairwell back to the floor where the Nave was. The sister led them down a hallway where, every few feet, torches hung from tarnished metal brackets. The fluttering flames did nothing to improve the dungeon-like quality of the corridor. The doors to the classrooms were open, and the light from the windows came spilling into the hallway, lighting up tiny, reflective flecks embedded in the floor's stonework.

"Potions class," Danny said as he led Kit into the room. "Sit with me and I'll make sure to explain what you don't know about."

"Danny, you can't even brew coffee, and you're going to help our new friend with potions?" Amara's tenor voice boomed out. She threw her hand over her mouth, not meaning to be so loud.

A short man with pale white skin and bright white hair stood at the front of the room behind a huge wooden desk. The desk was covered with jars and vials that were filled with all sorts of liquids and powders. He was wearing a white robe covered by a white apron, with only the slightest hint of stains on it. He smiled brightly at Amara's assertion as he waved the children to come into the classroom.

"Good morning, children. I see we have a new acolyte with us this morning." The priest's bright blue eyes fell onto Kit, making her feel even more self conscious.

"So, young girl. Father Hoarfrost told me your name is Kit and that, until very recently, you lived in northern Berrathia. Maybe you can tell me what you know of brewing potions?"

The man's voice was quite high-pitched with a slight lilt to it.

"Nothing," Kit said, casting her eyes down at the scarred and damaged table at which she was sitting.

"Acolytes must stand when addressing a priest," Brother Powder said, drawing laughs from the rest of the class.

Kit picked herself up from her bench and lifted her head high. "I know nothing of potions."

"Brother Powder," Danny whispered to Kit. "Always refer to him as 'Brother Powder.'"

A deep frown pulled at the corners of the priest's mouth. Kit swallowed and quickly finished her sentence. "My community did not make potions, Brother Powder, but I will work hard to learn."

"Very well then," the priest said as he rummaged through a pile of scrolls on his desk. "Let's start with a simple potion today then, shall we?"

Kit struggled badly as the priest droned on and on about plants, powders, and mixing techniques. Her eyes were getting heavier by the second.

"Don't worry," Danny whispered to her, making Kit jerk heavily when she woke up from her unexpected nap. "Our next class is martial training. It's a lot of fun if you don't mind getting a few bruises."

CHAPTER SEVEN

COMBAT TRAINING

Sister Nevara did not show up at the end of the potions class to lead them to martial training. As soon as the end of class bell rang, all the students charged from Brother Powder's class, overturning several tables in the process. Any other teacher would have been furious with this callous display, but the potions teacher was no disciplinarian. Kit offered a half-hearted apology before Danny dragged her out of the room and down the hallway. The boy used his broad shoulders to clear a path to the gray stone staircase that led to the Temple's back gardens.

"What's the hurry?" Kit asked as she struggled to catch her breath.

"The students at the front of the class are the ones Sister Gale chooses to spar with," the young Berrat explained. His flaming red hair and wild eyes made him look more than a wee bit crazy.

"And everyone is rushing for the back of the class?" Kit asked.

"Sweet Titan, no," Danny said, pulling Kit harder to make her hurry up. "It's a great honor to be chosen to fight with Sister Gale, and it's so much fun. She never holds back and she never treats us like children."

As soon as they exited the Temple's rear door to the gardens, Danny broke into a full-out run. Not wanting him to leave her behind, Kit put her legs to work, quickly closing the gap. To her left and right, acolytes pushed against each other as they tried as hard as possible to win a spot in the first row.

The training area was an expansive lawn of shortly-cropped grass. Acolytes had already taken up every available spot in the front row, forcing Kit and Danny to file into the space behind them.

"At least we'll get to watch the sparring up close," Danny said as he gasped for breath and wiped the sweat from his brow.

A moment later, a petite, stern-faced woman came strolling up a path on the far side of the garden. She was an Easterner, with honey-colored skin, and jet-black hair. Even though she wore loose-fitting linen shirt and trousers, she was clearly fit and covered with lithe muscles. Every movement exuded a quiet grace that spoke volumes about her confidence and abilities. Kit couldn't figure out why so many people were anxious to spar with the woman.

"Good morning, acolytes," the priest said as she pulled a quarterstaff from a barrel standing near a great oak tree. She spun the weapon in her hands until it hummed as it cut through the air.

"Who among you wishes to be a *warrior*?" she asked, as she brought her weapon to an immediate halt and tucked it up under her armpit. When nearly every hand in the class went up, including Kit's, she smiled a wicked smile and paced back and forth before the front row.

"For the three of you who do not want to be a warrior, who of you wish to become a *ranger*?"

Two of the three acolytes pumped their fists into the air, causing everyone to stare back at Amara, the only acolyte who hadn't raised her hand.

"And you, Gigas, what discipline will you follow?" Kit could have sworn that Sister Gale scowled when she asked, as though any discipline outside of being a warrior or a ranger was beneath her.

"I will be *a scholar*," Amara said, straightening her back, making the young giant that much taller. "After all, Sister, knowledge is power."

"Then why are you attending my class and wasting my time? Go to the library, where you can expand that giant-sized brain of yours."

"My people are pacifistic by nature," Amara said, showing no fear of her instructor, "but we still delight in martial combat. It is our favorite sport."

Sister Gale snorted and shook her head. "Your people could be some of the finest fighters in all of Orth, and yet you will not raise a weapon in combat. You idly watch while the world burns. If I could but light a fire beneath you, such a warrior you would make."

"There are ways to peace that do not require an ax or shield," Amara said, her deep voice making her sound quite sage.

Sister Gale gave the giant acolyte a dismissive wave before casting her gaze back over the assembled students. "I guess that only leaves healers. Are there any among you who wish to be healers?" She cocked an eyebrow as if daring anyone to raise their hand. There was a gasp among the acolytes when Kit shoved her hand high over her head.

"Step forward, little one," Sister Gale said. "I cannot see you behind the mass of muscled bodies standing in front of you."

Disregarding her reddening face, Kit stepped up through the boys in the front row. Each one of them was pushing his chest out and flexing his arm muscles, trying to look as impressive as he could manage.

"You're the new acolyte," Sister Gale said as she let her quarterstaff drop down to waist height. "You wish to be a healer, and yet I saw you raise your hand to be a warrior."

"Yes," Kit said, trying to appear confident as her knees wobbled underneath her. "I will be a warrior *and* a healer."

Sister Gale's jaw became hard as her emerald, almond-shaped eyes bore into Kit.

"You wish to be a warrior *and* a healer?" The woman chuckled loudly as she idly spun the weapon in her hands. "As priests, we can only choose one discipline." The crowd of assembled acolytes laughed behind Kit's back, mocking her with cruel taunts.

"Gaia has placed no such limitations on me," Kit said, taking a step toward the priest, craning her neck to look up at her. "I don't expect Titan to be any different."

Quick as a viper, Sister Gale struck out with her quarterstaff, catching Kit on her temple, sending her toppling onto the garden's thick green grass.

"How dare you!" the priest exclaimed, striding towards Kit. "How dare you speak of another god, a false god, here on the Temple grounds!"

"Is that how you teach your students?" Kit asked as she picked herself up off the ground, a trickle of blood pouring down from where the wooden polearm had struck her. She frowned down at her grass-stained robe and sneered.

"Have you ever considered that the disciplines you talk about mirror those of the four aspects of Gaia; The Warrior, The Hunter, The Wise One, and The Healer?"

Without so much as a warning, Sister Gale hit Kit repeatedly with her quarterstaff, striking her about the head, shoulders, and thighs. With each strike, Kit's face became sterner.

A thin-lipped smile crossed the priest's face when Kit refused to fall after taking her savage beating. Sister Gale took a step back and tossed her weapon to Kit. She dropped her hands by her side and stuck her chin out slightly. "You have spirit. Now let's see what you can do when you have a weapon in your hands."

Kit stared down at the weapon, not quite sure how to use it. Gritting her teeth, she brought the pole over her knee, snapping it into two equal-length clubs. Kit closed her eyes for a moment and took a deep breath.

"You prefer kali sticks to a quarterstaff?" Sister Gale asked. "They will force you to come into closer quarters if you wish to strike me with them, or perhaps you just enjoy receiving beatings?"

Disregarding the priest's words, Kit took a moment to calm herself. When she opened her eyes, she leapt forward, striking out at the priest's thighs and waist. With each swing the acolyte took, the priest either stepped out of the way or she redirected the attack so that it fell wide of the mark. With each failed attempt to strike her teacher, Kit's anger grew. Her attacks degenerated into wild, flailing swings meant to inflict ultimate damage, but they were so uncoordinated that the priest was having no difficulty defending herself.

"Why have you not yet cast a battle spell?" Sister Gale asked. Kit paused, desperately trying to catch her breath. Her lungs were burning so badly she could barely manage to get a word out.

"What?" Kit managed to say between gasps. "I don't understand."

"A battle spell. Combat magic. Surely you must know something about casting such spells." Kit could only shake her head, her cheeks reddening at the sound of laughter at her back. "We call them battle spells, but they are no different from any miracle that we request from Titan. They just happen to be effective in combat. There are four basic forms of battle spells: attack spells, enhancement spells, defensive spells, and, last but not least, healing spells."

"Attack spells, as you might have guessed, are used to cause harm to an opponent." The priest made a fist and a blue glow materialized. She thrust her fist forward, striking Kit in the chest, knocking her off her feet. "That was a frost attack. When you have learned to master this spell, you can form the cold almost any way you want."

Kit rubbed her chest and picked herself up off the ground. Fury was building up inside her, but a sharp look from the priest was enough for her to calm herself.

"Enhancement spells allow a priest to increase their speed or their strength. Had you used a speed spell, you might have been able to avoid the bolt of ice that struck you." Sister Gale cocked an eyebrow. "Or, you could have used a defensive spell, like a shield, which would have absorbed much, if not all, of my attack. Lastly, are healing spells. Using these spells, you can heal the wounds of yourself or an ally. They come in very handy when you're too slow or too dim to get out of the way of your opponent's attack."

"What about auras?" a student called out from somewhere behind Kit. "You didn't tell her about aura spells."

"True," Sister Gale said, a look of annoyance spreading across her face at the interruption. "Aura spells are quite special and difficult to master. They behave just like a standard spell, but they can affect everyone within two or three paces from the caster. Keep in mind, an aura of healing will not cure the wounds of everyone within its area of effect. But what benefit they provide might be the difference between you living or dying in battle. A very powerful priest can extend that range to fifteen paces if they put enough *faith* into the spell."

"Faith, Sister?"

"Faith is what we call the energy we are given by Titan to perform his miracles. And how did you become an acolyte without knowing any of this? Every novice must pass these tests before being promoted."

"She's Father Hoarfrost's pet," Iba bleated out. "She doesn't belong here."

Kit gripped her kali sticks and bolted for Iba, ready to teach the loud-mouthed girl a lesson. Before she took a second step, Sister Gale had used her quarterstaff to trip the girl. "We'll have none of that. The only fighting that will take place here is with me."

With a fierce growl, Kit sprang at the teacher; her weapons a blur as she unleashed a relentless barrage of attacks. Each strike met its match as her teacher skillfully parried with ease. When Kit's attacks finally slowed, the priest spun around, bringing the flat of her foot across Kit's cheek, sending her skidding along the grass. She tried several times to pick herself up, before finally collapsing with a groan.

The dumbfounded acolytes stared blankly down at Kit, having just witnessed the most severe beating a student had ever received. Sister Gale glided over to the fallen student, checking that she was still breathing.

"What can you tell me about her attacks?" the priest asked with indifference to the girl on the ground.

The acolytes immediately shouted out answers, saying things like her attacks were crude, or that they lacked discipline. They continued shouting out more answers, each more derogatory than the previous.

Just when they became silent, Danny said in a low, almost threatening voice, "Her attacks were both relentless and fearless. She was willing to take damage to inflict damage."

"Very good, Acolyte Fox-Dancing. I want you and Amara to take her to the infirmary. Tell whoever is working there today that this acolyte is to receive no healing potion. I want her to remember what her wounds feel like for the next moon. Also, teach this girl some basic combat spells. The rest of you start doing push ups. I'll tell you when you can stop."

CHAPTER EIGHT

BROTHER RIME

Kit spent the next four nights in the Temple infirmary. She could hear voices through the mists of her addled brain. She could not quite make out what was being said, but there was a woman who was clearly upset.

"... child... nearly dead," a woman said. The shrill of her voice was cutting into Kit's brain like the blade of a hatchet.

Kit opened her eyes slightly, the sun streaming in through the window forcing her to squint.

"I will not countermand Sister Gale's orders," a somewhat familiar male voice said. "If you want her healed, teach her how to heal herself."

Kit fully opened her eyes, and quickly closed them again. The light caused a stabbing pain that made her head throb. Father Hoarfrost was speaking with a woman dressed in the same sort of robes as the other priests.

"But she's only just arrived, Father. How can you expect her to call upon Titan's healing powers?" the woman asked, shaking her head.

"Give her a chance," Father Hoarfrost said calmly as his eyes fell on Kit. "She may well surprise you. But, under no circumstances are you to heal her yourself, or to use a healing potion, or a healing scroll."

"Father?" Kit asked. Her hands went to the sides of her head, as though trying to prevent it from splitting open.

"Hello, Kit. Nice to see you're awake."

Kit winced and scrunched her eyes tight.

"Oh, praise be to Titan," the young female priest said. "You've been unconscious for over three days. I feared you were going to join the Great Cycle."

"Sister Alyce," the old priest said, shaking his head. "Her life was never in any danger. Don't be dramatic."

"Dramatic? Dramatic?" the Nomad woman screeched. As her arms flailed about, her sleeves rose, exposing her heavily tattooed skin.

"My apologies, Sister. I should not have suggested that you were *dramatic* in any sort of way." Father Hoarfrost patted Kit's hand lightly, then turned on his heel and headed off for the door. As he glided along, the man made no sound whatsoever as his feet glided across the room's white-tiled floor.

"Would you like to try to heal yourself?" Sister Alyce asked. She scratched the top of her head and continued down to the back of her neck. In no way did she expect Kit to succeed.

"I don't know how," Kit said, looking up at the woman with chin-length black hair. The pain wracking her head subsided slightly.

The priest pinched the bridge of her hooked nose on her skeletal-thin face. "Calling upon Titan for his healing requires an advanced level of faith, but I will do what I can to teach you."

"Thank you," Kit said, wincing as the pain in her head flared up when the woman spoke.

"I want you to clear your mind," the priest started. "Reach out with your heart to Titan, feel for his grace. Let his power fill you. When you think you can feel him, say these words... *Titan, hear me.* As you speak the phrase, let your faith flow out to him and ask for his mercy to heal the wounds."

"Okay," Kit said, closing her eyes. She had no idea what it meant to reach out with her heart, let alone how to do it. She cast her mind back to the day this journey began, trying to remember how she felt in her dream when he stood before her. Suddenly, she found herself standing on a cliff-face, staring out over the northern sea, with its frosty blast of cold wind cutting through her. Tiny shards of ice stung her face and neck, but she refused to turn away.

"Titan, hear me," Kit whispered.

I made the journey to your temple. I left my mother behind, the only person who loved me, to seek you out, just like you asked. I am doing everything I can to find my way to you. Now I have something to ask of you.

The thought had barely coalesced in Kit's mind when the ground at her feet became covered in ice crystals. They gathered and grew, climbing up her ankles, past her knees, all the way up to her chest. Regardless of the agony it caused, it felt right, almost comforting.

Please, if it be your will, take this pain from me.

The deep, throbbing cold suddenly turned warm, like a blanket had been wrapped around Kit's body. The blinding headache that she'd felt just moments earlier drained away, replaced with a sense of calm and well being. When she opened her eyes, Sister Alice's face was white, her mouth agape. The woman stumbled backwards a few paces; her hands pressed against her cheeks.

"Sweet Titan," she said, blinking rapidly. "It's not possible."

"What happened?" Kit asked. She wobbled as her head swam.

"You... it's not possible," the priest repeated. "You called upon Titan, and he heard you."

"What's not possible?" a high-pitched, nasally voice asked.

Kit turned to see a tall, thin man with long chestnut hair heading towards her. "I see she's alive," he said with a sneer. "From the way the acolytes were carrying on, it sounded as though Sister Gale had killed Father Hoarfrost's new pet."

"Brother Rime!" Sister Alyce said, "that is..."

"That is *what*?" the priest asked, as if daring the healer to say another word. He glowered at the woman for a few more seconds before turning his attention back to the acolyte. The expression on his face made Kit think he had just sucked on a lemon. An unwanted snigger escaped, and she immediately recoiled at her own noise.

"You think me funny?" the priest said while he cracked his knuckles. "You should have been placed with the other novices. You should have earned your place before being made an acolyte. You have, for whatever reason, been treated like you are... *special.*"

As Kit shook her head, her mouth clamped shut. The foul man leaned over Kit, his unblinking, beady black eyes staring down at her. "You will receive no special treatment from me." A small bit of spittle hit Kit in the face. "I will make you wish you climbed the ranks like the other children. You can start by visiting Sister Miyuki in the kitchens. When you are not in class, that is where you will spend the rest of your time."

"Forever?" Kit asked. Fire burned her belly at the way this man was treating her. She had no idea who he was, but his unfounded hatred for her was all too familiar. How many days had she traveled to get here, all because of a dream. At that moment, Kit wished she hadn't left home. At least there, she had her mother, a woman who loved her when everyone else would have rather seen her dead.

"If I had it my way," Brother Rime said, "I'd leave you there to rot. You will be on kitchen duty until the new moon. Don't test me, girl. I'll happily extend the timeframe."

The surly brother stormed from the infirmary. A moment later, he popped his head back through the doorway, the sour look on his face as nasty as ever. "Speak of this, Sister Alyce, and I will make it my mission to ruin your life." As quickly as he arrived, the man exited the room.

The young healer recoiled at Brother Rime's words, clutching the side of Kit's bed to steady herself. The woman's face had turned deathly pale.

"Don't worry about that man," Kit said, sitting up on her bed, grasping Sister Alyce's hand. "I won't let him hurt you."

Sister Alyce pulled away and straightened the bedsheet. She gave Kit the smallest of smiles and shook her head. "You are a good girl. Get some sleep now and don't worry about such things."

Kit nodded and plopped her head back onto her soft pillow. A moment later, darkness engulfed her, and the young acolyte fell into a deep, peaceful sleep.

CHAPTER NINE

SISTER MIYUKI

The next morning, Kit woke up feeling better than she had in many moons. She yawned and stretched, and rubbed her eyes.

"Good morning," said a young western human priest with black hair arranged in a series of short braids. The way each braid stood straight up and bobbed from side to side reminded Kit of the snakes on a gorgon's head. "I'm Brother Snowpack."

"Good morning, Brother. I'm Kit Standing Bear." This man, with his smooth skin and wide eyes, stood in complete contrast to the nasty man who had visited her the previous. "I'm starving!"

"Well," he said, scratching the back of his head, "then perhaps I have good news for you. I was told to send you to the kitchens to see Sister Miyuki. She will give you your lessons today while you are on kitchen duty."

Every bit of joy that had filled Kit's soul drained away in an instant.

"Oh, don't fret," the brother said. "You'll love Miyuki. She's the best. I'm sure she'll make sure you're well fed, too. Nobody leaves the kitchens on an empty stomach. If you are well enough, I can show you the way."

The trip to the kitchens passed in a blur. Brother Snowpack wasted no time hustling her through the halls and down several flights of stairs. The temple seemed to be a vast labyrinth, designed to confuse and disorient anyone who dared to enter. The unearthly aromas told Kit they were nearing the kitchen. Her stomach growled in hopeful anticipation.

"Through these doors," Brother Snowpack said. "Sister Miyuki is expecting you." Without another word, the brother spun on his heel and disappeared down the hall. Another rumble from deep in Kit's gut spurred her into action. Blowing out her cheeks, she stepped through the doors and into a large room filled with rows of tables. An extremely fat woman at the far side of the room hopped from her chair, her arms wide.

"Welcome, Acolyte Kit. Come in. Come in."

Kit immediately recognized the woman from breakfast on her first day. Up until that moment, she hadn't remembered the sister's name.

⸎

After eating her fill, and then some, Sister Miyuki led Kit from the eating area into the kitchens. An intense wave of heat washed over her as she entered the room. There were several large stone alcoves in the walls, and within each of them was a roaring fire. Several smaller fires were burning in black metal boxes, the likes of which Kit had never seen.

The rotund priest walked Kit through the kitchens, explaining how the fireplaces and black-iron stoves were used to prepare the Temple's meals. She was introduced to numerous kitchen staff, but their names and faces blended together, making it impossible for the young girl to remember a single person.

The one and only name and face she remembered was Lump-on-a-log, who was snoring loudly, laying by one of the many hearths. Sister Miyuki had described the animal as a golden retriever wolfdog. Whatever he was, seeing him sleeping so peacefully warmed Kit's heart.

"Lump doesn't do much," the sister said with a laugh. "He showed up a few days ago, about the same time you did. I considered running him off, but he looked so sad and lonely. I thought maybe he could stay down here and chase off any rats who might find their way into the kitchens. The poor beast has barely moved. It's how he got his name, because he's not much more than a lump on a log."

"He's very handsome," Kit said. At her words, the dog's tail began thumping on the floor. Slowly, he picked himself up off the ground and made his way over to Kit, rubbing his face against her side.

"Well, my word, that's the most I've seen him move since he got here," Sister Miyuki said with a laugh. "Even the offer of boar sausages doesn't get this lively of a reaction."

"Can I feed him? Do you have anything for me to give him?"

"After you finish your duties," Miyuki said. "Then you can spend time with the dog. I've got ten baskets of potatoes that need peeling before lunch."

Kit's heart sunk at the thought of peeling potatoes all day, but at least it was a familiar task.

The morning passed quickly. While she peeled potatoes, Lump laid at her feet, keeping them warm. All the while, Sister Miyuki worked tirelessly, making a variety of breads and crusts for meat pies. Every once in a while, Kit stood to stretch, giving her multiple opportunities to pocket several chunks of meat which she slipped to the dog when no one was looking.

"You know, Acolyte Kit," Sister Miyuki said as they finished eating lunch. "If you keep feeding the dog the way you've been doing, he'll be too fat to be of use to anyone. Before we begin your afternoon lessons, I want you two to go into the back gardens. Try to get Lump to run around while you gather blooms for Father Hoarfrost's table."

"How do I get there?" Kit asked. "I don't even know how I got to the kitchens. The brother who brought me here... well, we moved through the halls so quickly..."

"Ah, yes. Brother Snowpack never seems to slow down for anything. In some ways, he is the exact opposite of Lump, but he is also one of the kindest people you're ever likely to meet. In that respect, I think he and this golden furball are quite alike." The baker patted her thighs, inviting the dog to come to her. Lump, with zero enthusiasm, walked over and stared up at the woman.

Sister Miyuki briskly rubbed the dog's head. "Would you like to go outside? Would you like Kit to take you?" The woman spoke the words, injecting as much excitement into them as she could muster. The big dog's tail wagged in slow, lazy circles. "He knows the way. Follow him." And with that, the dog trotted off towards the door. "You best hurry. I've never seen him move this quickly before."

Kit spent the next two weeks in the kitchens. She learned almost nothing about baking, except that she was completely inept at it. But while Kit peeled, sliced, and chopped her way through thousands of pounds of vegetables, the head baker filled Kit's head with many stories of the Temple and the people who lived there. All the while, Lump stayed at the girl's feet, following her everywhere she went.

Every day, after everyone was fed, Sister Miyuki took Kit to the orphanage. They brought all the leftover food from the meal, much to the delight of Sister Nevara, the first woman Kit met when she arrived at the Temple. She ran the orphanage. Despite how formidable, and downright scary the woman appeared, she welcomed Kit and Lump warmly, happily accepting the gifts they brought.

The children screeched with delight as the golden retriever wolfdog came into the room. They quickly fell upon the poor beast who simply rolled over onto his back while they gave him non-stop pets and belly rubs.

Kit reveled in the time she spent at the orphanage. When Kit left her village, she'd traveled to Aarall to become strong, to learn to be a warrior priest. But these small acts of kindness, spending time with the children, sharing in their laughter, creating bonds with them, gradually revealed to her a deeper connection between her quest and the simple pleasure of helping others.

The young girl had much to learn at the Temple, and not all of it was going to bring her joy.

Chapter Ten

THEOLOGY CLASS

For two years, Kit called the Temple of the Fist her home. But far from the sanctuary she had imagined, her days were now consumed by grueling and monotonous tasks. The excitement of becoming an acolyte had long dissipated, leaving her feeling trapped in a relentless routine. The temple's unforgiving teachers were solely focused on preparing their students to become priests; driven by the mission to break their god free from his icy prison. With every passing day, Kit's hope of a brighter future waned, and the weight of her responsibility grew heavier.

"Acolyte, wake up!"

Kit's eyes snapped open, revealing Sister Nevara, her mouth pressed so tightly that her lips had all but disappeared. She stared blankly for a moment at the woman, blinking her eyes, trying to focus. The look on Sister Nevara's face was colder than the blizzard that had been raging outside for the past three days. On multiple occasions, the priest sent the acolytes into the freezing temperatures to dig out the completely buried windows and doors. The way her teacher was looking at her, Kit would rather be out in the elements than facing Sister Nevara.

"I asked you for the names of the four Realms," said Sister Nevara as she repeatedly rapped her thin, Amberwood pointer in her hand.

"The four Realms, Sister?" Kit asked, stalling while her brain returned from the wonderful daydream she had been enjoying. Seeing a small puddle of drool on the table in front of her, Kit quickly wiped the corner of her mouth with the sleeve of her robe.

"Did you not finish the reading I set out for you?" Sister Nevara asked. Her tone made Kit think that the woman would likely beat her if she found out that Kit hadn't completed her reading assignment.

"Father's pet doesn't need to do takeaway work," Iba said from behind Kit, kicking the back of her chair with her hoof. "She thinks she's too special for such mundane tasks."

Lump, who never left Kit's side since the day they'd met, growled at the Tahr. While he voiced how Kit felt about the obnoxious girl, she didn't bother to respond to Iba's relentless taunts. Every day the gizmo found new ways to torment Kit and every day Kit just ignored her. Someday though, she was going to shut that girl's cud-chewing trap.

"No, Sister, I didn't," Kit responded, ready to accept whatever punishment the sister would dole out, drawing some sniggers from other class members.

"Let me guess," Sister Nevara said, pushing her badly bent nose into Kit's face. "Martial training?"

The woman scanned the room, looking for her training partner. When the priest's eyes fell on Silverleaf and the deep purple bruise around his eye, she shook her head and clucked her tongue.

"You didn't even have the decency to heal him?"

"I did heal him," Kit mildly objected before she lowered her head. "The first time. But he challenged me again after I repaired his broken mouth. I tried to heal him again, but I cannot call on Titan for healing more than once per day."

"Kit," the priest said as she slowly exhaled. "You're nearly fourteen years old. When you're fifteen, you'll be taking the Rite of Abandonment. You must learn when to use your healing gift and not squander it unnecessarily on minor wounds. You never know when you're going to need it to save a life."

Aiming her pointer at Silverleaf, the sister asked the half elf the original question. "Can you name the four Realms, Acolyte?"

"Autoria, Orth, Netherworld, and Helja," Silverleaf replied, trying his best not to wince when he spoke.

"Very good, Acolyte," Sister Nevara said with a mocking tone. "You are able to recite basic information that *every* acolyte should know by your age, and yet it seems that Acolyte Kit cannot be bothered to master even the basic tenets of our faith."

Kit groaned at her teacher's last comment. She just couldn't get into reading books. It was such a slow way of learning, and you couldn't ask a book a question. When she was little and the elders spoke of their village's history, they made the stories exciting, and the children could ask the storyteller anything they wanted. As much as she enjoyed those tales, it would infuriate Kit as she watched the elders patiently answer all the others' questions, while her own inquiries were ignored or met with stony silence, leaving her feeling unseen and unheard.

"Tell me about Autoria," Sister Nevara asked, directing the question at Kit.

"Autoria is the home of the gods," Kit replied in a lifeless, monotone voice. "Orth is the Realm we live on, the Underworld exists beneath Orth, and Helja exists beneath the Underworld."

Sister Nevara did not seem to appreciate her student's attitude, but cocked an eyebrow in surprise when Kit gave her a brief, albeit correct, answer. Quite frankly, Kit was equally astounded that she had been able to call on those facts. She didn't actually remember reading them. They must have come up in conversation at some point and she, miraculously, had managed to retain the information.

"So," Sister Nevara said, whacking her pointer across her hand. "What can you tell me of the Veil?"

The class became deathly silent at the sister's question, with many of the students looking dumbstruck. Kit's head swiveled about while she tried to understand everyone's reaction.

"And why is it that we don't speak of the Veil?" Sister Nevara asked, practically daring someone to speak up.

"Because it's the Veil that has trapped our god beneath the North Sea, and we don't speak of it because the Veil was created by Titan's wicked children, Ollin and Bael," Amara answered. Because of her immense size, she did not sit at the long tables with the rest of her class. She sat at a desk and chair, specially crafted to suit her needs.

"And why do we not speak of Ollin and Bael?" Sister Nevara asked. She smiled when almost every hand in the class enthusiastically rose.

"Slate? Would you like to answer this forbidden question?" Sister Nevara asked, resulting in disappointed groans from many of the acolytes.

"Sister," Slate said as he stood from his bench. He rubbed his hands thoughtfully over his thick orange beard. "We don't speak of it because what Titan's wicked children did was an affront to justice. Tricking their father in such a way was an act of cowardice."

Most of the class gasped at the dwarf's statement. Several even moved away from him, seemingly fearful that one of the gods may strike him dead where he stood.

"Quite right," Sister Nevara said, her eyebrows raised to comical heights. "Boldly stated, I might add."

After the class settled in slightly, Sister Nevara leveled her gaze onto Kit again.

"Tell me, Acolyte Kit, what is Father Hoarfrost's role in the Temple?" Sister Nevara asked, her tone sounding more like a challenge than a question. Kit's stomach flopped, unsure why the teacher was suddenly singling her out. The woman typically ignored her, treating her like she was hardly even there.

"He's in charge of the Temple and of the city as a whole," Kit said, her response sounding more like a question than an answer.

"Yes, I suppose that answer is not wrong," Sister Nevara replied, slowly pacing back and forth. "What is his role in regard to Titan?"

Kit stared blankly at her teacher, while behind her, she could hear Amara groaning, most likely thrusting her hand into the air repeatedly, hoping that she could answer the question.

"Yes, Amara," Sister Nevara said, "would you like to illuminate your friend here, who has not been completing her reading?"

"More like, humiliate her friend," Iba said, drawing a round of laughter from those sitting nearby.

Amara stood from her stool, its wooden legs scraping along the floor as she pushed it backwards.

"There is no shame in learning," the big girl said. "And you embarrass yourself with your flippant mouth, tiny acolyte." There was another short burst of laughter which died out as quickly as it started.

"Please answer the question, Acolyte," Sister Nevara said, her hard eyes raking over the outspoken Tahr.

"If my friend spent less time fighting and more time learning, I'm sure she'd know this as well." She gave Kit a friendly wink. "Father Hoarfrost is the embodiment of Titan on Orth. When Father Hoarfrost speaks, he speaks on behalf of our god." The Gigas' face beamed with pride.

"If Amara spent more time on the training field and less time with her nose in books, she probably wouldn't have known that answer either," Kit said, her voice sounding more than a bit sulky.

"Just because you don't enjoy learning the history of the Temple," Sister Nevara scolded, "doesn't mean that it isn't just as important as your martial training. Your understanding of Titan may be the key to your freeing him if you should ever take up the quest to do so. The secrets to passing the trials that a priest must face in order to free Titan can only be discovered by having a deep understanding of our faith."

"What's there to understand?" Kit asked. "Titan is trapped in a prison beneath the North Sea, and he has charged us with freeing him. How does knowing what happened before I was born help me to do that?"

Before Sister Nevara could respond, the end of class bell pealed and the entire class bolted for the exit.

"Before you all race out of here," Sister Nevara said, rolling her eyes, "you are to return to your rooms and dress in your leather armor, and bring your weapons to Sister Gale's class. She has a surprise for you today."

As the class bolted for the exit, Kit grabbed Danny by the arm and pulled him aside.

"I have no weapons or armor," she hissed at him. "What am I supposed to do?"

"Titan will provide," Danny said. "Go to your cell. You'll see."

SISTER GALE

The acolytes raced from Sister Nevara's theology class to their dorm room cells to prepare for combat.

Kit had no idea what Danny was referring to, but when she opened the door to her cell, she found a suit of light leather armor, an iron battle hammer, and a small wooden shield. When Kit picked up her armor, a small piece of parchment fell from it, fluttering to the stone floor at Kit's feet.

When she picked it up, she found it had four words scribed on it. "Fight well. Sister Gale."

Lump looked on with detached amusement while Kit practically bounced from foot to foot as she slipped out of her gray acolyte robes and pulled on her brown leather breeches and jacket. The jacket was padded on the shoulders and chest, with thick leather piping running down the sides. The holy symbol of Titan was engraved over the armor's left breast. Kit did a few quick stretches, finding that her movements weren't restricted in any way. It was surprisingly comfortable, too.

When Kit picked up the hammer, she tested its weight, finding it perfectly balanced in her small hands. The polished oak handle had thin leather strapping wrapped around its base, giving a secure grip. The iron head was small, flat, and bulbous on one side, with a sharpened pick on the other. Kit gave it a couple of practice swings. She quickly wrapped the sheath's leather belt around her waist and slid her hammer into it.

She picked up the shield and slipped it over her left forearm. It was made from thin strips of oak with iron banding around the edges. She tested its weight and balance as she feigned using the shield to block fictitious attacks. Like the hammer, it just felt *right*. Kit quickly slung the shield over her back, hooking it on a small clasp on her armor's integrated shoulder strap.

"You need to stay here, my handsome," Kit said, running her hand over the wolfdog's head. "You know how Sister Gale gets when you come to her classes." Lump harrumphed at the girl's words, hopped onto her bed, and curled up into a tight ball. She gave him a quick kiss on his forehead and bolted from her room.

Kit's heart soared as she raced down the hallway leading towards the Temple's back gardens. Today's session with the combat instructor promised something exciting. She could only hope it wasn't just another sparring class. Not that she didn't love them, but something different might be fun, too.

A smile spread across Kit's face when she caught sight of Sister Gale standing on the training field. The teacher had donned a full set of studded leather armor which covered every inch of her skin. Behind the woman were three large crates, each one covered in heavy beige tarps.

Today was going to be different. Sister Gale never showed up in armor.

✦

"In a circle around me, acolytes. We will not be sparring today." The priest's words drew many groans and protestations. She pushed the students back to create a ring of bodies around her. "Today, you'll be fighting for your lives."

With a flourish, Sister Gale pulled the tarp off one of the crates, revealing a rat that was the size of a small bear. The animal had beady black eyes, mottled gray fur, and a long bare tail with black rings running down the full length of it. The creature snarled, clawed, and snapped at the crate's wooden slats. With a nasty grin, Sister Gale leapt up onto the enclosure and drew a wicked-looking dagger. Several acolytes took a step, or four, away from the creature.

"For those of you who have never seen one before," Sister Gale said, stomping her foot on the top of the crate, "this is a dire rat. For those of you who did not do your assigned reading, you should be aware that the bite of the dire rat is extremely venomous, capable of paralyzing its victim in just a few minutes, and, like many of the dire animals, it has a potent frost attack."

"How will you decide who gets to kill it?" Kit called out as she stepped closer to the crate, with Danny and Slate doing the same. Amara and Silverleaf took up positions behind their friends. It seemed that neither of them wanted to directly confront the animal, but they appeared willing to support their allies as best they could.

"Step back, all of you," Sister Gale snarled. "I will not choose, the rat will. You will all form a tight circle around the animals. When I open the door, the rat will try to escape. Do. Not. Let. That. Happen."

She leapt down from the wooden box and promptly pulled the tarps off the other two crates, revealing two more dire rats. They looked like the first animal, except they were significantly larger, and their tails had bright-green rings instead of black.

"Besides their size, what sets the two larger creatures apart from the first?" Sister Gale asked, pounding on the side of the crate with her studded leather gauntlet.

"The black ringed rat is a juvenile," Amara said from behind the rest of the acolytes. "The green ringed tails identify the others as mature adults. The venom of the juvenile is weak and unlikely to cause severe harm."

"Very good, Amara," Sister Gale said, giving her a nod of approval. "I'm glad at least one of you took the time to do your reading."

Kit gave her giant friend a wink. In the two years since they'd met, Amara had grown at least another foot and her voice had deepened to a rich tenor that rivaled Danny's honey-sweet baritone.

Sister Gale's head swiveled about to get a better look at the circle of students. There was an evil gleam in her eye that made Kit's heart race with excitement.

"I will release the juvenile. If he escapes, I will let loose the adults as well. Unlike the juvenile who will seek his freedom, the adults will try to kill as many of you as they can before they seek refuge in a dark hole somewhere."

The combat instructor took hold of the latch which secured the cage door. "Ready your weapons," she called. "Don't disappointment me." When she opened the door, the animal bolted through the opening, immediately seeking its escape route.

The rat took several steps in multiple different directions, and each time it did, the acolytes closed ranks, giving it no room to pass. When it turned towards Kit, who was smaller than most of the students, it twitched its nose and barrelled towards her.

"Titan, hear me," Kit quickly whispered as she called forth a frost attack. Pointing at the animal with her battle hammer, the young acolyte released a thick stream of frozen air towards the rat, striking it fully in the face. Screeching in pain, the rat lowered its head and ran headfirst into Kit before she had a chance to pull her hammer back.

Kit watched helplessly as the rat leapt over her, making good its escape.

A moment later, there was a loud squeak and crunching sound. When Kit rolled over to get a better view, Amara was holding her eight-foot-long halberd as she stared down at the rat. Her eyes were blinking rapidly. Even with her hand over her mouth, her jaw trembled uncontrollably as she stood over the lifeless body at her feet. Amara dropped to her knees and wept.

"Forgive me," she croaked out. "I only meant to stun you."

The lifeless rat popped back to its unsteady feet. Before it had a chance to bolt, Amara grabbed it by the scruff of its neck and carried it back to the crate. She gently released it and carefully closed the door.

"Acolyte Amara," Sister Gale said, shaking her head. "The rat was not meant to survive its encounter. Your pacifistic ways are not... I mean... Holy Helja girl, we're warrior priests, yet you refuse to kill anything."

"My people, the Gigas, will not take a life, except to save another or to provide food for our clan," Amara said as she snapped upright, holding her heavy-bladed halberd at her side.

"Then why in the name of Titan do you want to be a priest?" Sister Gale asked, bellowing the question at the giant.

"I serve Titan because his house saved me," Amara said, her bright green eyes holding the priest's stare. "The Temple took me in after my caregiver passed away. If it weren't for Titan and this Temple, I don't know what would have happened to me."

"A noble reason," Sister Gale said through gritted teeth. "But, we live in a world where people kill to get what they want. They will cut you and your friends down without thought, without mercy. If you cannot learn to take a life, if you cannot accept the reality of your duties, then you are not suited to being a member of the Temple."

Amara's face twisted into a bizarre expression as she seemed to consider the priest's words. After a few moments, her mouth turned down in a frown and she shook her head. "Nowhere in all of my readings have I discovered that Titan requires us to spill blood. He only requires us to mete out justice in his name."

Sister Gale slapped herself on the forehead. Rather than continue the debate, she turned her attention back onto Kit.

"Who can tell me what Acolyte Kit did wrong?" the priest asked, causing Kit's face to redden.

"She chose the wrong battle spell," Amara answered after several seconds of silence.

"And what spell should she have used?" Sister Gale asked as her eyes scanned the rest of the students.

"Well," Danny offered with something of a grin. "She shouldn't have chosen a cold-based spell against a dire animal. They're practically immune to them. Since acolytes have an extremely limited number of battle spells, she would have been better to just use her hammer and shield."

"You're quite right, Acolyte," Sister Gale said, taking a few brisk steps towards the Berrat. "But that's not what I asked. I want to know which spell would have been the best choice under the circumstances."

"As acolytes, we have only three battle spells granted to us by Titan," Danny replied, straightening his back. At five feet, he was taller than most Berrat, yet Sister Gale towered over him by nearly a foot. "Since Titan limits the available choices to a frost attack, an aura of healing, and an aura of speed, she should have chosen the speed spell. It would have helped her to react faster, and it would have helped her allies within the aura to also receive the same benefit."

"Very good, Acolyte," Sister Gale said, her body now only a few inches from the burly Berrat boy. "And when should she have cast the spell?"

"As soon as you said you were releasing the animal," Danny said, looking up at his teacher with his infuriatingly infectious grin.

"That is quite right," Sister Gale said as she spun around and walked back to the crates. The priest placed her hand on the door to one of the adult rats and smiled.

"Not a single one of you prepared yourselves for combat. I suggest you do so now." As she finished her sentence, Sister Gale opened the door, releasing the adult rat.

⌘

Before the creature had a chance to escape, the priest leapt on top of its cage and took note as each of the students cast their battle spells. She cocked an eyebrow when Kit and Amara cast auras of healing, while every other student cast an aura of speed.

As the adult dire rat slowly stepped out from its cage, it turned its beady black eyes to Sister Gale and growled. It slowly circled the crate as long viscous trickles of slime-green venom dripped from its six-inch-long teeth.

"You're picking the wrong opponent," Sister Gale said as she slipped her dagger back into its sheath. She silently whispered a prayer to Titan. A gleaming two headed hammer appeared in one hand and a small silver buckler appeared in the other.

The rat spun around and lowered its head. With slow, careful steps it stalked towards the students, unleashing a wide blast of frost. The stream of ice-pellets knocked a few acolytes over and immediately froze several more. As it moved in to kill one of the prone students, Kit, Danny, and Slate burst forward, aided by the speed auras Danny and Slate had cast.

Before the rat had a chance to bite, Kit slammed into it with her shield, sending the rat skittering across the lush green grass. As the rat scrambled back to its feet, the nearby acolytes moved back, giving the creature as much room as they could.

"Why are you backing away?" Sister Gale scolded, spittle flying from her lips.

Danny immediately stepped in front of the rat, drawing its attention away from Slate who was trying to flank the animal.

"Amara," Kit said, motioning to the half elf. "I'll stay with Silverleaf, you cover Danny."

Before Kit could move into position, Danny launched himself at the rat, swinging wildly with his twin iron battle hammers. Considering the creature's bulk, it moved with surprising agility, avoiding each of the Berrat's attacks, biding its time until he revealed an opening.

Just as Kit arrived, the rat leapt at Danny, burying its teeth deep into the young man's chest. As the Berrat cried out in pain, Kit's healing aura immediately engulfed him, providing a small bit of relief, hopefully preventing the animal's venom from afflicting him.

Kit, now in an indefensible position, drew the attention of the dire rat. As it leapt from Danny to Kit, it squealed in pain as Slate delivered a deep gash into its hind end with one of his hatchets. When the animal turned its head towards its new threat, Kit brought the pointy side of her hammer down on its neck, severing its spine, killing it instantly.

Throwing her weapons to the ground, Kit knelt beside Danny and called unto her god. "Titan, hear me," she said as a pale-yellow aura engulfed her hands.

"Do not heal him," Sister Gale threatened as she leapt down from her crate.

"But he's dying," Kit said, as the glow on her hands intensified.

"He will live," the sister growled. "He needs to suffer for his mistakes, and so do you."

"His mistakes?" Kit yelled, the yellow aura on her hands disappearing as she jumped to her feet. Kit clenched her hands into tight little fists, and she bore down on her teacher.

Sister Gale released the two weapons she summoned back to the ether and threw her studded leather gauntlets to the ground. Seeing that Kit was about to attack, she put herself into a defensive position, ready to unleash a counterstrike as soon as the student committed herself.

In an unexpected maneuver, Kit leapt into the air and caught her teacher fully in the jaw with her knee. Both women landed in a heap on the ground, with Kit scrambling to get on top of her teacher. With her knees straddling the sister's chest, she rained a series of vicious blows down on the woman's face.

Thrusting her hips into the air, Sister Gale threw Kit off herself and popped up to her feet.

As Kit jumped up to continue her attack, the priest spun around, striking Kit solidly in the temple with her heel. Once again, darkness took Kit as she landed face-first on the soft, thick grass.

***

Kit's face was bright red as she and Lump skulked into Sister Gale's martial training class. Even though she had locked the dog in her room, he had somehow managed to free himself and follow her. Kit got the feeling he was not going to allow any further harm to come to her.

It was her first time back since the teacher had put the acolyte in the infirmary three days prior.

"Don't you dare hide in the back," Sister Gale called out to Kit. "We have some unfinished business to attend to."

Kit clenched her jaw as she weaved through the other students. Some were whispering that she was about to die, while others were surreptitiously congratulating her. By the time Kit made it to the front, her stomach was in a tight knot. Lump leaned against her, offering his support. The teacher's gaze was locked firmly on the girl, ignoring the dog completely.

"You surprised me, Acolyte," Sister Gale said, moving in close so she could look down her nose at Kit.

"I did not mean to disrespect you, Sister," Kit said, her eyes lowered.

"Disrespect?" Sister Gale laughed as she turned and walked away. "You showed exactly the sort of bravery I would expect from a warrior of Titan. You saw what you perceived to be an injustice, and you risked everything to stand against it.”

“And that surprised you, sister?” Kit asked, her anxiety switching quickly to anger.

“No, your behavior is exactly what I expected. What surprised me was your jumping-knee attack. I’ve never taught you, or anybody else, that type of maneuver.” The priest rubbed her jaw where Kit had kneed her. “You are to be commended.”

“Thank you, sister,” Kit said as her face flushed.

“And now,” Sister Gale said, a wicked, devious glint in her eye. “I want to see how you can manage against an invisible opponent.”

“Invisible?” Kit said, her eyes widening. “You can make someone invisible?”

“No,” Sister Gale said as she produced a scroll sealed with black wax. “Thanks to Brother Rime, I have a Scroll of Invisibility. All I need now is a volunteer from your classmates, somebody willing to fight you.”

The garden was immediately filled with shouts of excitement as the class clambered over each other, hoping Sister Gale would pick them to fight against Kit.

“Acolyte Iba,” Sister Gale said as she held out the scroll to the Tahr. “Do you think you can show Kit what it’s like to fight against an unseen enemy?”

Lump spun to face Iba, issuing a low, menacing growl.

“Keep your dog under control or I will have him permanently removed from the temple grounds,” Sister Gale said.

“Kit’s not so tough without her companion,” Iba bleated. “She’s afraid of me and the beast knows it. Can I use my axes?” Iba asked as she rocked back on her hooved feet.

“We won’t be using lethal weapons for this exercise,” Sister Gale said, her eyes bulging somewhat at the girl’s question. “You can choose either a quarterstaff or kali sticks.”

“Quarterstaff,” Iba said, squaring her shoulders. “I think I can use it to knock out a few of her teeth.”

Sister Gale's jaw flopped open at the girl's comment. Her lips moved as if to say something, but instead, she shook her head and groaned.

"And what weapon do you want?" Sister Gale asked, directing her question to Kit.

"Since I can't use a hammer," Kit said as she glared at Iba, "I choose a single kali stick."

"Very well then," Sister Gale said as she pulled a quarterstaff from one of the weapon barrels. She then walked over to a table with a wide array of one-handed weapons, and selected a thick, ironwood kali stick. With a flick of her wrists, she tossed the desired weapons to each of the acolytes.

"I'll be okay," Kit said to Lump. "You need to stay back. Do you hear me?"

"Form a circle," Sister Gale said. "No more than fifteen paces across. They need room to move, but no path to escape."

When the class finished forming a circle, Danny shouted out to Kit. "Listen for her movement. Use all your senses."

Not wanting Kit to succeed, several of Iba's friends clapped their hands in unison, making any chance of Kit *listening* to her opponent an impossibility.

"Are you ready?" Sister Gale asked each of the students. When they both acknowledged her, the priest unfurled the scroll and read the words. The parchment disappeared with a puff of gray smoke and Iba's form immediately became insubstantial.

Just as Kit took a fighting stance, her head snapped hard to the side and an angry red welt appeared on her cheek. Stumbling to her left, Kit swung wildly with her stick, hoping to clip Iba in the process.

After taking several more swings, each one wilder than the previous, Kit let out a grunt, grabbed her belly, and buckled over. A moment later, there was a loud crack and Kit dropped to the ground.

"Hold," Sister Gale called out. "Iba, stand back."

Sister Gale stopped just as she was about to help Kit get to her feet.

"Acolyte," she growled out, bringing her own quarterstaff down in a quick, downward arc, followed by a loud crack and a squeal. "If you make me tell you again, I will be the one giving this demonstration."

"Who can tell me what acolyte Kit has done wrong?" Sister Gale asked, slowly turning around to see all the students. "What should she be doing to help herself in this situation?"

"She never cast a battle spell," one of the acolytes shouted out.

"True," Sister Gale said, "but under this circumstance, which spell would aid her?" She continued to look to the class, but nobody answered.

"She isn't being mindful of her surroundings," Danny said. He caught the look Kit was giving him and he withered slightly. He glared back at her with a hint of a smile on his face. "She needs to use *all* her senses when fighting."

"Very good, Acolyte Danny," Sister Gale said, pursing her lips and bobbing her head. "The question is, what will our little acolyte do with this key bit of information?"

"She'll get her head split open," said the disembodied voice of Iba. "How long are you going to let her recover before we start fighting again?"

"Are you ready to continue, Acolyte Kit?" Sister Gale asked. A trickle of blood flowed down from Kit's scalp across her cheek.

"Yes," Kit said with a growl.

"Good. Now bow your head to me and then to your partner."

"Sister?"

"Do it, Acolyte," Sister Gale ground out. "Bow, to both of us."

Kit bowed slowly to her trainer. When she raised her head, she had a deep frown on her face. She then slowly turned and bowed to where Iba's voice had last come from. Mid bow, Kit stopped and stared, and then finished her bow. As she raised her head, she turned back to Sister Gale. The look of understanding replaced the previous look of disdain.

When the sister called for the fight to resume, Kit took on a fighting stance. She held her Kali stick out to her right side and put her left arm in front of her like a shield. She held this pose for several seconds before turning slowly to her left.

There was a sudden *whack* and Kit grimaced in pain. With her left hand, she struck out in front of her, catching Iba, possibly in her stomach, and followed through with an overhand strike with her kali stick that swung harmlessly through the air.

Kit took a quick step to her right and kicked low with her left foot. Again, she made contact, and Iba grunted in frustration.

"You're going to lose, Iba," Kit taunted, turning to her right. "You're invisible and I'm still going to kick your hairy butt."

As the words left Kit's mouth, she jumped backwards, ducked, and jumped backwards again. She then held her Kali stick out in front of her. There was the crack of wood on wood as Iba's attack made contact with Kit's weapon.

Kit promptly used a series of front kicks, each one catching Iba fully, repeatedly knocking her backwards.

There was another solid *whack* and a streak of crimson appeared on Kit's left cheek.

"Frost," Kit yelled as she produced a wide stream of frozen mist that clung to Iba and her weapon.

With a series of relentless attacks, Kit brought her kali stick and her fist to bear, striking the frost covered Iba repeatedly. With a similar move that Sister Gale had used, Kit spun around and brought the heel of her foot down onto Iba's shoulder, knocking her to the ground.

Kit slid down beside the fallen girl, her kali stick raised and ready to deliver a devastating blow.

"I claim victory," Kit said as she lightly rapped Iba with her stick. "I claim victory."

"Very good, Acolyte Kit," Sister Gale said, not so gently pulling Kit away from Iba. She produced another scroll from her belt, broke open the seal, and read the words. A moment later, Iba reappeared, laying on the soft grass, clutching her shoulder.

"Okay," Sister Gale called out, shaking her head at Iba. "Who can tell me how Kit defeated her *invisible* opponent?"

"She used her frost attack to reveal her enemy," Silverleaf said with a broad grin on his face. "The frost clung to Iba, making her sort of visible again."

"True," Sister Gale said, "that was a highly effective strategy, but acolyte Kit had turned the tide of the fight before then. How did she do it?"

"She paid attention to her surroundings," Danny said, bowing his head slightly to Kit. "She saw what couldn't be seen." Danny stepped back from his place in the circle and showed the dented grass he left behind.

"And?" Sister Gale said, patiently waiting for a response. When nobody spoke up, she raised her eyebrows to Kit.

"I could tell by her foot placements," Kit said with a small shrug. "The way she held her feet told me what type of attack she would use." The acolyte's fingers moved to wipe some of the blood from her cheek. "It mostly worked, at least."

While several of Iba's friends helped her to her feet, Lump moved to Kit's side. When Iba said something indiscernible to her, Kit rubbed the dog's head and gave the Tahr a coy smile. "We should do this again. It was fun."

Chapter Twelve

Fall From Grace

Kit sat bolt upright, her long black hair pasted to her face and neck, her entire body drenched in a cold sweat. A brisk wind whipped through her room's tiny slit of a window, raising goosebumps and sending shivers through her body. When Kit had turned thirteen, she had been moved from the children's common room to the private acolyte quarters. The rooms, or cells as they were referred to, were barely big enough to hold a bed, a desk, and a small chest to store an acolyte's limited amount of clothing.

While the kingdom was enjoying warmer than average temperatures, Kit's room remained ice-cold. No matter how warm it might be outside, it seemed to have a perpetual chill to it. Wrapping her arms around her tiny body, she looked to the narrow window slit, finding no sign of Pele rising in the east. Morning wouldn't be here for another hour, at least.

Kit suppressed a yell when a wet, cold nose nuzzled under her arm. Her hands lashed out, ready to defend against the attacker, only to find solace in the familiar touch of her beloved wolfdog companion.

While she lay in her cot, Lump pressed his chin onto her chest. She tried her best to get back to sleep, but to no avail. Between the oversized golden retriever wolfdog pinning the blankets and the disturbing dream she had been having, she knew the effort was futile.

As she slipped from her bed, she recoiled her feet as soon as they touched the ice-cold stone floor. Goosebumps covered her flesh as she scampered across the small room to the hook holding her rough spun acolyte robes. As she slipped them over her head, she started to quake uncontrollably as the memory of her dream broke through to her consciousness.

Kit raised her eyes up from the broken body of a young Nomad man. She was fighting a rage so deep, so visceral, that she feared it was going to consume her whole being. The man, covered in golden scales from head to toe, struggled to catch his breath. Blood sprayed from his mouth each time he coughed.

"I will rend you limb from limb," Kit said as she stepped over the fallen warrior, striding towards a great winged creature, with luminescent blue skin and great horns protruding from its massive head. Even though the creature towered over Kit, it took several steps backward, trying to keep the woman before him at a distance.

"He trusted you, dragon," Kit said as bright flames licked up the pale white skin of her arms. As the flames on Kit's body ignited, she caught her reflection in an ever-widening pool of blood spreading out from beneath the golden-scaled man. The reflection was Kit, and yet, it was not. What she saw was a woman with deep red hair, and huge, black-leather wings. Unexpectedly, the reflection looked back at her with eyes like swirling pools of molten gold.

"Cleanse the world with ice and fire. Break the cycle now, or all will perish," the reflection said.

When the memory of the dream passed, Kit found herself sitting on the floor with Lump's head on her lap.

"Hey, Lump," Kit said as she gently ran her hand over the big dog's head and ears. "How's about we go grab us some breakfast?"

⊱─────⊰

It was a fine spring day. The sun was shining brightly, and songbirds had begun arriving from their southern wintering homes. Whilst it was a glorious day, Brother Rime, the herbology teacher, insisted on holding a session in his dank, cold, basement classroom. Kit always hated this room, its smell being a mixture of moldy hay and old feet. To make matters worse, her teacher forbid Lump from accompanying her, claiming he was a distraction and a nuisance; both of which were completely ridiculous since the dog slept at her feet most of the time.

"Without looking through your notes, who here can tell me the three properties of Pele's Gift?" Brother Rime asked with his high-pitched, nasally voice. The Western Human priest ignored the half-dozen hands in the air and focused his beady, black eyes on Kit, who was desperately trying to be invisible.

"Did you not finish your assignment, Acolyte Kit?" Brother Rime said as he cracked the knuckles of his long, boney fingers.

"No, Brother," Kit said, staring up at him, her mouth twisting as she tried to come up with a reason he might accept. "I was..."

"Making yourself busy with martial training, no doubt," Brother Rime said with a sneer as his long, chestnut hair fell in front of his face. "You think because you are nearly sixteen years old, you can ignore the assignments I give you?"

"No, Brother, I..." Kit stammered, trying not to raise the ire of this middle-aged teacher who had been riding Kit since the first day she arrived at the Temple.

"She was performing a task for Father Hoarfrost," Iba said, disdain pouring from the girl's voice. "Everyone knows she's Father's pet."

"I see," Brother Rime said as he stroked the hair of his long, thin goatee. "When Father gave you *his* assignment, did he excuse you from all other classwork?"

"No, Brother," Kit answered, cringing internally while she waited for her teacher to mete out some form of punishment.

"Okay then," the priest said, puckering his lips while trying to imagine a suitable sentence. "You will join Sister Miyuki in the kitchens for the next moon. I will speak with her and make sure she gives you... suitable tasks to perform, ones befitting your lowly station as *acolyte*."

Kit breathed out a sigh of relief. She didn't enjoy kitchen duty, but she was happy to spend time with Sister Miyuki.

"And," Brother Rime added in a sadistic afterthought, "I expect to see three full scrolls by tomorrow on the methods of locating and identifying Pele's Gift, Medeina's Grace, and Sorrow Sage. With it, I want a complete outline of how each of the flora are to be gathered and prepared for the creation of at least *three* potions."

"Brother," Kit objected, her hands curling up into tight little fists. "You know that I am working in the Temple's infirmary, trying to hone my healing skills. How can you expect me to find time to do this? It's not like I'm ever going to be an alchemist or an herbalist. I have no interest or skill in either subject."

"Do you think I should give you special treatment, just because you're learning to be both a healer and a warrior? Is that what you think, Acolyte, that you're *special*?"

The words burned deep into Kit. She had never wanted to be special. She just wanted to fit in, to be accepted.

"And maybe you think..." Kit said, her fists turning white from gripping them so hard.

"Choose your next words very carefully, Acolyte," Brother Rime said, his eyes narrowing. "You are no longer a child under the protection of Sister Nevara."

"Is there a problem here?" asked a voice from the doorway, immediately drawing the ire of Brother Rime. A thick layer of frost instantly covered his hands, as though he was ready to attack whoever had just interrupted his lesson.

"Father Hoarfrost," Brother Rime said, his nasally voice jumping an octave. "No, Father, no problem."

"If you are concerned that Kit's takeaway work wasn't completed," Father Hoarfrost said, his voice smooth and easy, "then maybe it is something best brought up with me. Blaming an acolyte for my actions is... inappropriate."

"Yes, of course, Father," Brother Rime said, giving the High Priest an obsequious smile. "I understood the reasoning for Kit not having finished her assignment. I was just explaining how I have allowed her another day to complete it."

"Very well," Father Hoarfrost said, inclining his head slightly to the priest as he quietly exited the room.

"Pet!" Iba said. "Someday Father Hoarfrost won't be here to protect you, *Kitten*."

Without a word, or even a sideways glance, Kit's fist struck out, catching Iba squarely in the jaw, sending the gizmo backwards over her bench, her hooved feet kicking wildly as she toppled over.

As quickly as Kit had punched Iba, the Tahr sprung back to her feet with a three-inch blade in her hand.

"Brother, she has a dagger!" Silverleaf cried out, hopping off his bench to help his friend.

"Kit attacked first," Brother Rime said with a sick laugh. "The poor girl is just defending herself."

"Put it away," Kit said as she stood up from her bench. "You don't want to do this."

"I've wanted to carve off your pretty little face since the first time I laid eyes on it," Iba said, letting her knife sway slowly in front of her face. "I'm sick of having to look at it."

With a quick lunge, Iba stabbed out with her dagger. Kit sidestepped the attack and slipped in behind the blade-wielding girl. With a swift kick to the gizmo's butt, she sent the goat-girl stumbling into a crowd of students.

"You think you're so special," Iba said as she spun around, again waving the blade in front of her face.

That was the same comment Brother Rime had made. I don't think I'm special.

A wicked grin split Iba's face as blood dripped from the tip of her blade. Kit quickly checked herself and she found no wounds. Her face turned pale when she caught sight of Silverleaf crumpled on the cold, stone floor. His hands clutched to his stomach as blood seeped out between his fingers. He looked up at Kit with unseeing eyes.

"What have you done?" Kit asked as she leapt forward, bringing her fist down onto the girl's face, dropping her in a single blow. In two quick steps, Kit was beside her friend, placing her hands on the open wound. The blood was coming out much too quickly. The weapon was too small to cause this much damage.

"Vorpal blade," Silverleaf said as his face drained of color.

"Titan, hear me," Kit growled as she applied additional pressure to the wound. Kit knew that the magic in a vorpal weapon prevented the wound from healing. Even a small blade could be lethal when its cut continued to bleed.

Kit continued calling upon Titan as a deep yellow glow burst forth from her hands, quickly engulfing Silverleaf's wound. The small girl's entire body shook as she poured herself into her healing magic. She winced briefly as a sharp pain ripped through her own abdomen. A moment later, her pain subsided and with it, so did her healing aura.

"Thanks," Silverleaf said, his eyes blinking back tears.

With her friend safe, Kit popped back up to her feet, and she pulled the blade from the hand of the unconscious Iba. The tiny dagger appeared normal in every sense, but within its steel was potent, deadly magic.

"Do you think it was *just*," Kit said as she turned her stare onto Brother Rime, "that she should seek to kill me for punching her? I wonder what Father would say if I doled out the same justice to you for allowing her to attack me?" Kit was now pushing through the students as she made her way toward the front of the classroom. Each step was purposeful and sure.

"You dare threaten me, Acolyte?" Brother Rime said as a huge battle ax materialized in his hand.

"You're a pathetic excuse for a priest," Kit snarled as she continued to move forward.

"That will be quite enough, Kit," Father Hoarfrost said from the doorway. "Brother Rime, put away your weapon and wait for me in my office."

The irate teacher threw his ax towards Kit's feet, disappearing soundlessly before it struck the ground.

"You won't always be there to protect her," Brother Rime said as he pushed past the old man, knocking him back as he did.

"I'm not here to protect her," Father said as he grabbed the priest by his upper arm. "I likely just saved your life, Brother. Perhaps you should show me some gratitude."

"You? Saved me? From... her?" Brother Rime pointed at Kit, his hand trembling wildly. "She's... she's an abomination," he seethed as he yanked his arm free from Father's grasp. "Her parents should have drowned her when she was born."

As Brother Rime stormed off down the hall, Father Hoarfrost stepped into the classroom.

He held out his gnarled old hand. "The blade, Kit, if you would be so kind. Carefully, please."

As Kit gently pressed the blade into the High Priest's hand, he gave her a hard look. Kit couldn't tell if it was anger or pride, but whatever it was, it passed quickly when he examined the small dagger.

"Are you well, Silverleaf?" the High Priest asked.

"Yes, Father. Kit completely healed me."

"You healed a wound from a vorpal blade?" Father Hoarfrost asked as his gaze fell upon Kit again. "Unprecedented."

The High Priest continued moving towards the back of the classroom until he came upon the unconscious Iba. "Wake child," he said as he touched his hand to her forehead. As soon as the girl woke up, she flailed at the High Priest, her unfocused eyes looking to attack anyone within striking range.

"Pack your belongings," the High Priest said as he caught the girl's wrist in his hand. "You are done here. In the name of Titan, I cast you out. If you step onto Temple grounds ever again, you will be summarily executed."

With that one simple phrase, the high priest excommunicated Iba.

Chapter Thirteen

The Rite of Abandonment

It had been over a moon since Father Hoarfrost excommunicated Iba. There was a definite split among the priests and acolytes alike as to who was to blame. Brother Rime had been spending a good deal of time telling everyone how Kit was the instigator in the affair and how she had it in for the poor Tahr since her arrival at the Temple.

The acolytes, especially those who had witnessed the encounter, told a completely different story. Even still, there was a clear division between those who supported Iba and those who supported Kit.

On a particularly gloomy, overcast morning, Kit found herself with her best friend Danny, parked under a huge oak tree in the Temple's back garden.

"How long are you going to put off your Rite of Abandonment?" Danny asked as he twirled a long blade of grass between his fingers. "Amara, Slate, and Silverleaf have already attempted it."

"And they all failed," Kit said, frowning at the large bank of clouds that was completely obscuring the top of Titan's ice statue.

"They weren't ready," Danny said with a shrug. "You are."

"You weren't ready either," Kit said, a queasy feeling settling into her stomach. The fear of failure gnawed at her, even if she wasn't worried about her friend mocking her for it. Not wanting to continue the discussion, she quickly deflected the conversation. "Now you're too old to try again. You're washed out."

"Oh, Kitten," the Berrat said, rolling over onto his hip. "I never wanted to become a priest. I'm only here because my parents forced me to come."

"You never heard the call of Titan?" Kit's mouth dropped open. She had shared many private conversations with Danny, but he'd never revealed anything like this before.

"Not even a whisper," he replied, flexing the thick, sinewy muscles on his arm. "I'm surprised he even gave me acolyte-level spells. It's not like I actually ever pray to him."

Kit's mouth fell open as she blinked at her friend. "That's... well... that's blasphemy."

"What's the worst that could happen to me?" Danny said. "I'll get kicked out like Iba did. I'm sure I can find a more comfortable place to rest my head. Maybe I could even find a pretty young thing to share it with me."

Kit gave her handsome friend a look of disapproval before changing the subject.

"How did Amara fail? The Gigas are practically immune to cold. They are inherently attuned to living in high mountain conditions."

"The cold is... unnatural," Danny said, a small shiver wracking through his body. "When the priests dug me out of a snowbank, I was practically a solid block of ice. I didn't even last a full day."

The young Berrat's eyes became glassy as he remembered the experience.

"Sister Gale was dressed in thick furs. She wrapped them around me, holding me close against her body. It took nearly an hour before my blood flowed freely again."

Kit rolled her eyes at her friend. "She did no such thing. You just wish it were true."

"You think I'm lying? Ask Slate, Silverleaf, and Amara. When the priests came to get me, they were all dressed in thick furs."

"With my luck," Kit said with a laugh, "it will be Brother Rime who pulls me from the snow."

"If it's Brother Rime, he'll likely pile more snow on you."

"Excuse me," said a young western human priest with black hair arranged in a series of short braids. Brother Snowpack, a priest she had met many times in the Temple's infirmary, smiled warmly at her.

"Yes, Brother," Kit said, standing up before addressing the young man, looking him straight in his dark brown eyes. "You look well this day."

"Father Hoarfrost wants to see you." The young man tugged on one of his braids, not responding in kind to Kit's pleasantries. "He's in a pretty foul mood."

"He's likely upset you haven't taken the Rite yet," Danny said as he brushed dirt and grass from his breeches.

"He did not say what he wanted," Brother Snowpack replied, shaking his head lightly, causing his braids to dance about on his head. "He only ordered me to find you and ensure that you return with me to his office immediately."

"Well then," Kit said, giving the priest a playful push. "Let's not keep Father waiting. No need to make it any worse by being tardy."

Lump followed along as the priest and acolyte headed through the gardens towards the Temple. Just as they reached the rear entrance, Brother Snowpack grasped Kit's shoulder and raised his eyebrows like he was trying to find just the right words.

"Kit," he finally said, tugging one of the braids on his head. "I hope you pass the Rite. Nobody has been able to pass since I took the test a little over two years ago."

Kit swallowed hard. "You're the only person in two years to complete the rite? How did you do it?"

"I don't really know how I passed when so many others failed. I guess I built a good shelter, and the weather was favorable. By the time the priests came to get me after the third day, I was starving. I couldn't find any food the entire time I was up there."

"That sounds like a good plan then," Kit said, giving the man a genuine smile. "I'll just make sure I pack a lot of food for the trip up the mountain."

Brother Snowpack pursed his lips and shook his head. "You can bring your furs, your boots, and a knife. That's it, nothing else. Lump will have to stay behind, too. He will not be permitted to accompany you."

"Oh, okay then," Kit said as deep furrows creased her brow. "Freezing cold, no food, and no company for three days. I see why so few people ever pass the trial."

"If I can do it, Acolyte Kit, I know you can. You're the most accomplished child this Temple has seen in many, many years."

"You know I'm just a few years younger than you, Brother. I'm fifteen and I'm not a *child* any longer."

The young priest immediately turned scarlet and began tugging at his braids furiously.

"Let's go see Father," Kit said with a small laugh. "No sense in making him any angrier."

⁓⁓⁓⁓⁓⁓⁓

When the trio got to the High Priest's office, the door was open, raised voices coming from within. A moment later, two young acolytes stepped out of the room with their heads hung low. They gave each other a sideways glance and shuffled off down the hall.

A shadow of concern crossed the brother's face. "I think it's time for me to go," he said with a nervous laugh. "Peace unto you, Acolyte." Before Kit even had a chance to reply, the young man had already bolted down the hallway.

Coward.

"Hello, Kit. Please don't lurk outside my door," called the familiar voice of Father Hoarfrost.

The acolyte rubbed the sweat from her hands on her robe. Lump whined softly and gave the girl's hand a quick lick. It was a small gesture, but it was what Kit needed to get her feet moving. Motioning for Lump to follow, the pair slipped into the high priest's office.

As Kit entered, the smell of musty books and peppermint tugged at her nose. Bookcases covered nearly every wall in the High Priest's office, and each shelf was crammed with dusty old tomes, parchments, and scrolls. There were three large windows facing east, and through the windows Kit could see the statue of Titan, its head still obscured by a mass of roiling dark clouds.

The old priest was busy tidying a number of parchments on his desk. The wrinkles on his face appeared even deeper than normal. His bushy white eyebrows were knitted together as though the man was deep in thought. Whatever the acolytes had done, it had profoundly upset him.

"Please, please sit," Father Hoarfrost said, motioning to the large wooden chair in front of his gargantuan dragonwood desk. Lump had already found a quiet place in the corner to lie down and was peacefully snoring away.

Kit hated Father's guest chairs. They were designed for people considerably taller than she was. As she took a seat, her feet dangled above the floor, making her feel like a young child. Kit never felt small when she lived with the Berrat, but at the Temple, at slightly less than five feet, she was well below average in height.

Whatever emotion the old priest had been experiencing vanished, replaced with a thin smile as Kit struggled to position herself in the chair. "This is new," Father Hoarfrost said as he ran his bony fingers over his temple and down his long, gray hair.

"Excuse me, Father? New?"

"The deep red stripe in your otherwise obsidian hair." Again, he motioned with his hand on his own hair to describe the location of the red stripe.

"Oh, that." Kit screwed up her face as she tried to think about how to reply. "I had a bad dream one night, an unbelievably bad dream. The next day, I saw it in my reflection while I was washing up."

"A bad dream?" The old priest cocked his head to the side while he considered her words. "Tell me of this dream."

She shrugged her shoulders. "I don't remember it, not really anyway. I think I was dreaming of a sky dragon." She shook her head. "I'm not sure, Father, it's all very hazy."

Kit's breath quickened.

Why is my dream even worth talking about?

The High Priest was staring at Kit as though he was sizing her up. "Are you well?" he questioned in a flat sort of way.

"Am I well, Father?" Kit's anxiety immediately shifted to confusion. "Yes, I am quite well."

"Are you rested?" he continued.

"Rested, Father? Yes, I suppose so. I'm weary from classes. Sister Gale's martial training has been particularly taxing lately."

"You appear to be in excellent physical condition," the old man said, eyeing the girl from head to toe. "Apparently, Sister Gale has been making sure you put on as much muscle as your tiny frame will hold."

"I am doing my best, Father." Kit cocked an eyebrow as she wondered where this conversation was going.

"Good!" the old priest exclaimed as he slammed his palms down on his massive dragonwood desk, startling Lump, causing the dog to leap to his feet. "You will take the Rite of Abandonment trial tonight."

"Tonight, Father?" Kit squirmed in her chair. She felt a sudden desire to bolt from the room.

"You are nearly sixteen now. You have put this off for far too long and this may well be your last chance to complete the Rite," Father Hoarfrost said, rising up from his chair. "Unless you do not intend to enter into the priesthood..."

Kit jumped to her feet, not liking the way the High Priest was hovering over her. Not that it made much difference, as she wasn't much taller standing up than she was while seated in that oversized wooden chair.

"Of course, I do," she replied in earnest, the words tumbling from her mouth before thinking through what she really wanted to say. This was a common thing for Kit, and it was something that had gotten her into hot water more times than she could count.

"Excellent!" the High Priest declared. He clapped his hands three times, loudly and in rapid succession. A moment later, Sister Gale and Brother Rime stepped into the office, with Sister Alyce and Brother Snowpack standing be-hind them.

"She will begin the trial immediately," announced Father Hoarfrost. All four of the priests nodded curtly, understanding what they must do.

Brother Rime moved in beside Kit and scoffed. "You will not succeed. I look forward to pulling your dead, frozen body from the snow." The priest bent close to Kit's ear. She could feel the moistness of his breath as he spoke in a low, raspy whisper. "Mount Uha is already in the middle of a squall. You won't even last the night."

Lump immediately put himself between Kit and the teacher, a low rumble rolling in the dog's chest. With a sneer, the priest backed away.

"Brother Rime?" the old priest asked. "Is there a problem?"

"No, Father," Brother Rime replied with an obsequious bow. "I just want our young acolyte to understand what she's preparing herself for, and under no circumstances is this beast to accompany her." The man's voice dripped with disdain.

"I have fully prepared her," Sister Gale said, taking a position beside Lump, also putting herself between Kit and Brother Rime. "I have no doubt that she is ready for this."

Kit's heart thumped heavily. Her martial training instructor had never had a kind word for her, and yet, here she was, coming to her defense.

"I have no doubt that you have all contributed to Kit's growth," Father Hoarfrost said, "and now it's time to put that training to the test. And, as Brother Rime has so *eloquently* stated, your companion must remain behind. This test is for you and you alone."

CHAPTER FOURTEEN

THE MOUNTAIN

The high mountain winds were shrill and cutting, blowing snow around Kit with every gust. The priests had taken her to the upper slopes of Mount Uha, to leave her to the elements.

It took the group an entire day to reach the treeline, the place on the mountain where the extreme cold prevented most trees from growing. A heavy snow squall had made the climb far more difficult than it should have been for this season, but the weather was unpredictable and extreme at this altitude.

"Show me your knife," Sister Gale said, pulling her wolf-skin mitten off her hand.

"Brother Rime already searched me," Kit said, scowling at the brother. "I have no contraband."

"I know," Sister Gale said, flexing her exposed fingers, trying to keep the blood flowing. "I wanted to make sure you have it with you."

Kit rummaged into one of several pockets in her furs, pulling out the ulu her mother had given her. As soon as she produced it, Sister Gale rolled it over in her hand, inspecting its quality. With a quick nod of approval, she handed the knife back to Kit and pulled her mitten over her half-frozen hand.

"The sun will be going down in less than an hour. The temperature will plummet as soon as it does. Keep your faith and remember your training. Do that, and you'll do fine."

Sister Gale growled at the other three priests who had already begun to descend the mountain slope.

"Remember," Sister Gale said, turning back to Kit after taking a few steps down the mountainside. "You can do whatever you must to survive, but you cannot venture below the treeline. May Titan's strength protect you."

"His peace unto you, Sister," Kit said, turning to face the steep, snow-covered slope. Thick, gray clouds loomed overhead, obscuring the mountain's pinnacle.

Kit hunched her shoulders as a particularly fierce gust blew across her, the cold cutting straight through her furs, obscuring her vision even further.

Someone of another faith might have viewed this ritual as barbaric or cruel, but Titan demanded followers of a hardier sort. Kit had to show the same determination on this mountain that she would use to chisel her god out of his icy prison.

As another gust of wind set Kit's teeth to chattering, she vowed to herself and her god that by the time the priests returned, she would have found shelter, sustenance, and protection. If she failed, they would be pulling her frozen, lifeless body out of a snowbank.

Peering through the blowing snow, Kit was able to make out a small copse of stunted pine trees a little way up the slope. The dark verdant island stood in deep contrast against the swirling, unrelenting white. With a deep grunt, Kit took her first step towards her destination.

The copse was farther up the slope than Kit had expected, and with the ever-deepening snow, the climb was slow and exhausting. As her heart pumped the heated blood from her chest out to her extremities, she was thankful for the extreme training Sister Gale had put her through.

By the time she reached the pine trees, the squall had passed, and the sky had cleared enough so that the crisp white snow was lighted by the pale glow of a nearly full moon. As the moonlight chased away the last of the deep shadows, Kit gasped. She had been walking precariously close to a huge crevasse. Had her feet carried her a few steps to her right, she may well have become food for the mountain's insatiable hunger.

It was only after taking a few minutes to rest beneath the bows of one of the larger pine trees that Kit realized that perspiration had soaked the clothing under her furs. A blast of wind whipped up an icy cloud of crystalline snow. It somehow managed to find its way through every crease in Kit's furs, instantly chilling her to the bone. She needed to assemble a shelter and warm up fast.

The trees were old, gnarled, and tough. Kit's stone knife wasn't much use as a saw, but she hoped it might score the wood deep enough that she could break off some of the thick lower branches to use for shelter. After several failed attempts, Kit considered shimmying up a tree to try cutting the thinner upper branches, but the trees groaned ominously when the wind shifted, and if she fell, she'd hit every limb on the way down.

After considering the situation further, Kit realized that she could simply fashion a shelter out of the fallen snow. Deciding it was the best course of action, Kit found a place on the leeward side of the trees and dug out a hollow.

After an hour of hard labor, she gave a sigh of satisfaction as she admired her efforts. It quickly turned to ash in her mouth when one side of the cave she had dug collapsed, filling in the majority of the hole.

"It's better that it happened now without me inside," Kit said aloud, shivering so badly that her teeth ached.

"I will not fail you, Titan," she said, pulling her furs tight around her neck. "I will not fail myself."

Kit decided the best course of action was to snap limbs off the trees and assemble them into a crude lean-to. She inwardly hoped the show of strength would please her god, and that the exertion would help warm her body.

She grasped onto one of the thicker bottom branches of a tree, bending it with all her might. Even with her exceptional strength and excellent physical condition, the gnarled old limb refused to yield.

"Titan, hear me," Kit intoned, taking a knee beside the indomitable pine tree. "If I am to free you, I will need your strength."

A surge of cold rushed through Kit, wracking her body with pain so intense that she struggled to maintain consciousness.

"Fine," she said, looking towards Mount Toka, "If you're not going to help me, I'll do it myself."

Kit's joints felt like they'd seized as she picked herself up from the ground. After taking several deep breaths, she grasped the limb again, putting the full force of her tiny body into her effort.

With a sound like a thunderclap, the wood snapped, leaving her with the first of many branches that she'd need to build the structure.

Following the same pattern, Kit continued to break off limbs until she had produced a formidable pile of lumber. With the wind biting at her once more, she piled them against the trunk of the thickest tree she could find. Using the thinnest branches, she wove the larger pieces together until she had a solid structure. The mass of pine bows worked extremely well, creating an impressive evergreen wall.

Kit had oriented the back of the lean-to to face the wind. The blowing snow quickly accumulated against the body of the structure, adding additional insulation against the cold. Building a fire might have gone a long way towards keeping the bitter cold at bay, but with the clouds once again obscuring the moon, it was much too dark and windy to go out looking for windfall branches.

With her furs wrapped tightly around her, Kit crawled into her new shelter and curled herself into a small ball. It was only once she had found a comfortable position that she realized that it was through Titan's strength that she was able to complete the task.

"Thank you," she whispered as she waited for sleep to take her.

CHAPTER FIFTEEN

THE FIRST DAY

The morning broke cold and clear. Kit was relieved to find she was still alive, and quickly offered a prayer of thanks to Titan for keeping her safe through the night. Instinctively, she must have tucked her hands into her armpits while she slept, because the tips of her fingers were frost burned, but after a quick inspection, it was clear that nothing was dead.

On the other hand, everything was sore. She winced as she stood up and stretched her arms and legs, while blood slowly crept back into her extremities.

The night was bad, but it wasn't a true storm. On the heights, things could get much worse.

Kit's stomach growled. She really hadn't eaten very much in the last day. If she was going to survive, she needed to find something to eat before this clear weather changed. Her eyes scanned the area for any sign of food, but alas, all she could see was fresh fallen snow and a few barren, stunted trees.

Past her shelter, the sun rose over Mount Toka, the tallest and most dangerous mountain in all Arnnor. It was from this mountain that the greatest of all Titan's statues was carved. Nobody could say for sure just how tall Titan's statue was. Its head and shoulders spent most of the time in the clouds. Some believed that the statue wasn't made of stone at all. Instead, they believed it was made of some sort of *magical ice* that never melted, even during the hottest summer days.

As the sun cleared the top of Toka, the statue glistened in the morning light, illuminating every detail of the magnificent wonder. She estimated that her position was still many hundreds of feet lower than the top of the statue, and that she was near the very peak of the mountain on which she was standing.

When she finally snapped back from her musings, Kit found herself facing another choice; how she was going to go about foraging for food. She could search for small game, knowing there was not likely to be much above the treeline, or she could try to forage for wild edibles, frozen roots, plants, or maybe even berries trapped beneath the icy mantle of snow.

She hated the idea of rummaging through the snow for frozen bits, so she headed downslope towards the treeline, figuring it would maximize her chances of success in finding small game. Predators would sometimes chase smaller animals up-slope, and she hoped to be lucky enough to find an exhausted rabbit or maybe even a ram.

The morning sunlight gleamed off the snow as she searched, sometimes blinding her with its brilliance. All the while, the cold, thin air nipped at her exposed skin.

Several long, uneventful hours passed. She had started her hunt full of purpose, but by midday she had found nothing. She couldn't tell if it was the altitude, or the lack of food, but Kit was beginning to feel lightheaded. Her head snapped to the left when a shadow caught her eye. The shape resembled that of an arctic hare. One moment it was there, the next it was gone. With renewed vigor, the young acolyte bolted off in what she hoped was the direction the animal had taken.

Her knees pumped through the deep snow. She was quickly running out of energy. Kit's lungs were burning as she tried to catch her breath. She dropped heavily to her knees, on the verge of utter exhaustion.

Gaia, help me.

Kit didn't know why she called on the old god, the god of the Berrat. Perhaps it was because she was defeated and ready to turn back. Perhaps this rite was all about testing her faith in the face of adversity. Perhaps it was because she was starving, and she was willing to try anything for a chance at having a meal.

She had come too far, done too much. She would achieve her goal. She would not give Brother Rime the satisfaction of finding her frozen corpse in the snow.

Get up, you fool! Failure is not an option.

With a deep sigh, Kit pushed herself up out of the snow. The only indication anything had been there were her own footprints. Perhaps she could retrace her steps back to the trees where she had first spotted the shadow. She pivoted on the spot and followed her footsteps. Again, she caught sight of the animal.

⚜

There was a blotch of differently hued white against the snow, right on the edge of the treeline. If she didn't know better, Kit would have sworn it was waiting for her.

If it were a hare, there wouldn't be much meat on the animal, but *not much* was way better than *none.*

She steadied her breathing, and moved gradually, methodically, towards the hare. It was busy digging in the snow, perhaps hunting for frozen morsels of food for itself. Between the never-ending wind and the softness of the snow, Kit was able to close the distance to just a few paces. As she readied her ulu, the hare disappeared beneath the snow.

"Titan's snowballs," Kit cursed out loud. "I nearly had you."

Assuming that the rabbit had disappeared into his warren, Kit charged towards the spot where it had vanished beneath the mantle of white.

Peering down the hole, Kit found the winter hare staring back up at her, sitting atop the frozen carcass of a mountain sheep.

"Gaia," Kit exclaimed as the rabbit leapt from the hole and bounded off into the snow. "Great spirit, thank you." She had unknowingly called upon the old god once again. Surely Titan would punish her for this blasphemy, but right now, she didn't care.

The young acolyte dug frantically in the snow until she revealed the half-eaten carcass. There were great rents in the animal's wool-covered skin. Kit had heard tales of great mountain cats, sabretooth lions with fangs as long as her forearm, and phantom cats that vanished from sight, only to reappear moments later next to their prey. Though they rarely ventured this far north, Kit was confident these were the leavings of a wolverine, The Great Hunter, one of the four aspects of Gaia.

"I will take only what I need," Kit said as she snapped the hind leg off the frozen carcass. "The rest I leave for you and your kittens."

With her prize in hand, Kit covered the remains with snow, knowing that whatever had left it there would be able to find it. With renewed hope, the young acolyte trudged back up the mountain to where she had built her shelter.

The excitement of the hunt had burned up a considerable amount of what little energy Kit had left. She tossed the sheepshank into her lean-to, feeling the need to lie down. She dropped to her knees, ready to sleep, but she feared that if she did, she might never wake up.

Kit remained kneeling in the snow for several minutes, taking time to rest and to thank Titan for the hardships he was offering her, and for the understanding, even if it was only minor, of what her god must be enduring in his icy prison.

She wasn't sure how long she knelt in prayer, but when Kit opened her eyes, she felt refreshed and rejuvenated. A sense of wellbeing and belonging permeated her soul.

With renewed purpose, Kit went about gathering firewood from the fallen limbs of the trees that were now her home. Using her knife, she carved out a hollow in one of the thicker branches and filled it with dead pine needles. Placing a thin, straight branch into the hollow, Kit rubbed her hands rapidly, spinning the branch while she did. Within a few moments, a wisp of smoke appeared from the pile of needles. A moment later, tiny flames licked up, igniting the tinder. While gently placing thin, dry branches over the needles, she blew lightly over the flames, encouraging them until they were burning brightly, filling the air with the acrid scent of smoke.

While the fire was burning down to a blazing bed of embers, Kit used her ulu to carve off a substantial hunk of meat from the frozen carcass. So as to not attract animals, the young acolyte dug a deep hole in the snow to bury the remainder of the sheepshank.

While the small roast cooked over a crackling fire, Kit dug a shallow latrine and prepared the amenities required for a basic campsite. Despite feeling much more prepared, she was still extremely exposed. If an apex predator were to find her, there would be little she could do to defend herself.

As Kit ate a ration of roasted meat, she considered her options. She could try to create a shield from branches or put a basic enchantment on her stone knife to make it more deadly, or she could prepare herself both mentally and physically for combat.

Any wood I find that's suitable for making a shield would also make good fuel for my fire. If I can't stay warm, I'll die anyway.

She stared down at her ulu and shook her head.

Maybe if I had stayed awake during enchantment classes, I'd know how to make my knife more deadly.

Kit carved off another slice of roast and quickly licked the smoky juice running down her fingers. It wasn't as good as Sister Miyuki's cooking, but she devoured every bite like it was the best food she'd ever tasted.

Meditation and training. Titan expects me to be ready for anything, so that's where I'll start.

With a belly full of food and a renewed sense of purpose, Kit banked the fire, helping to ensure it would continue to burn and not smolder out. Satisfied with her efforts, the girl decided it was time to train. Moving deeper into the copse of trees, she started off by going through some of the basic patterns she had learned from Sister Gale. She was sluggish performing them, but with practice, Kit quickly learned how to adjust her footing and her style to work in the deep snow. After several hours, Kit's legs wobbled like jelly. There was no benefit in overexerting herself, so she headed back to her lean-to.

Kit stared into her humble abode and exhaled deeply. What currently passed for her bed beckoned to her. She rubbed her arms and legs, feeling the exhaustion in them. "Enough for one day," she muttered to herself. She tossed a few of the larger branches onto her fire before curling up in her bed, falling immediately into a deep sleep.

Chapter Sixteen

Tracks in the Night

On the morning of the second day, the air was again crisp and clear, yet warmer than she'd expected for this early in the spring. Kit could not let her guard down and become complacent because of the good weather.

She stepped out from under the cover of her lean-to and gasped. There was a multitude of paw prints around her camp. Judging by the size of them, a pack of wolves had likely found her. Their tracks were everywhere. Several of them may have even entered her shelter.

Why didn't they try to eat me? My food!

She raced over to where she had buried the remainder of her sheep shank and found it untouched. She cocked an eyebrow and surveyed the area. Whatever their reasoning was for not killing her, the girl was happy to be alive.

After Kit finished taking care of her morning needs, she got back to her training. Following the same idea of the previous day, Kit started with some of the simple fighting patterns taught by the Temple. As her muscles loosened up and her blood started to flow, she worked her way up to the more intricate patterns that required precise movements, heightened balance, and extreme flexibility.

By midafternoon, Kit was as comfortable fighting in the grove as she would be fighting in the training halls of the Fist.

During her exercises, she inadvertently revealed some snow-covered prickle-berry bushes. Regardless of the remaining berries being frozen solid, she gathered them all, adding the prized fruit to her remaining supply of roasted sheep. Prickle-berries were rare, and even if frozen solid, they were an amazing treat.

Kit built another fire and roasted the last of the sheepshank. While she waited for the meat to cook, she scraped off any remaining bits of flesh clinging to the animal's thick thigh bone, making sure to not waste even the smallest amount of food.

When evening came, Kit's body was once again utterly exhausted, but her soul was fully sated. She reignited the embers of her fire, fueling it with wood she had managed to gather over the course of her training. Sleep came easily that night, but it didn't last for long.

No sooner had she fallen into a deep slumber, Kit woke with an excruciating pain in her leg. A large animal was dragging her from her refuge, its dagger-like teeth embedded in her calf muscle. With a flick of the great beast's head, Kit was thrown up against a pine tree, its bows digging into her back.

Scrambling for cover, the young acolyte scampered underneath the tree, hoping to find a hole small enough for her to slip into. She cried out in agony as the beast sunk its teeth into her leg a second time, dragging her into the open.

With no weapon at hand, Kit used her fists to strike out at the animal. She landed repeated blows, but to no effect. With spots beginning to dance in front of her eyes, she kicked out with her free leg, striking the animal in its large, glistening eye. With a howl, the creature dropped her to the ground and roared out a challenge, the spittle from its mouth striking her in the face.

Under the pale light of the moon, Kit got a look at the sabretooth lion as it stalked around her, its huge paws kicking up puffs of snow with each step. A low, primordial rumble came from deep within its chest.

As the animal moved in for the kill, several pairs of jade-green eyes appeared on the far side of the lion. The wolves' threatening growls drew the giant cat away from Kit.

There was a sudden flurry as several animals jumped over her, engaging the lion. Barely able to stand, Kit gritted her teeth. "Titan, hear me," she growled out. A moment later, a deep-green aura exploded outward from her, engulfing the lion and the wolves attacking it.

Kit rolled out of the way as a huge gray wolf landed at her feet, a large gash across his face. In seconds, her aura engulfed the animal. Almost immediately, the blood gushing from its deep wound slowed. The wound was still horrendous, but the aura allowed him to continue fighting. The large animal gave Kit a quick, almost appreciative glance before jumping back into the fray.

For several minutes, the battle of the creatures raged on. The dim lighting mixed with the speed and ferocity of the animals as they fought tooth and nail, made it nearly impossible to tell what was happening. The great cat spit and clawed at the wolves, but their coordinated attacks gave them the advantage. Eventually, the wolves gained the upper hand, and the lion bounded off down the mountainside. Several of the wolves gave chase, making sure the lion had no interest in returning.

After the cat retreated, several of the wolves moved towards Kit. With their heads low and their ears pinned back, they circled. Had they chased off the lion so they could have her for themselves?

A great white wolf, by far the largest in the pack, moved towards Kit, its movement slow and deliberate.

"Thank you," Kit said, as she staggered a few steps away from the advancing alpha. Unlike her healing spell, which could almost entirely heal a wound, the battle spell only provided minor healing over a period of time, usually just enough to keep a warrior in combat. Like the wolf, she was far from healed, but able to continue. "Did you save my life, or were you just scaring him away so that I could be your meal?"

The alpha turned and walked back to a smaller gray wolf lying in the snow, its blood puddling out beneath it in a black pool. The great white wolf nosed the fallen pack member, trying to rouse it. It turned back to Kit, a deep sadness filling its jade-green eyes.

Kit stared down at the wounded animal, a huge lump in her throat.

"If you will spare me, I can heal your friend," Kit said, holding her hands out in a defensive position.

One of the wolves, a big gray, unleashed a series of panicked, high-pitched barks. It bounded over to the fallen wolf and laid at its side.

Hoping beyond reason that the pack had accepted Kit's offer, she hobbled closer to the injured animal. As she approached, two more wolves moved to the acolyte's side.

"Titan, hear me," Kit said as she knelt next to the wolf. When Kit's hands glowed a pale yellow, she placed them on the neck and side of the wolf, the most obvious sources of the bleeding. The glow from Kit's hands stretched out across the animal and died off as quickly as it had appeared. Her chest heaved with grief. The wounds were too severe for her power to heal them. The big gray that laid beside the fallen wolf whined and stared at the girl, begging her to not give up.

"Titan," Kit said, bellowing at Mount Toka in the distance. "You cannot let this creature die."

There was nothing left in her healing power, but she refused to accept that. She dug deep within herself. There had to be more. There had to be some way. Somewhere in the recesses of her soul, a tiny spark burned within her. With all her being, she reached for it, coaxed it, nurtured it, until it burst forth from her in a blinding flash of deep-yellow light.

Kit cried out in agony as the golden glow enveloped her and the wolf, extending out to surround the entire pack that had moved in so close that Kit could feel their combined warmth. Her healing spell wasn't supposed to hurt like this. Something was wrong. Very, very wrong.

As the golden aura dissipated, Kit fell face-first, unconscious on the snow.

Chapter Seventeen

The Final Day

When morning broke, the sky overhead was again unnaturally clear, and the sun was strong enough to melt the surface of the snow. Kit squinted and shielded her eyes as she peered out from her lean-to.

Had I dreamt it?

She quickly checked out her leg, finding her pants shredded and blood-soaked. She could only assume that she managed to crawl into her camp sometime in the night after she had regained consciousness. Peering past the tears in the cloth, she was surprised to find no visible wounds. Her own wounds should not have healed with her healing spell. She'd put everything into healing the dying wolf. Then again, the why of it wasn't important. What was important was that she was alive and whole.

Jumping from her resting place, Kit raced outside. Crimson stains and a mass of paw prints told the story of the great battle. The memory of the fallen wolf and the agonizing pain she felt when she tried to heal it came flooding back.

"Where were you when I needed you?" Kit said as she glared over at the great statue carved into the face of Mount Toka. "Why would you let such a noble creature die, one that had willingly sacrificed itself to protect me?"

A crushing sadness washed over the girl. She walked around the camp, searching for the dead wolf, but found no sign of it. There was still a great deal of blood staining the snow, but no corpse. Had she healed it? The wolves may have dragged their pack-member away, but there was no indication this had happened.

"Forgive me, Titan. Forgive me for doubting you." She swallowed down the lump growing in her throat. "Thank you for saving the animal. I will prove myself worthy. I swear it to you."

Feeling rejuvenated and full of purpose, the small girl smiled. She looked down the mountain slope and nodded.

I made it. The priests should be coming to get me by the day's end. If I can survive until sundown, I will finally be accepted within the temple, welcomed as a true priest of Titan.

Without any real idea of what she was going to do until they came to retrieve her, Kit returned to the impromptu training grounds she'd created for herself and resumed her activities. As before, she started off with her basic patterns as she normally would, but today she also took some time to practice with a heavy branch that she fashioned into a crude club. Its weight was lighter than her iron battle hammer, but it was more than adequate for its purpose.

Kit moved to a circle of small pines, placing herself in the middle of them. She practiced attacking and defending against multiple imaginary opponents. Using a series of elaborate maneuvers, she punched, kicked, and swung her club at the trees until they were nothing more than battered ruins.

She finally took a break, her chest heaving from the exertion. There was a thick bank of clouds gathering in the north. A sudden shift in the wind brought an icy breeze towards her. A storm was coming, and it was coming fast. Kit had been so engrossed in her training that she had failed to be mindful of her surroundings.

After wasting a few minutes admonishing herself, she quickly gathered up as much firewood as she could carry before racing back to her lean-to. When she arrived, the young acolyte quickly built up the fire in the hopes that it could keep her warm through the oncoming blizzard. The winds picked up and the blowing snow fell in earnest.

Pele had still not set in the western sky, but with the gathering clouds, it was becoming as dark as any night might be. The wind turned into a howling, living thing, throwing sheet after sheet of snow and freezing pellets over the trees while Kit hunkered down, trying to wait out the storm's fury.

The fire quickly succumbed to the barrage of snow and sleet. The winds shifted, sending the unrelenting flurry directly into Kit's shelter. As the snow piled up around her, Kit tried her best to push it back out. Disregarding the biting winds, Kit pulled her furs off her back and tried to use them as a windbreak. With any luck, she could hold the snow off long enough that it would pile up around her lean-to without completely burying her.

Just when Kit thought her luck was changing for the better, the branches of her lean-to began to groan under the weight of the snow piling up over her. In a last-ditch effort to prevent a cave in, Kit called out for Titan again.

"Titan, hear me," she bellowed, her blood boiling with rage.

The young woman's hands became coated in a thick layer of frost. Holding them out before her, Kit sprayed ice pellets at the walls of her dwelling, coating them with a heavy layer of ice. She didn't stop until she felt the structure could support the weight.

Just as she completed shoring up her lean-to's walls, the room went pitch black. Kit scrabbled around until she found her furs. As carefully as she could, she tried to yank them free from the snow. When she finally liberated her fur cloak, Kit wrapped it tightly around herself, thankful for the warmth it provided.

It was impossible to tell how much time had passed as Kit sat in her frozen cocoon. The priests should have been on their way. It had been a full three days, but considering the weather, they would likely make Kit spend a fourth night alone on the mountainside. With her head leaning against the frozen wall, Kit slipped off into a deep sleep.

"You have proven yourself worthy, priest," said a disembodied voice. "It's time to awake."

Kit's eyes slowly opened to the pitch-blackness of her shelter. She blinked several times before she remembered what had happened. She felt her way to where the exit of her lean-to should be. With her heart beating out of control, she pulled out her ulu and commenced digging her way out through the snow. After many minutes, her fingers were near frozen. She gutted through the pain and continued digging. A sudden panic struck her.

Sweet Titan, what if I'm under fifty feet of snow?

She was not going to give up. She was not going to die on this mountain. The ulu was too slow, but she was not going to stop until she breathed fresh mountain air again. It was only then that she remembered the club she had fashioned for training. After several minutes of scrabbling around in the darkness, she found the battered piece of wood.

Scrambling with it back into the tunnel she'd been digging, she used the end of the club to scrape at the snow. It was no more effective than using her ulu, but it was much less painful. She wasn't always wrist deep in the snow anymore. Her chest burned with each stroke of the club.

Don't pass out, you fool.

When the snow got a bit easier to dig into, she shoved the club hard upwards. It burst through the thin crust of ice above. As the fresh night air poured in through the hole, Kit inhaled deeply. The intense pain in her chest instantly dissipated.

"Thank Titan," she whispered as she pulled her furs a little tighter around herself.

Peering out at the star-filled sky, Kit considered her next step. The snow had stopped falling. She could stay cocooned in her cozy den, or she could step out into the night. Deciding that the priests may never find her, Kit dug with earnest, shivering badly when the loosened snow fell down her neck and back.

When she had finally made the hole wide enough for her slender body to squirm through, Kit poked her head out to get a better idea of her situation. When a snow-laden gust of wind bit at her skin, she quickly pulled her hood up and scrambled out of her hole.

⸺⸻❦⸻⸺

Desperate to stay warm and keep the cold at bay, Kit hopped lightly and rubbed her arms. Anything to get her blood moving again. Whatever cold she had experienced earlier was nothing compared to the cold that was ripping through her furs now. She stared longingly back at the hole she had just pulled herself out of. It was warm inside her den. There was no wind, only darkness and solitude.

"For you, Titan," Kit said as she turned towards Mount Toka and the giant statue of her god. As she offered her prayer, the bite of the wind didn't feel quite so vicious. The sun's rays had not yet broken over the mountains, but the sky was beginning to lighten, shifting from black to deep blues.

It was only then that Kit spotted the priests coming up the side of the mountain, their torches like small candles being carried in a procession. She had survived the trial. Not just survived, she had fully surpassed every expectation she had set for herself.

As Kit peered through the darkness, it seemed that the approaching priests were all fully armed and armored. By the light of their torches, she could see they were carrying ceremonial axes and hammers.

Why? Why would they need those weapons? Ceremonial weapons were pretty to look at, but not particularly effective in combat.

When Danny had told her of his story, the priests were wearing furs, like they had been when they delivered Kit to the mountaintop. It was only then that Kit caught the menacing grin of Brother Rime.

The girl's head snapped backwards.

They're not here to bring me down. They're here to make sure I never leave this mountain. No matter what I do, I will never be good enough for them. I will never fit in.

Setting her jaw, Kit huffed loudly.

Come and get me. Kill me if you must, but I'm not going down without a fight.

Kit glowered at her makeshift club, easing up on the death-grip she had been putting on it.

Stay calm. Consider your opponent. Prepare yourself.

The words of Sister Gale's martial training came seeping to the forefront.

They're carrying melee weapons, and I'm outnumbered. Find a place where they cannot use their numerical advantage against me.

Looking back over her shoulders, Kit considered returning to the copse of trees. There was no hope of hiding, but at least she could make it difficult for them to surround her. Spinning on the spot, Kit pumped her arms and legs as she climbed up through the thick, freshly fallen snow. By the time she slipped in behind the first of the pine trees, she was already breathing heavily.

The climb up the mountainside will be no easier for them. They'll be tired as well.

The snow inside the copse wasn't as deep as it was in the open, where the wicked winds had piled the snow in huge drifts. Where the snow was thinnest, the pine bows above were bending badly under the weight of the white powder.

After quickly racing about, trying to pack as much of the snow down with her feet as she could, Kit peered out between two of the larger trees. Now that the priests were much closer, Kit could see their faces quite clearly.

At the lead was Brother Rime. His eyes were locked on Kit, giving her an intense, fevered stare, his mouth curled into a deep frown. Behind him was Sister Gale, Brother Snowpack, and Sister Alyce. Their faces were grim, but they didn't seem to share the same loathing as Brother Rime.

None of the priests were saying a word as they reached the grove. Brother Rime motioned to Brother Snowpack and Sister Alyce, and they broke away from the group, moving around the outside of the copse.

They're going to try to cut off any escape to the rear.

Kit slipped between the pines, trying her best to make her location a mystery.

As soon as Brother Rime made it to the treeline, a burst of pale light engulfed his battle hammer, lighting up the surrounding area.

"Brother Rime, what are you doing?" Sister Gale hissed.

Ignoring the priest's question, the brother stepped into the grove, the light from his hammer illuminating his maniacal expression.

While Sister Gale was taking a direct line towards Kit, Brother Snowpack and Sister Alyce were working at flanking her. Their feet repeatedly broke through the snow, slowing their progress substantially.

As the sun broke over the peak of Mount Toka, it glistened off the snow-crystals, reflecting its cold light in a kaleidoscope of colors.

"Don't make this any harder on yourself than it needs to be, *priest*." Sister Gale called out as she picked up her pace.

As Kit edged towards the rising sun, she spotted Brother Snowpack racing up outside the trees. His feet were pumping hard through the deep snow, his face covered with perspiration. There was no sign of Sister Alyce.

Kit liked Brother Snowpack, but he was likely the easiest path out of this predicament.

"There is no escape for you," Brother Rime ground out as he closed in on Kit.

Seeing that the priest would be on her before she could make it to the treeline, Kit threw herself to the side, putting her back to one of the trees. Taking a defensive stance, she crouched low and readied her weapon.

"Titan, hear me," she whispered, calling on her god for increased combat speed, her nerves flaring with brief, intense pain as the spell took hold.

With the training she had done in the grove, Kit hoped she would be able to move easily and quickly amid her opponents. While they struggled to move through the deep snow, Kit moved with relative ease. She smoothly ducked under Brother Rime's wild hammer swing, returning a solid blow with her club to his midsection. A warmth filled Kit's chest at the sound of the priest wheezing, knowing that she had knocked the wind out of him. Pressing her advantage, Kit brought her makeshift club down on his back, sending the man face-first onto the frozen ground.

Kit was about to deliver a killing blow when she was struck in the ribs, searing pain radiating across her chest. As she turned to see her attackers, she caught a glimpse of a heel that was sailing towards her head. Quickly ducking under the attack, Kit counter attacked with her club, catching Sister Gale just below the knee, dropping her with a thud onto her back.

As Kit moved in on her fallen teacher, a bolt of ice hit her on the shoulder, sending her sprawling into the limbs of a pine tree, knocking the snow from its branches.

Sister Gale loomed over Kit with a strange look on her face.

Is that remorse?

Kit rolled under the bows, making it impossible for the woman to land a clean blow. On the far side of the tree, Brother Snowpack prevented her escape.

"You chose to enhance your speed," Sister Gale called out as she and Snow-pack circled her, cutting Kit off before she could find a safe exit. "An excellent choice, considering your circumstances."

"Why are you doing this?" Kit yelled as she scrambled about beneath the pine canopy, growling when she saw Brother Rime getting back to his feet.

"You will not walk down this mountain," Sister Gale said. "Don't prolong this, *priest.*"

"I don't plan on making this easy on you," Kit said as she scampered away from Brother Rime, emerging on the far side of the tree. The ground was quite sloped where she was standing, and as Brother Snowpack and Sister Gale emerged from opposite sides of the tree, Kit had an elevation advantage.

She moved quickly up the slope to the next tree. Its bows were heavily laden with the ice-covered powder. Using her club, Kit struck the tree's trunk, releasing its frosty burden. As the snow hit the ground, it tumbled down the hill, taking Sister Gale's feet out from underneath her.

While the snow swept Sister Gale away, Brother Rime closed in and dropped the head of his weapon onto her left shoulder. There was a loud crunch of bone causing Kit to cry out. Before she could react, the priest brought down another blow onto the same spot, sending a bolt of pain through her body. Fighting to maintain consciousness, Kit struck out with a kick, catching her attacker just below the knee, knocking him off balance. Pain exploded in her shoulder as she clambered up the slope to put some distance between her and her assailants.

As she climbed, a thought struck her. Sister Gale had referred to her as *priest.*

"Titan, hear me," Kit called out again. A moment later, her club was crack-ling with energy, lightning-like sparks dancing over the length of the makeshift weapon.

Placing her hand on the ground, Kit envisioned her god, his disappointment in his children, and his undiluted wrath. With all the faith she could muster, Kit brought her club down on the ground, releasing a shockwave that reverberated in all directions.

As the ground shook, the trees released the snow clinging to their bows. An avalanche tumbled down the mountainside, sweeping Brother Rime up with it, carrying him down the slope. Kit inwardly hoped the man would drop into the crevasse that she had passed on the way up the hill. A wicked grin crossed her face.

"Well done, *priest*," Sister Gale said as she stared down at Kit. "You fought well. Calling upon Titan for an earthquake was... inspired."

Kit turned to find her combat instructor standing beside her, a bemused ripple touched the woman's face. That was the last thing she remembered before a chainmail gauntlet punched her squarely in the head.

THE AFTERMATH

When Kit awoke, she found herself in the Temple infirmary with a scratchy woolen blanket pulled up under her chin. She moaned softly as she stared up at the thick wooden beams that supported the floor above her. Every inch of her body ached, and each breath was labored. She couldn't help but wonder why the priests had attacked her, or why they'd brought her back to the Temple and didn't bother to heal her. That was likely Sister Gale's doing, with her belief that pain was a great teacher.

Kit let out a small yelp as she tried to lift her head. A stabbing pain radiated out from her shoulder, making even the tips of her hair feel like they were on fire. She winced as she pulled the thin, gray shirt down from her shoulder, revealing a deep purple bruise.

"You're awake," said a young acolyte of maybe thirteen years. He was considerably heavier than most acolytes, marking him as a cook or a baker. He rolled himself over on his cot so that he was directly facing Kit. "Your friends are going to be disappointed they weren't here for you."

"Hey," Kit replied, her voice hoarse. "My friends?"

The boy nodded quickly. "Danny and Amara are the only two whose names I know, but there was also a dwarf and a half elf. They hardly ever left your side, at least not until Sister Alyce chased them away. I thought she was going to take a broom to Danny to get him to leave."

The notion that she had friends to watch over her warmed Kit's soul. It brought back the memory of the wolves who had put themselves at risk for her, watching over her as she slept. Never had she ever heard of such a thing happening.

"You beat the mountain," the boy said, his dark-skinned face lighting up with wonder, his chocolate eyes gleaming. "Nobody ever beats the mountain."

"What do you mean, beat the mountain?" Kit asked, lowering her back down to her thin, straw pillow.

"You hadn't suffered enough," a new voice said from the far side of the room. "Acolytes are meant to fail the challenge and suffer hunger and severe cold. This suffering is meant to help them understand what their god endures every minute of every year." Kit picked her head up high enough to see Brother Snowpack bouncing across the room, his crazy braids dancing on his head.

Lump bolted from Kit's bedside to meet the man. She didn't even know the dog was there until just that moment. She chuckled at the sight, sending a shooting pain through her skull.

"I didn't beat anything," Kit said, letting her head drop back down on her pillow. "I simply managed to survive."

"You didn't just survive, little *sister*," the priest replied. "You thrived. You could have endured an entire winter up there from what we saw."

Lump jumped onto the cot and curled up at the girl's feet. Despite losing the bottom third of her bed to the large dog, he comforted her in a way she couldn't begin to describe.

"What do you mean, from what you saw?" Kit asked as another bout of pain blossomed through her shoulder. She closed her eyes for a moment and took a deep, cleansing breath. A pale-yellow glow covered her body, and she let out a deep sigh. When she picked her head up again, there was only the slightest hint of discomfort from her shoulder.

"Your healing skills are remarkable," Brother Snowpack said as he pulled his gaze away from Kit and rubbed the back of his neck.

"Answer my question," Kit said, pushing herself up onto her elbows.

When Brother Snowpack's eyes fell on the acolyte next to Kit, he shook his head. "Not now."

With a huff, Kit swung her bare legs over the side of the bed. When the cold air hit her skin, she gasped and quickly pulled her woolen blanket over herself. She was not going to go walking around in just the thin gray infirmary shift she was wearing.

"Let me get your robes," Brother Snowpack said as he rummaged through a large chest at the foot of Kit's bed. He nonchalantly tossed a set of white robes onto Kit's lap.

"These aren't mine," Kit said as she stared down at the garment, running her fingers over the smooth, fine material. "My robe is gray, rough-spun wool."

"Father Hoarfrost delivered them yesterday. He told me to give them to you when you were well enough to put them on."

"But... these are priests' robes," Kit said, swallowing hard.

"Indeed, they are, Sister Kit. You passed the Rite, and now you are a priest, like me. Well, almost anyway. There are some formalities which must be observed first."

Brother Snowpack glared at the young acolyte beside Kit, gesturing for him to turn away while Kit pulled on her new robes. Lump's growl punctuated the man's signal, ensuring immediate compliance.

"Are you well enough to walk down to the kitchens, Sister?" Brother Snowpack said with a grin. "I'm thinking you must be hungry. You've been in here with nothing to eat for almost three full days."

"I'm famished," Kit replied, staring down at her fresh white robes. As she hopped down from her cot and her bare feet touched the cold stone floor, a cold shiver ran up her legs.

"I can cook you a meal," the young acolyte blurted out. He had his hands over his eyes, splaying his fingers, affording him a clear view of the young woman standing before him.

"After you poisoned yourself cooking up mushrooms?" Brother Snowpack said in a scolding tone. "I think our young priest has suffered enough, don't you?"

The acolyte flopped back onto his bed and rolled over. He mumbled something about it being an accident before falling silent.

"Now, tell me how you saw me," Kit whispered as the pair exited the room, Lump padding along at their heels.

⁂

The young man's eyes darted up and down the hallway. "You can't tell *anyone* that I told you this."

Kit nodded, spurring the priest to continue speaking.

"After we left you on the mountain, there was always one of us keeping an eye on you, making sure that nothing terrible happened.

"You mean like being attacked by a sabretooth lion?" Kit asked, her voice cracking.

"Yes, exactly. If something horrible like that were to befall upon you, there would be at least one of us to come to your rescue."

"Then where were you when I was attacked?" Kit asked as she rounded on the man. "If it wasn't for the wolves coming to my aid, I'd have never survived the encounter."

"What?" The man's mouth dropped open. "When?"

"On my second night," Kit said, her brows knitting together in a tight vee.

"Brother Rime," Brother Snowpack said, baring his teeth. "He was on duty that night." The priest's demeanor changed as his eyes became wide. "You were attacked by a lion and wolves protected you? That's unprecedented. Were you able to kill it?"

"No, we drove him off." Kit grimaced and scratched at her temple. "Something happened when I healed one of the wolves."

"You healed a wolf?"

"Yes," she said as she pulled her fingers through her hair. "He was severely injured and when I called for Titan, he wouldn't help me. I tried harder, and when I did, my healing power... it... well, it hurt so bad that I passed out."

"Healing another doesn't hurt," Brother Snowpack said, taking a step away from Kit. "That's not normal."

The two walked in silence for the rest of the trip down to the kitchens. When they entered, cheers sprang up from the gathered crowd. At the farthest side of the hall, Amara stood and waved Kit over. Her straw-colored hair was tied in loose braids and gathered into a tight bun on top of her head.

As Kit made her way towards her friends, Lump followed close while Brother Snowpack lagged behind.

Danny was the first to greet Kit, gently wrapping his arms around her, giving her a noisy wet kiss on her cheek. "Congratulations, *Sister Kit*," he said with a broad smile. "They decided to heal you?"

Kit shook her head and gave her Berrat friend a coy grin. "No, Acolyte, I healed myself." She stared at him for a long while before they both burst out laughing. Danny quickly wrapped his arms around her again, this time hugging Kit with enough enthusiasm that he picked her up off the ground.

Slate slid a plate of sweet biscuits towards Kit. "Sister Miyuki made these for you, in case you came down today."

Kit willingly accepted the gesture, slipping one of the treats to Lump. She took a seat beside her friends while the dog took his usual place at the girl's feet, under the table. Kit's hunger got the better of her, and she quickly took a huge bite from one of the fluffy, fruit-filled biscuits. The flavor was amazing. As she took a moment or two to savor each morsel, she inadvertently let out a soft moan.

By the time Kit finished telling her tale, there were several dozen people gathered around, priests and acolytes alike. The entire group crushed in on her as she described her fight with the *rescue party*.

"I was doing pretty well," Kit declared as she took a big sip of her coffee, "until I got punched in the face."

"Sister Gale!" the entire group yelled in unison.

"The way she told it," Danny said, his eyes wild with excitement, "they quickly overpowered you and you barely put up a fight at all."

Slate laughed deeply, his eyes seeking out those who were closest to Kit. "But the next day, in martial training class, when we all saw how badly bruised Sister Gale was ... you had clearly put up a good fight."

A wide grin broke across Kit's face as she raised her mug, "To Sister Gale, may she never punch me that hard ever again!" Again, the entire group broke into cheers.

When Kit had told her tale from every possible perspective, the group finally dissipated, leaving Kit alone with her friends.

"I'm surprised Sister Miyuki isn't here," Kit said, glancing towards the kitchens.

"Sister Miyuki's off buying supplies for the upcoming Feast of Titan's Bounty celebrations," Danny said, stretching back over his chair before tousling his bright red hair. "I can't wait to see what meal she'll be making this year. She always goes over the top."

"I'm going to go find her," Kit said, seemingly ignoring her friend's comment, widening her eyes for extra effect. "I'm a priest now, I can leave the Temple any time I like."

"Ooh. Aren't we special!" Silverleaf said, earning him a clap on the back of his head from Amara.

"Don't be jealous," the giant said in a deep threatening voice. "Just because we failed, doesn't mean we can't share in Kit's joy and newfound freedoms."

Silverleaf glowered at the giant before lowering his eyes in shame. "Sorry, Kit. Have fun with your newfound freedom." When the half elf lifted his head, a wide grin slowly spread across his face. "And that hurt," he said to Amara before giving her a solid punch in the shoulder. When she reached out for him, he slipped beneath her grasp and giggled wildly.

"I guess this also means you'll be moving to the priest's quarters," Danny said. "It won't be the same on our floor without you. We won't be able to pop in and visit anytime we want."

Kit gave the Berrat a quizzical look. "I'll just be a floor above you. Is that too far for you to walk?" Her comment made Danny laugh.

"I'd walk to the ends of Orth to visit you, Kitten. But we acolytes aren't allowed up there, not without a good reason at any rate. So, like I said, things won't be the same."

The new priest stood from her seat and gave her best friend a shrug. "I guess I'll have to come visit you then. My new title changes nothing. Not between us anyway."

"Sure," Danny said, shaking his head. "Except now that you're a priest, you're going to be so busy, you won't be able to find the time. It's just the way it is."

"No. It isn't," Kit said, giving her friend a hug. "I promise. Now, I've got to go and find Miyuki."

"Like I said." The Berrat boy chuckled and pushed his friend away. "Busy."

Kit promised to herself that she wouldn't let that happen. As she started to head out, Sister Gale came striding across the hall. Her loose, jet-black hair was laying across the front of her traditional white priest's robes, well past her chest. She was holding a small wooden shield and an iron battle hammer in her hand.

"You did extremely well on the mountain, Sister Kit." A small, thin smile crossed the woman's lips. "You were clearly trained by the best."

The combat instructor held the weapon out to Kit and motioned to her to take it. "Now that you're a priest, you will need these, especially for the next phase of your training."

"My next phase?"

"Yes. Your *blooding*."

"I don't understand," Kit said, accepting the gifts the priest had offered. "What's my blooding?"

"It's a way of proving that you are up to the challenges of being a priest. You must complete three missions in three days," Sister Gale said. "Father Hoarfrost is waiting for you in his office. Now that you're out of the infirmary, you need to see him to receive your first task."

"But..." Kit was about to object, but the stern expression on Sister Gale's face said that this was not a request. "Yes, Sister. I'll see Father Hoarfrost immediately."

Chapter Nineteen

Amilta, the Lost Daughter

As Kit approached Father Hoarfrost's office, she spied an acolyte with long dark hair, worn loosely over her shoulders. She was several years older than Kit. Though she was dressed in the typical rough-spun gray robes of an acolyte, she carried a bright silver war hammer on her back. It was the sort of weapon reserved for full priests. When the woman saw Kit, she ducked her head and scuttled off down the hall.

"There's always someone lurking, eh boy," Kit said. Lump gave her a blank stare in response. "Do you not think that's odd?" The dog continued to stare causing the girl to roll her eyes. "I wish you could talk. I'd really like to know what you're thinking about when you look at me like that."

The High Priest's door was closed when Kit arrived. She paused a moment, considering what the acolyte might have been up to, skulking outside the man's office.

"Come in, Kit," Father Hoarfrost called out, startling Kit in the process.

"How could he know I'm here?" Kit whispered. Again, she looked to Lump, and again, received the same blank stare. The girl checked under the door to see if perhaps the old priest could see her boots or something, but she doubted that was it.

As she pushed open the door, the familiar smell of musty books and peppermint met her nose. The High Priest was deep in thought as he stared out at Mount Toka and the great statue of Titan. Lump slipped inside, quiet as a mouse, and curled up in front of Father's large desk.

"You wished to see me, Father?" Kit asked, fidgeting with the sleeve of her robe.

"Yes," the priest replied, his gaze out the window never wavering. "I have a task I need you to perform."

"For my Blooding?" Kit asked as she ran her hands over the fabric of her new robes, trying to remove wrinkles that didn't exist.

"For your what?" Father Hoarfrost asked, turning to face the young priest.

"My Blooding, Father," Kit said, swallowing hard. "Sister Gale..."

"Sweet Titan," Father Hoarfrost said, slowly closing his eyes. "I hate that expression, but apparently your martial training teacher insists on continuing with it."

"Father?"

The priest moved purposefully from the window to his desk, before taking a seat. He pulled out a small scroll and a long silver quill. The sharpened tip hovered over the parchment when he paused and motioned to one of the two guest chairs.

Kit groaned inwardly as she studied the massive pieces of furniture. She really hated sitting in them.

"Suit yourself," Father Hoarfrost said as he scribbled on the parchment. "I will not be long here."

Kit's eyes wandered about the room while the old priest continued to scratch out a message with his quill. Her eyes paused for a moment when they fell on an ornate hammer and shield displayed over the room's fireplace. She blinked several times as though doing so might provide some clarity. Kit had been in this office many times and never once had she noticed either.

"Are those yours?" Kit asked, her voice a bit shaky.

"From a time long since past," the old priest replied as he folded the parchment. "I have not removed them from their resting place for many years."

For the briefest of moments, a wistful expression crossed the man's face. After releasing a deep sigh, Father Hoarfrost cleared his throat to get Kit's attention.

"Take this, and seek out Sister Miyuki," he said, holding out the parchment. "This is your first official task as priest."

"Thank you, Father," Kit said as she accepted the parchment. Her heart was beating so fast she could feel it in her throat. When she unfurled the scroll, her mouth parted slowly, and she plopped down at the edge of one of the guest chairs. She stared at the words for a good long while before letting out a low groan.

"Is there a problem, Sister?"

Kit raised her gaze to the old man, her brows furrowed in perplexed annoyance. "Is this a joke? This is nothing more than a shopping list. For my first official duty, you want me to go to the market and buy food?"

"Sister Miyuki is there now," Father Hoarfrost said, with a hint of mirth in his voice. "If you hurry, you can catch her there. She can help you fill out the list."

The old man opened one of the many drawers of his desk and pulled out a small leather pouch. He tossed it to Kit and said, "This should be more than enough to cover the costs. You can procure something, a treat, for yourself if you wish. You get something for your dog, too, since he's likely going to follow you."

"But... Father..."

"Move along now, priest. Daylight is burning."

Without another word, Kit slipped down from the chair and shuffled towards the door. Several times, she took a deep breath as though to speak, and each time she exhaled slowly and kept her thoughts to herself. Lump quietly moved in beside the girl, rubbing against her thigh as though to spur her on.

⚜

The Temple was located at the farthest point from the main gate, and Kit often wondered if the city's layout was intentionally designed to lead visitors on a journey through its entirety before making the pilgrimage up the Temple's grand stairs.

As a new priest, Kit was taken aback by the constant greetings she received from the people as she walked through the bustling streets. The warmth of their welcome was a stark contrast to her childhood, where she had been hated and ridiculed for simply being herself. Now, she found herself embraced by the city's inhabitants, their kindness and respect showered upon her solely because she wore the priest's sacred robes.

The young girl's heart warmed as she took in the sights of people going about their daily routines and the sounds of children's laughter. The smells however, especially those coming from the poorer districts like Old Town, were something she could do without. Not that the people in these parts of the city were unclean, but many of the activities that took place in these areas, like tanning, were powerfully aromatic. The fact that many of the families kept livestock on their properties or in their homes with them, did nothing to improve the odoriferous experience. More than once, Kit needed to check her gag reflex as she passed through.

As she headed out the main gates toward the market district, new smells came to greet her. The scent of fresh vegetables, baked goods, and roasting meats were a wondrous delight, driving away any remaining bad olfactory memories of Old Town.

"Smells good," Kit said. Lump licked his chops in response making the girl chuckle. "At least I understood you that time. I'll see if I can't find you something to eat. After all, Father did give me a little extra coin, and he did say I could buy you something." Again, Lump licked his chops, his big pink tongue leaving a trail of drool over his snout.

Kit moved through the crowds, jostling with vendors and patrons alike, and made her way to the spice tents. Her list didn't include anything that might be found here, but the aroma of fresh spices always brightened her day. She picked up a small pouch of saffron and delighted in its sweet, musky fragrance.

A Berrat woman standing in the middle of the street caught Kit's attention. Her chest hitched as she tried to control her sobs. The flow of her tears had stained her face, and she was frantically looking about.

Kit put down the pouch of saffron, walked over, and bowed lightly to the woman. "Titan's peace upon you. What's the matter? Do you need help with something?" The Berrat woman's shoulders slumped. She was perhaps four feet tall, with olive skin and white hair that was pulled back in rows of tight braids. She was dressed in the shell beads and goat hide of a Berrat nomad. There were several families who herded goats and hunted in the flatlands around Aarall.

Sometimes they sent representatives to the city to sell pelts, wool, or carved bone, or to buy metal tools for their kin. The woman before Kit had no stack of goat hides thrown over her shoulder, and no bag of new tools at her waist. Instead, her eyes were damp, and her voice shook when she asked, "Are you a priest?"

Kit nodded and inwardly smiled. She *was* a priest now, at least unofficially. "I am Sister Kit Standing Bear, with the Fist of Titan. Do you require counsel?"

The Berrat woman shook her head. "I am Linnim. My daughter..." she stopped, unable to get the rest of the words out.

The noise of the bustling market clamored loudly around the pair, drowning out their words. If this was going to be a long conversation, it was better to have it somewhere quieter. Kit gently guided the woman to the edge of the market square, where her shaky voice wouldn't be drowned out by hopeful merchants bellowing about salted fish. "Tell me what troubles you," Kit said, as gently as she could manage.

The Berrat took a shaky breath and steadied herself. "My daughter, Amilta, is gone." Gone could mean a lot of things. Kit gave the woman a moment to gather herself, and she continued.

"She's a young girl of only eight years, and headstrong. She likes to wander, so we gave her a few of the older goats to look after." The woman paused and wiped her eyes with the back of her hand. "These animals know the land as well as any of us, and they'd have brought her back if Amilta had become lost. Except they didn't. When we eventually went looking, we found two of them grazing on top of a rocky outcropping. The other one was down below." The woman's face contorted with fear. "The one down below had been eaten, organs and skin and everything. Bones cracked, marrow gnawed..."

"And Amilta?" Kit asked, fearful of what the answer might be.

"No sign," the woman croaked, shaking her head. "We've been looking for her a day, a night, and a day. We found signs of her near the stone knoll, but nothing beyond that. There were tracks leading away, but only of wolves. They led into the distant forest."

Kit turned to the statue of Titan and considered what this woman was asking. She fingered the note in her pocket and cringed. Father had given her a task, a boring, mundane task, and if Kit helped this woman, it would draw her away from the city, and she would fail her mission.

Just as Kit was about to decline to help, Sister Miyuki waddled up, mopping sweat off her bright red face. As usual, her expression was one of pure joy.

"*Sister Kit*," the jolly priest called out as she approached. "I was hoping to run into you. Hello, Lump. I'm surprised to see you here."

Sister Miyuki motioned to the half dozen acolytes that were trailing behind her to take a rest. They each had a small, over-filled cart strapped to harnesses on their backs, making them resemble drab gray oxen. From the linen sack she was carrying, she produced a leaf-wrapped treat. She tossed it to Lump who eager chowed it down, leaves and all.

Kit pulled out Father's parchment and gave it a forlorn look.

"What do you have there?" Sister Miyuki asked, holding her pudgy hand out. "Is this your first Blooding task?"

"I guess," Kit said as she pressed the parchment into Sister Miyuki's hand. "Father asked me to go shopping for him."

"Tut, tut," Sister Miyuki said as she perused the list. "I've already gotten all of this, and much more."

The overweight baker considered the tear-stained face of the Berrat woman standing close to Kit. "It looks like you have much more important things to do than gather groceries. Let me take care of your list and you help this lovely woman with whatever it is that's troubling her."

"Really?" Kit said, her voice jumping several octaves. Without warning, the young priest threw her arms around Sister Miyuki and gave her a deep, thankful hug. "You're the best, Miyuki. I'll make it up to you, I promise."

"No need, child," Sister Miyuki said with a motherly smile. "Serve the people. Serve Titan. That is reward enough. I am only glad to do my little part."

Sister Miyuki waved her hand over her head in a wide circle and waddled off into the crowd, her acolyte oxen struggling to keep up.

"Take me to where she disappeared," Kit blurted out. This may not have been the task set out for her, but Kit couldn't leave a young girl lost in the woods, even if she was prone to wandering. She feared how Father Hoarfrost might react to her shirking the task he gave, but an opportunity to help someone had fallen into her lap, and the new priest was not going to let it pass.

"Thank you, priest. It's not far from here. I will guide you to where we found the tracks."

The Berrat woman led them away from the walls of Aarall and into the surrounding flatlands. The area around the city was not especially dangerous as it was easy to spot predators from a good distance. The worst creatures, the most dangerous ones, preferred the mountains, forests, and riverbanks over the open country. In the vast grasslands, prey had room to run, making them much harder to catch.

Still, *few* predators did not mean *no* predators.

As Kit and Linnim traveled along, Lump stayed several paces behind, his nose pressed close to the ground, sniffing anything and everything along the way. When they arrived at the foot of the knoll, Kit recognized the tracks of the wolves right away.

They were small prints, but even a young wolf could take a person if it got hungry enough. Add to that the comparatively diminutive size of the Berrat race and the fact that Amilta was only a child, and…

Kit shook her head, trying to dismiss the gruesome visage, but it lingered all the same.

Linnim and her family were lucky not to have found the chewed remains of a corpse here.

The rest of the Berrat community arrived shortly after Kit did. Some were carrying babies in their arms or in small shoulder-packs made from cured hide, adorned with beads. Others were leading groups of ten, twenty, or forty goats.

They called somber greetings to each other in their lilting family dialect, and a few made hand-signs that the young priest interpreted as frustration or helplessness. Kit may have been raised by a Berrat woman in a Berrat village, but the accents and regional dialect of these herders made them exceptionally difficult to understand.

She looked to Linnim. "Will you translate for me?" The woman nodded.

"I am Kit Standing Bear, a Priest of Titan. I am here to help you find Linnim's daughter."

After conveying her message, the herders started talking, frantically flashing hand signs to one another. She could only understand bits and pieces of what was being said, but their anger was unmistakable. More than once, Kit picked up the word, 'outsider,' a word she'd heard a lot as a child. A large knot formed in her stomach.

Linnim took a deep breath. "My daughter is a willful child. Amilta has always been a wanderer. Against our wishes, she'd often go into the city." The faces of Linnim's kin were a mixture of sorrow and resentment. "One time, after visiting the city, she came back speaking in the common tongue. She refused to speak in her native language."

"So, you're suggesting that she's smart?"

"Not just smart, she's... gifted." A worried look crossed Linnim's face as she said the words. "She speaks with the animals. Many of our people have a strong connection, but hers goes much deeper."

Just then, two of the male Berrat stepped up. They were speaking at a feverish pace, and Kit did her best to understand. Linnim was about to translate, but Kit held up her hand.

"Peace to you, brother," Kit said in her own Berrat tongue. She knew that this was a common greeting among all tribes. She quickly flashed hand gestures at them, inexplicably remembering everything she'd learned as a child while she lived with the Berrat in northern Berrathia. The men were astonished at her fluency. Like the greeting, hand gestures were often used when people of different tribes needed to communicate.

"You speak Berrat?" an old woman with weathered, wind-burned skin, said in the common tongue. The two men bowed their heads to her as she stepped out from the rest of the family. Judging by the way the others showed the woman profound respect, she was most likely their Elder.

"Tell me child, how is it that you know our language?" the old woman continued as she stared up at Kit with dull, gray eyes.

"Honored one," Kit said, bowing slightly to the woman. "I lived in Berrathia, in a village near Lilloet. My mother, the woman who raised me, is Berrat."

"Lilloet?" the old woman pressed her lips together and nodded slowly. "That explains your dialect then. The northern regions have done well to uphold the ancient traditions of *Sprak*, the language of the hands." She moved closer to Kit, craning her neck to look up at her. "Perhaps then, you understand why we must find Amilta?"

Kit tilted her head to the side, considering the question. "You fear she is on a binding quest, that she will seek to meld her spirit with that of a wild animal?" The old woman closed her eyes and nodded. "But she's only eight years old. She's too young to be able to challenge anything *too* dangerous."

"My granddaughter is quite gifted," she said, the pride in her eyes beaming as she spoke. "She would probably try to join with a *Yeti* if she could find one."

Kit turned back to Linnim, speaking in the common tongue. "I will find your daughter, if it is Titan's will."

Linnim translated to her family, letting them know that Kit would take up the search for Amilta. Several of the family members wanted to join the young priest, but Kit explained that this was something she needed to do on her own. After a heated debate among the family and extended family members, two of the Berrat men moved next to Kit, insisting that everyone accompany her on the search.

As much as Kit wanted to go without the family, there was no way she was going to talk them out of it.

Chapter Twenty

A Hopeless Quest

The wolf tracks led across the flatland. It had rained recently, but the ground here was hard and rocky. Regardless, the herders were apparently able to find prints in little more than scrub grass, lichen, and disturbed rocks. They walked to where trees reared up from the ground and the dark body of the forest loomed overhead. They pointed to a small, dry clumping of wolf scat on the loam.

The leavings were matted with what Kit assumed to be goat hair. Although, on second glance, it could have belonged to a Berrat instead. One of Amilta's family members murmured something, and Linnim translated: "No beads." Kit tapped her finger to her lips while she considered the significance of that statement. A shaky laugh escaped her lips. If there weren't any beads from Berrat clothing in the leavings, then it would be unlikely that this wolf had eaten the young girl.

Kit breathed a sigh of relief and stepped forward, but none of the Berrat followed. When she beckoned them forward, several of the men took a few steps backward.

"It's too dangerous," Linnim said, shaking her head. "When the goats go in there, they die. And when we go in there, so do we."

The old woman spoke up, her tone firm. "We are hoping your god can help us. That is why our sister asked you here. If we had just needed another pair of eyes, we would not have sent Linnim to find a priest."

The Berrat were presuming a lot, and they misunderstood the role of the priests of the Fist. The members of the temple existed to labor on behalf of

Titan, not the other way around. Still, meditating on the situation may provide some insight, as the girl's trail had already gone quite cold.

Giving the group a nod, Kit and Lump moved into the forest far enough that the Berrat could no longer see them, but not so far that they could not make a hasty retreat if the Berrat's concern about danger in the forest was real.

Kit looked to Lump, who had been quietly moving with her, following the girl's lead. "I might have taken on more than I can handle," she said, rubbing the big wolfdog's head. Lump whined, took a step back, and lowered his head. This simple action might have meant a thousand different things, but the girl chose to believe her friend was suggesting she pray to her god, because she had no idea what to do next.

Giving her companion a smile and a nod, Kit drew her battle hammer and took a knee. Closing her eyes, the young priest opened herself to the world around her. She embraced the coolness of the earth beneath her, somehow giving her a closer connection to Titan. She took a deep breath, inhaling the smells of new grasses, budding plants, and springtime blooms. She focused on the injustice of her god's imprisonment, on her will to free him, and on the mortal limitations that were holding her back from doing so. To liberate her god, Kit would need to become stronger. To become stronger, she would need to triumph here.

All at once, warmth flooded through her.

It was not the gentle reassurances of a weaker god. It was wrath, pure and undiluted. It coursed through her so fast that she clenched her jaw, shivering momentarily with the need to pick a fight.

Titan's guidance was with her. Kit would not need the Berrat, or anybody else, on this mission. She rose from the ground, a sense of purpose coursing through her veins. She took a deep breath and commenced the search, confident that she would find Amilta.

Kit moved deeper into the forest as she searched for clues; a hank of hair, or a path. She found nothing. No sign or trace that the Berrat child had come this way. With each passing step, the weight on her chest pressed harder. Kit's tracking skills were abysmal.

"Can you find her Lump?" Kit blew out a long sigh when the dog stared blank faced at her. "You're not being much help, you know. I thought you had a good nose?" Her companion continued to stare for several more seconds before lying down on the ground.

"Oh Lump, why didn't I pay better attention to Brother Rime's classes?" Kit laughed at her question. "Because he was a giant butt-crack, that's why." The girl sighed again and shook her head. "I'm not giving up. I refuse. I'm going to find the girl."

Clenching her teeth together, Kit pushed down her worries and pressed forward. She had little more to go on other than 'head in the direction of the wolves.' It didn't take long before Kit was walking aimlessly, hoping that she might simply stumble upon Amilta.

As she slipped between the trees, their massive trunks wider than the arms of three men standing in a ring, doubt grew in her mind. Perhaps Kit's utter faith in Titan had led her to a place from which there may be no return.

"Why isn't Titan helping me?" Kit mused aloud. She looked over to Lump who was busy snuffling at the ground, completely ignoring her. "Because Titan expects his servants to be self sufficient."

Kit stood tall and scanned the area. The canopy overhead was thick, and it rattled intermittently with the cold wind. The leaves had barely begun to bud on some trees, but even still, there was hardly any light penetrating down to the forest floor. It may have been midafternoon, but it was dark enough now that it was beginning to feel like twilight.

Kit berated herself. Every second she wasted on this fool's errand was a sin against her god. If there was nothing to find here, or if she lacked the required skills to locate the child, it would be best to cut her losses.

The young priest shook her head, wondering how these negative thoughts permeated her consciousness. Her task to free Titan had not changed, but this was the challenge set before her. She would need to succeed here if she was to have any hope of surviving the quest to liberate her god.

One must be resilient in the face of adversity. Had Sister Nevara said that in theology class?

Locate and rescue a young girl who had been taken by wolves; that was her mission. She committed herself to the task and vowed that she would not fail.

Without much of an idea on how to proceed, Kit wended her way through the trees, calling out Amilta's name. The birds and woodland creatures were obligingly silent for a few seconds after every yell, but no sooner did the echoes of Kit's voice fade, than the chiding of jays and cowbirds and the chittering of squirrels replaced them.

If there were any signs of wolves in these woods, she had missed them completely. So had Lump. Either that, or he didn't care. Then again, how could he possibly know what she wanted of him? Even if he was of no help, she was happy for the company.

Hunkering down while she tried to get her bearings, Kit discovered a small cluster of weeds on the ground. Something about their leaf pattern was familiar, and she wracked her brain trying to recall the context in which she had last seen them.

Kit cursed quietly, reprimanding herself for not being a better student.

If only I had paid closer attention, I might recall what this plant is.

Whenever Brother Rime droned on about the various flora, Kit usually found herself staring out a window, wondering what life there might be for her outside the Temple.

Kit followed the brother's descriptive process, something she was able to recall from her classes. Staring intently at the plant, she described it out loud, hopeful that hearing the words might help jog her memory.

"A bright orange blossom with thin willowy stems, long wilted leaves, and fine white hairs on the undersides of each leaf. A scentless milk-sap that oozes out any time the plant is broken..."

This is Pele's Gift!

As excitement blossomed in her chest, she quickly looked around, hoping someone might have witnessed her ability to identify this rare and valuable plant. What did it matter if no one but Lump witnessed her discovery? She successfully completed the task, and that was enough.

Pulling her dagger, Kit quickly harvested it, roots, and all. She carefully placed it in one of her robe's many pockets.

Feeling more than a little proud of herself, the young priest brushed the dirt from her knees and continued her search. Something was different about this part of the woods, but the change wasn't obvious at first. She paused and held her breath, standing quietly. She closed her eyes and tilted her head back, slowly exhaling, opening herself up to her surroundings, taking in every smell, every sound.

That's it!

The background noise of the forest had gone utterly silent. Kit spun about, looking in all directions. The hairs on her neck stood stiffly at attention. As she took a few strides, she became acutely aware of how loud her footsteps were, the crackling of dead leaves, the snapping of twigs and fallen branches beneath her feet. She was the only thing in the forest making any noise. That was until a low growl rumbled in Lump's throat.

A moment later, the first wolf appeared; a young female.

Chapter Twenty-One

The Wolf in the Girl

The wolf's fur was tan colored, with hints of red around her head and neck. She was smaller than many of the wolves Kit had seen before, but even at this size, she could easily kill someone. The animal circled, each step drawing her closer.

"Lump, stay back," Kit said, her gaze never leaving the steel-blue eyes of the wolf stalking her. Slowly, she reached down to her hip for her battle hammer. She had her weapon half-drawn when the wolf rushed her. As the animal leapt, Kit tried to barge it aside with her shoulder to give herself some breathing room.

That was a mistake.

Two of its pack-mates hit Kit from behind, and two sets of jaws closed on the backs of her legs, worrying at the flesh, trying to work their way towards one of the channels where her heart's blood flowed fastest.

Using her drawn weapon, Kit struck out at one of the wolves at the back of her ankles, connecting hard enough to force it to release its grip on her leg. As she was about to strike at the second, the small female leapt at her chest, the impact sending Kit crashing down onto the forest floor. Despite its small size, the wolf was relentless in its attack, its foam-covered fangs snapping repeatedly, mere inches from her face.

The young priest managed to shove a forearm into the wolf's mouth, keeping it from immediately tearing out her throat, but now its companions were shifting their attention, going for Kit's face or her armpits. They tried to wrench her forearms away from where they were, guarding the tender flesh of her neck.

"Titan, hear me," Kit shouted as the small wolf shook its head, intent on tearing flesh and ripping tendons. As the healing aura took effect, an immediate wave of relief spread through her. The young female dropped her grip from Kit's arm as she too became engulfed in the deep-green glow surrounding them.

Confusion crossed the small wolf's face, and her hesitation gave the young priest a brief window of opportunity. Kit slammed the butt of her hammer into the wolf's snout. With a whimper, the young female retreated a few steps, her eyes still focused on the aura surrounding Kit.

Taking a moment to check on Lump, Kit saw that he was standing before four wolves, his head low, his hackles raised. The typically quiet and submissive golden retriever resembled a demon-hound the way he peeled his lips back, baring his impressive array of teeth. Foam poured from his mouth as he snarled and snapped, keeping the animals at bay.

The priest bellowed out in agony as one of the other wolves dug its fangs into her thigh, her white robes instantly stained crimson. Fighting through the excruciating pain of the wolf tugging at her leg, Kit swung her hammer feebly at it, striking it with barely enough impact to force the animal to retreat.

Using her bare fist, Kit lashed out at one of the wolves that had a grip on her shoulder. It was only after several punches to its face that it finally released its hold, giving Kit an opportunity to fully swing her hammer.

As the wolf moved back in, a sickening mix of blood and saliva dripping from its mouth, Kit brought her hammer to bear, striking the animal cleanly in the ribs. It howled as it tumbled across the ground. It tried to stand back up, but quickly fell over onto its side.

The young priest grimaced as she tried to pick herself up off the ground, only to be knocked down again. Her head slammed into a large rock, sending a searing bolt of pain down her back.

Kit was certain that the last thing she'd ever see was the tooth-filled maw of the large male that was now standing on her chest. His mouth was full of foam and drool from the excitement of the hunt. He was about to move in for the kill when there was a short, sharp whistle.

The entire pack immediately came to a halt.

Whimpering, the wolves withdrew, their ears flattened back against their heads. Lump quickly moved to Kit's side, whining and licking at the wounds on her leg.

At the wolf's lead was the small female. Her shape slowly shed the features of a wolf, melting like candle wax, as the fur and fangs were gradually absorbed into the body of a Berrat child wearing goat-hide clothing. She bore a striking resemblance to Linnim, except for the bright red hair tied back in many rows of tight braids. Though the child was only eight years old, she was significantly taller than her mother.

"Amilta?"

⌘

The Berrat girl covered her mouth with a cupped hand. Huge tears welled up in her steel-blue eyes. "You didn't have to hurt them," she said as she took a knee beside one of the wolves, gently caressing the spot where Kit had hit it with the hammer. Her lower lip was trembling uncontrollably.

She wasn't speaking in her family's impenetrable dialect. The child could have easily passed for a merchant in Aarall, albeit with a hint of an accent. Kit shook her head in wonderment at the simultaneous notion of a Berrat child protecting the wolves, and of this herds girl talking like she came from the city.

Kit gave the small girl an incredulous look. Her head spun as she picked herself up off the ground, staggering as she tried to regain her balance. Lump immediately moved beside the priest, offering what support he could.

"Are you kidding? They were going to kill me," Kit said, gesturing towards the wolves. "I didn't have a choice."

Kit rolled her shoulder where one of the wolves had gotten a particularly deep bite on her. The ongoing effects of her healing aura continued to slow the bleeding and ease the pain, but it was going to take some serious effort to fully repair her wounds.

The girl nodded curtly. "Neither did they. Your people drove them off the plains many years ago. They remember it in their songs. And now..." Amilta sniffed and wiped the blood from her nose where Kit had struck her. "And now they are being hunted and killed for no reason."

A feral growl rumbled deep in Amilta's throat, the muscles in the girl's tiny neck strained against her skin. "Those who are actively slaughtering the wolves must be stopped. The world depends on the animals' survival. If it isn't me who stands against them, who will? Will you, priest of Titan? Will you and your dog protect the wolves? Will you save the world?"

Protect the wolves? Save the world? Right now, all Kit wanted to do was get this child back to her mother, return to the Temple, and care for her wounds. She didn't heed the call of Titan to save the world. She did it to free her god and receive the boon he promised her.

Had he already granted her that which she wanted more than anything? For the first time in her life, Kit realized that she fit in. She was a part of a community that welcomed her, embraced her. Was this why she came to Aarall?

Amilta folded her arms and backed away from Kit. Her eyes narrowed as she continued to put distance between them.

The wolves had all moved in around their tiny leader, the largest male taking his place at the front. It didn't look like they were going to attack, but several of them were snarling, ready to pounce on command.

In a similar fashion, Lump moved in front of Kit, putting himself in harm's way. The priest renewed her grip on her hammer. If things went badly, she wanted to be ready this time.

"We mean your leader no harm, son of the wilds," Amilta said. The wolves immediately settled, their demeanor suddenly shifting. "Be at peace."

Lump strode forward, bypassing the wolves, stopping when he stood in front of the small girl. Amilta scratched the dog's neck, placing her forehead to his. "He cares deeply for you," she said, raising her gaze to Kit. "Are you here to take me back?"

"Don't you want to go back to your family?" Kit asked as a pang stabbed at her heart. She would do almost anything to see her own mother again. Despite feeling like she was fitting in, for the first time in her life, she would do anything to be back with Riva. The pain inflicted by the wolves was minor in comparison to the heartache she carried.

The girl stared down at the forest floor, shuffling her feet in the leaf litter. "I do, but…"

"But what?" Kit prompted as gently as she could.

"I shouldn't."

"Why not? Do you not understand how worried they are about you?"

Amilta shifted her weight between her feet, never looking completely at ease. "I was chosen," she said. "The wolf god came to me one day while I was tending to my goats. She told me that I am special, that I can't herd goats anymore. She said that I must live in the woods and be family to this wolf pack until my training is complete. Then I would be free to wander, doing great deeds in her name." The girl's ears were quite red, but there was also more steel in her voice than Kit might have expected.

"The wolf god?" Kit asked, still stuck on the first thing she'd said. "Do you mean Fenrir? You believe that you were chosen by Fenrir?"

Fenrir, along with Ymir, were two warriors Titan had charged to find someone capable of freeing him from his icy prison. The god had bestowed divine status upon them, so that they might serve him better.

The girl shrugged. "She came to me as a white wolf. Her pelt was painted, and her hair was braided." Amilta's fingers moved, sketching in the air symbols for woad-paint, tribal tattoos. "She didn't say her name, but yes, I believe it was Fenrir."

It certainly sounded to Kit like it was the wolf god, based on the beautiful statues of her that she'd seen at the Temple. If Fenrir had involved herself in the life of this girl, it should not be Kit's place to question the actions of one of Titan's greatest disciples.

Still, it appeared that the wolf god had intentionally isolated Amilta from her family, and that deeply bothered the priest.

Kit cared deeply for the woman who had raised her, but she would also have liked to have known her birth parents, even if just for a short while. And she would have resented Titan if he had intentionally torn her from them.

Maybe Fenrir had lived so long that she had forgotten what mortal life was like.

"Will you come with me, back to your family?"

Amilta raised her chin, and paused, seemingly unsure of how to respond to the question. "I will go to them, but I cannot stay."

The tiny Berrat moved forward, while Lump stayed at her side. She absent-mindedly scratched him behind his ear. "I will let them know that I am well, and I will say goodbye to them."

Kit took the gesture as being a positive one. Perhaps when she was reunited with them, she would change her mind and return to her family.

Together, they walked out of the woods to where Kit had left Amilta's mother and the rest of her kin. The wolf pack was no more than a few feet behind them.

The Berrat nomads gasped when Kit, Amilta, and Lump emerged from the forest. Most of them drew back in fear when the wolves came stalking out behind them. All except Linnim, who ran forward and clasped her daughter in a deep, powerful hug. The tiny girl looked uncomfortable as she patted her mother on the back.

Over the next while, Amilta explained what the god had asked of her. Although Linnim calmly listened to her daughter's words, Kit doubted the herds-folk's reception would be favorable, given they had no particular love for wolves. Nevertheless, her work was done.

As Kit turned to leave, Amilta's grandmother rushed over to her.

"You did a good thing, Sister," the old woman said, taking Kit's hand in her own. She rolled Kit's hand over to look at her palm, humming lightly to herself as she did. "Titan has made you fierce, but Gaia, she has made you compassionate." After taking a quick glance down a Lump, who had taken up his place next to Kit, the woman continued. "It seems even Fenrir has taken a keen interest in you. May you walk in their light, all the days of your life."

The mention of the wolf god's name gave Kit pause. Wolves had protected her on the mountain. Had Fenrir played a roll in her passing the trials? The priest shook off the notion, chalking it up to coincidence. The lion and the wolves were natural enemies, nothing more. Even still, the elder's words echoed in her mind.

"Thank you," Kit said in her own Berrat tongue as she touched her forehead to the woman's. "May Gaia keep you and yours safe and well fed."

"And may she forever see you safely on your travels," the woman replied, giving Kit a wry smile.

Kit thanked her again and bowed slightly to the rest of the clan, at least those who were paying any attention to her. She then walked away, leaving the Berrat to decide for themselves whether or not the young girl would follow the destiny Fenrir had set for her.

Lump bounded ahead, spurring Kit to hurry along or be left behind.

CHAPTER TWENTY-TWO

AN UNWELCOME RETURN

As Kit walked through the main gates, two City Watch guards approached her. They both had the traditional look of Nomads with deeply tanned skin, long black hair, and dark brown eyes. Like all members of the Watch, they were wearing brown leather armor with white trim and a patch of a red castle-tower on a field of white.

"Halt!" the taller of the two men said. He held his hand out, as though threatening to grab Kit should she not comply to his command. The way he looked down at her, as though she were a blight on the city, got the priest's back up. Based on the way Lump was growling, he, too, didn't appreciate the man's tone.

The guard had two silver pips affixed beneath his patch, identifying him as a lieutenant. Sister Nevara had taught the acolytes what the ranks meant and how the City Watch's hierarchical structure was organized. *"Regardless of their rank,"* the old priest had instructed, *"As members of the Temple, we stand apart. The Watch holds no authority over us, except in their role as the city's protectors. We work with them, not for them."*

The second guard, a heavy-set man whose armor was several sizes too small for him, crossed his arms over his chest in the traditional greeting of a follower of Titan.

"Hail, Kit Standing Bear!" the shorter guard said. His words and actions showed respect for Kit's priestly robes, unlike his disrespectful superior. He swallowed hard at the sight of the young priest's torn and bloodstained robes. He quickly averted his eyes and took a step away from the girl.

Seeing the portly guard's reaction to her disheveled state, Kit ran her hands down her white robes, trying to smooth down the blood-stained rips in her clothing. When it was clear there was no hope of improving her appearance, Kit gave the two men a curt nod. "Gentlemen? Are you in need of assistance?"

The tall guard sneered at her use of language. "We are not *gentlemen*. We are emissaries of our captain, and we certainly don't need assistance from the likes of you." He stepped closer, towering over Kit. Lump immediately moved to block his progress. "Keep your mutt in check or I'll end his miserable life."

The entire encounter brought back a flood of memories, of how Alyn and Coltyr accosted her, of how she felt unwelcome even in her own home. Her priest's robes and protective dog reminded her that she was both loved and respected. Kit placed her hand on Lump's back and stepped forward, putting herself between the golden retriever and the man whose face she wanted to cave in with her hammer.

"You look more like errand boys right now," she blurted out. Kit's heart began to race. She knew better than to antagonize bullies, but the day had already worn her out and, at this point, she really didn't care what they thought of her. Besides, he threatened her dog, and she wasn't going to let that go unchallenged.

"I am Lieutenant Karr, and I am no errand boy." His words came out like an ominous rumble, a low and threatening tone that sent a chill down her spine. He moved closer still, stopping when his toes were practically touching Kit's. He was a good deal taller than she was, and he was using his size to intimidate her.

It didn't matter how big or how threatening the man was, the small priest refused to back down. Placing her hands on her hips, she replied with more than a hint of superiority. "Errand boys rarely make the rank of lieutenant. You must be exceptionally good at it."

When the heavy-set guard sniggered at the insult, the lieutenant's face turned grim. It appeared he was about to explode, but he managed to swallow Kit's insult.

"Follow me!" he barked.

Kit was fairly certain that this was not a request she was allowed to refuse, but as he turned away, she retorted. "Tall, dark, and lackey is not my type. I'll pass on that."

"Have it your way," the lieutenant said, without bothering to turn around. "Take her!"

The heavy-set man slowly closed in on the priest, ready to force her compliance. From behind, Kit could hear Lump's growls. She lowered her hand and splayed her fingers, wordlessly telling the dog to hold his ground.

"If you're trying to frighten me," Kit said, stepping towards the heavy-set man and putting as much venom into the words as she could muster, "then you're going to be extremely disappointed. I am a Priest of Titan and I fear nothing, for my god is with me."

The lieutenant chuckled. He turned back toward her, disdain filling his eyes. He looked Kit up and down and sneered. His feet pounded on the cobble-stone street as he stormed closer. With a quick shove, he knocked the portly guard aside.

"You're no priest. You are an acolyte at best, but to me, you're nothing more than a common street rat. My guess is, if you didn't have that animal for protection, you'd have likely soiled yourself." He spat at her feet, a good amount landing on the hem of Kit's robe.

"A street rat?" Kit recognized that insult. It had only ever been used once on her, by a City Watch guard as she tried to enter the city for the first time as a small child. She was still small, but she was no longer a child.

The Lieutenant ignored her question and walked away. "If she doesn't want to follow, kill the dog and drag her by that rat's nest on her head."

Kit glanced down at herself and tried to quickly run her fingers through her mane, only to have them snag on one of the many knots in the tangled mass of black locks. Raising her chin, she glared at the heavy guard, attempting to conceal her reddening face while daring him to step closer. However, despite her initial defiance, curiosity now gnawed at her. Kit found herself strangely intrigued by the lieutenant's intentions – wanting to know where he was taking her and why.

"Lead on," she said. "We're coming."

Lieutenant Karr led Kit towards the City Watch's barracks. As they approached, a mountain of a man came out from the barracks' gate, which separated it from the rest of the city. The barracks themselves made up one of the largest building complexes in all of Aarall, perhaps second only to the Temple of the Fist. It was made of stone and iron and appeared to be something of an impenetrable fortress.

"Are you injured?" the man asked, his eyes turning to the lieutenant as though accusing him of accosting the girl.

Kit craned her neck to gaze up at the ruggedly handsome man. Based on the gold piping of his surcoat and the three gold pips beneath his City Watch patch, she identified him as a captain. He reminded Kit of the man who'd helped her so many years ago, the guard who showed her kindness when she first arrived at Aarall.

"No," Kit said, again trying to iron her robes with her hands. "I, um, had a small encounter with some wolves." The girl scrubbed her fingers through the ruff of Lump's neck, finding reassurance in the dog's presence.

"A small encounter?" the man asked, his dark brown eyes alight with amusement. "With wolves?"

With a curt nod, the big man addressed Karr. "Thank you, Lieutenant. I'll take it from here."

The man held out his large, heavily calloused hand to Kit in greeting. "Captain Ray Harding. I'm incredibly pleased to meet you."

Kit took the man's hand and replied, "Kit Standing Bear, Priest of Titan." As she did, she gave Karr a sarcastic smirk.

The Lieutenant gave Kit a hard look, nodded to the captain and moved to leave. Before he was too far away, he said in a voice just loud enough for Kit to hear, "She'd do well to spend some time in the dungeons. She's got far too much attitude. Maybe it would teach the street rat some humility."

Kit wasn't the only one to hear the retreating guard's words.

"Lieutenant!" The captain's voice rumbled out, low and powerful like a thunderstorm on the horizon.

The intensity of his voice startled Kit, causing her to wilt slightly. "Speak to my guest like that again and I'll have you scrubbing the latrines until the next moon."

The lieutenant stared flatly at the captain, like he was pondering if he should reply. Before he opened his mouth, his shoulders drooped, and he walked away.

"And you must be Lump," the man said. "I've heard a lot about you."

The golden retriever sprung forward at the sound of his name, rubbing his body against the big man's legs. Kit could only cock an eyebrow at the encounter.

"You know my dog?"

Kit's question made the big man laugh. He gave the wolfdog a healthy scratch behind his ears.

"My apologies for their rudeness, Sister Kit. The guards have been under a lot of pressure lately, and they don't like that I'm looking to hire outside help."

"Hire new help? Do I look like a mercenary to you?" Kit cocked an eyebrow and folded her arms across her chest.

The captain let out a booming laugh at her comment. "Father Hoarfrost told me you were, umm, spirited. He also told me to expect this big fella to be attached to your hip."

"You've spoken to the High Priest about me?" Kit was suddenly aware that she was speaking to someone well above her station and her face reddened slightly. Next to Father Hoarfrost, the captain of the City Watch was the most powerful man in Aarall.

"Don't worry, Sister Kit, there is nothing amiss. I need some help and the High Priest suggested you might be willing to put your talents to good use."

Kit's body visibly relaxed at his comment. She really didn't know what to expect her final trials to be, but working for the City Watch never crossed her mind.

"Another Blooding task? What do you need of me?"

The captain looked around, seeing that a good number of citizens had stopped by the gates to see what was going on. "This is not a good place for this discussion. Let's take this to my office so that I can speak more freely."

The trio headed through the barrack gates, past the expansive grounds, and into the massive building. As they entered, there was a large open area where at least twenty guards were busy training. The overwhelming stench of body odor reminded Kit of their own indoor training facilities. It must be why Sister Gale preferred to train outside when the weather permitted.

Kit paused for a moment to observe. She wrinkled her nose as she tried to figure out what they were doing. It appeared as though they were shooting arrows at each other. When an arrow struck one of the guards in the chest, Kit was about to run to his aid, but the captain caught her just before she could move away.

"Don't worry, he is not injured. Not badly at least. They're using blunted arrows, designed so as not to inflict any serious damage."

Kit watched the guard picking himself up off the sand floor. She winced slightly as he reached in under his tunic, rubbing the spot where the arrow had hit him.

"Nice shot," the young Nomad yelled out to his training partner. "Let me try again."

Kit tilted her head back to look up at the captain. "Why are they shooting each other with blunted arrows? Why not shoot straw dummies like everyone else does to practice archery?"

The captain paused for a moment, seemingly reluctant to speak further on the subject. His head wobbled on his neck as he considered whether or not to answer the question.

"They're not practicing their archery skills. They're practicing their abilities to protect themselves against incoming arrows. They must either dodge the arrow or block it in some way." The captain then waved his hand like he was trying to shoo away a fly. "That doesn't matter right now. What matters is that I need your help."

CHAPTER TWENTY-THREE

THE CAPTAIN OF THE GUARD

Captain Harding led the priest off to a small, heavily cluttered office just off the training grounds. Kit rubbed her finger under her nose when the pungent smell of leather, dried blood, and body odor hit her like a hammer in the face. There were bits of armor and sheaves of parchment strewn about the room. In front of an enormous rough-hewn double pedestal desk, were two guest chairs that dwarfed the chairs in Father Hoarfrost's office. Clearly, the City Watch liked to hire men who were well above average height and weight.

"My men are busy dealing with a serious matter that threatens our entire kingdom. While they are engaged in this task, there are too few left to deal with the day-to-day problems faced by our city and our barony."

Exhaling loudly, the big man flopped into his oversized, black leather chair. He motioned for Kit to do the same. He failed at suppressing a laugh when Kit practically had to climb onto her chair to take a seat. While the priest took her place, Lump immediately settled himself in, curling up at the feet of the girl.

The young priest watched as the captain considered the state she was in. With a groan, he ran his large, meaty hand over his face. "The High Priest said you're up to the challenge, but... I'm dubious."

Harding's comment got Kit's hackles up. "Dubious? If the High Priest said I'm ready, then I'm ready." Kit pushed her shoulders back and her chest out. "Let me prove it to you."

She raised her eyebrow when the smallest of grins curled up at the corner of the captain's mouth. The man was playing her, and she walked right into it.

The captain nodded his assent, almost like he was having a conversation inside his own head. "Okay," he said. "I do have a small task for you. If what the High Priest says about you is true, you should have no difficulty with it."

Kit's face hardened somewhat as she narrowed her eyes. "You doubt the word of the *High Priest*?"

The captain pushed up from his chair, slamming it against the wall behind him, knocking it over in the process. He leaned across his desk, towering over Kit. "The High Priest's word is *gold*, but when I give a mission, *I* am taking responsibility for the soldiers involved. If they are injured, or worse, die, it's on my conscience. I'm the one who breaks the news to their loved ones. I take my responsibilities seriously and I don't do anything without having a full understanding of the potential outcomes."

The captain then turned around, picked up his chair and eased himself back into it. He was breathing hard, but his face softened.

"I need your help, but I will not unnecessarily send you to your death," he said, a hint of resignation in his voice.

In an attempt to mimic the captain's dramatic flair, Kit stood up abruptly, intending to send her chair toppling. But her war hammer got caught up in it, sending both her and the chair tumbling backwards into a tangled heap on the ground. Lump, thinking that some sort of game was afoot, barked wildly and bounded over the fallen girl, enthusiastically licking her face.

The captain let out a deep belly laugh that shook the room. He moved quickly around his desk, grabbed Kit by her upper arm, and lifted her up like she was nothing more than a straw-filled rag doll.

"I get it," he said, his voice still full of mirth. "You are exactly the person the High Priest described. You are headstrong and full of... enthusiasm."

When Kit managed to untangle herself from her chair, he walked over to a large cork board on his wall. It was covered with small parchments, each with some writing on it. He perused them, then plucked one of them off and pressed it into Kit's hand.

"Here," he said. "This came in this morning. The city has always had rat problems, but apparently a *dire rat* has been seen in the Merchant's District.

If this is the case, it will be... bad for business. It's my understanding that you have some experience in dealing with such creatures."

The captain drummed his fingers on his desk as Kit read the parchment thoroughly. Lump quickly became bored and immediately found a new place to curl up and sleep.

"Don't forget that dire rats are dangerous. They can carry nasty diseases, and the venom in their bite can be lethal," Harding added while he waited for Kit to finish examining the parchment.

The captain moved over toward one of many shelves in the cramped room. He pulled off a small scroll and waved it in front of himself.

"This is a blessing scroll. If you fear the rat is more than you can manage, use this scroll to cast a *Protection from Poison* blessing upon yourself. The rat's bite will have far less effect on you if you do." And with that, he tossed the scroll to Kit.

Opening his office door, the captain addressed the young priest loudly enough that anybody within a hundred paces could hear him.

"Come back when you've completed the mission. If you do well, I'll have many more tasks for you to carry out." He motioned to the cork board on his wall. He did, indeed, seem to have a long list of unfinished duties.

Kit paused before she left the room, continuing to review the text on the parchment. "What can you tell me about the shop owner?"

The captain took a moment to think about it. He seemed to appreciate that she was trying to gather up additional details before heading out.

"The owner's name is Samm Larder. The shop has been in Aarall since long before I was born. His father died some fifteen years or so ago, along with his business partner, a Berrat businessman. They both up and died, seemingly without reason. It was the first case I oversaw when I was promoted to lieutenant." The captain's face turned grim. "I was never able to figure out why or how they died."

The big man shook off the memory and continued. "The Cheeserie is renowned for its rare and exotic cheeses. Samm produces some himself, while others are shipped here from all over Orth. Until recently, it was the only place in the entire kingdom where many of these rare delicacies could be purchased."

"You said it *was* the only place. Where else can they be purchased now?" Kit asked as she tucked the parchment and protection scroll into one of the many folds of her robes.

"Well, I don't recall the name of the shop, but my wife has told me that the Berrat woman running it has an uncanny nose for amazing cheese. Why do you ask?"

Kit shrugged slightly. "Because you brought it up. You said there was another store also selling expensive cheeses..."

The captain waved his hands in a dismissive manner. "Maybe you should be getting to the Cheeserie? Perhaps you'll find the answers during your investigation?"

Kit nodded and headed for the door. Lump immediately moved in beside her, ready to follow her on the priest's next mission.

"Um, little sister," Harding said. His mouth opened, paused for a moment, and then closed again. He motioned to the girl's clothing. "Maybe you should visit the Temple infirmary and change into less... bloody clothes before you head off to the Merchant's District? It's late in the day. This task can wait until tomorrow morning."

Kit grimaced at her ripped and bloodstained clothing. She gave the captain a bit of a grunt and headed out the door.

"I'll deal with the problem before the sun sets," Kit said, as she ran her hands over her disheveled clothing.

"Um, captain?" Kit asked, before she exited. "Have we met before? Both you and the lieutenant seem familiar to me."

"You have a good memory, little sister," Harding said. "Put it to good use and deal with the task at hand."

Kit gave the captain a bright smile and strode confidently out the door. Just as she was about to exit Harding cleared his throat. "You might want to leave the dog behind. I doubt his presence would be appreciated in a cheese shop."

"I'm not sure I can make Lump stay away. He pretty much does whatever he wants."

Kit's comment made the commander laugh. "Well, that explains why you two are so close. You're kindred spirits. That being said, find a way."

"The captain is right," Kit said to Lump, her voice filled with excitement. The big dog wagged his tail expectantly. "It's probably best that you don't come with me this time."

Lump's tail instantly stilled, and he lowered his head. With his head drooping, he raised his gaze, his big brown eyes reflecting his disappointment. The tiniest of whines escaped his lips and shattered Kit's heart.

"I'll tell you what," Kit said, mustering as much excitement as she could manage. "Why don't you wait here with Captain Harding? Would you like that?" The dog's head snapped up and his tail wagged in slow, lazy circles.

"He's not staying here," the captain said. "Absolutely not."

While Lump moved to the big man's side, rubbing his body against his leg, Kit plead his case. "Captain," she said, giving the man her most apologetic smile. "It's either he stays here or I walk him all the way back to the Temple. If I do that, I'll lose at least two hours that I could be spending helping to solve your problem."

The big man groaned and let his hand fall on the dog's head. "I swear to Titan. You'll be the death of me, Kit. I really need to find someone else to help me out. I'm just not sure you're worth the trouble."

"Of course, I am, Captain," Kit said brightly. "Besides. You'll love having Lump around. He's a lot of fun." As if on command, the big dog found his way into the corner of the office, curled up, and immediately went to sleep.

Chapter Twenty-Four

The Cheeserie

Four guards dressed in plate armor with silver and gold surcoats blocked Kit's entrance into the Merchant District, the richest section in the entire city of Aarall. They were all wielding heavy-bladed halberds, and based on the way they moved, Kit could tell they knew exactly how to use them.

The guards were not wearing the insignia of the City Watch. Instead, they wore a patch displaying a silver shield with a single gold coin in the middle of it. The tall female guard who approached Kit had two silver pips beneath her patch, identifying her as a lieutenant.

"What is your business here?" the lieutenant asked as a lock of dark blonde hair fell across her bright blue eyes.

"I am Kit Standing Bear, Priest of Titan," Kit declared. "I am here on City Watch business."

"You are not dressed as a priest," the woman said as she tightened the grip on her halberd.

Kit had just changed out of her tattered robes into her leather training armor. She had thrown a cloak on over it in the hopes that it would dress it up. She groaned silently. It hadn't helped, not one iota.

"This is my second mission of the day," Kit blurted out. "My robes didn't fare well during my first." She pulled the sleeve up on her white cloak, exposing some angry red wounds on her arm where one of the wolves had bitten her. Kit quickly remembered the parchment that Captain Harding had given her. After pulling it out from a pocket in her cloak, she shoved it into the guard's hand.

"I see," said the guard as she returned the parchment to Kit. "Be sure to maintain discretion, young priest. This is not the sort of thing the merchants would want made public."

"Titan's peace be upon you," Kit said as the guard waved her past the high marble arches that marked the entrance to the district.

While the best roads in the city were rough cobble stones, the district's streets were formed of tightly fitted flagstone. There were highly manicured flowering bushes lining the edge of the streets, giving a garden-like appearance to the entire area. The buildings themselves were almost exclusively made of granite and marble, with huge arched windows and heavy ornate columns to mark the building entrances.

The wide thoroughfares opened to an expansive square, with a large circular platform which Kit assumed was used for auctions or some other mercantile function. The platform stood empty today, save for a single Berrat youth, speaking in harsh tones to a gathered crowd. Some of the people assembled were shouting in agreement with the young Berrat, where others were shouting obscenities, demanding the piece of *gutter trash* be removed immediately.

Not wanting to get caught up in the excitement, Kit jostled her way through the crowd until she made it to the far side of the square. As she finally cleared the mass of bodies, she looked for a shop named, 'The Cheeserie.' She chuckled to herself, thinking about how there was a rat problem in a cheese store. It all seemed a bit too cliché, but life was like that sometimes.

Her internal ruminations were abruptly cut short as a pair of oxen pulling a large cart bore down hard on her. Kit barely got out of their way in time as they continued to rush through the assembled crowd, scattering people in all directions. They shook their fists and shouted obscenities at the driver and his oxen, but he just kept on plowing through them with no regard for the people's safety.

Kit shook her head, concerned that this idiot was going to kill somebody with his antics. When she turned away from the mayhem, she discovered she was standing in front of *The Cheeserie.*

That's a good start to things.

Kit pushed open one of the highly polished teak double doors, thinking that this business must be doing very well to afford such a luxury. Unsurprisingly, the cheese shop was impeccably clean and tidy. Most every surface was either granite or marble, except for the front counter which also appeared to be the same high-quality teak as the front doors.

A young Berrat was actively sweeping the floor, though it appeared to be utterly spotless. The boy looked to be about the same age as Kit, with sandy-brown hair cut close to his scalp. He was dressed in fine linen clothes of white and green, and well-crafted black leather boots. A crisp white apron covered him from neck to mid thigh. He gave Kit a brief smile before returning to his duties.

Kit was about to speak to the Berrat when an extremely fat, and mostly bald Nomad Human came bursting in through a door behind the counter. "Welcome, welcome, welcome," he was practically shouting at Kit. "Welcome to the Cheeserie, Aarall's finest cheese establishment. What can I get for you today?"

Pulling back her overcoat, Kit showed the battle hammer hanging from her waist. "I'm not here to buy your cheese." She sniffed the air. "But it does smell good."

"Sweet Titan, are you here to rob me?" The fat man appeared flustered, seemingly unsure whether to run screaming or to raise his hands in surrender. The young Berrat stood motionless, carefully watching to see what Kit might do next.

The priest's eyes widened at the man's panicked reaction. She waved her hands furiously in front of herself, desperately trying to assuage the man's fears.

"No, no. Peace unto you. Titan, save us. I'm no robber." After a moment or two, the man's face lightened up, and he wiped a copious amount of sweat from his brow. The young Berrat continued his sweeping, while still maintaining a close watch on Kit.

"Forgive me, please, I had not intended..." Kit continued to stammer. Finally, she took a deep, cleansing breath and started anew. "My name is Sister Kit Standing Bear, a Priest of Titan, currently helping Captain Harding with some City Watch duties."

"Oh, that's wonderful!" The fat man promptly grabbed a tray off the counter and waddled his way over to Kit. "Here, try some of my cheeses. You'll agree, they're the best in all of Aarall."

Kit took a small piece from the tray, giving it a sniff before popping it into her mouth. She moaned unexpectantly as the flavors sang in her mouth, creating a culinary experience the likes of which she had never before enjoyed. She reached out again, this time taking a much larger sample. Before realizing it, she had devoured half the tray. The cheese had a delightful warming effect, causing the tension in her body to drift away. Lost in the revelry of the flavor sensation, she was oblivious to the shop owner's look of shock. When she finally realized that she was overstepping the offer, her face burned. In an attempt to hide her embarrassment, she blurted out the first thing that came to mind.

"I'm here about the dire rat problem you raised with the City Watch."

The fat man's eyes immediately became as big as dinner plates. The young Berrat stopped sweeping as he gawked at the priest. The shop owner blinked rapidly, his face turning a brilliant shade of purple.

"Dire rats? We have no rat problem, dire or otherwise," he blustered, his gaze quickly scanning the room. Seeing that Kit was the only patron present, his face turned stern. "How dare you speak of such things where the public might hear you! I'm going to have a long, hard talk with your Captain. Your stupidity could have ruined my business."

Kit's face reddened. She knew better than to act without discretion. She stared down at the half-eaten tray once more and briskly rubbed the back of her neck.

What is in that cheese?

Once she gathered herself, Kit straightened her back and put on her best official face. "I am Sister Kit Standing Bear, Priest of Titan. I am here as a courtesy to the captain, to help him clear a backlog of complaints. If you'd prefer, I can go back to the captain and take on a different task. The City Watch seems to be extremely busy right now. It might be a few moons before somebody gets around to your... problem."

The fat man frowned and shook his head, causing his jowls to flop about beneath his mouth. Kit was likely his only hope to get this problem addressed promptly. His jolly demeanor returned in a heartbeat. He carefully put down the cheese tray and beckoned her to follow him behind the front counter.

As they went through the doors into the back room, Kit was immediately assaulted by a huge array of cheesy aromas, the smell nearly overwhelming her senses.

CHAPTER TWENTY-FIVE

SAMMUEL F. LARDER

"I'd say you'll get used to it, but I don't think you will. I've been running this cheese shop since I was a young man. I took it over from my father and his business partner after they mysteriously passed away." The fat man's eyes welled up a bit while he reminisced about his father's death. "It's been almost fifteen years, and I am still not used to the smell of these cheeses. I love it, but I'm not used to it."

Unexpectedly, the man's eyes widened, and he bowed gracefully to Kit. "Please forgive my rudeness. I have not formally introduced myself." With a flourish befitting the finest bard in the land, he raised himself up fully. "I am Samm. Sammuel F. Larder." He promptly grabbed his massive belly, giving it a good shake. "Larder is a most excellent name for me, don't you think?"

Rather than get pulled into what could only be an extremely uncomfortable conversation, Kit took on a more businesslike air. In a controlled and quiet voice, she whispered, "Like I said, I'm here about a *dire rat* problem. Have you seen it? Where can I find it?"

Samm moved further into the storage room, away from the door. "I have only seen it once. It was pulling wheels of cheese from my shelves. I can only assume it was trying to take as much as it could back to its nest."

Okay, now we're getting somewhere.

Her eyes scanned the area, looking for anything that could potentially be meaningful. "Where did it go after you saw it?"

"When I interrupted it, the foul creature growled at me and then burst out the back door. It ran right past my delivery man. It nearly scared him out of his wits." Sheepishly, he looked around and lowered his voice to barely a whisper. "I had to pay him double his normal wage for a month to get him to promise to never speak of it."

"Does this delivery man use a team of oxen to pull his cart?" Samm nodded to Kit's question. "I think he nearly ran me over when I was approaching your shop. He was pushing them hard."

Samm was genuinely surprised. "He did? He knows better than to move quickly through the market." The fat man furrowed his brows. "Why was he leaving my shop? He's not scheduled for a delivery until tomorrow morning."

Waving his hand in front of his face he said, "that's not important right now. I'll speak to him about it tomorrow when he comes with his next shipment."

Kit tried to bring the conversation back in line. "You mentioned the rat bolted out the back door?"

"Yes, yes. Right out the back door. That door is almost always locked. I don't know how or why it was open."

"Is that the only time you've seen the rat?" she pressed on.

"Yes, the only time. But that horrible beast keeps getting in. I know it. I've been losing stock at a horrific rate for the past moon. If I can't catch him, he'll empty out my entire storeroom. I'll be ruined." His face lit up with a memory of days past. "We had a dire rat in here once before, you know. It broke through the storeroom window and gorged itself on the cheese. Karim found it in here, its belly so full it could barely move. Karim stabbed it through the chest with a large gaff that we use to reach the cheese on the top shelves." He grabbed one of the poles. It was about ten hands long with an impressive-looking iron spike at the end of it. When he handed it to Kit, she marveled at its balance.

"That is a fine weapon, and you use it to skewer cheese?" she commented, handing the spear back to Samm. "You must have some pretty scary cheese if you need such a thing in order to subdue it."

The rotund shop owner chuckled lightly at Kit's attempt at humor.

"Samm, if it's okay with you, I'd like to look around on my own. You know, get a feel for the place and maybe I'll discover how the rat gets in and out of your establishment."

"Suit yourself," Samm said with a flourish. "I should be out front, anyway. I don't want to miss a customer, now do I?" And with that, the fat man shuffled his way out the door and into the storefront.

After Samm exited, Kit commenced her investigation. She walked along the perimeter of the room, searching for possible entry points, both obvious and secret. As far as Kit could tell, there was no other way into the building except through the alleyway back door, or through the front door, into the storefront itself.

Perhaps, if there was only one way into the storeroom from the outside, then maybe that, in of itself, means something.

She moved to the door leading to the alley, examining the handles, the hinges, and the locking mechanism.

If the only way the rat is getting in here is through this door, then there should be some signs, something to show how it is breaking in.

Kit ran her hands along the edges, hoping some random clue would jump out at her.

There were no signs that the rat had broken in through those doors. There wasn't so much as a scratch on them.

She let out a small groan. This wasn't going to be as simple as she had hoped. Kit expected to show up, kill a rat and then be on her way.

Okay then, if there is no obvious point of entry, perhaps the cheese itself holds a clue.

Kit wandered up and down the aisles, inspecting the cheese as she went. In doing so, she found something interesting. The inventory was stacked oddly, but maybe that was just the way the cheese wheels rolled here. It appeared that it was organized to make it seem like there was more cheese in the storeroom than there actually was.

Kit poked her head into the storefront, motioning to Samm to join her. He was just finishing up with two elaborately dressed women. When he caught sight of Kit, he became flustered. "Thank you, thank you, thank you," he said enthusiastically as he guided the customers towards the exit. "I know you'll be pleased with your selection, a most wonderful selection indeed. It will pair nicely, very nicely, with that vintage south-elven wine of yours. Try it! Try it, you'll see!" As soon as the customers exited, the fat man spun around and glared at Kit. "What? Couldn't you see that I was with customers?"

Undaunted by Samm's reaction, Kit called him over again. As Samm came into the storeroom, she pointed up at one of the shelves. "Is this the way you typically stack the cheese? I found it odd that your shelves have a lot of empty space, completely hidden by these wheels of cheese."

Samm pondered the question for a moment. He rubbed his massive belly, like it somehow helped him think. "It's irregular," he frowned. "We use the empty space as an indicator of when it's time to bring more cheese from the factory."

"The factory?"

"Well yes, the factory. It's where I make and store all my cheeses, as well as the cheese I import." There was a hint of pride in his voice as he described his operation.

"Have you been missing any cheese from your factory? Has the rat tried to break in there?"

Samm shook his head violently, causing his ample rolls of neck fat to jiggle in a humorous fashion. Kit barely managed to hide her mirth. "Oh, no!" he said with enthusiasm. "I have over twenty guards at the factory. They're very skilled and they're very well armed. If a rat got in there, it would be dead before it took twenty paces."

"Hmm," Kit said as she considered the information. "If you have guards at the factory, why don't you have any posted here in the storeroom?"

The fat merchant shrugged his ample shoulders. "They're expensive, awfully expensive. I keep about ten times more cheese at my factory than what I have on hand here. Besides, Karim and I are here all the time. We live upstairs. Karim's got the best ears of anybody I've ever known. He can hear a beetle walking across the forest floor. If something was going on, he'd have alerted me in moments."

"Who's Karim?"

Karim

"Karim's my helper. He's the Berrat you met when you came into the store. He's like a son to me. I took him in after his father died. Well, after both our fathers died. His father was my father's business partner."

"As you mentioned earlier." Kit scratched at her forehead. The fat man's assertions weren't lining up. "If his ears are so amazing, then why didn't he hear the rat when it broke in?"

The fat man shrugged his shoulders in response.

Kit toed the ground with her boot. "Do you mind if I speak with him, alone?"

"What are you insinuating?" Samm became immediately defensive. "Karim's a good boy, a very good boy, I tell you."

Kit held her hands up and shook her head. "I'm insinuating nothing. I just want to speak with him. Alone."

"Fine. I'll get him. I should be out front, anyway. I've got customers, important customers." And with that, Samm waddled off to fetch the boy.

A moment later, Karim entered the storeroom, clearly wondering why he had been summoned.

"Hello. My name is Sister Kit Standing Bear. I would like to chat with you about the *issue* Samm is having."

The Berrat calmly leaned his broom against the wall. "I am Karim. I am pleased to meet you."

"Titan's peace upon you," Kit said, inclining her head. "I was hoping you could tell me about the *problem*, you know..."

"I'm not sure what to say," Karim's voice was calm and measured. "Samm told me he's seen the rat, but I've never seen it myself."

Kit was wondering why he was being so careful with his words. "You've never seen it, but surely you've heard it stealing cheese from the storeroom?"

Karim slowly shook his head. "No, I've never heard anything. I'm a deep sleeper. Maybe the rat had come in through the night and I slept through the event."

That didn't fit well with Samm's description of Karim's supernatural hearing. Even if he was a deep sleeper, Kit expected he would have picked up on a large animal rummaging through the storeroom. Kit folded her arms across her chest and pressed her lips into a long, thin line. There was nothing more he was going to offer her, freely or otherwise.

"Thank you for your time, Karim. I'll let you get back to work." The young man calmly took his broom and headed back into the storefront. After a few minutes of considering what she had found, Kit followed the boy through the doors.

"Samm, do you think we could take a trip to the factory? I'd like to take a look around, you know, to make sure everything's okay there."

Samm picked at his cuticles while he considered Kit's question. The fat man's head slowly started to bob as he considered his options. The bobbing turned to nodding, which Kit could only assume meant that he agreed with her suggestion.

"Mind the store while I'm gone!" Samm said to Karim as he shuffled his bulk towards the front door. "I don't expect us to be too long. The Moreden twins are going to be coming in any time now. Make sure their order is ready for them when they arrive. You know how they get if you make them wait." While saying that, Samm made a frenzied motion with his hands, causing Karim to laugh lightly.

As they made their way towards the factory, which was apparently just outside the merchant district, Samm asked, "Why do we need to go to the factory? I've told you it's perfectly safe."

"During my investigation, I found very little evidence, but I have an idea," Kit replied, her face stoic.

Samm's face went dark. "You dragged me away from my store to tell me you know nothing? How can you have a plan if you have no idea how that damned… *thing* is getting into my shop?"

"Samm," Kit spoke slowly, trying to carefully formulate her words. "I think there is nothing to find because any clues have been carefully removed."

Samm rubbed the back of his head as he pondered Kit's comment. "You think the rat is cleaning up after itself?" He laughed like Kit was insane. His jowls swung about with each guffaw. "Like I told you, I saw a rat once in my cheese shop. It was not careful about cleaning up. All it wanted to do was gorge itself into oblivion."

"And yet, you have seen *this* beast, and it ran away when you entered the storeroom. The previous rat just continued eating like you weren't even there."

"That is strange," Samm replied. "But what does it mean?"

"I can't say for sure, but if you'll let me, I'd like to spend the night in your storeroom. If the rat comes back, I'll either capture it or kill it. Either way, your rat problem will be over, and you can move on with selling your cheeses."

The doubt-filled expression on the man's face clearly stated that Samm wasn't sure if Kit's idea was a good one. The bulky shop owner blew out a breath. "I see no harm in trying. How do you propose we proceed?"

Kit told him of her plan, making up most of it as she went along. "I'd like us to pick up the best, most expensive cheese you have at the factory. A full wagonload of it if you have enough."

Samm was far less enthusiastic about that part of her plan. "I've got a palette of Blue Yeti cheese that is ready for sale. It's exceedingly rare and extremely expensive."

"How's its aroma?"

Samm laughed weakly. "Remember what the storeroom smelled like? Well, a single wheel of this cheese has a more powerful bouquet than everything else in my shop. Combined."

Kit's head swam as she recalled just how aromatic the storeroom was the first time she entered. "That should do nicely," she said with a thin-lipped grin. She was already gagging on the inside.

Chapter Twenty-Seven

The Blue Yeti

The Cheeserie's factory was in a large section of the city adjacent to the merchant district. This area was where the city's merchants stored all their goods before they were shipped out or held those that had arrived from other baronies but had not yet moved into the storefronts. It was also the location of all the city's artisans. Woodworkers, masons, armorers, enchanters, and the like, could all be found here. Kit had never ventured into this part of the city, and she had been amazed by the amount of culture to be found here.

The streets themselves were wide and extremely well maintained. There were no booths or vendors, but she could see dozens of master-artisans working in the open air outside their buildings. They passed by a sculptor who was fashioning the likeness of Father Hoarfrost out of a yellow-white stone of some kind.

"Peace unto you," Kit offered as she admired the man's artisanship. "Is your creation to be donated to the Temple as an offering to our god, Titan?"

He didn't even bother to raise his eyes from his work. "Not bloody likely. If the Old Goat wants me to create a likeness of himself to adorn the Temple, well then, he'll bloody well pay me like everyone else does."

His voice was becoming more and more agitated as he spoke. "Just because something is for the Temple, they expect it to be an offering of some sort. I have bills, you know, children to feed, a house to maintain."

Finally, he slammed down his hammer and chisel and glowered up at Kit. His angry gaze weakened when it fell upon the holy symbol of Titan engraved on her training leathers. "Forgive me, little sister. I meant..." quickly he jumped to his feet, realizing it was impolite to speak to a member of the Temple while seated. "I meant no disrespect."

Seeing the look of dismay on his face, Kit chose not to make him feel any worse than he already did. "Peace unto you," she repeated. "The fault is my own. I made a poor assumption, and for that I must be the one who apologizes to you."

The tension drained from the sculptor's face.

Kit continued to examine the art. "If this is not meant as an offering, why are you creating such a beautiful likeness of the High Priest?"

He shrugged his shoulders. "I was offered twice my normal fee if I could create this statue before the annual celebration at the Temple. If someone's willing to pay, I'll carve just about anything."

"Celebration?" Kit asked. Then it dawned on her. "Do you mean the Feast of Titan's Bounty celebrations?"

"The one and only," he replied. "To be honest, getting paid extra is a nice bonus, but it will do me well to have my work on display during the Feast. Father Hoarfrost invites many of the city's wealthiest to attend, and hopefully donate to the Temple. When they see my work, I'll likely get more business coming my way."

"I hate to interrupt," Samm said as he nudged Kit's arm. "If you're going to chat all day, we're not going to get our work finished."

"Peace unto you. May Titan guide your hands in your efforts." Kit would have liked to speak more with this artist, but duty called. Duty always called.

When they approached Samm's factory, it was exactly as he had described. It was an exceptionally large, nondescript building, with no less than eight guards standing out front. "There are a few more in the back and even more inside," Samm offered. "I run them in shifts, to make sure there are always fresh eyes and ears on duty."

As they entered the factory, Kit's stomach heaved. The aroma of old cheese was so strong that she covered her mouth, desperately trying to keep her gag reflexes in check. "Here," Samm offered. He was pointing to a small sack near the entrance. "They don't fix it, but at least they help keep the overwhelming olfactory assault at bay."

Kit opened the bag to find that it was full of tiny bulbs. "Onions?" she asked him. "How are they going to help?"

Samm chuckled to himself, reached into the bag, and pulled out two of them. He promptly stuffed one up each nostril. "They help block and mask the aroma," he said with an extremely nasally voice. "They burn a bit too, which seems to help dull your sense of smell."

Kit found this whole thing a bit ludicrous, but she had to do something, or she was going to have to find a place to hurl. She quickly grabbed two of the biggest onions in the bag and rammed them up her nose. "A bit of burning?" Kit blinked rapidly as tears formed in her eyes. "It feels like I've got a swarm of hornets in my nose!"

"If you'd rather wait outside, I can get some of my staff to load up a wagon of Blue Yeti for us." Samm was doing everything he could not to laugh.

"No, I'm okay." Kit's lips were saying she was okay, but her face was telling a completely different story.

Samm grabbed her by the arm and helped her back outside. Even with the door closed, and the onions jammed up her nose, the smell of the cheese was still making her feel like she was going to lose her breakfast. She pulled the onions out of her nostrils and took a deep breath of the fresh air.

"Sorry," Samm offered. "I suppose it's much worse than I realize. You wait here while I get somebody to load up a wagon for us."

As Samm headed back into the factory, Kit found a lamp post to lean against a bit further away from the building. The dark spots that were filling her vision were just beginning to clear when Samm came back out. He was clearly amused at her inability to deal with the stench.

⁂

Samm took care of all the details, setting up the wagon and having the workers load it up with his prized wares. Fortunately, the trip to the cheese shop was mostly into the wind, so the ripe smell of the cheese was being carried away without Kit having to endure its aroma.

When they returned to the shop, Karim was clearly excited to see what had arrived. "Is that the Blue Yeti?" He was hopping about, unable to contain his excitement. "Nobility is going to come in droves for a chance to buy some of it. We should limit how much people can buy at one time, to make sure all of our best customers get some." Karim took one of the wheels off the cart. Holding it close to his nose, he drew a deep breath. "This cheese has a most wondrous aroma." And with that, he carried the wheels into the building.

By the time they finished unloading the Blue Yeti into the storeroom, Kit was ready to pass out from the smell. For the life of her, she could not figure out how Karim could stand the aroma, let alone bask in it.

Now that the cheese was in place, it was strictly a matter of finding a place to hide without anybody knowing she was there. In her mind, she had two choices. She could wait inside the storeroom and try to catch the dire rat 'in the act,' or she could wait outside in the hopes that she could discover how the rat was getting in. The overwhelming stench of the cheeses forced Kit to choose the latter.

After a quick survey of the area, Kit found a quiet, out of the way location on another store-top that allowed her to see both the front door and the side entrance into the storeroom. There was only one way into the side of the building, and the front entrance was open to the marketplace.

As she waited, the sights and sounds of the district filled her senses. The night-bugs were chirping out their mating calls. The street hawkers had been replaced with street walkers, offering their patrons both company and pleasure, whatever that may be. A pair of drunken sailors were stumbling about, either trying to find their way back to the docks or just trying to find the next tavern to experience its liquid fare.

Kit laughed quietly when the two drunks acted like they'd been struck by something, and they both fell face-first onto the street. Her attention was completely drawn off the task at hand, and she nearly didn't notice that the sounds of the night had come to an abrupt stop. Her eyes immediately scanned the area, but she found nothing.

The two drunks picked themselves up off the ground and waved their arms about. It looked like they were yelling at each other, but she heard nothing. *She. Heard. Nothing!*

It was at that moment that Kit realized she was in the middle of a *silencing spell*! The store was being robbed!

The young priest bolted across the roof to the staircase. She didn't bother trying to be quiet since the area was already silenced. She raced down the stairs, bolting for the storeroom entrance.

Just as Kit was running full-out towards the door, she slammed into what could only be described as a wall. She dropped like a stone on the spot, feeling completely disoriented. As she laid there, trying to regain her senses, a warm, moist *something*, dragged across her face. As she tried to ward it off, her hand brushed the soft hairy snout of an animal.

It seemed that she was also inside an invisibility bubble of some sort.

Kit picked herself up off the ground and carefully felt her way to the back of the 'animal.' It was then that she put her hand on a rough wooden object. The animal was a beast of burden, and the rough wood was a piece of a wagon of some sort. Her head was still ringing from having run headlong into the beast when a foul odor assailed her nostrils. There was no mistaking the pungent, revolting aroma of Blue Yeti cheese.

She tried to find her way around the wagon to the storeroom door. Just as Kit made her way to the end of it, she was once again knocked off her feet by an unseen force. She screeched in frustration, but her voice went unheard by anyone.

Picking herself up off the ground, she moved into the storeroom. The room was completely dark, except where a lantern was lying on its side, its flame guttering, casting strange spectral shadows across the room. Before she could react, one of the phantom shapes headed straight for her. She was about to ready her weapon when the shadow bowled her over. It was like a block of stone had slammed into her. Once again on her back, Kit watched helplessly as the shadow leapt over her and headed for the door. By the time she got outside, the shadow was gone, and so was the invisible cart. Moments later, the sounds of the night once again filled the air.

Kit raced back to the storeroom. She picked up the lantern that had been knocked over onto the floor. Fortunately, the lamp's oil bladder hadn't burst open. If it had, it likely would have set the entire building on fire. Scanning the surroundings, Kit found Samm sitting on the ground, leaning against one of the shelves, a large gash across his forehead, blood pouring over his face.

When she tried to rouse him, Samm's eyes fluttered open. "I tried to stop them."

Pressing her hand against the wound, Kit attempted to staunch the bleeding. "You could see who it was?"

⫷⫷⫸⫸

She quickly applied a bandage to the wound. As a trained healer, she always had a supply on hand. As quickly as she could wrap it, blood from his wound soaked through. Kit turned back at the door and growled. She wanted to continue her pursuit of the robbers, but she feared that if she left Samm there, he would die from blood loss.

The shop owner struggled to maintain his focus. "I hid here, in the storeroom. When you said you were going to keep an eye outside, I decided to wait here. My Blue Yeti..."

Kit could see that he was having difficulty staying awake and that his skin was turning a deathly shade of gray.

"You've been poisoned," Kit said, thinking perhaps the wound on his head came from the teeth or claws of the dire rat. As quickly as she could manage, she pulled out the small scroll that Captain Harding had given her. Typically, protection spells were cast before a person was injured, but maybe it would work to slow any spreading infection.

Kit broke the seal and carefully examined the writing within. The words made no sense to her at all. Whatever language it was, it was neither Common nor Berrat. Slowly, she read the text aloud, hoping that she was pronouncing the words properly.

As she finished the last sentence, the scroll disappeared in a puff of green smoke which traveled from her hands to the wounded man. The smoke slithered over Samm, tiny tentacles probing every inch of his skin. When a tendril found the gash on his head, it disappeared into the wound with the rest of the smoke following it.

Almost immediately, the color returned to Samm's face, but he still appeared to be groggy, on the verge of losing consciousness.

Calming her mind, Kit called out, "Titan, hear me." As she said a prayer to Titan, asking for his strength to heal the wound, her hands burst forth in a pale-yellow glow. The bleeding slowed as the aura covered the wound. Moments later, Samm's eyes opened once again. They appeared to be much clearer now.

"I couldn't believe my eyes!" Sam said, his voice much stronger. "I was hiding over there," he said, pointing to where a large pile of crates stood. "The storeroom door opened and moments later, cheese was simply disappearing off the shelf. I was about to come out of hiding when I saw Karim come bursting through the door. He... changed! Right before my eyes he turned into a dire rat!"

Kit was beginning to think that this head wound was more serious than she realized, but Samm continued.

"Karim, the rat, crashed into something that wasn't there. He floated up off the ground, clawing violently at the surrounding air. Then, he flew across the room, and crashed hard into the crates I was hiding behind. I ran out, you know, to confront whoever was in the room... then... that's all I remember. I guess I passed out."

Samm pushed Kit's hand away from his head, trying to feel the wound. Outside of a nasty red welt, it was completely healed. Still, Samm winced when he touched it.

"And then what happened?"

Samm shook his head, trying to clear any remaining cobwebs. "When I opened my eyes, you were hovering over me."

The shop keeper's words suddenly made sense. "Karim changed into a dire rat." Thinking back to Samm's story of how Karim stabbed the animal with the spear, she remembered tales from her past, from when she lived in the Berrat village. "Karim defeated that rat in single combat, and in doing so, took the animal's spirit into himself. He learned how to assume its form."

Only then did Kit remembered the dire rat jumping over her, giving chase to the robbers.

Hopping to her feet, Kit told Samm to rest and recover, then raced for the exit.

She searched the ground outside the storeroom. There were a number of cart tracks there. She followed the one that appeared to be the most recent. As she moved out into the market square, the tracks were more difficult to identify, obscured by the dozens of other cart tracks and other foot traffic. Just when Kit was ready to give up, the sun broke over the horizon, illuminating the ground. One set of tracks clearly stood out from the rest. Her pace quickened as she easily followed the trail. A breeze picked up, and the unmistakable scent of Blue Yeti stung her nose. She smiled, knowing she was definitely on the right track.

Chapter Twenty-Eight

On the Scent

The priest ran as fast as her feet allowed, following the cart trail and the stench of Blue Yeti across the market district, only stopping when she arrived at another cheese shop. There was an oxcart sitting out front, along with two Berrat locked in a heated argument.

As Kit got closer, she could see that one of the Berrat was Karim, and the other was an older woman. She had gray hair with tinges of red in it, woven into rows of tight braids. She was wearing simple clothing of cloth and leather. Deep wrinkles etched her forehead, likely a result of the heavy scowl that looked to be a permanent fixture on her face.

The discussion came to an abrupt stop when the pair noticed Kit's arrival.

"Karim, what's going on here?" the young priest demanded, her eyes locked on the old Berrat.

The woman gave Karim a scathing glare, and he withered under her gaze. With that same loathsome scowl, she moved away from the boy, stalking toward Kit. "This is none of your business *human*. If you know what's good for you, you'll leave now."

Karim stepped between Kit and the elder. "Mother, this is Kit Standing Bear, a Priest of Titan."

He said the words like they should carry great weight, but the woman was undaunted. "You heard me the first time, *priest*." Her voice was pure venom. "LEAVE!"

"Karim, is this your mother?" Kit's hand had already moved to take hold of her battle hammer.

The old woman spat on the ground. "You would draw your weapon on me, priest?"

She muttered something unintelligible when the surrounding air shimmered and her form became blurry. Kit stumbled backwards as the woman grew to be more than twice Kit's height. Thick brown hair covered her body while great, long claws grew from her fingers. When the transformation was complete, a grizzly bear stood before her. It roared out a challenge, its wide maw exposing some hugely impressive fangs. Kit took a fighting stance, her weapon at the ready.

Karim's shape also changed. His Berrat form melted away as he transformed into a dire rat, quickly moving between Kit and the grizzly bear. Even as a rat, the animal could still speak the common tongue.

"Mother! I will not allow you to attack her."

The bear's paw struck Karim with such speed that Kit barely saw it happen. The impact knocked the dire rat through the air, crashing hard into the wagon's wheel. There were huge gashes across its ribs. The bear's shape shimmered again as Karim's mother rushed over to his side. She was speaking now in Berrathi, using a dialect that Kit mostly understood.

"Forgive me, my son," she said, her hand tentatively moving to the boy's blood-soaked fur. "It is for the good of our people. It..."

Karim's shape also returned to his normal form. His tunic was in tatters and his side was drenched in blood.

Kit was about to come to Karim's aid when she saw that his mother was casting a spell on him. A deep green glow poured forth, engulfing the mother and son in moments. The bleeding abruptly stopped as the gashes knitted together. The wound was completely healed but the boy's shirt was still shredded where the bear's great claws had ripped through it.

The woman clutched the boy to her, sobbing uncontrollably. "I'm sorry, Karim. Please forgive me."

"Mother, why?"

"Samm Larder stole our family's business right out from under us. When your father died, you should have received half of the shop and Larder the other half. Instead, that foul human took it all, and you became his *servant*." Tears welled up in Karim's mother's eyes. There was no sorrow in her expression, only rage. "All the while, I've been pushed to the side and forgotten about. It was my husband who died, and I received nothing."

"Why did you not get your husband's share of the shop?" Kit asked, interrupting the woman's tirade.

"She got nothing because she left my father. She left him to take up with that radical..." before Karim could finish his sentence, his mother cuffed him across the face, splitting his lip in the process.

"Don't you ever speak of Pental with that tone. He is a great man!" The woman's eyes were wild with fervent fanaticism.

Karim wiped the blood from the side of his mouth. "That great man broke up our family, and then he threw you in a ditch when he was done with you."

Karim pushed himself to his feet, running his fingers over his tattered shirt. "You, mother. It was you who destroyed our family, and you would try to kill me? For what? Because you think you're owed something? Samm raised me as his own son. He treats me with respect and I'm proud to be a part of his family." Karim's face contorted with rage. "And you would steal from him? From us? For your own personal gain, you would again hurt me?"

Karim and his mother were about to go to blows again when a regiment of eight City Watch guards approached. Their boots clomped on the ground in perfect precision as they neared.

"What is the meaning of this disturbance?" asked a short, stubby guard with a single brass pip beneath his patch, identifying him as a corporal. He leveled his spear tip at Karim. "Boy, what is your purpose here? Why are you harassing this businesswoman?"

The stubby guard turned his stubbled face to Karim's mother. "Are you well, Yenda?"

Kit calmly stepped in front of the guard, gently moving the spear tip to the side. "I am Sister Kit Standing Bear, Priest of Titan. I am here on Watch business. This woman is a thief, and I am bringing her in."

The short man scoffed and eyed Kit up and down. Clearly, he did not believe her story.

⁐⁖⁖⁖⊹⁖⁖⁖⁐

"Please help me bring her to justice." Kit hoped that by asking for the guard's assistance, he would see that she was, in fact, acting on behalf of the City Watch.

The guard's face was completely flat. "Nice try. I don't know who you are, and I don't believe what you're saying. You're all coming in with us. We'll let the magistrate decide your fate. Until he does, you can all enjoy the *hospitality* of our dungeons."

The man took his spear point and leveled it once again at Kit's face. In unison, the other guards moved against Karim and his mother, using their spear-tips to bar any chance of escape.

The short guard's mouth twisted, as though he had just tasted something... off-putting.

"Kit Standing Bear, you say? I recognize that name."

It appeared the other guards recognized the name as well now. Kit stood up a bit straighter. It seemed that her good work for the Fist of Titan preceded her. Warmth blossomed in her chest. It felt good to be seen as a valued contributor to the City Watch's force.

The stubby guard gave his comrades a knowing glance before turning his condescending glare back on Kit. "This is Kit Standing Bear, the little shrew who called our Lieutenant an *errand boy*. Well now, little shrew, you suddenly find yourself in need of our help."

He gave Kit an evil glare. "We'll take them all in and leave the business of sorting them out to the magistrate. I think Karr is going to enjoy throwing this little *street rat* in the dungeon himself." He grinned at the little priest, regarding her with a hate-filled gaze. He moved in closer, his sour breath smelling of cheap wine and garlic. "There's not much to you, but the dungeon rats aren't too picky about who they gnaw on."

Karim's mother spat at the guard with remarkable accuracy. "I do not recognize your authority over me or my son. We are Berrat. You and your people are interlopers in our land. Look to the horizon. This morning, you are witnessing your last sunrise." While she was speaking, she once again shifted into her grizzly bear form.

Kit was now standing between the guards and the challenge the great bear was roaring out. Its lips were quivering as saliva flew from its mouth, its wicked teeth ready to rip flesh from bone.

"Form a wall!" the leader yelled as he spun to point his spear tip at the grizzly. With a quick swipe, the bear knocked the weapon from the man's hand. Before he could draw the short sword from his belt, the great bear swiped again with its six-inch claws, rending the man's throat open, his lifeblood gushing from the wound in a horrific torrent.

Kit now had her hammer in her hand, unsure of what to do. The guards had all but lost interest in her, each of them concentrating their efforts on the bear.

When one of the men buried his spear into the shoulder of the animal, it bellowed out in agony and spun around to meet the attacker. When a second guard sunk his spear into the bear's side, Kit threw herself at him, knocking the soldier to the ground. She quickly rounded on another guard as she moved in closer. Kit used her hammer to knock the spear from the man's hand.

"Enough!" Kit shouted. "You are not charged with delivering justice!"

The bear, now with two spears lodged deep into its flesh, barrelled past Kit, sinking her fangs into the neck of the female guard standing in front of her. With a twist of its neck, the bear ripped her open. Blood, gushing from the gaping wound, covered Kit's face and hair.

Again, the grizzly bellowed out. Kit spun to see two more guards twisting the tips of their spears that they'd impaled the creature with. The bear swung weakly at them. The ferocity of her attacks was no longer present.

Two more guards stepped up and buried their spears into the animal's chest. It barely even reacted, its eyes rolling back in its head. With a sopping thump, the bear fell to the ground, her final breaths coming in raspy gasps.

Kit fell to her knees beside the gravely wounded guard. The extent of the damage was beyond Kit's healing abilities.

"May Titan guide you to the Great Cycle," she said as she placed her hand upon the woman's breastplate. "You died in the service of Titan's people. There is no greater calling."

"Get off her, shrew," one of the male guards said, kicking Kit in the side of the head, knocking her onto the blood-soaked ground.

"Enough!" another of the guards cried as Kit jumped to her feet, ready to attack. "There has been enough death this day. Be at peace, little sister."

Kit nodded as she wiped the dripping blood from her face. The priest's heart shattered for Karim as he stared down at his dead mother. His face was a picture of torn loyalties. He grimaced as the bear's form changed back into her natural Berrat shape. Every bloody wound was now easily visible.

"You brought this upon yourself, mother."

The young man shed no tears at the woman's death, but Kit could see in his face that his heart was breaking.

Moving next to him, Kit put her hand on Karim's shoulder. She could feel the conflict within him, rolling off in waves of despair. "She was a troubled woman, but now she is at peace. She has taken her place in the Great Cycle, returning to whence she came."

The guards wasted no time turning their attention back to Kit.

"March!" a heavily muscled guard bellowed at her. "Move now or face the same outcome."

Kit would normally have found a quick response to his orders, but she was too busy looking out for Karim. She worried that he might try to retaliate against the guards, but instead, he lowered his head, ready to accept his fate.

Chapter Twenty-Nine

A Deeper Problem

When they arrived at the City Watch barracks, the heavily muscled guard ordered the body of Karim's mother to be taken away and to be prepared for burial rites. Kit was surprised that they were taking the time, and the effort, to ensure the body was treated respectfully.

"What?" asked the guard. "Regardless of her behavior, she was a citizen of this city, and she will be given a proper burial."

Karim was as dumbfounded as Kit was. "Thank you," he managed to say. "She was once a good woman, before her mind was poisoned."

The guards roughly pushed their prisoners towards the entrance to the dungeons. Kit figured that once they started that trip into the bowels of the structure, she would never again see the light of day.

"Take me to see the captain!" she blurted out, her voice full of authority. "I was acting on his orders. Take me to him and I'll prove it to you."

"Sure, little shrew. I'll take you to the captain," a horse-faced woman said as she slid her hand under Kit's chin, tilting her head up to her. "And when he exposes your lies, maybe he'll let me dole out some punishment before I throw you in the dungeons. We haven't had a public flogging in a long time. I very much think I'd enjoy flaying you while the temple's faithful watch."

Kit held the woman's gaze, her eyes narrowing slightly. "And when I prove that I am working for Captain Harding, maybe you'll be the one taking the trip to the dungeons." The guard's face blanched slightly at the small priest's comment. It appeared that Kit's confidence in the outcome had cast some doubt on what the soldier had previously perceived as a lie.

As requested, Kit and Karim were dragged to see the captain, more forcefully than the priest would have liked. The horse-faced woman pounded on the heavy wooden frame. Before she could finish knocking, the door swung open, the captain's enormous bulk filling the entire entrance.

"Welcome, Sister Kit," the captain said. "Please come in."

The guard was unable to hide her surprise, her voice raising an octave as she spoke. "You know this girl?"

A grin pulled at the edges of the captain's mouth. "Of course, I do. She's been on an assignment. I'm assuming she's here to tell me that she's killed the dire rat that's been infesting the Cheeserie."

Karim mumbled to himself, his voice barely audible. "I was not infesting the store. I was protecting it." Nobody but Kit seemed to have heard the boy. Either that or they were choosing to ignore him.

The guard bowed slightly to the young priest. "Forgive me for not believing you, Sister. You don't look much like a City Watch guard, let alone a priest, for that matter." Before Kit had a chance to respond, the guard nodded to the captain and bolted down the hallway, her heavy plate armor clattering as she did.

"So," the captain said, turning to Kit. "Tell me how you defeated the rat."

"Where's Lump?" Kit asked, ignoring the captain's question.

"I took him back to the Temple last night," he replied with a groan. "He practically emptied the kitchen of food."

"He's a big dog," Kit interrupted. "And he worked hard yesterday."

"That wasn't the worst of it," the man said with a growl. "He wanted to crawl into my bed with me. I need my sleep, Kit. I need every bit of strength to deal with *you* and he was robbing me of that very precious commodity. So, I took him back to the Temple and left him with Father Hoarfrost. You can imagine how happy he was to be bothered in the middle of the night."

"You woke up Father?" Kit swallowed hard.

"You bet I did. If he's going to subject me to you, then I am going to give him a taste of what you're putting me through." A heavy weight was growing in the pit of Kit's stomach. Returning to the Temple wasn't going to be a pleasant experience. No, not a pleasant experience at all.

"Now," the captain said, scrubbing his meaty hand down his face. "Answer my question and tell me how you defeated the rat."

Kit's voice broke slightly as she recounted the tale. Karim stayed silent, except for the one instance when he blew his nose into his handkerchief.

The captain's eyes were wide by the time she finished the story.

"You did well, Kit. You did very well." He gave his chin a thoughtful rub. "It's a shame what happened, but you kept your head and solved the real problem behind the dire rat incident."

"Thank you, Captain, but I fear there is a bigger problem going on in the city."

"And what problem might that be?" The exasperation in the man's voice clearly indicated he didn't want to hear about it.

Unsure of how to continue, Kit looked to Karim and then back to the captain. What she witnessed was important, so, regardless of how he felt about it, the girl pressed on. "I think there is an undercurrent of hatred spreading through the city, specifically between the Berrat and the humans."

"I am aware," the captain said. The words came out like Kit's concern was a relief. "We're doing what we can, but the City Watch has limited resources, and we have serious problems that need to be dealt with. Maybe you'd like to take one of the many outstanding tasks off my job board to help me out?"

Kit didn't say a word, but her dubious look came through loud and clear drawing a groan from the captain.

"Yes, yes. Of course, you are a Priest of Titan, and you serve the Temple." He tilted his head slightly and raised his eyebrows. "That being said, you may want to reconsider your point of view. The work I have for you benefits the people of this city, both within its walls and across the kingdom. By serving the City Watch, you are serving the Temple as well as the people."

Kit was torn by what the captain had said. Serving the people was to serve Titan, but it was her job as a Priest of Titan to devote herself to freeing her god from his icy prison. Being a priest wasn't as straightforward as she expected it to be. Unsure how to respond, she nodded her head. "I will pray to Titan for his guidance."

The captain chuckled and raised his eyebrows at the girl. "You do that, Sister Kit. You might also consider asking the High Priest. Does he not speak for your god?"

Kit didn't bother responding to the comment. She knew he was right, but she didn't want to admit it.

The captain walked over to his desk and pulled out a small piece of parchment. Using a stubby, half-chewed quill, he started writing. When he finished, he rolled up the piece of paper and handed it over to Kit.

"Next time, show this to anyone in the City Watch to prove you are working on my behalf." A small smile was growing on his face. "Or you can use it the next time you get yourself into a bind. Consider this a 'get out of trouble' scroll."

She took the furled parchment from the captain's hand. Her mouth fell open while she furrowed her brow. "That's it? I get a note saying that you know me?"

The captain's face turned to stone. "You expect payment for serving your god?"

"I serve my god in my own way. When I work for you, I expect payment. If you pay me in gold, I will give it to the Fist." She frowned at her worn-out, light-leather armor. She then looked over her shoulder, out the captain's door, into the training area. "I could use some better gear. I wasn't prepared to fight a grizzly bear."

The captain leaned to the side, looking out into the training area. He gave a small motion with his head. "Why don't you take that studded leather armor off the practice dummy outside my office? It's decent quality, and I'm sure it will serve you well."

Kit walked out of his office to check out the armor, removing it from the dummy. She tilted her head slightly in acknowledgement of payment. "Thank you. This will serve Titan well."

The entire experience had left Kit feeling cold inside. First, she had discovered that there was an undercurrent of hate being spread across the country. It wasn't just perverting the minds of the young, it was also strong enough to break the bonds between a mother and her son. Karim's mother had mentioned the name, Pental. Who was he, and what role was he playing in spreading this hate?

With that, Kit and Karim left the captain's office and headed towards the exit. Along the way, several of the guards acknowledged Kit with arms crossed over their chests, the traditional sign of peace among Titan worshipers.

"Peace unto you," the young priest offered in response. "May Titan's strength protect you."

As they stepped out into the city streets, Karim followed closely at the girl's heels. The quiet of the early morning had long since passed, and the streets were bustling with activity. Kit turned to Karim, unsure of what to say or do. "I'm so sorry for your loss. What will you do now?"

The young Berrat appeared lost in his thoughts. "I'm not sure. First, I need to go back to the shop and explain to Samm what happened. After that, I don't know."

She placed her hand on his shoulder, offering him her strength. "Who knows what is in the heart of people? Your mother's actions may have made sense to her, even if they hurt you deeply. Today, her choices caught up with her. She has taught you an important lesson in her passing."

Karim's head bobbed as Kit spoke. She believed he understood, but there was no way to know for sure.

"The winds are changing," the boy said. "Soon, the world as we know it will be no more. I can feel it." Without another word, the young Berrat simply walked away.

Kit peered up and down the street, wondering what to do next. Whatever it was, it would be in the service of Titan. Father Hoarfrost needed to hear what happened. Like Karim had said, change was upon them, and she feared it was for the worst. The Temple needed to be prepared for what was coming, whatever it might be.

Chapter Thirty

No Rest for the Weary

Kit once again found herself at the base of the stairs leading up to the Temple. Even though she had made this climb dozens of times, she paused, staring up at the task before her. Just like every other time, she squared her shoulders to the massive staircase, took a deep cleansing breath, and began her ascent.

By the time she reached the top, she was breathing heavily, but her conditioning was sound, and she was ready to visit the High Priest. Physically ready, at least. She wasn't looking forward to the tongue lashing she was going to get for having Lump dumped on his lap in the middle of the night. She would explain that it wasn't her choice. The captain had sent her on another mission, and he didn't want Lump to come along. What else could she have done besides leave him in the captain's care. It wasn't her fault if Harding didn't want to share his bed with the pup. He could have told Lump to sleep on the floor.

With something of a plan on how she'd deal with the high priest's anger, Kit pressed on. As she walked through the Temple's nave, priests and acolytes alike greeted her. All the while, citizens were actively praying to Titan, hoping to gain his favor.

Ducking her head, Kit quickly moved past everyone, doing her best to avoid any conversation that might distract her from making it to her destination. When she arrived at the high priest's office, his door was open. She poked her head in, asking softly, "Do you have time to see me, Father?"

"Just the person I wanted to see," the High Priest said as he waved Kit in and motioned for her to take a seat. As she did, he pulled a tightly furled parchment off a shelf behind him. Without a word, he handed Kit the paper and took a seat behind his massive, highly polished dragonwood desk. She was still actively reading while the High Priest told her about the task.

"I want you to visit one of the local fishing villages. Two more children have fallen mysteriously ill. This makes almost ten who have contracted this illness. All the others have died. If you cannot heal these children, your job will be to help comfort the villagers."

"But Father," Kit was uncomfortable with his request, "I, I just..."

"Returned from completing a task for Captain Harding?"

Kit blinked at the High Priest in disbelief.

How could he possibly know these things? I only just got back.

Then she remembered that the captain had woken Father in the middle of the night to bring Lump to him. He must have told him that she was out doing work for the Watch. That weight in the pit of Kit's stomach reappeared and doubled in size.

The high priest chuckled quietly to himself. "I suppose you're wondering how I know where you've been?" Kit shrugged. The ball resting in the pit of her stomach suddenly twisted. The young priest lowered her gaze, her fingers fidgeting uncontrollably. "I know because..."

"Father," she said, cutting the man off mid sentence. "I know about Captain Harding waking you in the middle of night. I'm really sorry he did that. Lump was annoying him and he... Father, I swear to Titan, it wasn't my fault." Everything she had rehearsed fell from her head. "I mean to say..."

"Sister Kit. I need you to stop talking." The old man's voice was stern and commanding. With no idea of how to defend herself, Kit did the smart thing and clamped her mouth shut. Moments ticked away in silence. Finally, the young priest looked up to find a very confused high priest standing in front of her. "I have no idea what you're going on about. I haven't seen the Watch commander since yesterday morning when we discussed your delicate mission."

Kit felt the blood drain from her face. The captain had played her, and she walked right into it.

The old priest chuckled. "I was going to say that I knew where you were because you reek of cheese. You're also carrying a suit of studded leather armor that bears the City Watch symbol on it." His bewilderment abruptly changed to annoyance. "I'm guessing Captain Harding was having some fun with you, little sister. But what I would like to know is why Lump was with him in the first place?" Kit scrambled to come up with a good explanation, one that wouldn't worsen the situation. Fortunately, the high priest spared her the effort. "Whatever the reason, you have a mission to complete, and I suggest you get going."

Kit looked down at the armor and cringed. "I am so tired, Father. Surely there is somebody better rested who you could send?" Kit sighed quietly and headed for the door.

"Get back in here!" the priest's voice boomed. "I am giving this task to *you*. It is the third and final assignment of your blooding. We can't always be fully rested when duty calls upon us. Regardless of our condition, we must always be ready to act. If you do not wish to take it on, then maybe your devotion to Titan is not what I believed it to be."

Bowing her head in contrition, Kit managed to squeak out a few words. "Forgive me, Your Grace. I've put my own needs before that of the community. It won't happen again."

The High Priest's mood did not lighten. "Little sister, you will learn that being a Priest of Titan is a life of sacrifice and hardship. If you will not, or cannot accept this, you will have to learn how to live a life without Titan's graces."

Kit's face reddened somewhat. The High Priest had always been tough on her, but this threat to kick her out of the Temple was real. With her eyes staring down at her feet, she acknowledged her understanding.

"I will leave at once." Kit stood straighter and put on a strong face. Inside, she felt like a puddle of goo, and she desperately wanted to get reacquainted with her bed.

"Do you know the way to the village, or do you require an escort?" The High Priest's tone was still full of steel.

"No, Your Grace, I know the way. The village is less than a half-day's journey west of here, on the shores of the Gaelinora Sea. I'll stop by the City Watch barracks and get Lump from Captain Harding."

"Leave the dog with the captain. It would take you much less time if you took a horse," Father said. "You do know that they are available to all priests."

"A horse, Father?" Kit shook her head adamantly. She wasn't afraid of horses, but she was a poor rider and the likelihood of the horse throwing her was enough to convince her to not even try. It would be embarrassing enough to fall off, but it would be worse if she returned to the temple on foot. "I would prefer to walk. It will afford me more time to contemplate the mysteries of Titan."

The high priest covered his mouth to suppress his laugh, but it did nothing to hide the humor in his eyes. Kit wasn't exactly sure what he was smiling about but it was much better than him being angry with her.

"Prepare what you need for the trip, but don't dawdle," he said.

"Yes, Father." As Kit turned to leave, he called out to her, his voice much gentler now.

"Sister Kit, be careful while you're there. There is a great deal of unrest brewing across the kingdom these days. Be mindful of the people around you. These are strange times."

With a curt nod, the exhausted girl left the High Priest's office and headed back to her small quarters in the Temple dormitories, the ones assigned to acolytes. She had never seen a priest's quarters, but she secretly hoped they were more substantial, and now, she technically deserved one. She really would love to take a hot bath and catch a couple of hours of sleep, but if she was going to make it to her destination before dark, she was going to have to head out as soon as possible.

Chapter Thirty-One

Brother Powder

When Kit entered her room, she quickly tossed her new suit of armor aside, grabbed her knapsack from the corner, and dumped its contents onto her bed. As she rummaged through her belongings, she tossed anything she wouldn't need for her journey onto the floor. It was a long walk, and she needed to travel as lightly as possible if she was going to arrive at the village before nightfall. She quickly slipped out of her filthy white cloak and bloodstained leather armor and pulled on her new suit of studded leather. She marveled at the fit. It wasn't perfect, but it was better than she expected.

Remembering what Father Hoarfrost had mentioned, she pulled out her dagger and removed the City Watch patch from her left breast. Thinking it might come in handy some time, she slipped it into one of the pockets of her knapsack.

The weary young priest looked longingly at her bed. It was only a thin mattress on a stone platform, but right now, it was calling out to her. It had been well over a full day since she last slept, and her recent adventures had taken a toll on her body and soul. It was at this point that she wished she had asked Father Hoarfrost for a rejuvenation potion. They were not good for you, but once in a while they could get you through a rough patch when sleep wasn't an option.

Perhaps the apothecary might give her a potion or two since she was leaving on a mission in service of the Temple. She smiled inwardly, hoping Brother Powder was still working there. Regardless of Kit being a terrible student in his class, he always seemed to have a soft spot for her.

Kit moaned at her reflection in the mirror and winced at the state she was in. Her face was fouled with smeared and dried blood, her long black hair was a tangle mass of knots, and her dark brown eyes were severely bloodshot.

"How can Brother Powder resist me?" she said with a laugh.

In her line of work, personal hygiene was a luxury one could seldom afford, but if she was going to try to coax Brother Powder into giving her some potions, she might want to look her best. Taking a few moments, Kit tried to untangle her hair, but without some hot water and a good deal of soap, she was not going to be able to do much more than just flatten it down.

Finally, Kit gave her shoulders a shrug and decided to visit the apothecary as she was. After all, if she looked like she had been hard at it, maybe she'd be more likely to get some sympathy from Brother Powder.

A quick check out the window-slit told her the daylight was burning fast, so she'd better hurry. Kit threw her knapsack over her shoulder and raced down the halls of the dormitory, and then down seven flights of stairs to where the Temple artisans worked.

In her haste, Kit nearly bowled over two acolytes carrying trays of what looked to be herbs. When she finally got to the apothecary, she was relieved to see that Brother Powder was indeed still working there. His eyes brightened as Kit burst into the room.

"Greetings, Sister Kit," Brother Powder announced in his high-pitched voice. "I hear that you are *unofficially* a priest now."

"Brother Powder, it's been too long since we've had a chance to talk." She gave him her best, cutest pout. "I'm afraid it's going to have to be a while longer. I'm here on business." She gave him a coy smile, hoping that its sudden appearance would help seal the deal.

Brother Powder frowned slightly at her, running his fingers through his short-cropped white hair. "What sort of trouble are you trying to get me into, little sister?" He raised his eyebrows expectantly, waiting for her response.

Kit considered laying it on a bit thick, appealing to his sympathy, but instead she chose to be straight with him. "I have been asked by the High Priest to visit a fishing village on the Gaelinora. It seems that my task is urgent, but I haven't slept in nearly two days. I was hoping you might be able to spare..."

"A rejuvenation potion?" Brother Powder asked, already knowing the purpose of her visit. He looked Kit up and down, a thin smile appearing on his lips. "They can be dangerous, if abused. You know that, right?"

Kit nodded, looking down at the floor. "Yes, brother, but I don't know if I'll be able to complete Father Hoarfrost's mission in my current state."

"You do look like you could use a good night's sleep." His nose crinkled a bit. "And a bath too, a long hot one."

"Please, Brother Powder, can you help me? I need to leave right now if I'm to have any hope of getting there before sundown. There are sick children who need my help."

The man shook his head and headed over to one of the many rows of shelves. "You should have started with that, you know. I'll do anything to help children in need."

He returned a moment later with two vials in his hands. They both contained a golden-orange liquid, one of them being deeper colored than the other. He handed Kit the deeper one first. "Here, drink this now. It's particularly potent, so it should fix you right up."

Kit took the potion, uncorked the stopper, and drained it in one gulp. The liquid tasted like honey and smelt like orange blossoms. Before she even had a chance to put the stopper back into the bottle, its magic surged through her. A rush of warmth ignited in her mouth, chest, and belly. It immediately radiated through her entire body. Kit wobbled a bit when the potion took full effect. She felt... amazing!

"Titan's snowballs, Brother Powder. That was intense. I don't think I've ever felt this good before."

"Do you remember how tired you felt before you took the potion?" Brother Powder asked.

Kit nodded as she continued to lick the potion's sweet flavor off her lips. She didn't want to waste a single drip.

"When this wears off, you are going to feel at least twice as exhausted. These potions can leave you incapacitated, especially if you overexert yourself while under their influence."

He handed her the other potion. "This one is less potent, much less potent. If you feel unable to function when the first one wears off, take this one, but only as an emergency. It will take the edge off and make it a bit easier on you while you recover."

"Thank you, Brother Powder, you're the best." Kit gave him a wink before bolting for the door.

The young priest dashed down the halls and up the stairwells until she reached the Nave. She slowed as she passed through the great hall, pausing momentarily to say a quick prayer to Titan as she passed beneath his statue. As she exited the building, she broke into a full run, barely able to keep her feet beneath her as she flew down the imposing flight of stairs that led up to the Temple. After clearing the Temple's square, she continued running all the way through the city streets, past the front gate, and through the colorful tents and crowds of the marketplace.

It was only after Kit had been running hard for about an hour that the young priest finally let up. Her chest was heaving badly, and her tiny body was drenched in sweat. Remembering the warnings of Brother Powder, Kit slowed to a steady jog, something she could do even when she was tired. She hoped it would be okay if she kept this pace for the rest of her journey to the village.

Along the way, Kit considered her conversation with Father Hoarfrost. The information on the children's illness was vague at best. She was going to have to wait until she arrived at the village to get any additional information.

Kit took note of the sun again. The day was more than half over and she still had a long way to go. The land here was fairly flat, open grassland with occasional bits of light forest. She picked up her pace again, increasing her speed from a steady jog to a full-out run. The potion was working wonders. She felt absolutely *awesome*!

CHAPTER THIRTY-TWO

THE VILLAGE BY THE SEA

The fishing village itself was quite small, consisting of no more than a hundred homes. As Kit approached, she cocked an eyebrow. There stood a structure that might be described as a gatehouse, yet it lacked both a gate and a surrounding wall. She thought it might be where people selling their catch met, but she couldn't be certain. Seeing that the small building was vacant, she continued on her way into the village proper.

Kit came to a fork in the road. One direction presumably led to the main street, and the other led to the docks. The main street was the most likely direction for her to take if she was heading to where the sick children were, but there appeared to be a large disturbance happening by the waterfront. She turned to head in the direction of the disturbance. Following the noise, she came upon a father weeping over his dying son. When he saw Kit approaching, he called out to her.

"Please help! My son found a spider's nest under the dock ..."

Kit quickly knelt beside the boy, checking for bites. There were no visible puncture wounds anywhere on his body, but the child was clutching onto a half-eaten apple. Kit inspected the fruit, finding it had an unmistakable odor, one she recognized from her potions classes. Water hemlock, a plant that was readily accessible in the north, can be brewed into a deadly poison or, with care, a powerful antitoxin. This was the poison used on the boy. She was certain of it.

"I don't believe your son was attacked by dock spiders, but I'm quite certain he's been poisoned. I should be able to reverse the effects easily enough."

The bystanders gaped in awe as Kit called upon Titan to heal the young Nomad. A soft yellow light emanated from her hands as she placed them on his small body. Slowly, the glow spread up Kit's arms and across the boy's chest. Moments later, the light dimmed, and the child's eyes fluttered open.

The sun was low in the sky at Kit's back, casting her in an otherworldly orange glow. Her black hair framed her fine facial features, accentuating her dark brown eyes.

The small boy furrowed his brow as he looked up at Kit. "Are you an angel?"

Kit took the child's face in her hands, gently caressing him. "No, sweet child. I am a soldier of Titan, and he sent me to watch over you."

His father clutched the boy to his chest, his face now wet with tears. "Thank you!"

"You should have let the human die," someone said from behind Kit.

As she turned, a rough-looking Berrat stepped up and pushed Kit away from the father and his boy. He was perhaps fourteen years old, with dark brown hair, braided in the traditional Berrat manner. He was wearing a cloth tunic and breeches with a bright yellow smock, the simple clothes of a baker.

"We don't need your type here. This land was once a sanctuary for the Berrat people. Now, it's been polluted by humans and elves, and other assorted *lesser* beings."

Kit was about to protest when she caught the glint of a blade flash. The young man was wielding a large dagger, but in his small hands, it more closely resembled a broadsword.

"Be at peace," Kit said, hoping to diffuse the situation. She slowly got to her feet, her five-foot frame towering over the young Berrat. "I am Kit Standing Bear, on a mission from the High Priest of Titan himself. I have no quarrel with you."

The young Berrat spat at her feet. "You and your kind are ruining our lands. You take our people. You turn them into blood slaves."

"Blood slaves?" Kit calmly held out her hands, taking no hostile actions against the young man. "I have no idea what you're talking about. I am here to heal this child, nothing more."

"On'nak, don't!" somebody from the gathering crowd yelled out. "She's here to help!"

The young man lurched forward and stabbed at Kit with his blade. She easily moved out of the way of the attack, turning to face him again. "There is no need for violence," Kit said in a calming voice, while raising her hands in a submissive display.

"We will rid our lands of you, even if we have to poison every single one of you!" The young man scanned the gathering crowd, his eyes moving to each *human* in the group. "We will rid our lands of all of you!" Again, he stabbed at Kit with his dagger, and again she brushed him aside, this time with enough force to knock him to the ground.

Kit stood over the Berrat. "So, you willingly admit that you poisoned this boy?"

He rolled onto his back, his face covered with dirt, and his eyes wild with zealous fervor. "I admit nothing!"

Before he had a chance to stand, Kit placed her foot across his wrist, grinding it into the ground. The knife fell from his grip, but he still tried to claw at her with his free hand.

Kit dropped her knee onto his chest, whilst simultaneously striking him across the face with her fist. The light in his eyes went dim. "You will all be cleansed," he said weakly, just before he fully lost consciousness.

⸎

"I will need something to bind this man for the trip back to Aarall. The City Watch will determine his fate." Two fishermen came over, one of them carrying a length of heavy rope. "Here," he said as he held it out. "If it can hold our boats at dock, it can hold this bit of *scum* while you take him to the dungeons."

Two women came over just as Kit finished binding the Berrat. "His name is On'nak," one of them offered. "He and his family have lived here for many years now. His parents manage the Sea Spray Inn." Kit stood up so that she could face the two women without having to strain her neck looking up at them.

"Has On'nak always been so... enthusiastic?" Kit was going to say something different, but she decided at the last moment to, uncharacteristically, hold her tongue.

"You mean crazy, right?" offered the second woman. "He used to be a good boy. He came down to the docks any time ships were returning. He brought the fishermen hot coffee to drink and freshly made sandwiches to eat. That was all before he got the fool notion that all humans, even us Nomads, had to be forced to leave Arnnor. Leave, or die!"

"What caused the change?" Kit asked.

The woman sneered. "A Berrat man passed through here, spreading his hateful lies. It seems On'nak bought into them."

Kit remembered her encounter with Karim's mother, how the words of some man named Pental had swayed her. "Do not judge this young man too harshly," she offered. "He is responsible for his actions, but he is not in his right mind."

"What will happen to him now?" the first woman asked.

"I'll be taking him to Aarall to face judgment for what he's done." Kit considered the young man a boy, really, and shook her head. "I'll see what I can do, so that he doesn't end up taking a trip to the gallows."

"The gallows?" gasped one of the women. "He's to be executed?"

"I believe he tried to murder this boy. I suspect he is responsible for the deaths of the other children as well."

"And he tried to kill you, too," the man who gave Kit the rope interjected. "Don't forget that!" He clearly had no love for the boy.

"Tell his parents that he's being taken to Aarall. He will be in the City Watch dungeons until he faces trial."

"What of the other children? They need your help as well." Kit turned to the woman who was asking her the question. "What are their symptoms? Is their sickness like this boy's?"

"Yes," she replied nodding her head. "I've tried almost every herb combination that I know of, but nothing has helped."

Kit's eyes lit up, and she rummaged through her knapsack. She pulled out a small bundle and handed it to the woman. "Make a weak tea using just two leaves, no more. Plant the remainder in a sunny location, hopefully out of the wind.”

The woman took the small bundle from Kit and opened it up. When her gaze fell upon the contents, she gasped. “This is Pele’s Gift! Are you giving this to me? To keep?”

Kit smiled at the woman, happy that she understood the value of the plant she had given to her. “It is yours,” she said with an easy smile. “For you and your people. Care for it. Keep it safe.”

The precious gift brought the woman to tears. “Thank you. Thank you for, well, everything.” She gave a quick bow before running off, likely to where the children were, to make them the antidote.

Turning her attention back to the young Berrat, Kit roused him by slapping his face, perhaps a bit harder than necessary. He struggled briefly against his bonds, but when he couldn’t free himself, he went back to spouting his hateful rhetoric again.

“Nobody here is buying what you’re selling.” Kit moved in close, making her voice as threatening as possible. “If you keep it up, you’ll spend the trip back to Aarall with a gag in your mouth.” The young man turned away, no longer willing to meet the priest’s stare.

“You will be cleansed,” he muttered one last time.

Just as Kit was about to leave, the father of the boy she had saved approached. “Thank you for healing my son.” Looking at the Berrat who had attacked her, he shook his head. “He’s only a child. Why? How could he do such a thing?”

“You will all be cleansed,” On’nak replied. “You will see the light, or you will perish.”

Three other villagers came up as well. “Thank you! Hopefully, this will be the end of the mysterious illnesses.” One of them held out a package to Kit. “Here. Take this. It’s not much, but maybe when you wear them, you’ll remember what good you have done here today.”

Kit protested, but they’d already shoved the parcel into her hands. When Kit opened it up, she found a well-made pair of leather boots. They were certainly higher quality than what the Temple provided, and hers were so worn that they were barely holding together. "This is not necessary. I serve Titan and the people of this land." A small smile tugged at her lips. "But I will wear these boots with pride." Kit wasted no time pulling on the new footwear. They were soft and comfortable, even if they were a bit too large for her.

A second villager held yet another bundle out to her, this one wrapped in large leaves and tied with string. "For your journey back to Aarall." Kit took the package and held it up to her nose. "Is this smoked tuna?" Her question made the villager smile.

"My husband's favorite meal," she said with satisfaction. "The catch lately hasn't been as plentiful as previous seasons, but we have more than enough to feed the village."

Kit's mouth watered. "Thank you," she said, grateful for the gifts they'd shared with her.

CHAPTER THIRTY-THREE

THE LONG TREK HOME

The journey back to Aarall was quiet, giving Kit some time to speak to the young prisoner. It took him several hours to stop ranting about how the Berrat were going to cleanse their lands of the interlopers who were threatening their way of life, and perhaps their very existence.

When the sun started to set, they were still several hours away from the city. They could travel the remaining distance in the dark, but it was better to make camp. A small clump of trees with a fast-flowing brook made a decent place to spend the night.

There was enough flat ground and leaf litter to make a comfortable bed. It was then that Kit realized that she only had her own bedroll with her. She had not expected to be returning with a prisoner. She tossed the bedroll to On'nak. "Here, you take the bedroll. I'll sleep on the ground."

On'nak kicked the bedroll back at Kit. "I am Berrat. I do not need such *comforts.*"

"Suit yourself," she said with a shrug. Kit took the bedroll and spread it out over the leaves. She took a moment to try it out, just to make sure there were no roots or stones that she might have missed. As she laid there, the young priest discovered just how exhausted she was. If she didn't pick herself off the ground, she was going to be asleep before she knew it.

Groaning loudly, she dragged her exhausted body off her make-shift bed. Kit tied the rope that was binding On'nak onto a low-hanging limb from one of the trees. There was enough slack in the rope that he would be able to prop himself up against the tree's trunk, but not enough that he could lay down.

"I'm going to gather some wood for a fire. You just... hang here and wait for me."

The young Berrat was not amused by Kit's choice of words.

It didn't take long to gather enough wood to make a decent campfire. The sun was already setting, and the temperature was beginning to dip. Even though it had been unseasonably warm lately, it was still too cold to be out in the elements without a source of heat.

As Kit sat by the fire, basking in its warmth, she took the package of smoked tuna from her knapsack. Even wrapped in leaves, it smelt heavenly.

There were four large portions of fish. She took a small piece and brought it to her nose. Kit closed her eyes for a moment, thanking Titan for the bounty she was about to enjoy. She was ready to pop the morsel into her mouth when she stopped.

Kit held the fish out to her prisoner. "If you would like to share this meal with me, I will untie you so that you can eat."

"I do not want any of that befouled fish." On'nak turned his head away so that he didn't have to look at Kit or her meal.

"Suit yourself," Kit replied as she quickly ate the piece of fish in her hand. It tasted even better than it smelled. "It will do you no good to starve yourself, and this fish is absolutely divine."

Kit finished off the first piece of fish, licking her fingers like it was the best meal she'd ever eaten. "I have plenty to share," she tried again. "Don't let whatever delusions you have cause you to miss out on this."

"I am not deluded. My people are dying. They're dying by the thousands. They're being taken into slavery and sold like cattle." Once again, the same fervor that Kit had witnessed earlier filled his words. The reflection of the fire in his eyes amplified his zealous look.

"Before your people came to our lands, we lived in harmony with Gaia, the god of nature and life. We lived in harmony with the animals. We were happy."

He pulled on his restraints as if to make a point. "Now, we are bound and gagged and carried off for the pleasure and amusement of you *humans*."

"You are bound because you tried to kill me." Kit moved away from the fire to where the Berrat was being held. "Whatever terrible things are happening to your people, I'm not the one doing it. I would help you if I could, but I'm only one person. I couldn't even help my own mother when her people turned against her."

"Humans in our land deserve to be turned against. They deserve to be removed and sent back south where they belong."

"My mother is Berrat, just like you!" Kit yelled at the boy. Whatever he had been saying had gotten deep under her skin. She managed to settle down enough to speak with control. Her words still came out as a growl. "I grew up in a Berrathian village. I was raised by a Berrat woman." She took a deep breath and slowly let it out. "I was not welcome in my own home."

"If you grew up in Berrathia, then you should know and understand our plight – the constant raids on our villages, the killings, the taking of people against their will."

Kit shuddered as the memories of her youth came flooding back. "I was only eleven years old when I left Berrathia to come to Aarall. My village was constantly on guard, and even still, we suffered at the hands of the raiders." As she said the words, Kit unexpectedly found herself having far more sympathy for the young man than she'd have ever thought possible. "I personally suffered as a result. Being a human, the villagers, children, and adults alike treated me like I was one of the raiders."

Before she realized it, Kit had untied On'nak. His wrists were raw from where the rope chaffed against his skin. He stared down at his wounds like they were a badge of honor.

"I am sorry for the pain your people are suffering, but not all of us are bad. You cannot blame everyone who is not like you for your troubles."

"Who should we blame then? When we allowed your ancestors entry into our country, you were like us. You were Nomads who lived *with* the land. You didn't try to change it, to bend it to your will." A sneer crossed his lips. "Now, you bend the land to suit your purposes. You create great walled cities, just like those people who drove you from *your* homeland. You keep beasts in pens, slaughtering them when they are no longer able to serve you, or simply to feed yourselves. All the while, they suffer under your bondage. We *feel* what they *feel*."

The fervor in his voice was gone, replaced with deep sadness.

Kit put her hand to her breast. "When Titan is freed, he will fix everything that has gone wrong. He will return the Berrat to their homes, and you can return to your way of life."

"Titan? You think that false god will save us? He and his kind are the reason everything is the way it is."

On'nak was about to go off on another rant, but Kit was unwilling to listen to him speak ill of her god. With lightning speed, she punched him squarely in the jaw. His body became stiff as his eyes rolled back into his head. He toppled, unconscious, to the ground.

Kit took the rope and bound him to the tree. She wrapped it around him and the trunk multiple times, tying it off in the back, ensuring he would not be able to free himself. She took several of the leaves that were used to wrap the smoked fish and stuffed them into his mouth. She was not going to listen to any more of his rantings. Not tonight.

The young priest lost her appetite. What the boy said made no sense to her. Her god could not be the source of the problems. Titan was the *solution* to Orth's troubles.

She tossed a couple more branches onto the fire and laid down on her bedroll. The last bit of exertion sapped the remaining energy from her body. She became so incredibly tired that she couldn't even raise her arms.

The potion must have just worn off.

Just thinking was exhausting. She was about to go hunting for the second potion, but since she was ready for bed anyway, she didn't bother. As soon as her head hit the ground, she fell into a deep slumber.

Sleep may have come quickly, but Kit spent the night battling with disturbing dreams. They were filled with memories of fire and hate, of people being ripped from their homes, and babies being torn from the arms of their lifeless mothers.

Chapter Thirty-Four

Through Berrat Eyes

When Kit woke up, the sun had not yet risen, and the fire had burned down to a smoking bed of coals. There wasn't much light, but she could clearly see that On'nak's eyes were open, his loathing burning deep from within. Just when she hoped she had made a connection with him, he had to speak against her god.

Kit quickly ate another piece of the smoked fish before breaking camp. She took her time to cover the smoldering coals with sand, and then doused them with water from the brook. She took a few additional minutes to deal with *personal duties*. Afterwards, she washed her hands and face in the cool, fast running water.

When she was ready to leave, Kit untied the Berrat from the tree. She bound his feet together, leaving enough slack that he could walk, but he wouldn't be able to run. Kit removed the gag from his mouth while issuing a stern warning. "If you need to relieve yourself, now would be the time to do it." The offer was met with a sneer.

"Suit yourself." She shoved him in the direction of Aarall. "Let's get moving then."

By the time the two arrived at the gates of Aarall, the sun was up, and the marketplace was buzzing with activity. Two children came running to greet Kit, or more specifically, to beg from her. "Are you hungry?" Kit asked as she knelt down beside them. Both of the children nodded vehemently. The priest reached into her knapsack, producing the last two pieces of smoked fish. "Here you go. May Titan's blessings be upon you."

The two children stared up at Kit, confusion in their eyes. They had expected her to give them candy or some other sweet. The first of the children eyed the fish apprehensively, but eventually took a small bite. His eyes lit up with joy. "Try it!" he urged the other. A moment later, they were both licking their fingers and running off into the crowd.

A guard eyed Kit up and down as she passed through the gate with the young Berrat in tow. "What have you got there, young girl?" He was about to get into her business when another guard grabbed him roughly by the arm, whispering in his ear. The first guard's eyebrows rose in disbelief. "Sorry, little sister. May Titan's grace go with you."

Kit smiled brightly back at him. "Peace unto you, good sir. May Titan's light shine upon you."

On'nak scoffed at the lot of them.

The pair continued past the city gates and walked up to the guardhouse outside the City Watch barracks. The Watch members stationed there wasted no time letting Kit and her prisoner pass. Without any hindrance, they continued into the main building.

The captain was training with several of the other guards. From what she could tell, he was engaged in a four-on-one combat. The guards were attacking him from all directions, and he was aptly blocking and deflecting their blows. When he caught sight of Kit with the young Berrat trailing behind, he lost focus, allowing one of his opponents to get a solid strike across his ribs. Kit could only assume that they were using practice blades, otherwise the captain's insides would be spilling out. Even still, the large man winced in pain as he clutched at his side.

Immediately, Harding spun to face the guard who struck him. He assailed him with a series of slashes and overhand strikes. The corporal defended himself well, but he couldn't stand against the onslaught. The repeated, vicious blows finally knocked the guard to the ground.

The captain immediately let out a deep booming laugh and reached out to help the fallen combatant to his feet. "Well done, corporal! Well done, indeed!" He turned to the other three he was sparring with. "That is how you take advantage of your adversary's lack of focus." He rubbed his ribs where the sword struck him, wincing again as he did. "Well done, indeed."

The Watch commander waved his blunted blade about, motioning to the group he was sparring with. "Break up into pairs and resume your exercises."

He continued rubbing his ribs as he walked towards Kit. "You're going to pay for that," he said as he brushed past her and walked off the training field. Kit stood there for a moment, unsure of what to do, when he called out to her.

"It wasn't my fault you looked," Kit called out, following the captain, her captive in tow.

⁂

Kit stomped into the commander's office, holding her prisoner by the scruff of his neck.

"What have we here?" The captain looked amused when Kit roughly pushed the Berrat inside.

Lump came bounding across the room, startling the boy. The young priest immediately forgot about all her troubles and wrapped her arms around her furry friend while the big dog covered her face and neck in slobbery kisses.

"Lump, down," the captain ordered. The wolfdog immediately broke away from Kit and flopped onto the floor. The girl had never seen the dog so obedient in her life. She looked up at the captain who was glaring at her, waiting for a response to his question. His initial amusement had been replaced with a deep scowl. The young priest immediately straightened, taking on a more serious demeanor.

"This is On'nak. He thought it might be a good idea to push a knife into my ribs. I taught him otherwise." Kit proceeded to tell the City Watch commander about what had happened.

The captain's stern expression deepened, changing from annoyance to frustration. "This is happening all over the barony. We've imprisoned several such hate-mongers in the past moon alone." He motioned to one of the guards standing outside his office. A grizzled-looking woman, with severely cropped black hair, dressed in brown studded leather armor, stepped in. She took the rope that bound On'nak and dragged him from the captain's office, a little rougher than what Kit believed necessary.

As the boy was led away, Kit turned back to the captain, folding her arms over her chest. "That wasn't very nice, what you did to me. You made me look like an idiot when I apologized to Father Harding for you waking him up."

"Let it go. I don't need any extra headaches this morning," the captain said, his voice filled with annoyance.

"Let it go? What you did to me was downright cruel. I thought Father was going to send Lump away or something... worse."

The stone-faced stare the captain leveled on Kit was enough to make her shut up. The commander pulled out his chair from behind his massive rough-hewn oak desk and plopped himself down in it. The furniture groaned under his bulk. "Take a seat," he said.

The big man's face was showing more wear than usual. Kit's first instinct was to push the situation harder, but the captain already looked to be on the verge. "Is everything okay?" she asked as she pulled up one of several oversized chairs in his office.

The captain shook his head as he leafed through a stack of parchments on his desk. Finally, he pulled one out and read quietly to himself.

"Would you prefer I leave? You seem... distracted." The commander glared at her over the top of the notice that he was reading. She expected to see playful irritation, but instead his face was filled with outrage, with a hint of gloom. Kit had never seen him like this. "What is it?"

He passed the notice over to the priest. Before she even had a chance to examine it, the commander described its contents. "Someone, or something, is making the wolves around Aarall sick. They're becoming extremely aggressive, attacking anyone or anything in sight. I need you to track down the infected wolves and put them down. And..." he said as he raked his calloused hands over his face. "I need you to find out where this sickness started."

Sweet Titan. Was she ever going to get a break? She had slept well enough on the return trip from the village, but she was exhausted. She wanted a proper meal and a much-deserved sleep in her bed.

"How am I to do that?" Kit asked, throwing herself into the back of her chair. She tilted her head back and closed her eyes. "I'm a Priest of Titan, not a City Watch detective."

The captain stood from his desk, towering over her. "Yes, Kit, I know you're a priest, no need to remind me. Father Hoarfrost has told me your trip to the village would be your final blooding test. Since you're here with a prisoner, I'm assuming you've passed the final piece of your initiation process. I'm counting on your formal title as priest to help you track down the source of this outbreak."

Kit cocked an eyebrow at the captain. "Um... what?"

"The people of Aarall are almost exclusively Titan worshippers," Harding continued, "and when a Priest of Titan asks them a question, they'll be quick to answer for fear of angering you and their god."

When Kit *sort of* agreed with him, he grunted something unintelligible. From a drawer, the man produced another parchment. Even from the far side of the desk, Kit could plainly see that it was a map.

"This is where the most recent sightings have been," Harding said as he made several marks. He pushed the parchment across his desk, motioning for Kit to take it. She hopped down from her chair with her eyes still glued on the parchment.

"These are all on the outskirts of the city," she mused out loud. "One of your marks is at a local village just south of here. I'll start there. Maybe I can get some specifics on where the wolves might be."

The captain gave Kit a flat stare. "There's the person I was looking for. When you're engaged, you're like a she-wolf on a trail. It's hard to believe that you've created a reputation for being formidable when you're such a small girl of only fifteen years."

"Almost sixteen," Kit quickly corrected, smiling up at the captain. There had been a compliment somewhere in the captain's words and she was more than happy to accept it.

"Too true," he said. It was the first time since she came into his office that he wasn't scowling at her. "In just a few more weeks, if my memory serves me correctly."

He knows my birthday?

Thinking the storm had passed, and not wanting to miss out on this bit of casual familiarity, Kit chose to have a bit of fun with the man. She craned her neck up at him and batted her eyes, straining to maintain eye contact. "Well, if you'd like to buy me something nice for my birthday, I could really use a set of chainmail gloves." She gave the commander her absolute best smile.

An inscrutable expression crossed the big man's face. Kit feared her bit of joviality was not taken in the spirit in which it was intended. "I suggest you be on your way. The mission I gave you is time sensitive."

"I'll go check with Father Hoarfrost immediately," Kit said. "I need to report back to him, to let him know what happened at the village."

"I am aware that I have no authority over you, only the Temple does, but I can assure you that when I give you a mission, it's with the high priest's blessing." Kit was about to object when the man held up his hand. "If Father Hoarfrost gives you any grief over this, you can blame me and tell him that I gave you no choice but to comply with my orders."

She didn't want this task, but she could see no way of talking her way out of it. Had she taken On'nak directly to the Temple, perhaps things would have gone better. Father would have recognized how tired she was, and how hard she'd been working to complete her blooding. Surely, he would have seen things her way.

Kit was just about to suggest that she take On'nak to see the high priest when the captain's face turned grim. He pointed his big, meaty finger at the door to his office. "Go. Now."

The girl swallowed hard, nodded briskly, and bolted for the door with Lump hot on her heels. Despite the captain's words still ringing in her ears, she couldn't help but smile as the warmth of the morning sun hit her face. It was going to be a fair hike to the village, but the weather was unseasonably warm, and she was going to relish every moment of the journey. After all, how hard could it be to put down a sick wolf?

Chapter Thirty-Five

Mangy Wolf Hunt

After Kit exited the city gates, she entered the marketplace where vendors hawked their wares to anyone within earshot. The market itself was huge, covering a large swath of land just outside the city walls. The tents were brightly colored, giving the entire market a festive charm. Merchants would have been arriving through the night, setting up their stalls in preparation for the morning's rush. Kit's stomach growled when the tantalizing aroma of freshly roasted boar wafted towards her from one of the carts.

Unable to resist the allure, she purchased a couple of meat-laden sandwiches for her journey, the first of which she wolfed down before she made it through the market area. She had asked the vendor to double wrap the second sandwich, as she planned on stowing it for later. As she tucked it into her pocket, Lump whined, nudging at her elbow.

"Fine," she said, giving the dog the leaf-wrapped sandwich. "Eat up. Who cares if I'm hungry later on." Lump ripped through the leaves and downed the food, barely chewing. "Come on. Let's get going."

It was an absolutely beautiful day, and the walk south to the first village was quiet and peaceful. Kit let her eyes scan the horizon, looking for any trouble, like wolves. Thank Titan, the entire hike passed without incident.

As Kit entered the outer limits of the village, an area where the farmers sold their wares to the locals, the children came running out to greet her and Lump. She had a strong connection with children since joining the Temple. The way they rushed out to greet the arrival of a visitor always reminded her of puppies.

The children ranged in age from five to eleven years old. They were primarily Nomad, but two of them, obviously twins, were dark-skinned southerners. They both had identical bright brown eyes, curly black hair tied up in pigtails, and matching light-wool, moss-green dresses.

She was enjoying the moment, playing, and laughing with the children when the face of one of the twins became slack. She trembled and babbled incomprehensibly, her eyes glued onto something across the field.

Kit searched for where the child was looking, and that was when she spotted the sick wolf off in the distance. Even from so far away, the severity of the animal's affliction was obvious. Large patches of fur had fallen from its body, and what remained was badly matted. Foam dripped from its mouth as it stared at some invisible object. Regardless of its current condition, it was obvious that the wolf had once been a magnificent creature.

The little priest barked orders at the farmers to protect the children and to take cover as she readied her battle hammer. One of the children grasped onto Kit's leg, begging her to come inside. The priest practically snarled at the poor girl as she told her to hide. Just then, the words of the captain rang in her ears. *You're like a she-wolf.* Despite the danger, she chuckled to herself as she prepared to deal with the diseased animal.

"Lump, stay," Kit commanded. "I'll deal with the wolf." Slowly, the young priest walked away from the village. After checking back to ensure the parents had safely removed the children from harm's way, she called out to the gray wolf in the distance.

Its ears perked up at her voice. As its milky white eyes fell on Kit, the diseased wolf pinned its large, pointy ears back and snarled. The priest assumed her best option was to continue moving toward the beast, trying to get it to engage her head on. Slowly, the wolf moved towards her. Its head was bobbing from side to side like it was trying to measure her up.

As they got closer to each other, it became obvious the wolf was a year or two old at the most. But, like most wild animals, they were dangerous creatures even at a young age.

At the sound of a dog barking, the wolf's head snapped to its left. Across the field came Lump, his teeth bared, his hackles raised.

"Lump, no!" Kit shouted, breaking into a run. "Lump, stay away." The girl's heart thrummed in her throat. She had to make it to the wolf before her dog. Pumping her legs as hard as she could, she raced forward.

"Titan, please hear me," she said, calling upon her god to grant her enhanced speed. Kit was desperate to reach the wolf before her dog did. Lump was a big dog, easily as large as the wolf, but the sick animal was wild and a natural born killer.

With her battle spell in full force, Kit's speed increased substantially, but even still, she was slow compared to her dog. Seeing no other option, the priest slammed her hammer against the side of her shield. The sharp sound distracted the wolf for barely a moment, but it was enough to allow Lump to ram into the animal, sending the pair toppling across the grass.

The sight of Lump risking his own life to save hers made Kit's heart swell. Nobody had ever done that for her before, putting her life ahead of their own. It was a gift like no other, one that she was not ready to accept. With renewed vigor, Kit gritted her teeth and surged forward.

Just as the wolf regained its footing, Kit was on it, slamming her shield into the animal's head. There was a loud crack and a small whimper as her shield made contact. The wolf dropped to the ground beside Kit, its head twisted into an unnatural angle. The milky white that had filled the animal's eyes faded away, returning to their natural amber.

Lump padded forward, his lips peeled back, a low growl rumbling in his throat. He looked to Kit as though seeking instructions from her. When the wolf whined, the dog's demeanor instantly changed. He dropped to the ground and lowered his head.

The wolf was panting heavily. The fight was gone from him.

Not wanting the animal to needlessly suffer, the young priest quickly pulled out her dagger and plunged it into the thick ruff of the poor creature's neck. As the animal's life drained away, a profound pain stabbed at Kit's heart.

With a hitch in her breath, Kit placed her hand on the fallen animal's head and offered a small prayer, sending its life force back to the Great Cycle. "Your pain is over now," she whispered, her heart aching for having destroyed the noble creature. "May you forever walk in the light of Fenrir's grace." Kit stood up and wiped her hand across her cheek. It was unexpectedly wet with tears. What if this had been Lump? Would she have been able to kill him, just because he was ill? It suddenly felt like something had clutched onto her heart, squeezing it to the point of bursting.

Kit remembered a time at the Temple. She had only been there for a few seasons when she was ordered to help Sister Miyuki in the kitchens. Acolytes brought in two spring lambs. They were bawling, fighting against their restraints. One managed to destroy a large clay pot full of potatoes. "Kit, you need to slaughter these lambs before they destroy the kitchen," Sister Miyuki said in the matter-of-fact tone she often used when giving orders. "Use the long-bladed knife on the counter here. Make your strokes deep and sure, so the animal doesn't suffer any more than necessary."

Kit looked up at Sister Miyuki, her face scrunched up, shaking her head. The jolly priest's face became very stern, her foot tapping rapidly on the stone floor.

"It is not a request, Acolyte."

Kit's first attempt at slaughtering the sheep was a disaster. All she managed to do was severely wound the poor animal. It cried out in pain as it bled all over the kitchen. Sister Miyuki snatched the blade from the girl's hand, ending the lamb's life in a single stroke. Without any sign of emotion whatsoever, she handed the knife back to her. "Don't do that again," she scolded. "One deep stroke, and it's done." Kit's hands were shaking badly as she took the blade back from Sister Miyuki.

The second lamb was bucking hard, trying to stay clear of the girl. With the horrific memory of the first animal fresh in her mind, Kit quickly grabbed the young sheep, holding it as tightly as she could. It took every ounce of her strength to keep it still. Like the sister had instructed, Kit drew the knife across its throat, making sure the blade went as deep as possible. As quickly as she had made the cut, the lamb went limp in Kit's arms. "Thank you for your sacrifice," Kit choked out through a stream of tears.

"I'm sorry you had to do that," offered Sister Miyuki. She, too, was crying. Not for the lamb, but for the young girl holding the dead sheep in her arms. "There are things in life, difficult things, that we must do. But remember this, don't let your actions lead to undo suffering. Not of animals, and not of people."

As Kit's mind returned to the here and now, she continued to wipe the tears from her face. She found herself wondering why, at that moment, she had invoked the name of Fenrir, the wolf god. Perhaps she felt a connection with her because of her interaction with the wolf? Perhaps it was because Fenrir was also one of Titan's servants?

"Perhaps it's because I overthink things," Kit mumbled to herself.

Chapter Thirty-Six

Indigo Willowbrook

The farmers had been watching the confrontation, and they were now running out to celebrate the victory. Several were wielding pitchforks, while others carried axes and hatchets.

"Death to wolves," they were shouting as they approached. When they saw the somber look on Kit's face, their jubilance quickly waned.

"The creature was sick. He was not in his right mind when he attacked." Kit's voice was trembling, still thick with emotion at the death of the wolf. Lump seemed to echo the girl's disposition, staying close to her side, his head low.

"Knowing they're not in their right mind does not bring back the sheep and cattle that the pack killed," one farmer yelled at her. He was a Nomad in his late forties, with hanks of black hair sticking out from beneath his straw, wide-brimmed hat. His eyes were bulging from his head, and he was practically foaming at the mouth. "They come day and night. They have no fear. They have even killed some members of the community."

"There is a pack of them?" Kit interrupted, raising her voice to ensure her question cut through the fog of their anger.

"Yes, a pack," several of the farmers answered in unison. "There were at least six of them at the start. We killed two, but they just don't stop."

"Six you say?" Wolves rarely traveled alone. If this wolf was with a pack, the remaining three were likely nearby. "Burn the carcass. If the animal is carrying a disease, we can't have it being spread. While I continue my hunt, get everybody back to the village and don't leave again until I tell you that it's safe to do so."

Kit's stay-at-home orders were met with resistance, but eventually the farmers relented, understanding the merit of her demands.

As the crowd dispersed, there was one young man left, likely a couple years older than she was, eighteen at the most. He had long black hair braided into a ponytail, and black paint across his eyes, a traditional marking of Nomad warriors. He was dressed in light leather armor and carried a well-crafted short sword.

"They killed my family, you know. Those beasts tore them apart, and all I could do was watch. I was too frightened to help defend my parents, my little sister! When they came, they caught my father alone in the field. After they killed him, they came straight for our house. I tried to call my mother and sister inside, but the wolves were on them before they could make it to the door."

The young man clenched his fists by his sides as he recounted the story. Tears flowed freely down his cheeks, his words now coming out in short, ragged breaths. "I shut the door so they wouldn't kill me, too. I should have tried to help my family but instead, I hid like a coward."

Kit walked up to the young man, placing her hand upon his shoulder. "You can't save everyone. It's one of the first lessons we're taught as an acolyte. Even though I have the power of Titan behind me, I cannot save everyone, and neither can you. Had you fought the wolves, you'd have likely done no good, and you'd have joined the Great Cycle with the rest of your family."

"So? What if I had? I have nothing to live for anymore." He took a deep breath as he tried to calm himself. "I'm coming with you." There was so much conviction in his voice that Kit knew there was no way she was going to talk him out of it. Quick as a viper, she swung her battle hammer at him. He deftly ducked the blow and slashed at Kit with his short sword, which she easily blocked with her shield. Lump bounded at the man, knocking him off his feet.

"What are you doing?" he shouted, holding his forearm in front of his face, trying to keep the wolfdog at bay.

"Lump, off," Kit commanded. The large dog immediately backed away, his gaze never leaving the young man. "I needed to be sure that you know how to use that weapon you're carrying." She stated the words as a simple matter of fact.

"By trying to kill me?" The young man popped to his feet, immediately moving into a proper battle-stance. His weight distribution and pose were that of a trained warrior.

"I would not have injured you badly. At most, I would have knocked you down... maybe made you unconscious." As Kit holstered her hammer she asked, "Who trained you? Your skills are raw, but you have clearly received some quality instructions on how to fight."

The young man was still breathing hard, adrenaline pumping through his body. "My father... my father started teaching me when I was sixteen years old. He promised that if I worked hard in the fields as a child, he would begin my training on the day of my *Ascension to Maturity*."

The comment took Kit by surprise. "Ascension to Maturity? That is the rite taken by a follower of Ymir, the ice god. Your father worships Ymir?"

"He did, before he was killed by those beasts. And not just him. My whole family. My father served as Temple guard in Jotunheim. He was released from service on the anniversary of his fortieth year." The young man stood a bit taller and puffed out his chest as he spoke with pride of the man. "He was twice honored with the Medal of Bravery, and upon his release from service, they gave him enough coin to buy some land of his own. We moved here just after my sister was born." The young man's face grew dark again. "My father was rewarded for his bravery, but I hid like a coward."

Kit gave the young man a light punch in the shoulder to snap him out of his gloom. "Since you'll likely follow me, even if I say you are not welcome on this hunt, you might as well keep me company on the search." Without waiting to see if he'd follow, Kit walked to where she first spotted the wolf. Without looking back, she called out, "What's your name?"

"My name is Indigo Willowbrook. My friends call me Indie."

Kit gave him the traditional sign of peace. "I am Kit Standing Bear, Priest of Titan."

Kit really loved adding the title *Priest of Titan* when she said her name. She remembered back to her days as an acolyte, listening to the brothers and sisters referring to themselves as Priest of Titan and then watching the look of awe on the faces of the Temple visitors. Unfortunately, Indie did not seem all that impressed with her new title. With the slightest of pouts, Kit completed her introduction.

"My friends call me Kit."

CHAPTER THIRTY-SEVEN

TRAPPED

It was only a short walk back to the location where Kit had encountered the wolf she killed. According to Indie, there were multiple tracks there.

"One headed off due north. The other three went to the north-west."

While Indie wanted to follow tracks with the largest of the paw prints, likely from that of a dire wolf, Kit insisted they deal with the lone animal first. It bothered her that the farmer had said nothing of dire wolves. She had never seen one before, but she'd heard tales of them as a child. They were the size of a grizzly, capable of biting a man in half.

"I don't care if the smaller one is easier to kill," Indie said, objecting to the priest's suggestion. "The order we kill them in is irrelevant. I'm going to slaughter them all."

"You will heed my word, or you will travel alone," Kit said. "I don't want you with me if you're going to run headlong into danger. Getting us killed isn't going to bring your family back." Indie held Kit's gaze for several long seconds until he finally relented. Without another word, the young man took off at a slow jog.

Even without the help of Lump's nose, the tracks were easy to spot. The ground was soft from a recent rain and the wolf's paws had sunk deeply into the fresh mud. They continued to follow the tracks for less than an hour when they came upon their quarry. Just like the first wolf, this animal was clearly ill. He was pacing in circles and snarling, as though being tormented by somebody or something that only he could see.

"Lump, stay!" Kit hissed. The dog tilted his head, seemingly unsure of why she might tell him that. The girl knew in her heart the dog wasn't going to listen to her. She saw the determination in him during the first encounter.

"I'll be okay," she whispered. "Stay close to Indie. Keep him safe." Seemingly satisfied with the new instructions, the dog padded over to the young man.

"Stand directly behind me," Kit said, motioning with her hand to where she wanted the man and dog to take up position. "Wait for my word and then start moving to flank the wolf." Unlike Lump, the young warrior wasted no time in following her orders. She could feel him directly behind her. His breathing was rapid and ragged.

"Calm yourself!" Kit said. Her scolding tone only served to heighten his already erratic breathing. She wished he wasn't here. His presence was only making things more difficult. It was one thing to put her own life on the line, but to risk another's wasn't something she was prepared to do.

As she readied herself for the attack, the priest quietly whispered out a prayer. "Titan, guide my hand this day. Do not let ill come to those who stand with me."

With her shield held firmly in front, Kit banged her hammer against its iron rim. Immediately, the creature turned his attention their way. Without hesitation, the animal broke into a dead run. As it neared, the wolf's milky-white eyes came into view, revealing the same sickness as the first.

Bracing herself behind her shield, Kit raised her hammer high. "Hold," she said. "Wait for my command!"

The wolf closed ground at a frightening pace. Froth sprayed from its mouth, as it snapped at the air.

Just before the creature came into striking range, Kit yelled out, "Flank left!"

Indie immediately stepped out from behind the girl, with Lump tight to his side. As they did, the wolf's gaze shifted to the new opponents, allowing Kit a free strike with her hammer. The weapon landed solidly across the side of the wolf's head, sending him sprawling across the ground directly in front of Indie. Wasting no time, the man struck with his short sword, delivering a killing blow to the animal.

Lump and Indie both stood over the body of the wolf, staring intently at it. Slowly, the young man raised his head, loathing in his eyes. "You used me as bait! I was nothing more than a distraction! If you had missed, that wolf would have been on me instead of you!"

Kit completely ignored the young man's rantings. She walked over to the wolf to inspect the carcass. "It was standard combat tactics, to force the enemy to split its attention between the two of us. If he was watching us both, then he was watching neither of us. If your father had lived long enough, I'm sure he'd have taught you that." The last comment struck a nerve. Indie hacked at the fallen body, slicing it deeply with every cut. In moments, the wolf was nothing more than a sickening pile of gore.

Kit's face and clothes were covered with blood splatter. Swiping it away, she bore down on the man.

"Well, thanks to your loss of self-control, any chance of discovering new information from this wolf is hopeless. If you cannot keep your emotions in check, we'll part company here and now. Am I making myself clear?"

Just as Indie was about to say something, Kit caught sight of a second wolf that was about to attack him from behind. She quickly threw her body against the young man, knocking him out of the way just before the animal's jaws closed on the back of his neck.

Adjusting for the changing target, the wolf snapped at Kit's face. She was barely able to get her arm up to ward off the strike when it bit down hard on her forearm. Kit yelped and dropped her hammer as she fell to the ground with the wolf on top of her. The creature's maw opened and closed repeatedly as it ripped into her skin.

With its muzzle directly in Kit's face, she noticed the milky white color of its eyes. Although it was looking right at her, it seemed the animal's mind was elsewhere, distracted by something that only it was able to see.

Lump, in a desperate attempt to save the girl, clamped his jaws around the wolf's neck. He shook his head violently, worrying his teeth into the flesh beneath the animal's thick fur. The diseased creature quickly pulled away, breaking free of Lump's hold. It completely disregarded the dog, snapping wildly at the surrounding air. He was foaming at the mouth as he spun, madly attacking some unseen adversary.

With surprising speed, Indie moved in with an overhand strike. With a single blow of his short sword, he separated the animal's head from its body. The wolf dropped to the ground, a lifeless lump at his feet. Almost instantly, the milky white color of its eyes disappeared, returning to a deep jade green.

Kit was still on her back, staring at the wounds on her arm. Lump moved in beside her, whining.

"Need a hand up?" Indie asked, holding out his hand for her to grab on to. He pulled Kit up to her feet with ease. Beneath the simple exterior was a powerfully built man.

"Thank you for saving my life. I need to learn to be more aware of my surroundings. I was too busy..."

"Grieving for your family?" Kit interrupted. "No need to apologize." She grimaced as she examined the wound on her forearm. "And thank you for saving my life," she said with a small wink.

"You know I did no such thing," the young warrior stated, although he seemed happy that Kit offered the praise. "What in Helja was that wolf doing?"

"I have no idea," Kit said as she gave the wolf's mutilated corpse a cursory examination. "Outside of the lost fur, and the odd behavior, this wolf appeared to have been in good health. Perhaps we can open his stomach to see what this decapitated wolf's been eating?" Kit drew her dagger and cut open the carcass from crotch to neck.

As the wolf's innards poured out, she removed the stomach and opened it up. Normally, one would expect to find half-digested animals; squirrels, rabbits or maybe even a fox, but all Kit could see was a deep purple mash.

She was about to examine it when Indie yelled, "Stop, don't touch that!"

⁂

Kit quickly drew her hand back and gave him a quizzical look. "Titan's snow-balls, what's the problem?"

"He's been eating death-cap mushrooms. They're bright purple and extremely poisonous. They grow in the marshlands around here. When the weather is warm enough, that is. Animals usually stay clear of them though. They can cause vivid hallucinations. I've heard that enchanters use them to make poisoned weapons." Kit raised her eyebrows at his surprising level of knowledge on enchanting. "My mother was an enchanter, and a rather good one, I might add. She often talked about ingredients that she used." The warrior shrugged his broad shoulders. "Apparently I was listening."

Kit gawked at the amount of gore that was on the two of them and the blood seeping out of her arm. "We need to find some water to clean ourselves off, and I need to dress these wounds before I grow weak from blood loss."

"Can't you just heal yourself? You know, say a prayer to Titan and make yourself whole again?"

"I can." Kit paused, trying to find the right words to make him understand. "I can only call upon Titan's healing powers once per day. Father Hoarfrost, the High Priest, explained it to me like this. 'If you keep asking for Titan's help, you'll sound like a petulant child in his ear. Eventually, he'll tune you out and he will never hear you speak to him. Save it for when it's important.'"

Apparently, Indie found this funny. He started off chuckling, but before long, it turned into a full-on belly laugh. "Now I know how my mum felt when my sister was forever tugging on her apron asking for *something*. She was relentless, but my mother learned to tune her out." The laughter soon drained from his eyes, only to be replaced with sadness. "I would give anything to hear my sister pester my mother just one more time." He tightened the grip on his short sword and his breathing slowed.

Kit moved next to Indie, taking his hand in hers. She recalled what it was like when she first came to the Temple. Even though her mother was alive, Kit somehow felt she'd never see her again. "It's okay to be sad and to miss your family. Hold on to the memories of the time you had with them. As long as you do, they'll be with you forever." Clearly, Kit's words did not have the intended effect. Indie yanked his hand away from her and stormed off.

"There's a river this way," he called out to Kit as he continued stomping away.

Indie kept his head down and his mouth shut for most of the walk. Several times Kit tried to offer him comfort, but he only glared at her. The pain in her arm was getting worse by the second. She had managed to bind the wound before heading out to the river, but the blood was seeping through much faster than it should have been. Kit paused for a moment to take the wrapping off and examine the damage. As soon as the last of the bindings came off, she could smell the rot. "Indie, stop!" she called out. Although Kit was a trained healer, the smell made her legs wobbly. "Indie!" she called out one more time before taking a seat in the tall grass they were walking through.

What kind of disease acts so fast?

She poked at the wound. "If I had some shimmer bloom root, I could make a poultice to slow the effects..." the girl said to nobody in particular. Kit was feeling lightheaded, like she might even lose consciousness. She laid back in the tall grass, her head resting on a thick knot of roots.

"Titan, hear me." She called up to the clear blue sky. Several birds were flying above her, too high to tell what they were. A cool breeze blew on her face.

"Titan, I need your help." The cool breeze quickly changed to a deep chill that coursed through her body.

"Titan, your servant is in dire need. I beseech thee, render aid unto me this day." Kit had never spoken with the flowery words that other priests used when they conversed with their god. She had always assumed that Titan was more interested in actions rather than some sycophantic rant that one might spew out in prayer. The deep chill in Kit's body intensified to an unbearable cold. It was so severe that her body convulsed. She was not sure how, but the sun became dark, as though blotted out by a great shadow. Darkness filled her senses. She struggled to catch her breath, like she had been thrust into the depths of the North Sea. As quickly as the cold took her, it was replaced with a cozy heat, like she had been wrapped in a blanket that had been warming by a fire for hours. Her body relaxed as the last of the chill melted away from her bones.

The gentle touch of a hand caressed her cheek. She turned into it, gently taking the hand in her own.

"Has it passed?" The words were warm and comforting. "Are you well?" Again, it was as though Titan was whispering directly in her ear. Even in her dreams, she had never heard his voice before with such warmth, such clarity.

Reality came rushing back in a torrent. Kit's eyes snapped open, finding Indie's face inches from her own. She blinked a few times, trying to process what was happening. "Get off me!" she screeched, pushing the man off to the side. "Titan's snowballs! What are you doing?"

The young man practically sprung away from her. His face was a mixture of happiness and shame. "You're well?" he stammered. Suddenly, his words gushed out of him. "You were shaking so badly. Your skin was turning blue. I thought you were freezing to death right in front of my eyes. I tried to warm you."

Indie backed up, trying to keep his distance as she sprung to her feet. She shoved him hard, sending him flying onto his back, disappearing into the tall grass. It was only then that she noticed that her arm was fully healed. There was no sign at all, save for the tear in her shirt, that she had ever been injured. A voice tentatively called out from where Indie had disappeared into the tall grass.

"Can I stand up, or are you going to attack me again?"

"I'm not going to attack you," she muttered. Kit cast her eyes to the north, where she believed Titan's icy prison laid beneath the North Sea. "Thank you!" Titan had come to her in her hour of need, curing her of whatever poison or disease was wracking her body. Kit often questioned her decision to become a priest, but on this day, she was thankful she had a god who actually listened to her.

"*Kit?*" a voice that sounded like it was leagues away barely pierced her consciousness. "*Kit? Are you okay?*" She quickly snapped out of whatever trance she was in.

"What? Yes, yes, I'm okay." She turned to see Indie staring off to the south. "What are you looking at?" she asked as she moved next to him.

"There's another wolf in the distance," he replied without looking at her. Kit strained her eyes to see what he was staring at, but she couldn't see anything. "If we stay down-wind," Indie said, while still looking off into the distance, "we should be able to approach without being noticed." Keeping his body low, he trotted off through the tall grass.

Lump appeared in the tall grasses from out of nowhere, staying close on Indie's heels. It appeared he was still following Kit's instruction to make sure he stayed safe.

Even though the priest could see Indie and Lump directly in front of her, they were hardly making any noise at all as they wove their way across the field. Moments later, the wolf the man was talking about came into view. It was one of the largest wolves Kit had ever seen, most likely a *dire wolf*.

Chapter Thirty-Eight

The Wolf Spirit

The dire wolf was snapping and snarling at the wind. Sparse patches of matted fur clung to its bony frame. Based on the advanced signs of its illness, Kit assumed that it had been infected for a while. The other wolves, as sick as they were, were sticking close to the wooded areas. This animal was in the open, in broad daylight. Kit was not an expert on their behavior, but this was definitely not normal.

With any luck, this was the beast that had been spreading the infection. If they could put it down, it might bring the blight to an end.

"We can't let it put its mouth on us," Kit said, remembering how quickly the infection had spread through her body when her arm was bitten. She called Lump to her side, her gaze boring into his. "I know you want to help, to protect me, but I'm begging you, stay back and let us handle this. Please, Lump. Don't go near this wolf."

The dog stared into the girl's eyes, holding her gaze for a long while before giving her a quick lick on the tip of her nose. Soundlessly, he moved off into the tall grasses and disappeared from sight. The way he took up his position reminded Kit of her mother, Riva, on the night of the Rite of the Way. Far enough that she could be on her own, but not so distant that she couldn't come to her aid if necessary. Memories of the woman made the girl's heart ache.

Swallowing down her emotions, Kit returned her attention to Indie and the dire wolf.

"I will draw it to me, while you flank it and attack from the rear." She held her shield up, emphasizing she was the only one with defensive equipment. "Stay wide until it engages directly with me. Once it does, slip in behind and slash at its hind legs. Maybe you can cripple it and slow it down."

The wolf caught sight of them and trotted their way. Its ears were flat against its head, with its lips curled up, displaying an astonishingly large set of teeth.

Wasting no time, the young warrior immediately moved into flanking position, putting distance between himself and Kit. Unlike the other wolves, this one didn't rush straight at them. It was trying to circle around. Perhaps the wolf viewed Indie as the easier target.

Kit's pulse quickened. Her plan wasn't going to work as she'd hoped, and she feared she was putting the young man's life in peril. The great beast was completely focused on Indie, ignoring her completely. Calling upon her god, she activated her speed spell, sending a rush of warmth through her muscles.

"Take a defensive stance," Kit yelled, just before bursting forward. Her sudden rush caught the wolf off guard, allowing the priest to slam her shield into its side, causing the animal to roll across the ground. The wolf immediately sprang to its feet and fully turned its attention back to the girl. It snapped recklessly, its milky-white eyes unfocused.

Again, using her shield as a weapon, Kit slammed it into the beast's face. The attack had little effect except to infuriate the monstrous animal.

The wolf redoubled its efforts to separate the girl's head from her shoulders. Despite the ferocity, its attacks were careless and chaotic, allowing Kit to easily block or evade its bites. The priest didn't expect the animal to use its claws. With a single swipe across her ankles, the strike knocked the girl prone, her guard exposed.

Great gobs of saliva poured from the beast's enormous maw. It pulled back its lips, exposing its massive teeth in a macabre smile. With a shake of its head, the dire wolf moved closer, ready for the kill. Just then, it howled in agony and staggered.

Indie stepped from behind the animal, his short sword dripping with crimson. As the enraged creature tried to spin around and attack the warrior, it collapsed in a heap, its back legs gushing blood. Kit hopped to her feet and wasted no time bringing her battle hammer to bear. With a full overhead swing, she brought it down on the animal's head, killing it instantly with the single blow.

"Were you bitten?" Indie cried out. "Did it bite you?"

Kit quickly gave herself a check. With the heat of battle pumping through her body, it was entirely possible she had been bitten, but she didn't feel it. "I don't think so," she replied as she ran her fingers over her face and neck. "You? Were you bitten?"

"No," Indie said, shaking his head. "It never had a chance to try biting me. You took the brunt of its attack." The young man was standing beside Kit, checking her over to make sure there were no obvious wounds. The warmth of his hand against her skin made the girl's face heat up.

"I'm okay!" Kit said as she pushed him away. A goofy grin spread across her face, which she quickly fought to rein in.

"Do you think she was the one?" Indie said, staring down at the corpse of the massive female. "She looks far sicker than the other wolves we saw." He was trying to keep his emotions in check, but his anger and self-loathing were obvious. The man's jaw quivered as he toed the remains.

Lump appeared out of nowhere, startling Kit. He paused next to the fallen wolf and whined. The big dog pushed against Indie, but the young man ignored the effort, his fists tightening at his side.

Grabbing the warrior by his sleeve, Kit turned him away from the dead animal. "Let's get to the river. I have even more blood on me now." She gave the man a nudge and a sad smile. "We can continue the search, just to be sure."

⁂

Once again, Indie took the lead. He was clearly in his element as he easily moved across some rough terrain. Kit found herself staring at him, watching the grace in his movement, when he called out. "There is an outcropping of rocks up ahead. The river is just beyond that."

"You must know this land well," Kit called back as she struggled to maintain his pace. "You move across it like you've done this every day of your life." Moments later, the hillock came into view.

"This is where she lived," Indie commented as his path shifted toward the large mound. "This is where her den was." Kit was about to question him when Indie picked up his pace and headed straight into a narrow opening in the rock face.

"Indie! Get out of there!" Kit yelled at him, but he had already disappeared. "Lump, go. Stay with Indie." Without hesitation, the dog charged forward, and like the young man, vanished from sight.

When Kit arrived at the entrance, a light shone from within. Muttering a curse under her breath, she quickly drew her weapon and readied her shield before following.

A winding tunnel led into the cave's depths. Kit wasn't sure where the light was coming from, but with it, she was able to move through the darkness with relative ease. She still managed to trip a few times on the refuse on its floor. She stepped over the huge skull of a great elk. As she rounded the last corner, Indie came into view. He was holding what appeared to be a suit of studded leather armor in one hand and a glowing ball in the other.

"What is that?" Kit asked, motioning to the glowing orb in the young man's hand.

"Something my mother created," Indie said, his eyes trained on the suit of armor. "Why would a wolf have armor in its lair?" he asked. "There are other trinkets in here as well."

"What do you mean, your mother created it?"

"Like I said, she was a gifted enchanter. She created this sun-orb for me to keep by my bed..." Even in the dim light of the orb, Kit could see Indie's face flush. Not wanting to embarrass him further, Kit examined the cave.

There was clearly a resting place of grasses and large clumps of matted fur. There were no signs that there was anything living here other than two small mice that had been ducking in and out of the shadows.

"What would that wolf do with the armor?" Indie asked again. "Why would she bring it here?"

Kit shrugged her shoulders at the question. "Keen fashion sense?" she retorted with a grin. "Maybe she was going to eat it?" Kit chuckled to herself despite the way this day had gone.

"Gather up what you think is valuable and let's get out of here," Kit said as she wended her way back to the entrance of the cave while Indie continued searching for any remaining valuables. She couldn't help but wonder why a sick wolf would feel compelled to horde things.

Just before Kit reached the exit, she turned back to call for Indie to hurry up. From behind, a deep, visceral growl broke the silence. Kit slowly turned to see an even larger male wolf darkening the entrance to the lair.

Standing just a few paces away was an enormous beast, easily twice the size of an average wolf, capable of looking Kit straight in the eye. His fur was black as obsidian, save for a white star on his forehead. In the animal's mouth was the carcass of the infected female they had just put down. The wolf carefully placed the remains on the ground and paused. After staring at the corpse for several seconds, the great beast raised his head. Saliva poured over his quivering lips. The animal glanced down one more time at what Kit guessed was his mate. He carefully stepped over the remains before lunging at Kit. With no weapon at the ready, Kit unleashed a bolt of freezing air at the wolf.

As the bolt tumbled toward the creature, it coalesced into a large shard of ice, striking the wolf full in the chest. The animal's body shimmered on contact, with the shard simply exploding in a shower of tiny ice crystals. It didn't even seem to slow him down. Barely a moment later, the wolf crashed into Kit, knocking her hard against the stone wall.

The priest struggled to maintain consciousness as the wolf circled her. He glared at her with the same milky-white eyes that his mate had. The wolf's moment of indecision allowed Kit to unsheathe her battle hammer, but she had no time to take her shield off her back.

"Hey, wolf!" Indie called out. "Hey, over here!" His attempt to draw the wolf's attention from Kit had no effect. Finally, he charged the wolf, slashing at his hip with his short sword. His strike was true, but it appeared to have done almost no damage at all. He did manage to draw the wolf's attention. The animal turned and snapped wildly at the young man.

Lump raced past Indie, nipping at the wolf's heels. Despite the dog's efforts, the beast behaved like he hadn't even seen the dog. The animal was solely focused on the man. With a single leap, he was on him.

The wolf's attacks were ferocious and unrelenting. Indie tried to fend off the assault with his short sword, but the animal was just too quick, too powerful. In a heartbeat, the creature got multiple bites in, tearing open Indie's sword arm. The next bite ripped open his side. The young man's tunic immediately became drenched in blood. If the wolf managed just one more bite, Kit was certain he would kill the young man.

There was no time to think, only react. Kit barrelled headlong into the beast, catching him fully with her shoulder. The impact knocked the animal away from Indie. As the wolf attempted to regain his footing, he stared intently at the girl with its glazed-over eyes.

A strange feeling washed over Kit. She couldn't tell if she was witnessing regret or thanks in the animal, but in that heartbeat, it was as though the beast was communicating with her, begging the girl to end his life, his suffering.

Throwing every ounce of her being into the attack, Kit brought her hammer around with a wide-arcing swing. The weapon caught the wolf directly on top of his skull. There was a deafening crack as the hammer's iron head met bone, killing the creature on impact.

The wolf's lifeless body dropped to the ground, sending a wave of sadness through the girl. She could have sworn it was what the beast wanted.

Taking no more than a moment to ensure the wolf was dead, Kit rushed to Indie's side. She tried desperately to staunch the bleeding with her hands, but the wounds were extremely deep. Without thought, she called upon Titan, pleading for his help. Seeing the shape her new friend was in, she wished she had not wasted her divine healing on herself.

"Titan, I beg of you." The words were coming out of Kit's mouth before she could consider the consequences of her action. "I am but your humble servant, once again asking for your assistance. This man does not deserve to die this day, not as a result of saving mine!" She gaped down at the blood gushing between her fingers. "Please, Titan, help me save his life. In his place, I offer up my own."

A burst of blinding white light filled the room. *"You would offer your life to save a stranger, a man you only met hours ago?"* The voice was quiet and smooth, but still, it echoed through the chamber. *"I accept your offer."*

A moment later, a warm hand caressed her cheek. "Kit! Kit, wake up!" Her eyes fluttered open, and suddenly widened at the sight of Indie kneeling beside her. "I feared I had lost you."

"You're okay!" Kit bawled, practically knocking Indie off his feet as she sprung up from the ground. She quickly pulled him into a deep hug, pressing her face against his chest. "I thought you were going to die."

Indie pushed Kit back to look at her. "Why would I have died? The wolf never got near me. You were like a crazy person, swinging your hammer about like a berserker in a full rage."

"But you were bitten!" Kit examined his side and his arm. He was completely intact with no sign of injury whatsoever. She looked down at Lump laying next to the body of the wolf. At the sight, a profound sense of loss and an overwhelming sadness washed over her. She knew in her bones that he was a magnificent creature before he was ravaged by this terrible affliction.

Lump looked up and whined. It seemed he was also swept up in the emotion. Indie, on the other hand, showed no sign of remorse at the great wolf's passing.

As she bent down before the beast, offering a prayer for its passing, a strong presence manifested beside her. Both sorrow and anger emanated from it. She then heard a word, clear as a bell and full of rage. "Avenge!"

This was not the same voice Kit heard earlier. The first voice had been sweet and melodic. This voice was male and filled with raw fury.

The power of the word muddled Kit's brain. A vision of an old Berrat woman sitting at a simple wooden table working on a pelt came into her mind. She was tiny, even by Berrat standards, with long silver-gray hair tied with thin strips of leather into several loose ponytails. Her neck and forearms were covered with light blue woad-paint and tribal tattoos. Kit was immediately overcome by an irresistible urge to visit this person. The woman looked up from her work, tears streaming down her face. She gently bowed her head to Kit before returning to her task.

When the vision disappeared, Kit was standing outside the lair, carrying the wolf's pelt. She had no recollection of ever having skinned the animal. She found herself running her hands through the long, thick fur, all the while feeling a deep, profound sorrow.

"Kit?" A nudge on her shoulder brought her back to reality. "What is going on with you?" Indie's face was a mixture of confusion and caring. "Let's wrap up that pelt and head back to my village. We need to tell everyone that you've taken care of the wolf problem."

"No," Kit said as she continued to run her fingers through the fur. "I can't go back. I have something to do."

"What is it? Whatever it is, I'm coming with you."

She shook her head as she stood up, still clutching the wolf pelt to her breast. "Thank you, but no. This is something I need to do alone."

Indie tried to talk Kit out of leaving without him, but she was resolute in her decision. "Take Lump with you. I will come back and find you," she said to him. "For now, I need to do this on my own."

"I'll hold you to that," warned Indie. "If you don't seek me out, I'll come looking for you." And with that, Indie left the lair with Lump in tow, allowing Kit to consider the path she had chosen for herself.

As Kit prepared for her journey, a powerful vision once again assailed her mind.

There was a clearing in the forest with a small hut made of earth and grasses. Outside the hut was an extremely large white wolf. Even though she was down-wind of the beast, it appeared to know she was there. Just as its eyes met Kit's, the beast lowered its head, acknowledging her presence. A moment later, it turned and strode into the hut.

Kit's desire to visit the location was utterly overwhelming. Again, the voice in her head called out.

"Avenge!"

CHAPTER THIRTY-NINE

THE HUT IN THE WOODS

Kit wasn't sure how long she had been traveling. Her brain had been in a dense fog for the entire journey. When the veil finally lifted, she found herself standing in a small meadow with a thick pine forest surrounding her. A sea of wildflowers completely engulfed her, their scent rejuvenating her body and mind. In the middle of the meadow was a small house constructed of grass and mud. Everything looked and *felt* just like it did in her vision. As she approached, the great white wolf appeared from behind the hut. It was huge. Without a doubt, the largest wolf Kit had ever seen, dwarfing even the black dire wolf she had encountered in the cave.

It had markings on its fur, like the tribal symbols she'd seen the Berrat warriors paint on their skin. The long ruff of its neck had multiple braids in it, adorned with small colorful beads. Like in Kit's vision, as soon as the wolf's eyes met hers, it bowed its head to Kit and then entered the hut.

The young girl remained motionless for several moments, trying to decide what to do next. The voice in her head urged her on.

"Follow."

As Kit approached the door, she paused for a moment, trying to decide if she should knock. The door was made of thin branches with grasses and vines woven between them. As she continued to ponder her next course of action, the door slowly opened. The light inside was dim, but Kit could make out the tiny old woman, hunched over her table, with gray hair, and tribal tattoos. She was most certainly the same person as in her vision. Kit's eyes quickly scanned the room. There was no sign of the wolf. The hut smelled of wood, earth, and wildflowers.

"Peace unto you," the old woman said in greeting. "Do you have something for me?" Her voice was clear and melodic, not what Kit would have expected from a woman of her advanced age. Unknowingly, Kit had moved into the small house. She was fairly certain that the old woman was speaking of the wolf pelt.

Kit handed the wolf pelt to the old woman. She gently accepted the offering, and buried her face into the soft, thick fur. When she pulled the pelt away, there were tears streaming down her face. Her voice was thick with emotion. "You did a noble thing saving him from his suffering. His spirit is extremely strong, and it lingers in our realm." She turned her head away, "Yes, I understand, and I will help," the old woman promised, before she turned her attention back to Kit. "Leave me now and return when the time is right."

Kit was about to ask her when it would be time to return when the voice in her head spoke yet again.

"Murderers!"

A moment later, another vision assaulted her mind. This time, it was violent and gruesome. A large group of people were attacking a dire wolf and her pups. The wolf had unleashed a barrage of cold attacks, but they had no effect on her assailants.

When the vision ended, the old woman was at her table, working on the black dire wolf pelt. She waved her hands at Kit as though to shoo her from her home. Without a word, Kit headed for the door of the hut. As she exited, a warmth spread through her entire body. The feeling was pleasant, like being wrapped in a warm blanket, sitting by a roaring fire on a cold winter's day. When it passed, Kit's wounds had been entirely healed; her gear and clothing were perfectly clean. She turned back to the hut only to discover that it was no longer there.

Had the entire encounter been a hallucination? The voice once again thundered in her mind, filled with urgency and an unbridled fury.

"Avenge!"

***

Before she knew it, Kit was running headlong into the forest with her weapon and shield at the ready. She crashed through the trees with reckless abandon until she came across the group attacking a dire wolf. When the priest approached, most of them scattered, but a few turned from their quarry to challenge the girl directly. The wolf was near death. From somewhere nearby, the frenzied cries of its pups stabbed at Kit's heart.

"Oh, look what we have here," spat the largest member of the group. He was a bald, thickly muscled, and heavily scarred Westerner. His shirtless body was covered in thigh-length chainmail, and in his hand, he wielded a large double-bladed ax. The weapon was stained with blood, most likely from the dire wolf laying on the ground.

"In the name of Titan," Kit bellowed. "What are you doing?"

"Earning a living," a feral-looking woman said. "We're slayers. We get paid to kill wolves. What's it to you, bitch?"

"Shut it," the bald man growled, giving Kit a grim smile. "Not that it matters. Once we finish up with these pups, I think I'm going to spend me some *quality time* flaying this here girl. I don't appreciate uppity little whelps sticking their snouts in my business." Spittle flew from his stained, chip-toothed mouth as he spoke.

"Perhaps we can spend some *quality time* right now," Kit quipped back as she let her hammer spin in her hand. "I'm guessing you're the addled one of this group. The rest of your friends were smart enough to run."

"Not all of us," retorted a filthy woman with greasy blonde hair, dressed in ragged leather armor, brandishing a pair of chipped and rusted dirks.

Kit rolled her eyes at the woman so hard that she was quite sure they made a noise. "Sweet Titan, anyone with half a brain can see that you're not *smart enough* to run."

The feral-looking woman really didn't seem to appreciate the comment. She quickly threw one of her dirks. Kit practically laughed as it sailed past, nowhere near its intended mark.

"Maybe you should put the sharp things on the ground. You *clearly* have no idea how to use them," Kit mocked.

The woman flew into a rage. She charged straight at Kit, unleashing a series of cusses that would have made a sailor blush. She raised her blade to bring it down on Kit's head, completely opening her defenses. Kit smoothly swung her shield up, catching the woman fully in the jaw. The impact created a large *snap*, and the woman crashed to the ground. Kit could only guess that the blow had broken her neck. Two of the other attackers immediately threw their weapons on the ground and bolted into the forest, leaving Kit alone with the group's shot caller.

"It looks like it's just you and me, little girl," he sprayed at her. He absent-mindedly wiped the drool from his chin with the back of his arm. He dropped his ax on the ground, deciding to replace it with a small leather sap he had hanging from his hip. His willingness to give up his ax gave Kit cause for concern. He clearly believed she offered little threat to him, and he'd rather end this fight with her alive.

"If you're trying to intimidate me," Kit said, "then you're failing miserably." Her voice wasn't as sure as she would have liked it to be. An unexpected resolve suddenly blossomed from within. The resolute priest stood as tall as she could, squaring her shoulders to her assailant. "*I* am Kit Standing Bear, a Priest of Titan and I will be delivering justice upon you this day."

"You?" laughed the hunter. "You're a *priest?* of *Titan?*" The big man was practically buckling over with laughter. "It seems that old goat, Father Hoarfrost, is digging at the bottom of the barrel trying to fill his annual quota of new priests for the Temple of the Fist. You don't look tall enough to order an ale at a bar. We need another serving girl, and once you learn your place, you'll do just fine."

Now this bully was causing Kit's blood to boil. "You know nothing of the Temple or my god; you, who prey on Fenrir's creatures for your own personal glory or profit. You are not fit to even speak my god's name."

"Not fit?" The foul man was making no attempt to hide his contempt. "I was one of the old goat's acolytes. I trained under him for over eleven years. After watching so many of my friends lose their lives in search of a way to free *Titan*, I took my leave from the forsaken place."

The hunter's eyes brightened up. "I do hope you are who you say you are," he said, his lips curling up in a wicked grin. "If you're a full priest, maybe sparring with you will even give me some entertainment before I truss you up like a spring lamb and use you as bait." He strode toward Kit, rolling his shoulders. There was an unmistakable swagger to his movement. "I can't remember the last time I've enjoyed a decent fight."

The way this man claimed to have once been an acolyte of the Fist completely repulsed Kit. If he wasn't lying, he was likely friends with Brother Rime. She quickly muttered a prayer to Titan and released an ice bolt at her attacker. It hit him square in the chest, but it had no effect on him at all.

"We deal with dire wolves on a daily basis, little sister. Do you really think we're not going to have protections from cold attacks?" He shook his head at her. "You're very pretty, but not too bright, eh?" He gawped at the dead woman on the ground. "Apparently though, there is no shortage of *dumb* in my group." He chuckled to himself, apparently enamored with his own brand of witless humor.

Kit took a few steps back and put herself into a battle stance. This man was huge, and he was well armored, but he had nothing but a sap for a weapon. She shifted her weight to her back foot, allowing her to react quickly to any attack. Sure enough, the large man threw himself at her, trying to grab Kit by the throat. She deftly moved to the side, preventing him from grasping her by the neck, but he still managed to get one of his massive hands on her upper arm.

His strength was astounding. It was like trying to grapple with a grizzly. He effortlessly picked her up off the ground and held her at his eye level. Using her free arm, Kit tried to hit him with her shield, but he easily brushed the attack aside. He cocked an eyebrow and shook his bald head.

"You disappoint me, girl," he said, spraying spittle all the while. "I had hoped to get more of a fight out of you."

"You want more of a fight?" Kit asked as she twisted herself enough within his grip to unleash a full-powered kick into his nether regions. "How's that?" she said as he gaped, wide eyed.

With a whimpering grunt, he released his hold and dropped her to the ground. While the big man buckled over, trying to catch his breath, she struck him with her knee, full in the face. Blood exploded from the man's nose and mouth on impact.

Kit knew that if this man had time to recover, he was literally going to squash her. Fearing for her life, she took her hammer and delivered a devastating blow onto the middle of his back. She put all her might into the swing, but it only managed to cause him to drop to one knee. He looked up at Kit through a bloody, toothless smile.

"That's more like it, but I'm afraid letting you live might not be an option. I fear you'll be more trouble than you're worth."

Before he had a chance to get up off the ground, Kit followed up with another overhand strike. "Titan, give me strength!" she yelled out as she brought the hammer down squarely onto the top of his head. She put so much force into her swing that his skull practically exploded on contact.

At the sight, Kit buried her face into the crook of her elbow, trying desperately to suppress the urge to vomit.

Her stomach heaved as she looked down at the dead man at her feet. She had been trained by the Temple to deliver justice, but never before had she taken a human life, let alone two. Kit knew it was kill or be killed, but it did nothing to lessen the vice-grip squeezing her chest.

The young priest shuddered as she gawked at the gruesome scene. Her stomach flopped.

As she turned away to retch, Kit looked upon the dire wolf that had started this whole confrontation. She was desperately trying to stand up. Unable to bear her own weight, the beast fell back to the ground with a heart-breaking whimper.

The small girl cautiously moved closer to the fallen creature. She was a large female, likely the mother of the bawling pups. When Kit perceived that the animal posed no threat, she knelt next to her, trying to ascertain the extent of her injuries. The poor creature's fur was matted, soaked in her own blood.

The priest ran her hands over the huge wolf's body, finding many shallow cuts across her neck and back, none of which appeared to be life threatening. It was only when the wolf coughed, causing blood to spray from her chest, that the grievous wound became apparent.

Carefully, Kit pulled back the fur, uncovering a deep, foot-long gash, likely from the shot caller's double-bladed ax. At that moment, the girl came to the somber realization that this once-magnificent animal was well beyond her healing skills. The only humane option was to end the poor creature's suffering.

"I'm sorry," Kit said as she pulled her dagger from its sheath, her hand shaking badly. What she felt for taking the lives of these two killers paled by comparison to the grief she was experiencing at this moment. "I cannot save your life. Your wounds are beyond my ability. I can end your suffering, though, if that is what you want."

The wolf's eyes focused on Kit for a long moment as though she was trying to convey a message of some sort. Tears flowed freely down the young priest's cheeks as the wolf lowered her head, quietly closed her eyes, and waited for her end.

"Fenrir, take this wondrous animal to your bosom. Care for her and guide her to the Great Cycle." With a single thrust, Kit gave the poor creature a quick death. As she put her dagger away, the voice once again spoke to her.

"Polaris, my love. Be at peace!"

The profound sorrow in its voice shattered the young priest's heart. Moments later, the yips of the pups started up once again, a stark reminder that life goes on, never pausing, never moving backward.

It didn't take long to locate and free the bawling pups. They appeared to be starving and near death. Despite having been with their mother who would have cared for them, they looked like they hadn't eaten in many days.

It was only then that Kit noticed that the mother had a broken manacle attached to her hind foot. She could only surmise that the hunters had chained the wolf up, making it impossible for her to feed her young. At some point, she must have broken loose of her bonds and attacked her captors.

Even though Kit was in a state of rage over what had happened here, she found herself facing an extremely tough decision. She could likely find some food for the young dire wolves, but she was not equipped to raise them. However, the thought of them roaming the halls of the Temple made the priest chuckle to herself.

All but one of the pups were lying at their mother's side, howling. It was the most forlorn sound the girl had ever heard. Were they, too, praying to Fenrir, asking for her to care for their fallen mother?

The last pup, which Kit could only assume was the runt of the litter, was pawing at her boot. It whimpered softly and then yipped at her. As Kit picked him up, he bit gently at her hands. He meant no harm, but his needle-sharp teeth were quickly drawing blood. Kit clutched him by the scruff of his neck and brought him up eye to eye with hers.

"Would you like me to look after you?" she asked him.

"Yip!" he replied, as though he actually understood what she'd said.

Kit took a deep breath, trying to steady her resolve. "Okay then, it looks like I'll be your new den-mother." At the sound of her voice, the wolf pups came rushing over, brimming with newfound energy. They clambered at Kit's feet, nipping at her pants and boots. "I guess the first order of business is to find a better place to make camp, and then I'll get you some food. We can't stay here and you look like you haven't eaten in days."

"Why don't you let me look after the food?" Indie said, the young man's sudden appearance startling Kit. He waded through the pack of pups, carefully avoiding stepping on any of them.

"What are you doing here?" Kit raced over and threw herself into his arms. Her face immediately flushed, and she pushed herself away. It suddenly dawned on her that Indie was alone.

"Where's Lump? Why isn't he with you?"

Chapter Forty

RESONANCE

"Lump took off," Indie said, looking over his shoulder. "There were some people that ran past us and he gave chase. I didn't know if I should follow him or try to find you." The young man shrugged and gave Kit a shy smile. "I chose you."

Kit blushed hard at the man's words. Her gaze darted about, and her hands fidgeted while her face heated. Thankfully, the small wolf-pup interrupted the awkward moment, jumping at her legs. The girl quickly scooped him up and held the furry animal to her chest, using him like a shield.

"Thank you for coming," she said, the words coming out much faster than normal. "These people. They slaughtered Polaris."

"Polaris?" Indie asked, his brow deeply furrowed.

"The dire wolf," Kit said, pointing to the fallen animal. Not wanting to explain how she knew the fallen animal's name, she waved her hand dismissively. "It's not important. What's important is, these pups need food and we need to find Lump."

Indie took Kit's hand in his. "Lump will be fine. He's the smartest dog I've ever seen. There is a place to make camp beyond those trees. Go there with the pups and I'll bring back some food for them." The young man walked over to a bow and quiver that a hunter had dropped. "I'm not the best archer, but I'm good enough in a pinch."

A moment later, the young man disappeared into the forest. As the sea of green swallowed Indie, the mob of unruly pups swarmed Kit.

Wasting no time, Kit shepherded the pups through the forest, stopping at a small clearing nestled in a thick stand of pines. The girl's spirit was low, her body exhausted. Taking a seat on the ground, the priest soaked up the unfettered affection the animals happily gave her. Their carefree behavior stood in stark contrast to the brutal violence that had just unfolded, and to the death that surrounded them.

Did they feel no sense of loss at their mother's passing? Their howls had marked the end of the dire wolf's life, but now, they showed no signs of sadness. None whatsoever.

"They live," said the disembodied voice in her head. "My children have a chance at life, thanks to you."

"Your children?" Kit asked, searching for the source of the voice. "Are you the wolf in the cave?"

The voice went silent. The pups suddenly moved away from her, bounding across the clearing. There, not more than a dozen paces away, the young wolves mauled a somewhat perplexed golden retriever.

"Lump!" Kit screeched out, racing to join the pack. "You're okay!"

The dog greeted Kit by knocking her to the ground, covering her with copious amounts of slobber. As the girl squealed in delight, the pups joined in, licking the fallen girl until she could not longer breathe.

Time passed as the priest soaked in the canines' celebrations. They lived life in the moment, not dwelling on the past. This was a lesson that Kit struggled to learn. She had forever been stricken by past events. She couldn't go back and change them, and yet, she dwelled on them.

Her life had been a tapestry woven with threads of disdain—first for being human in a Berrat village, then for being an outsider in a city of her own kind. The weight of those judgments clung to her like a shadow, a burden that threatened to crush her spirit.

Watching the dire wolf pups playing with Lump, Kit realized, in a perfect moment of clarity, that the past was what it was; its chapters were written, the ink dried. Nothing could ever change it.

The dogs' joyful actions whispered to her soul, a reminder that the value of life isn't in the opinions of others but in the sincerity of one's intentions. It was a revelation as potent as a dawn's first light. Her desire for acceptance had driven her from her home and her mother; the one person who had accepted her and loved her in the face of hatred. It blinded her to the true source of fulfillment – family, love, helping people for its own sake. If she was going to live life to its fullest, she must first cast aside the chains of the past and embrace the present.

Lump and the puppies suddenly stopped playing and barked frantically.

Indie, whose smile was as big as the haunch of meat slung over his shoulder, was forced to fight off the onslaught of Lump and the pups.

"I found an elk," he said, wading through furry frenzy. "I took as much as I could carry and buried the rest. I'll start a fire and you carve up the meat."

Truthfully, Kit believed he assigned the tasks the way he did to avoid the mayhem. If he was ever to have children of his own, he would need to learn to embrace the chaos. The wolves' overly excited behaviour reminded the priest of the children at the orphanage, practically mauling her whenever she brought food from Miyuki's kitchens.

Even though they were only three or four months old, each puppy likely weighed between thirty and forty pounds. With Lump's help, they were going to overwhelm her.

"Enough," she bellowed out, her voice coming out like a ferocious growl. Lump, and pups alike, immediately ceased their foolish behavior and took a seat. They stared at her, their attention unwavering.

"That's better," Kit said. "You'll eat when I give it you, and not a moment sooner."

A long string of drool hung from Lump's mouth. As though on cue, the pups followed suit, releasing their own streams of viscous slobber.

Kit took a knee beside the enormous haunch and drew her dagger. She carved off a large section, an amount she believed would be enough to feed the lot of them. Carefully, thoughtfully, she carved off bite-sized pieces from the hank of meat.

The pups were rapidly growing impatient while she meticulously attempted to cut the elk into equal sized portions. Fed up with waiting, one of the pups jumped at the main body of meat, snatching it from Kit's grasp. Quickly, he bolted a few feet away and ripped off a large portion to chew on. The other pups immediately joined in on the feast, all except one of them. The runt of the litter sat patiently at Kit's feet, right next to Lump, waiting for her to give them some food.

Kit's heart swelled at the sight of the two canines, one large and one small, giving her their undivided attention. She looked down at the bits of meat in her hand before carving off another large chunk from the shank.

"For you, my handsome," she murmured to Lump as she offered the food. The dog looked to the wolf pup, not accepting the exceptionally large treat. "Don't worry. He'll get his share, too." Still, the golden retriever refused to take the meat. The simple gesture made Kit's heart swell.

Taking one of the small chunks, she offered it to the pup. He gently took the morsel from her hand, swallowing it without bothering to chew. She offered him another, but like the big dog sitting beside him, refused to take the food.

"True friends already," Kit mused, offering the larger piece to Lump. This time, the dog didn't hesitate. He accepted the offering and laid down at the girl's feet, aggressively ripping chunks from it. While Lump devoured his meal, Kit continued to feed the remaining smaller chunks to the pup, his gentle behavior never changing.

With the meat supply exhausted, the pup nuzzled his head against Kit's leg, curled up next to Lump, and drifted into a content slumber. The other pups, their bellies full, were busy cleaning the blood off themselves and their littermates. Kit marveled at how caring they were for each other, giving her a new appreciation for these majestic animals.

"Fire's ready." Indie's voice shattered the tranquil interlude. He gazed upon the pack of over-stuffed animals sprawled out before him, a broad grin splitting his face. "Is there any left for us?"

Under the starlit canopy, the crackling fire cast dancing shadows, creating an intimate bubble of warmth and companionship. As they shared stories and laughter, Kit felt an unexpected sense of camaraderie with Indie. Despite their disparate backgrounds, they seemed to harmonize effortlessly, finding common ground in the midst of their personal journeys.

Lump's rhythmic breathing added a comforting backdrop to the night's symphony. The young wolf pup, nestled beside the golden retriever, occasionally twitching in his sleep, his innocent dreams a testament to the sanctuary Kit had provided. The other pups had settled near each other, their playful antics replaced by the tranquility of slumber.

Gazing at the stars above, Kit's mind drifted, reflecting on the choices that had led her to this point. The scars of her past seemed to fade in the gentle glow of the fire, and she realized that her path was no longer defined by the disdain she had endured. She was forging her own destiny, one step at a time.

In the midst of this serene interlude, the forest's symphony seemed to change its tune. The rustling leaves carried a whisper of unease, and Lump's ears perked up, his instincts sensing the shift in the air. Kit's gaze sharpened, her senses alert as a distant snap of a twig punctuated the night.

"Weapons," Indie whispered. Kit nodded and scampered across the campsite, scooping up her hammer. By the time she looked back, Indie had his bow nocked and drawn.

The young priest strained to listen, but all she could hear were Lump's low, throaty growls.

Chapter Forty-One

BETRAYAL

"What have we here?" said a thin man dressed in leather pants and vest. The firelight highlighted the scars that covered his body, giving him a deadly appearance. A large group of hunters emerged from the forest, forming a semi-circle, surrounding Kit and her cohorts.

The priest strode forward and held up her hand, wordlessly telling Indie and Lump to stay where they were. She needed to size up her opponents, to know who the leader was, and which ones were the most dangerous.

The skinny man walked forward with a cock-sure swagger that evoked a gag-reflex. Fingering his blade, the leader coolly said, "We'll be taking those puppies now. Step away or die."

Lump stepped forward, his hackles raised, his teeth bared. He barely made a sound, but his deadly intent was clear. With a single command from Kit, the wolfdog held his ground, waiting for his chance to strike.

While Indie slowly moved into a better defensive position, the pups scrambled behind Kit, all except for the runt. Kit could feel him pressing against her leg, trying to be as menacing as possible while protecting her.

"We'll be taking that large mutt as well," the skinny man said. "I'd prefer him alive, but if you can't get him under control, we'll just take his pretty coat."

The threat to Lump set Kit's blood boiling. She continued to study the group. From what she could see, not one of these thugs appeared to be a particularly skilled fighter, but there were still too many of them to defeat, even if they barely knew which end of a spear to use. Two of them had longbows, and at this range, it was unlikely they'd miss very often. One of them had been with the shot caller earlier on. Rather than face Kit, he had turned tail and ran at her arrival.

"You!" Kit called out to the coward. "Do you feel more confident now that there are eight of you? You left your boss to die. I expect that once I open a skull or two, you'll turn tail and run a second time."

The hunter shifted nervously from foot to foot as he eyed the others. His gaze darted between Indie and Kit, his resolve crumbling.

One of the bolder hunters pushed closer to the front of the group. "You never killed Cleaver," he said. Had he not been one of these despicable hunters, Kit might have even considered him handsome. "Cleaver would cut you from top to bottom before you even had a chance to blink."

Kit aimlessly twirled her hammer in her hand and gave the bold hunter a small shrug. "Don't take my word for it," she said with the ease of somebody clearly in control of the situation. "His body, and what's left of his head, are only a few hundred paces away." Kit pointed to where she had left the two dead attackers. "Perhaps you'd like to see for yourself. We're in no rush. Go ahead, we'll be right here."

Kit picked up the puppy at her feet. He'd been snarling at the hunters through the entire exchange. As she gently rubbed the fur around his neck, Kit casually shrugged her shoulders again. "Well?"

Two of the men bolted off in the direction to which Kit had pointed. "I don't think they're coming back," Indie said, smirking at the remaining hunters. He leveled his bow at the two archers. "I'll bet I can kill both you before you can get off a single shot."

Indie had said earlier that he wasn't the best archer around, but the calmness in his voice said otherwise. The young man's expression was completely stoic, showing no signs of fear.

The group didn't seem quite as keen to fight as they were a moment ago. Seizing the moment, Kit decided to attempt a more diplomatic approach. "We seem to be at an impasse," she said, eyeing each of the six hunters. "I suggest you all slink back to wherever it is you came from. Either that, or you can stay here and die."

"We're not leaving without those pups," the skinny man said, his back suddenly straighter than it had been a moment ago, that same cock-sure attitude appearing out of nowhere. A moment later, six more hunters stepped out from the trees. Like the others, they didn't appear to be particularly skilled, but the numbers were against them.

"I'll tell you what," Indie offered. "You take the pups, and leave me, the girl, and the dog behind. I doubt we can kill you all, but we'll take a good number of you down with us."

The runt stared up at Kit and whimpered. He clearly did not like Indie's suggestion, not one bit. Neither did she. Was the young man actually a coward, ready to sacrifice the lives of others just to save himself when things got difficult? She didn't want to believe it, but that was exactly what it looked like. "We're not giving up the pups," she growled, glaring at Indie. "I'll die first."

"Yes, you will," the cock-sure man said. "I'll do it myself."

"You can try," Kit said. "It didn't go so well for your friend. Maybe you'll fare better."

"Take the pups and go," Indie said, turning his arrow on the man threatening Kit. The hunters looked at each other, wondering if the offer was nothing more than a trick. Before they could fall on a decision, the two men returned. Their faces were white, and their chests heaved as they tried to catch their breath.

"We accept your offer," one of them blurted out, buckled over with his hands placed firmly on his knees. There was a moment of bickering amongst the group, but eventually they relented, concluding that they were getting what they wanted without any more of them being killed.

"What are you doing?" Kit asked, turning to Indie. "I'm not giving them the pups. Why are you doing this?"

With his bow still pointed at their leader's chest, Indie turned his gaze on Kit, his eyes pleading. "Trust me," he mouthed. Something in the man's eyes cut through the fog of anger that had been enveloping the young priest. He was begging her to give the hunters what they wanted.

"Take them and go," Kit snarled. "Get out of here before I change my mind."

Two of the hunters tried to gather up the pups, but the little wolves were not willing to go easily. They bit and clawed at their captors, drawing blood in multiple locations. As one of the thugs came to collect the runt, Kit held him close and shook her head, daring the man to try and take him.

"Leave him," the cock-sure man said. "He's just a runt and not worth our time."

The puppy in Kit's arms squirmed, trying to free itself to go help his siblings. The priest maintained her grip and whispered softly to him, "Not yet, Runt." The pup looked up at her, his eyes a combination of questioning and trust. Reluctantly, he settled in her embrace, but never stopped growling at the hunters. Kit cringed inwardly, concerned he may not like the name she'd given him. After all, he really did seem to understand when she spoke to him.

Chapter Forty-Two

Where There is Life

As the group of hunters left with the pups, Kit rounded on Indie. "What were you thinking? Do you hate wolves so much that you'd let them be slaughtered? You're a coward. You'll do anything to save your own hide."

The look of shame on the young man's face instantly diffused Kit's anger. Indie's face crumpled and he dropped to the ground in a heap.

"I don't hate the wolves," he said, his face buried in his hands. "I hate myself." When he pulled his hands away, the man's face was filled with rage. "But I'd sacrifice a thousand wolves if it meant protecting you. Had we fought those hunters, they'd have killed you. We all would have died, and they'd still have the pups. What good would have come from it?"

The girl stared at the man; her lips pressed into a hard, thin line. She didn't want to admit it, but he was right. They were alive, and where there was life, there was hope.

"I'm sorry," she said, holding the whining pup close. "I shouldn't have said what I said. You're not a coward. You were being smart."

Indie turned away, his head hanging low. "No. I am a coward. My first instinct is always to save myself. I lied. I didn't give up the pups to protect you. I did it because I didn't want to die."

"But you did save me. You saved me, and Lump, and this pup. And now we can hunt down those heartless bastards and kill them all. We deliver justice upon them. Together."

Indie nodded but he refused to look back. "We need to wait a while. They need to feel like they've escaped. Their guard will be up right now. Lump will have no trouble following their trail. I don't think they've bathed in months."

After what felt like an eternity, Kit decided she could wait no longer. "Lump, follow their trail, but go slow. We need to be as quiet as possible, in case any of them decide to ambush us." Indie gave Kit a doubtful look for talking to the dog like he understood the common language. "He understands me just fine, don't you, Lump?"

The golden retriever wolfdog immediately put his nose to the ground and headed into the forest, the runt close on his heels. He kept his pace to a slow trot, making it easy for Kit to keep up. Indie took up the rear, his bow at the ready.

The group traveled through the forest for several hours, finding no sight of the hunters. Kit was worried that her plan to move at a slow but steady pace was a bad idea, thinking she was giving time for the thugs to escape. If they had been running hard, they could be miles ahead of them by now.

Lump stopped suddenly, Runt bumping into his legs. While the wolf dog's head was turning left and right, the dire wolf pup was sniffing the ground, walking in circles.

"Did they lose the scent?" Kit asked as Indie strode up beside her. The young man moved closer to Lump, examining the ground and the plant life. He shook his head.

"They were here. They're not far ahead of us." He lifted his gaze to Kit. "They've split up. Some have headed off north. The others continued west."

"Which way did the pups go?" Kit asked, straining to see the signs that Indie had found. She saw nothing but grass, leaf litter, and thorned bushes. Gods, how she wished she had paid more attention in Brother Rime's class. He often spoke of tracking while she dozed off.

"There's no way to know for sure," Indie said, still examining the forest floor for signs. "They're carrying the pups, so there are no prints for me to follow, and nothing for Lump and Runt to scent."

"We split up then," Kit said. "I'll go north and you go west. We'll find a way back to each other once we've rescued the pups."

"Absolutely not! You're not going off on your own. We have no idea how many more of those hunters there are. Splitting up is suicide." Kit gave the man an incredulous look. "I'm not doing it because I'm a coward, if that's what you're thinking. I'm saying we stick together because it may be the only way either of us survives."

"And while we're safe, the pups might die." Kit set her jaw. She was not going to accept no for an answer. "Take Lump with you. We'll find the hunters and kill them all."

"I can track them on my own," Indie said, shaking his head. "You can't see anything. Without Lump, you'll be lost in ten minutes."

"I've got the runt. We may not be able to smell the other pups, but I'm sure he can. They're his family."

"If he can follow his brothers and sisters, then we stick together and let him lead." The pup gave a small yip, as if in agreement.

Kit stared blankly at the man. She didn't want to admit it, but his logic was sound. When no better plan came to mind, the girl whispered to the pup in her arms. "Okay, Runt, I sure hope you'll be able to help sniff out your littermates." She could swear that the pup nodded in response. Kit cringed inwardly, concerned he may not like the name she'd given him. After all, he really did seem to understand when she spoke to him.

The priest took a deep breath to center herself and placed the puppy on the ground. "Okay, let's go find your family. Show us the way." Runt immediately dropped his nose to the ground and ran off, taking the path that led north.

"Trust the nose," Indie said with a shrug and a half-smile. His demeanor instantly improved now that he was staying with Kit. Truth was, she was happy for the company.

Even though this pup was barely more than a season old, he was running much too fast to allow Indie to check for signs that they were on the hunters' trail. With little choice, they were forced to completely trust that the small wolf could keep the scent. It felt like hours had passed by the time Runt finally came to a stop, his chest heaving, his tongue hanging out the side of his mouth. Lump was also panting hard, but he looked like he could run forever.

Runt motioned with his snout and gave a low growl.

"I think he's telling us they're up ahead," Indie whispered, a hint of wonder in his voice. Kit raised her eyebrows, giving him a wordless *I told you so*. "Stay here with the boys, I'll take a look."

"You're not going alone. You don't have to prove anything. Either we go together, or you can stay here with the boys."

"Together then," Indie said. "At least let me lead. I'm a better tracker than you."

Kit scooped up the pup and nodded. She patted her hip, instructing Lump to stay beside her. "Go. We're right behind you."

The young man slunk off, nary making a sound. She gave Lump a wide-eyed glance. He gave her a smile in return.

As Kit pulled back a pine branch, she caught sight of Indie. He was on one knee, giving her a shush signal. Nodding her understanding, she slipped in beside the young man and peered into the clearing.

Up ahead, a small camp came into view. One of the hunters who took the pups was sitting alone by a fire. She was in the midst of skinning yet another slaughtered wolf. She had one of the puppies tied to a tree.

"They're using the pups as bait," Indie whispered. "Their cries are luring in adults."

Indie's words made Kit's blood boil. The voice in her head had gone silent, but she could still feel its hatred burning from within. Without giving it much thought, Kit drew one of her daggers from its sheath preparing to throw it at the hunter. The woman was at least twenty paces away, a near impossible feat. As the priest drew back her arm, Indie shook his head and brandished his bow.

She gave him a quick nod and slid her knife back into its sheath. Indie held his breath as he drew back his bow. His hands were shaking as he took aim. Kit could only guess that he had never killed anyone, and it wasn't something he wanted to do. Just as she was about to stay his hand, he released the arrow.

The bolt stuck the hunter with a wet thud, catching her fully in the throat. She clutched weakly at the shaft, a look of shock on her face. A moment later, the life went out of her eyes as she toppled over onto the ground.

"Thank you," whispered the familiar voice in Kit's head. Gratitude mixed with a burning hatred flooded Kit's mind. There was more she needed to do. This hunter was just a small part of a much larger picture. "You have a worthy mate."

"Nice shot," the priest said, patting Indie on the shoulder. While the young man's skin looked pale, Kit's face was burning from the wolf-spirit's words. Taking the woman's life had not been easy and she feared it would take its toll. "Are you okay?"

Indie nodded without turning to Kit. Blowing out a breath, he nocked another arrow and moved into the camp. After doing a quick survey, he slipped the arrow back into the quiver and slung his bow over this shoulder. The man slowly moved over to the dead woman. He seemed to pause for a moment before grabbing the fateful arrow and yanking it out. Not giving it a look, he slipped the blood-soaked bolt into the quiver.

"Indie," Kit said, placing her hand on his back. "I'm sorry you had to do that. Taking a life... even from someone so despicable, it's no easy thing." She waited a few moments, but the young man refused to turn towards her. "I don't know why or how, but I believe what we're doing here is going to save lives."

"Wolf lives, maybe," Indie said, his voice thick with emotion. "I know the wolves who killed my family were sick, but I don't care. I hate them all."

"If you hate them, why are you helping defend them?" The man shrugged at the question. The girl turned Indie to face her. "Listen. I get it. I grew up with it. I was hated because I was human. The raiders, the people who came to our village and stole our people, they were human, too. Everyone despised me because I was like them."

Indie turned, avoiding Kit's gaze, and her words. A fire rose in the girl's belly.

"I wasn't like them, Indie. I was never like them, but the Berrat people in my village despised me anyway. It wasn't right, and I suffered for it. These animals, these wolves we're helping, they don't warrant your anger. The people who would hunt and kill them for their own gain, they're the ones who deserve your wrath."

Leaving Indie to work through his emotions, Kit did a quick search through the small camp, revealing cages made of branches and twisted vines. Most of them had been destroyed, but a couple remained intact. There were tracks leading away from the camp of what might have been from a half-dozen wolves or so. Some of the tracks were huge, likely dire wolves.

"My pack fights back," said the voice in Kit's head. "We will not go quietly. We will bring balance back to the lands."

"Why are they doing this? It makes no sense." Kit asked, turning in a slow circle, hoping to see from where the voice was coming. She waited several moments but the wolf spirit had gone silent, choosing not to answer her questions. Maybe he didn't know the answer.

The young priest continued to inspect the camp. It quickly became obvious that, amidst the wolf prints, there were a number of human tracks as well, three sets at least.

"I think the wolves found the camp," she said to Indie. "They were destroying the cages to free the pups. The hunters must have caught them in the act and gave chase." The theory might have explained how the dead woman had a new kill so quickly after leaving with the pups.

There was a loud yelp, followed by the screams of a man.

"Follow!" the anxiety-filled voice shouted. "Kill them. Kill them all! Save my children!"

Lump barked and dashed off, barreling headlong into the forest. "Free the pup," Kit shouted, putting Runt on the ground. "Stay with Indie, I'll come back for you."

CHAPTER FORTY-THREE

HUNTER HUNT

Kit readied her shield and tightened her grip on her battle hammer as she pushed her way through the thick pine branches. She was running blind, hoping that she was still on Lump's path. A moment later, Runt raced past, giving a small yip as he did.

"Find Lump!" Kit said, doing her best to keep up with the pup. In seconds, he, too, was swallowed up by the forest, leaving the priest to find her own way. Assuming she was on the right path, she forged forward, running as fast as her legs could carry her.

Seconds passed like hours as she ran through the trees. Fear that Lump was going to get himself killed fueled her, drove Kit to run beyond her limits. Unexpectedly, she burst through the woods and into a clearing.

Runt stood motionless in the clearing while Lump and a pair of grey wolves were actively dismembering another hunter. When the wolves caught wind of Kit, they abandoned their kill and moved on her. Runt immediately took a protective stance, moving between Kit and the wolf-pair. With their hackles fully up, they were putting on an impressive display of aggression. The two wolves stared at the wolf-pup for several moments before lowering their head. It looked to Kit like they were showing respect to the pup.

Lump moved to Runt's side, barking out a series of high-pitched sounds. The wolves barked back, whined, and quickly returned to their kill. Moments later, Indie arrived, a dire wolf puppy nestled in the crook of his arm.

"One less hunter," Kit said, motioning to the dismembered carcass. "The wolves are fighting back, and I'm going to help them. I'm going to see this through to the end. Are you with me?"

The young man nodded, not saying a word. He held the small female wolf pup to his chest, giving it a gentle squeeze before putting it on the ground. "Until the end. I'm sorry for what you went through. You didn't deserve it and neither do they."

While Lump was cleaning the blood from his muzzle, the two pups had their noses pressed to the ground, snuffling through small plants and fallen pine needles. The female yipped, drawing Runt's attention. He stuck his nose to the ground by his sister, yipped, and bolted into the forest. The larger pup immediately gave chase, as did Lump.

"Go," Indie said. "I'll guard the rear."

Over rock and under log, the puppies' pursuit was relentless. Kit's chest was on fire, her breaths coming out in loud wheezes, when the two wolves finally came to a stop. The pair sat and stared at the girl, their tiny chests heaving, their tongues lolling out the side of their mouths. Lump was lying on the ground next to them, panting uncontrollably.

"Why'd they stop?" Kit asked, buckled over, her hands on her knees. She didn't want to let on just how winded she was, but it was impossible to hide. She stole a glance at Indie and groaned to herself. He was breathing was slow and steady. Swallowing hard, the priest stood tall and wiped her sleeve across her sweaty brow.

"There's another camp nearby," Indie whispered, sniffing the air. "I smell smoke." He motioned with his head in the direction of the scent. He slipped an arrow from the quiver and nocked it. As quiet as a shadow, the young man slipped between the trees.

"Lump," Kit whispered. "Stay here with the pups." The big dog stopped panting for a moment, licked his chops, and resumed his heavy breathing. The two wolves appeared to be just as tired as their larger counterpart. "I'll come back for you."

And with that, Kit stepped into the woods, sniffing the air for the scent of wood smoke. She smelled nothing but pine trees. It was as though the man's senses were supernatural. He could see what she couldn't see, smell what she couldn't smell. She hoped he could teach her to do what he did, something Brother Rime had never been able to accomplish.

Stepping through a bush that had remarkably long thorns, Kit found Indie crouched behind the trunk of an ancient oak. He motioned for her to move forward, pressing a finger to his lips.

"Outside of the fire, the camp appears deserted," he whispered. "I can hear some wolf pups crying, but there is no sign of any hunters. They might be inside their tents though. I count at least twenty, along with a large pavilion."

With slow, careful steps, Kit stalked forward, doing her best to remain silent. She peered past Indie to the clearing beyond.

This was a much larger camp. There were tents that Kit presumed to be living quarters, but there were also wooden structures and something that she could only assume was a tanning apparatus, with multiple hides stretched out on it.

"You go left and I'll go right," Indie said, slipping out from behind the tree. With an arrow nocked and ready, he glided from his place of cover and slunk into the camp. Carefully trying to mimic the man's movements, Kit crept out. Beneath her foot, a large stick snapped, setting off a cacophony of yips and high-pitched whines.

Indie gave Kit a wide-eyed glare. She mouthed "sorry" in response and continued into the camp.

The pups' cries were relentless, getting louder by the second. Moments later, Lump and Runt came barreling into the camp, the large female pup hot on their heels. The group sped through the middle of the compound, presumably heading to where the cries were coming from.

With a stealthy entrance now out of the question, Kit threw caution to the wind and followed the trio into the camp, running headlong into whatever trouble there might be.

Chapter Forty-Four

Instinct and Courage

The young priest raced across the camp, finding the remaining pups in a single makeshift cage. The bars were made of green branches and twine. The supple nature of the wood made it remarkably hard to break into. A large lock and thick chain held the door closed. Kit considered smashing it with her hammer, but the sound would surely alert anybody nearby of her activities. While Lump and the pups gnawed on the wood, Kit dropped her shield and used her dagger to saw at the fibrous wood and ropes holding the cage together. She was making progress, but it was much slower than she'd have liked.

The rhythmic stamping of approaching boots warned Kit that her time was nearly up. There was no way she was going to get the cage opened before the hunters returned. She looked over her shoulder, wondering where Indie was.

"Quiet now," she whispered to the pups. "Be still."

She may as well have told the rain to stop falling. As the footfalls came closer, their incessant noise only became louder and more frantic. Lump's actions were becoming frantic as he continued chewing and clawing at the bars.

Kit did her best to quiet the canines, but it was hopeless.

"Check the cage," someone said. "Something's wrong."

While Lump continued working his way through the wooden bars, Runt and his sister bolted towards the voice. The stopped some ten paces from where Kit was and put on their best display of snarling and growling. It was, unfortunately, cuter than it was threatening.

With no other options, Kit picked up her shield, readied herself for combat, and stepped into the open. One of the hunters, a tall, reedy man with filthy brown hair, had a wolf carcass slung over his shoulder. Bile rose in the priest's throat when he tossed the body onto the ground like it was a piece of garbage. Three more hunters joined him. The sight of the two pups seemed to confuse them.

"What have we here?" the willowy man said with a laugh. He pointed at the two snarling pups and shook his head. "Grab them, you idiots. I'll take care of the stupid girl."

Kit quickly glanced around, wondering where Indie was, desperately hoping he had not been captured or killed already. She grimaced as two more hunters stepped from the woods, joining the reedy looking man.

"Throw down your weapons and surrender," Kit shouted. If Indie was nearby, she wanted him to know that there were others here. Despite her desire to rend these men limb from limb, the girl's legs wobbled beneath her.

"Have courage," the wolf spirit said, the voice offering his support. "I am with you and we will prevail."

"Who wants to die first?" Kit said, boldly stepping forward. She raised her chin in defiance, eliciting laughs from her would-be attackers. "Come, gentlemen. I don't have all day."

Kit considered the battle spells she had learned at the temple. Her frost attack would most likely be useless. Her healing spell wasn't right for the situation either. "Titan, give me speed," she whispered. The familiar rush of warmth that came with the spell coursed through her muscles.

One of the new arrivals drew a deep-bellied sword from his belt and stepped forward. He barely made it two steps before an arrow appeared in his chest. Crimson bloomed from the wound. The man took another step forward before his legs gave out and he dropped face first onto the ground.

Kit renewed her grip on her battle hammer and bolted forward, running headlong for the tall, reedy man.

A second arrow whizzed past the girl, striking another of the new arrivals in the face, sending him toppling backwards. Behind the man were more hunters, at least five, likely more. Kit didn't have time to count.

The reedy man screeched out commands, ordering the new arrivals to find the archer and kill the girl. With her attention split, Kit's progress faltered, unsure of what to do next. Lump made the decision for her, rushing into the midst of the new arrivals.

Hoisting her shield high, Kit sprinted forward, ready to join her stalwart companion. She surveyed the hunters, choosing the largest of them as her target. She was, a large, beefy woman, wearing a full breast plate and steel gauntlets. At the sight of the girl, the bear-sized woman charged forward. She was wielding a long, blood-covered, spiked club. She clapped her open hand against her breastplate, a tactic often used to frighten an opponent before the melee started.

Normally, Kit would have taken a passive approach to her attack, but the wolf spirit's unbridled rage exploded within her, driving the priest into a frenzy.

"My strength is your strength," said the voice in her head.

Just as the enormous woman raised her club, Kit stepped to the side and took a full cross-swing with her hammer. It hit the hunter flush in the chest, crushing the woman's light plate armor into her ribs. She let out a gasp of pain before crashing to the ground, her fingers ripping at her armor that was likely crushing her lungs.

The two hunters behind the woman kept their distance and nocked arrows to their longbows. Together, they loosed their arrows, their attacks barely missing. One grazed Kit's forearm. Blood pooled where it nicked her, but it was hardly even a scratch.

Not wanting the archers to get off another shot, Kit quickly closed the gap, engaging them both simultaneously. The two hunters dropped their bows and drew their swords.

In the brief moment between heartbeats, Kit flashed back to her time at the Temple when she learned how to fight against multiple foes at once.

"When the numbers are stacked against you," Sister Gale would say, "it's important that you keep track of every opponent. When they are behind you, you

cannot see them. You must listen for them. You must feel them. Strike when you can. Defend when you must!" A smile tugged at Kit's lips, her body instinctively knowing how to deal with this situation.

⤜⟡⤛

As the priest darted between the pair of foes, she feigned an attack against one, pulling the second off balance. She brought her hammer around for an underhand swing, catching him neatly on the chin. As the hammer arced upward, she quickly pivoted around and brought the hammer down on the second opponent in an overhead swing, catching her just beside her shoulder. The woman squealed in agony upon impact. The hammer-blow likely shattered her collarbone, possibly doing additional internal damage as well. With a spin, Kit used her shield's iron edge to cave in the woman's face, instantly ending her wails.

The priest held her hammer high, searching for her next target. There were at least five hunters dead on the ground, arrows protruding from their lifeless bodies. Lump had another by the throat while the pups ripped at the man's hands and arms. It was then she spotted Indie, fighting off two hunters with his broadsword.

Fear gripped the girl's chest, worried the young man was out of his depth. But, even in combat, he moved gracefully, dodging one attack while parrying another. Kit stood transfixed, gawking as Indie slid his blade into the larger hunter's throat while ducking the swing of the other.

A fireball sizzled past Kit's head, its intense heat drawing her attention back into the battle. The last of the hunters, the tall, willowy man, was standing off away from the mayhem, preparing to cast another spell.

Everything went into slow motion as the man's hands worked their way through an intricate pattern of movements and poses. He snapped his palms outward and released a ball of fire that crackled and tumbled through the air. Kit threw up her shield at the last moment. The fireball exploded in a brilliant burst of oranges and reds. The light of the explosion blinded her while the impact knocked the girl off her feet.

With a shake of her head, Kit picked herself up off the ground. She looked up just in time to see a stubby arrow sailing for her. She threw up her shield hoping to fend off the bolt.

There was a sharp crack as the arrow struck her shield, followed immediately by a white-hot pain in her arm. The bolt pierced through the wood, embedding itself deeply into her forearm.

Gutting through it, Kit raced for the willowy man, running headlong as he prepared to shoot her again. He was wielding a strange bow, unlike anything the priest had ever seen before. Fearing her shield could not protect her, Kit threw her hammer, hoping to disrupt his actions.

Although her weapon missed the mark entirely, it had the desired effect. The man had ducked down to avoid the hammer, which bought Kit just enough time to jump at him, preventing him from getting off a second shot.

The two tumbled on the ground for a while before Kit finally gained the upper hand. With the man on his back, she straddled his chest. She pulled back her shield, ready to send him to the Great Cycle.

The man's resolve melted. His lower lip quivered. With his eyes wide, he shook his head violently.

"Mercy!" he begged. "Please, don't kill me!"

The voice of the spirit in Kit's ears cried out. "Kill him. He does not deserve mercy." Before she even realized what she was doing, the priest slammed her shield into his throat.

With a grimace, Kit stood over the broken body of the spell caster. "You showed no mercy. You received no mercy." She was practically spitting out the words, but the willowy man had already joined the Great Cycle.

"I think we got them all," Indie said, startling the battle-worn girl. "Are you hurt?"

Kit shook her head. "No. Not at all." The young man motioned to her shield and the stream of blood pouring off down her arm.

"I think you are," he said. "That's going to start hurting very soon. A lot."

The priest raised an eyebrow as she stared down at her arm, and the stubby bolt tip sticking out of it. Fortunately, it was a smooth iron tip, designed for penetrating. She'd be able to pull it out, but as Indie said, it was going to hurt. A lot.

"Hold the shield," she said, "while I undo the straps. When I'm done, pull it straight back."

Indie nodded and waited for Kit's signal. As she finished unfastening the last buckle, she whispered a prayer of healing. As the familiar yellow aura appeared on her hands, the priest nodded to Indie, telling him to pull the bolt from her arm.

Pain exploded as the arrow was extracted. Kit quickly put her hand over the now-gushing wound, the bright yellow aura immediately engulfing her arm. Despite the instant relief the spell offered, the priest stumbled forward. Indie's powerful embrace ensconced the girl, offering her comfort and support while her spell mended her injury.

"Thank you," Kit said, her face pressed against the young man's chest. "I'll be ready to continue in just a moment. We're not done. Based on the size of this camp, there are more. A lot more."

FROM THE BEYOND

After a quick search, Indie pointed out several well-worn paths that led away from the camp. Whichever they chose, it would be easy to follow. The hunters were making no effort to conceal themselves. As they made ready for departure, Lump and the pups were sitting and staring at nothing. They appeared to be listening carefully to something. Then, in unison, they jumped to their feet and moved in behind Kit, barking and yipping.

"I know," Kit said with a laugh. "You're all coming!"

Indie quickly checked his gear before heading off. He grabbed as many arrows as he could stuff into his quiver before deciding to choose the path that ran north. While Indie carefully followed the path, the pack of wolf-pups clambered over one another, trying to take the lead. All except for Lump and Runt who were running easily at Kit's side.

The group ran through dense forests, thick underbrush, and the occasional clearing. Kit might have even enjoyed the scenery if it weren't for the constant voice of the wolf spirit in her head, urging her to run faster. Ever since they freed the pups, he seemed more agitated, more insistent that *the murderers be dealt with*.

After an hour or so, Indie came to a halt, signaling the others to hush. Kit nodded and took a knee, her chest heaving from the exertion. As a group, the pups all laid down, looking impatient, waiting for their den-mother to give them direction.

"I wonder how the others are making out?" said a voice coming from behind a small outcropping of stone and bush.

"Don't know. Don't care," replied another voice. "We got our kill here, so da boss ain't gonna have no grief wit us." The two laughed like they hadn't a care in the world. "Not good to have da boss mad at ya. Better ta be a dead wolf den ta have da boss mad at ya." That last comment made them laugh all the harder.

With Lump and the pups all lying in the grass, Indie waved at Kit to follow him, taking the opportunity to move in closer. He motioned that they should split up and approach the hunters from either side of the hillock.

The two thugs were making so much noise that sneaking up on them would be simple. Kit figured she could probably stroll right up to them before they would even notice her. Still, the little priest moved as quietly as she could to try to improve her chances.

As she came out from behind one of the larger bushes, one of the two hunters caught sight of her. He reached out to grab the spear he had laying beside him, but as he did, Kit brought her hammer down on his hand, crushing it against the boulder he was sitting on. The laughter from the second hunter came to an abrupt halt at the sound of his cohort's pain-fueled shrieks. The man managed to get his longbow picked up, but before he could nock an arrow, Indie ran him through with his short sword.

Cradling his ruined hand, the remaining hunter continued to cry out. In an act of desperation, he reached for his spear, only to receive a punch in the face for his efforts. The man was already missing a good number of teeth before Kit struck him. Now, he was missing a few more.

The hunter wailed and moaned as blood poured out from his ruined mouth. Indie stepped forward, ready to finish him off.

"Not yet," Kit said, glaring at Indie. The young man's face was twisted in rage, his eyes wide and crazed. "I want to talk to him first."

Indie pressed the tip of his sword against the man's chest. Both of them were breathing heavily and Kit feared the hunter would be dead if he so much as wiggled.

"Answer my questions and you'll live," Kit said. "Otherwise, my friend here is going to send you to the Great Cycle."

The man was babbling incoherently as Kit snatched up a length of rope from the hunter's supplies. He offered no resistance as she bound him to a tree. As the girl tightened the knots, he continued to babble, spraying blood from his mouth with each incomprehensible word. Once fully secured, she slapped him hard across the face to bring him to his senses, or because she simply wanted to.

The hunter's gaze flicked between Indie and Kit. He struggled momentarily against his bonds. He stopped shortly after, and a grimace spread across his face.

"Hand still hurts, eh?" Indie said to him. "It's going to get much worse if you don't answer the lady's questions."

The hunter slowly nodded, acknowledging his understanding.

"Okay then. Who's in charge of this operation?" Kit asked, still managing to keep her voice smooth and even.

"Da boss," he replied with a bit of a shrug. Even though his life was in mortal peril, the fool answered the question like Kit was some sort of moron.

"Who's your boss?" she asked slowly, her blood already boiling. Kit did her best to control her temper, but at that moment she wanted to ram the heel of her boot into his ugly, disgusting face.

"Him da guy that tells me what to do," he said. "Everybody knows dats what da boss do."

"Titan's snowballs! You can't possibly be that thick," she bellowed at him. "What is the name of your boss?"

"Never! I never tell ya dat." His voice was weak, but he tried to get his point across nonetheless. "Dere ain't nuttin you can say or do dat will make me to tell ya anyting." The man's eyes flitted to Kit's left.

Kit stole a quick glance, finding Lump and the pups coming around the corner. Behind the pups were three gray wolves. The largest of the three slowly moved forward, its growl menacing beyond belief. It padded up beside the priest, but its attention was locked on the hunter.

She didn't know why, but Kit didn't fear the wolves. She looked over at Indie, who did not appear quite so comfortable. Only when Lump and the pups moved in beside him, did the young man noticeably relax. The girl turned back to her prisoner and gave him a feral grin.

"It seems they want to help convince you to answer my questions. Did you know that these wolves can feed on you for days, keeping you alive the entire time? With or without your help, I will find whoever is in charge. Speak up and save yourself."

As Kit turned to leave, the hunter whimpered softly, pathetically.

"Please, don't let dem eats me. I'll tell you whatever you want." The hunter's eyes lit up, and he gave Kit a bloody toothless smile. "Da boss' name is Jaycob, but we ha' ta call him Boss."

Kit took another step away and the three wolves moved in closer. She turned back, giving the man one last chance.

"Da boss, Jaycob dat is, said we to meet up wit him at Two Forks. Weeze about to go there when you show'd up."

Kit looked to Indie, wordlessly asking if he knew where this place was. He shrugged and shook.

"We has a map," the prisoner said, his voice panicked. "In dat knapsack over der."

Indie strolled over and pulled out the bag's contents, stopping when he came upon a tattered parchment. He held it up, showing a crude map of the area.

The priest moved closer to the hunter and spoke very slowly. "I'm going to release you from your bonds so that you can show me where to go. If you try to run, the wolves will eat you. After you've shown me where this Two Forks is on the map, I will tie you back up. If you tell me true, I will come back and release you. If you lie to me, the wolves will eat you."

The hunter nodded weakly. He may not have liked it, but he understood that he had little choice in the matter.

As Kit untied his bonds, the terror in the hunter's eyes said that he wanted to run, but he managed enough courage to hold his ground. He looked over the map and pointed out where the camp was located. Each time the man touched the parchment, he left a bloody fingerprint on it.

"Thank you," Kit said. "I'm going to tie you up again, and like I said, I'll come back and release you if you have told me true." The largest of the wolves pulled back his lips in a visceral snarl.

"Dey's gonna eats me," the man said, his face devoid of color. "You lies ta me. I'll tell you true, but you lies." Before Kit could stop him, the man bolted, screaming incoherently. He hadn't made twenty paces when the wolves descended upon him. Claw and fang brought a quick end to the man's life, a fate that was likely better than he deserved.

Shaking off the effects of the gruesome attack, Kit called Lump and the pups over to her, checking to make sure they were safe and whole.

"There isn't much daylight left," Indie said. "I estimate Two Forks is at least an hour from here."

Kit shook her head. She didn't want to wait. The girl was weary all the way down to her bones, but she couldn't rest. Not now. Not when the end was so near.

"I'm going. You can stay with Lump and the pups if you want, but I refuse to give these monsters a chance to get away. I will deliver justice on them this day, one way or another."

With a groan, Indie ran his hand over his face. He blew out a long breath and chuckled. "I'm coming. I'm not going to abandon you just because I'm tired."

"Thank you," Kit said, inclining her head. "It means a lot to me." She was just about to start off when the disembodied voice again made itself present.

"Lay the fallen upon the boulder and call unto Fenrir."

"Who said that?" Indie asked, spinning about. He held his short sword in front of himself, ready to defend against the voice.

"It's a long story," Kit said, motioning to the carcass of the wolf the hunters had killed. The priest didn't understand, but the spirit's words were compelling. Doing as instructed, the small priest picked up the dead animal and gently placed it upon the largest of the boulders. As she tried to imagine how she might go about calling Fenrir, an unknown voice, something sweet and gentle like the wind whispering through the trees, floated on the breeze.

"You who would help my children, I am here for you. I will aid you in your quest to right the wrongs that have been done to those who only seek harmony in this world."

And with that, the dead wolf came to life. Its eyes were wide with panic. It did not understand what was happening. The unknown voice spoke yet again. "Be calm, my child, for I am with you. Call out to the world. Let your presence be known."

The wolf slowly calmed and closed its eyes. Tilting its head back, the resurrected creature let out the most mournful howl Kit had ever heard. The loneliness and despair in its song sent shivers down her spine. After the wolf finished, it leapt down from the boulder and laid peacefully on the ground, once again rejoining the Great Cycle.

"They come!" There was a new excitement in the voice of the spirit. "Make ready, for battle is at hand!"

Chapter Forty-Six

Jaycob and the Wolves

Five hunters wielding longbows came crashing through the bushes. They had already nocked their arrows, releasing them as they cleared the woods. Four of the arrows flew wide of the mark. The fifth, Kit deflected with her shield. The three wolves that had finished off the prisoner came bounding past her, each of them taking a different archer.

"Stay with the pups," Kit said to Lump just before sprinting across the grass. Indie was already a dozen or more paces in front of her. A second arrow whizzed past, narrowly missing him.

Raising her shield high, the priest bellowed, "Aura of Healing!" The words were part prayer, part battle cry. A deep green aura burst forth, emanating out to encompass any cohorts who were nearby. Indie was already engaged by the time she moved into the melee. The remaining two archers had both drawn longswords. Indie cried out when his left arm was sliced open. The healing aura immediately took effect, the wound slowly starting to mend itself.

Kit quickly ran headlong at the hunter fighting Indie, trying to buy him some time to recover. The priest struck the woman's knees with her hammer, shattering bones on impact. Kit reacted just in time to catch the second hunter's overhand strike with her shield, deflecting the man's sword, knocking him off balance. A quick flick of her wrist, Kit brought her hammer crunching into his ribcage, dropping the man to the ground, wheezing.

"Are you okay?" Kit asked Indie as he held his hand over his wounded arm, blood seeping through his fingers.

"We're not done," Indie said, motioning to a new group of hunters who had just emerged from the trees. He quickly checked the wound on his arm. "It's stopped bleeding already," he added before bolting off to engage the new arrivals. There were too many enemies to count. The five hunters they originally faced had significantly grown in number.

A wolf's pained yelp drew Kit's attention back to the fight. It had taken a deep slash across its neck. Indie had already dispatched the man he had engaged with and was running headlong at the group fighting the wolves. For a man who professed to hate the wolves, he wasn't showing it now.

It didn't look like the two hunters Kit had been fighting were going to get up anytime soon, so she abandoned them and raced towards Indie and the wolves. As soon as she neared, her healing aura engulfed the injured animal. Its wound immediately stopped bleeding, but it was still in rough shape.

From out of nowhere, an unseen attacker rained blows down on Kit. With her shield held high, she was able to keep him at bay, but his attacks were vicious and relentless. With each strike, Kit's ability to hold him off dwindled. Her defenses were about to fully fail when Lump jumped into the fray. He grabbed the hunter by his sword arm and dragged him off Kit. With a couple of quick shakes of his head, the wolfdog ripped through the hunter's muscles and tendons. The man wailed out in agony before dropping to the ground.

While Lump held fast, a wolf joined in, descending upon the man. It wrapped its great jaws around his windpipe and clamped its mouth shut. The man's cries were abruptly cut short.

As quickly as the battle started, it came to a bloody end. All three of the wolves had taken serious damage during the battle, but with Kit's healing aura in full effect, none of their wounds appeared to be life-threatening.

"Thank you," Kit said as she inclined her head to wolves. The words didn't fully convey the deep sense of gratitude she was feeling at that moment. "You, too, Indie." She gave the blood-soaked man a crooked smile. "I couldn't have done this without you."

Runt and the rest of the wolf-pups came bounding through the bushes. They were yipping and howling and carrying on in true puppy fashion. After spending some time in celebration, the pups visited the wolves that were busy licking their wounds. All except for Runt, who was now sitting at Kit's feet, staring up at her. The young priest's heart swelled.

"You did well today, little wolf. You did very well."

He gave her boot a small nip before bounding off to inspect the bodies of the fallen hunters. Moments later, he returned dragging a bandolier of potion bottles, his tail wagging furiously. A quick examination of the contents revealed four healing potions, a potion of frost defense and another potion that Kit could not identify. She ran over to the injured wolves and poured the potions directly over their wounds. As expected, the wounds immediately began to knit together, leaving no sign that there was ever any damage at all.

One by one, the wolves jumped to their feet. They raised their hackles and growled at the forest.

"Stay!" Kit ordered them, but they weren't paying any attention to her. They all fanned out, their gazes never leaving the edge of the woods.

Seven men strode out through the trees, shouting obscenities, waving their weapons over their heads.

Kit could only assume they were coming to the aid of their fallen cohorts. With her healing aura still in full effect, she walked purposefully in their direction. She slowed her advance when five more hunters emerged from the trees, a dozen paces away.

Sweet Titan, the odds are getting worse by the second.

Kit groaned as another group of hunters emerged from the forest. There were well over two dozen of them. At their lead was a man who had to be at least seven feet tall. His head was clean-shaven, covered in tribal markings. He was so large, and so heavily muscled, that he had to be part Gigas.

"We can't win," Indie whispered. "There are too many."

Lump and Runt strode in beside Kit, their gazed locked on the enemy ahead. To them, the odds didn't matter. They would fight with their last breath.

"You must be Jaycob!" Kit called out, trying not to let her fear show. "You saved me a lot of trouble showing up like this. Now I don't have to hunt you down."

The group of hunters continued to close in from multiple directions. The wolves continued to spread out, trying to block their progress.

"You can't be the mythical warrior my men have been blathering on about. You're barely old enough to breed!"

Kit cringed at the crass manner in which Jaycob was speaking to her. She tightened her grip on her hammer as she walked out to meet him. She was about to break into a run and charge when Runt sat down, threw back his head, and howled. The noise that came from the small pup was not sadness or fear, it was a call to action.

Immediately, Lump, the wolf-pups, and the three gray wolves joined in.

The priest's heart swelled.

"It's a shame I'm going to have to kill you," Jaycob called out again, seemingly confused by the wolves' behavior. "You have spirit. I like that in a person." The monstrous man motioned this cohorts forward. "Kill the wolves and gather the pups. Do what you will with the boy, but the girl is mine." He drew thumb across his throat in a revolting display, his eyes gleaming with sadistic delight. "I'm going to relish her screams, like honey drizzled over fried bread."

⚜

"Spread out," Kit said. "Don't let them flank us."

The huge man broke into a run, covering ground at a phenomenal pace. There was a comfort and ease to his strides that said he was an experienced fighter. He had absolutely no fear of the enemy standing before him. About twenty paces away, Jaycob's charge came to an abrupt halt. He practically skidded across the grass as he dug his heels into the ground.

The man's eyes were wide as his head scanned left and right. Kit took a quick peek behind her to find that there were twenty or more wolves at her back. Several of them were dire wolves. She turned back when she heard the screams of the other hunters. Emerging from the woods behind them were another forty or more wolves. Many of them were also dire wolves.

The wolves encircled the hunters, forcing them into a tight group. Several tried shooting arrows at the encroaching animals, but they all sailed harmlessly over their heads. With fear and adrenaline pumping, it was impossible for them to calm their nerves enough to be effective with their long-range weapons.

"It's not a good day to be a hunter." Kit called out to Jaycob. "I can try to call them off, but I don't think they'll listen."

Several of the hunters bolted. They ran in multiple directions, bawling for mercy. Wolves loped along side of them before cutting their legs out from underneath them. Cries of terror and pain issued out from the tall grasses. They didn't last long. The wolves who brought them down returned. Their muzzles thick with the blood of the fallen.

Jaycob tossed his weapons on the ground. "Drop your weapons! Everyone, drop your weapons!"

As though they were on fire, the entire group of hunters threw their weapons to the ground. In doing so, they might as well have rung a dinner-bell. In a blink, the wolves descended upon them, ending their miserable lives in mere seconds. Kit would have liked the honor of bringing justice to Jaycob personally, but she recognized that this was the wolves' fight to win.

Despite the hunters being dead, the wolves continued the carnage for several more minutes. They moved from body to body, ensuring there were no survivors. The way some of the wolves eviscerated the corpses, Kit assumed that these animals belonged to the families of the wolves the hunters had taken.

The priest felt no sorrow for the fallen. They chose the life they were leading. They got what they deserved. The visceral joy of the wolf spirit marked his agreement.

As the last of the wolves returned to Kit, Fenrir appeared in the form of a great white wolf, a black dire wolf at her side. Just like the wolf Kit had encountered in the lair, his fur was black as ebony, save for the white star on his forehead. Fenrir rested her forehead against his.

"Peace unto you, my child. Your suffering was not in vain. Come to me now so that you may know life everlasting."

A sudden warmth filled Kit's body. The voice of the wolf that had been urging her on, spoke to her again.

"Warrior of the North, you seek justice and deliver retribution. My thanks are forever with you, as will I be. My strength is your strength, my heart is your heart. These hunters were only the tip of the spear. Find whoever it is that controls the hunters. They are the true menace that must be dealt with. We do not know who they are, or what purpose they have, but we trust that you will bring their actions to an end."

The wolves gathered around, forming a loose circle around Kit, Indie, and Lump. Each one bowed its head before the wolf god and the spirit manifestation. All except for the pups, who were bouncing around, running in and out of the legs of the larger wolves. One of the wolves gave a pup a light nip, immediately settling it down. The other pups followed suit. All except Runt, who bolted to Kit's side, practically wrapping himself around her leg.

Kit took a knee beside the small dire wolf and scratched the fur on his neck.

"You cannot stay with me, little friend," she said as her eyes welled up with tears. "This is *your* family. You need to stay with them." At her words, the pup moved closer, practically climbing into Kit's arms. A large female dire wolf moved up beside the pup, urging him to return to the pack. Reluctantly, the pup left Kit's side and joined his siblings.

At that moment, a silence fell over the entire pack. They were all staring at Kit with their soulful jade-green eyes. In turn, they each inclined their head to her in thanks. One by one, they turned and disappeared back into the forest. The runt pup added a quick spin before he, too, ran off after the rest of them.

"I love you!" Kit yelled, barely able to choke out the words, instantly regretting not keeping Runt with her. Sweet Titan, how her chest hurt. She hadn't realized just how quickly the young pup had filled her heart. "Be safe."

"He's with his own," Indie said, wrapping his arm around her. "With his own kind."

"Home is where you're loved," Kit said, not looking at the young man. "Being with your own kind isn't important. Not in the slightest."

With that, the visage of the wolf and Fenrir vanished. A sense of satisfaction and wellbeing filled Kit's soul, but she knew there was more she must do. The memory of the old woman she met in the woods popped into her mind. She was not sure why, but she was certain that it was time to go see her again.

"I have something to do. Someone to see. I won't be long if you want to wait."

"We're coming with you," Indie said. "I'm staying with you until we're back in Aarall."

Kit nodded and turned north. She was about to begin her journey when her feet became entangled, causing her to flop onto her face in a most ungraceful manner. As she tried to right herself, she was tackled back onto the ground as wet, warm kisses covered every inch of her skin.

"Runt!" she cried out in delight. The young dire wolf bounced around, yipping with joy. "I can't believe you came back." She picked him up and buried her face into his silky-soft fur. "I'm so glad you came back." She couldn't wipe the tears fast enough from her face.

With a broad smile, she dropped him to the ground. "Come on, there is someone I want you to meet, someone I want you all to meet." As though he already knew where they were headed, Runt loped off towards the forest, Lump hot on his heels.

CHAPTER FORTY-SEVEN

RETURN TO THE HUT IN THE WOODS

The journey back to the hut in the woods went without incident. Lump and Runt played constantly, chasing anything that moved, especially each other. They often wandered off, their noses pressed firmly to the ground, but the pair never ventured too far.

Indie had been quiet, contemplative. In contrast, Kit felt better than she ever had. A deep sense of well being had calmed her mind and nurtured her soul. The sun was warm, and the sky was blue. A gentle breeze brushed against her face, causing her unruly tangle of black hair to sway behind her. The fields were full of wild blossoms, their fragrance carrying her on a carefree cloud of bliss. Her heart soared.

This must be what it feels like to fly.

Kit paused as she stepped from a dense stand of pines. They were at the edge of a small clearing. The small hut she had visited earlier was there once again. In front of it, the great white wolf sat as though she had been awaiting her arrival. The majestic creature bowed her head in greeting and entered the hut.

"This is the place I was telling you about," Kit said. "The hut with the old woman."

"Go," Indie said. "I'll wait here with the boys." The small priest grabbed the young man by the sleeve and dragged him forward.

"You'll do no such thing. You're all coming with me. I'm sure the woman will be happy to meet all of you."

She continued dragging Indie forward while the boys raced on ahead. They both waited impatiently by the entrance, Runt running around in tight circles, unable to contain himself.

"Behave yourself," Kit gently said to Runt as she pushed open the door. The small wolf burst past, disappearing within.

Shaking her head, Kit followed the wolf into the small mud and grass building. Like her first visit, the hut smelled of wood, earth, and wildflowers. As expected, she found the old woman. She inclined her head slightly and gave Kit a broad, toothy smile. Runt was sitting at her feet, gazing adoringly at the old Berrat.

"Welcome, friends of the wilds," she grinned. The small dire wolf pounced at the woman, desperately vying for her affection. "And greetings to you, too, Runt!" She bent down and rubbed the pup briskly behind the ear.

Kit wondered how the old woman knew the name she had given him. Her curiosity piqued further when the old Berrat woman called Lump over to her, by name. After giving the boys a heartfelt greeting, the woman turned her attention to Kit and Indie.

"Your acts of selflessness were observed and noted. You risked your lives to protect wild creatures because, in your heart, you knew it was the right thing to do." The old woman shuffled across the room, which seemed to be much larger than it appeared from the outside. She reached out with thin, bony arms and picked up a package that was wrapped in large leaves and bound with a fine rope. "This is for you. As you protected the forest creatures, so too will this gift protect you."

Heat rose in Kit's cheeks as she graciously accepted the package. She stole a glance at Indie. His expression was inscrutable.

"I have something for you, too, Indigo Willowbrook." The tiny woman looked up at the young man who was two feet taller than she was. She smiled up at him and tutted. "But you're going to need to take a knee before me if you are to receive my gift."

When the young man took a step back, Kit glared at him. The inscrutable expression suddenly shifted to one of reluctant acceptance. The young man lowered his eyes and knelt before the old woman.

"You carry a great weight, a burden that threatens to drag you into the abyss." The Berrat placed her hand on Indie's forehead and traced a pattern on his skin with her thumb. Tears welled up at the corners of his eyes before finally spilling down his cheeks. "The sadness you feel for the passing of your family, this you will carry with you forever. Your love for them was deep and never-ending. But the guilt that consumes you, it is misplaced. I free you of this yoke."

Everything stilled for several long minutes. Finally, Indie stood and wiped the tears from his face.

"Thank you," he said, inclining his head. "But I am undeserving of such a gift. Please, take it back. I understand what you tried to do, but I need what you took from me. It serves as a reminder of who I was and who I want to become."

"As you wish," the old Berrat said. She pursed her lips and gave a small nod of approval. "You surprise me, young Indigo. That isn't something that has happened to me in a very long time." A shadow crossed over Indie's face and his body slumped. He took a shuddering breath before standing tall. "You have the heart of a dragon, young man. And that is a compliment I don't give lightly."

Kit stepped beside Indie and leaned into him. "I've known that all along," she whispered.

"And for you, my courageous Lump, what gift shall I bestow upon you for having saved the wolves?" The old woman's eyes were alight with joy as she spoke to the golden retriever wolfdog. Lump, immediately dipped into a play-bow and barked sharply three times. The Berrat's head snapped back in surprise. "As you wish."

The old woman turned her attention back to the dire wolf pup, calling him to stand in front of her. "As for you, Runt," she said, shaking her head as she took a knee beside him. "Your big friend is quite right. I cannot let you accompany our young hero. You are much too small for such adventures."

Kit's mouth fell open and unbidden tears immediately stung the corners of her eyes. What had Lump said to her? Was she planning on keeping the pup?

Kit knew deep down that this woman was good, and only had the wolf's best interests at heart, but she'd rather give up the priesthood if it meant not keeping the pup with her.

Runt whined, his head immediately turning to Kit.

"I have no intention of taking you from Kit," the old Berrat cooed, guiding the pup to look at her. "I only said you are much too small." The woman took the dire wolf's face in her hands and stared into his eyes. As she did, she blew gently over his face. The pup's body glittered and shone. In seconds, he transformed from a young pup into a fully grown dire wolf. His mottled black-gray coat fell away, leaving him jet black, save for a white star on his forehead. The old woman giggled, a sweet melodic laugh that filled the room with joy and wonder.

She stretched up as high as she could and patted the gigantic wolf on the top of his head. "Now you are ready to travel with our young hero!"

She turned her attention back to Kit. "I think he'd like it if you still called him Runt, but the name seems a bit misplaced, don't you think?" She then nodded toward the gift in Kit's hand, prompting her to open it.

As Kit unwrapped the gift, she found a fine set of armor made from the hide of the great black wolf. It was remarkably lightweight, undoubtedly the finest workmanship she had ever seen. The leather had been cured, making it extremely tough, yet still pliable. Kit pulled her gaze away from the gift to thank the woman, only to find that she was once again standing outside, in a clearing in the woods. The woman and the hut were both gone. A sweet, melodic voice whispered in her ear.

"You will be forever known as Wolf Friend."

"We should make camp here," Indie said with a wide yawn. "There is no way we'll make it back to my village without rest. And we're going to need some food. My stomach won't stop growling."

Kit rubbed her belly and nodded. "I don't think there is anyplace nearby to get any food. Besides, I have no coin. I didn't expect to be away from the Temple for so long." The girl's comment drew a snigger from the young man.

"If you can make a fire, I'll take the boys and find us some food." He patted his bow. "You can make a fire, can't you?"

The young priest pressed her lips into a thin line and gave the young man a curt nod, drawing another snigger from Indie. "I survived three nights atop Mount Ula," she said. "I'm sure I can manage to set up a camp in a nice, warm forest."

The man gave Kit a warm smile before gliding off into the woods, the boys hot on his heels. Not wanting to fail at setting up camp, she immediately set to work, gathering small twigs and branches. Before long, she had a cheery fire blazing. She had also gathered enough grasses to make bedding for the two of them. She made two piles near the flames, close enough that the bed of coals could keep them warm, but not so close that they could catch fire.

It felt like an eternity before Indie and the boys returned. Indie had two large rabbits slung over his shoulder and an annoyed expression plastered on his face.

"You had problems?" Kit asked. Both Lump and Runt had blood smeared across their muzzles.

"Runt needs to be taught how to hunt," he said, shaking his head. "I tracked a deer and a wild boar but before I could get a shot off, he scared them off. After I lost a second deer, I told them to get their own dinner – which they did. All I was able to get were these rabbits."

Runt trotted next to Indie, eyeing the carcasses slung over his shoulder.

"Don't even think of it. These are not for you."

It didn't take long for Indie to prepare and cook the rabbits. He had filled his pockets with herbs and berries which he turned into a mash to coat the meat. The end result rivaled Sister Miyuki's food. Although, Kit was so famished that a stick might have been tasty.

"Thank you," Indie said as he licked the last of the grease from his fingers. When Kit gave him a quizzical look the young man lowered his gaze. "For letting me come along. I needed this more than you'll ever know."

"It's I who should be thanking you," Kit said. "I don't think I could have done this without you. What you did here, it saved hundreds of wolves. You saved me, too."

Again, a shadow crossed the young man's face. He blew out a breath and shook his head. "We should get some sleep." And with that, he laid on his side, tucked his arm under his head, and closed his eyes.

"I gathered grass to sleep on," Kit said. "You don't need to sleep on the hard ground."

"Tell that to our companions," Indie said, a small smile pulling at the corner of his lips. "They've already claimed their spots."

The priest peered over to the beds she had made, finding Lump stretched out on one and Runt curled up on the other. She considered sending them away, but she didn't have the heart. Following Indie's lead, she curled herself into a small ball by the fire.

With the memory of the day's events playing in her mind, she drifted off into a fitful sleep.

Dreams took her back to when the black dire wolf had mauled Indie. She offered her life to save his. A beautiful, powerful voice had said, *"You would offer your life to save a stranger? I accept your offer!"* The voice was familiar, but she couldn't recall from where she had heard it. She also couldn't help but wonder what it meant.

Chapter Forty-Eight

The Reunion

As they crested over a grassy hill, the outskirts of Indie's village came into view. Kit ran her hands over her new armor, smoothing out non-existent wrinkles. She marveled at the workmanship. It was, quite literally, the most comfortable bit of clothing she'd ever worn.

The trip back had been uneventful, outside of the entertainment provided by Runt along the way. Though he was the size of an adult dire wolf, his behavior was anything but. On multiple occasions, small animals and buzzing insects sidetracked the oversized puppy. The colorful insects provided Runt with an endless supply of things to do on the last leg of their journey. Kit could have sworn they were tormenting him on purpose, flying just outside the reach of his snapping jaws.

But now, from her perch atop the hill, Kit watched down on the farmers working in their fields, going about their daily business, living their lives the best way they knew how. In the distance, on the road that led back to Aarall, a caravan of empty wagons was approaching the village. Kit assumed they were returning from having sold their wares in the city.

A commotion in the village drew Kit's attention. She could hear panicked cries as people were running about gathering up farm implements. One farmer was loading his children into a hay wagon, urging the driver to leave.

"What's going on?" Kit asked.

"Come on," Indie said, breaking into a run. "They're running for cover. Something's wrong."

While Indie sprinted ahead, Kit did her best to keep up, trying to see what was causing the ruckus.

Three farmers were running their way, two with pitchforks and one with a long sword. It was only then that it dawned on her that *Runt was* the source of the disturbance. The oversized puppy raced ahead, his hackles raised, and his teeth bared.

"Titan's snowballs! Runt! Get back here! They're not going to hurt us!" The dire wolf immediately stopped and waited until Kit moved in front of him. The farmers' threats died off somewhat as Indie tried to explain what was happening.

"Peace be with you!" Kit yelled to the farmers. "We have news to share with you!"

The farmers, with Indie at their side, slowly approached. The look on their faces shifted from fear and anger to confusion and wonder.

"This wolf is yours?" one of them shouted as he raised his pitchfork, placing its tines directly in Runt's face. "He obeys your commands?"

"As I already explained," Indie said, his words harsh.

The other farmers took up a similar stance. The one with the sword looked to have seen at least sixty years. His sword-hand was steady, but his eyes shifted about like he was ready to bolt at a moment's notice.

"Peace!" Kit said to them again. "You know me. I am Kit Standing Bear. I was sent by Captain Harding to help with your wolf problem." She turned to Indie. "Can you ask your friends to lower their weapons? It's making the boys nervous." As she said this, Runt turned his attention to Indie, showing him his ample set of enormous canines.

"Runt, lay down." Indie's order was part command, part request, but the dire wolf obeyed and laid down on the grass. Lump, on the other hand, moved in front of Kit, shielding her from the farmers. Completely ignoring the threat, Runt rolled onto his back and twisted and turned, all the while, his feet kicked playfully into the air.

"What's he doing?" one of the farmers questioned. "Is he okay?"

Kit rolled her eyes at Runt. "Yes, he's okay. He's saying he likes the smell of your land, and he wants it to stay with him." Runt paused his activities long enough to stare at Kit, his tongue lolling out the side of his mouth. Just as quickly, he went back to his antics.

The farmers all quickly lost interest in Kit, and her wolf, and prepared to return to their duties. In the distance the parents removed their children from the hay wagons, and people once again comfortably moved about.

"I need to go to Aarall and let Captain Harding know what's been going on," Kit said, absentmindedly. She was still watching the people going about their business. "Something's brewing. I don't know what it is, but we need to be ready for it."

Indie nodded, staring wistfully at his home. "If you're willing, I'd like to accompany you back to Aarall. Since my parents died, I don't have much keeping me here. The village elders will probably be able to find a family to look after my land while I'm away." His eyes teared up when he mentioned his farm, the loss of his parents, and his normal life. It was all still too fresh in his mind. Runt and Lump instinctively moved closer to him, offering him their comfort and strength.

"You're welcome to come to the city," Kit said. "But I'm going to need to return to the Temple. You can help me explain to Captain Harding what happened here though."

Indie's eyes suddenly brightened, and he dashed into the village, leaving Kit and the boys on their own. She shrugged her shoulders and followed the young man. Runt and Lump were both bounding at her side, excited at the prospect of heading toward the village.

The sight of trio running after Indie sparked another flurry of activity amongst the village community. Adults were quickly putting themselves between Kit and the children, and livestock were quickly herded into their pens. Runt's gaze turned to the animals.

"Leave it," Kit said in as stern a voice as she could muster. "They're not for you." Not wanting to cause any more commotion than she already had, Kit took a seat on a patch of thick, soft grass. The boys followed suit, laying close enough that Kit could pet them both. While she scratched Runt's back, he sniffed the air, his eyes still wide with excitement. It was then that Kit spotted several children racing toward her, with their parents hot on their heels yelling at them to stop. The children were squealing with anticipation. Their arms were outstretched, their little fingers convulsing rapidly while they squealed repeatedly, "Puppies!"

"You two behave yourselves," Kit scolded, long before the children even arrived. "They're too small for you to play with."

A parent managed to scoop up one of the children, but the other two maintained their distance and ran directly up to Runt. There was no fear in them at all. "Can we pet your dog?" the smaller one asked.

"Absolutely not!" yelled the parent who had one child already tucked up under her arm. "Stay away from that monster!" Unlike the children standing next to Runt, her eyes were wild with terror.

"Do as your elder tells you." The words were to the children, but they were also directed at the parents. Kit stood up and offered them her hand in friendship. "I am Kit Standing Bear, Priest of Titan. These big fellows are Lump and Runt." She couldn't help but smile when she said his name. The dire wolf's shoulder came up to Kit's chest, with his head being about the same height as hers. He easily weighed three times as much as her, if not more.

"Please, mommy!" pleaded the younger of the two children. The second followed, creating a chorus of pleas.

"I can assure you they are perfectly safe."

While Lump appeared happy enough to lie undisturbed in the grass, Runt pulled his eyes away from the children and turned towards the adults, adding his own pleas to theirs.

Before the parents had a chance to fully answer, the younger of the two children reached out her hand. "My name's Hilly. It's a pleasure to meet you, Mr. Runt!" Her voice was squeaky as she introduced herself. Runt lifted his paw, offering it for her to hold.

"Careful!" said the other parent. The woman had one hand clamped over her mouth and another over her heart. She was terrified, but she didn't want to startle Runt.

As though he sensed the adult's fears, Runt dropped to the ground and rolled on his back. He had that same wild look of joy in his eyes that Kit had seen so often from him. His tongue, again, lolled out of his mouth.

The children immediately descended on him, scratching his belly with frenzied jubilance. The child being held squealed and thrashed about in her mother's arms, obviously wanting to get in on the puppy-action.

As the children continued to interact with Runt, the adults were visibly beginning to relax. Kit moved to stand beside them, taking in the sight from their perspective. "The wolves harassing your village were sick. Somebody poisoned them," the words poured out of Kit's mouth like she was discussing the day's weather. "Healthy wolves don't pose a risk, so long as they're treated respectfully."

There was grumbling from the parents. They clearly doubted Kit's words.

"If I hadn't witnessed it with my own eyes, I would have never believed it." One mother's eyes remained glued to the children as she offered her hand in greeting. "Peace unto you, Kit Standing Bear."

The group had been exchanging pleasantries for several minutes when Indie came running up. He had a heavy rucksack slung over his shoulder. "I'm going with Sister Kit to the city," he said to one of the women. "I don't plan on coming back."

The women took Indie's hand and nodded. "We'll let Elder Chenoa know you're leaving. Your parents' land will be cared for in your absence. You can take your place as landholder when you decide to return."

Their words, and offering of assistance, clearly meant the world to Indie. He tilted his head in thanks. "Peace unto you, my family," and just as he had done several times in the past, Indie headed off, not waiting to see if Kit was following. The small priest shrugged her shoulders, and the villagers smiled in response. It seemed this was not uncommon to them either. Kit didn't need to ask the boys to follow. They were up and ready to go, but before he headed out, Runt quickly gave Hilly a lick across her face, causing the young girl to squeal with joy.

As Kit made her way back to Aarall, the dream she'd had continued to tug at her. *My life for his.* That was what she had offered and that was what someone had accepted. She was still alive, so whoever that mysterious woman was, she hadn't actually wanted to take Kit's life. So then, what did she want? She shook the thoughts from her head. Runt's antics, his nipping and jumping at Lump, gave Kit a welcome break from her concerns.

"What are you going to tell Captain Harding?" Indie asked, as he threw a stick for the boys to chase.

Kit could only shrug her shoulders. She had no idea what she was going to say. She would need to tell him of the hunters and the poisoned wolves, but she didn't think she would want to share her experience with the old woman in the hut. Then again, how was she going to explain the dire wolf that she had accompanying her? Her thoughts were coming at her faster than she could process them. There were too many unknowns.

"I'm not exactly sure what I'm going to tell the captain," she finally said in reply. "But I'm planning on telling him everything. If those hunters truly are just the tip of the spear, then we need to find out who's been wielding them."

CHAPTER FORTY-NINE

THE RETURN TO AARALL

Kit and Indie couldn't help but laugh while watching the antics of Runt, as the dire wolf chased anything and everything that caught his attention. He particularly seemed to enjoy chasing butterflies. Perhaps it was their bright colors, perhaps it was the haphazard way they flitted about, or perhaps it was because chasing them simply brought him joy.

Lump, on the other hand, was content to keep at Kit's side. He seemed to be feigning disinterest because every now and again, he'd check to make sure Runt didn't stray too far from the group.

As the outskirts of Aarall came into focus, a sinking feeling settled in Kit's stomach.

"I'm really worried that Runt is going to cause quite a stir when the people see him," Kit shared with Indie, just as the oversized pup came back to walk beside her. "Even though he's with us, they're going to react badly to him."

Runt's eyes seemed to indicate that he, too, was worried about how people might perceive him. Kit gave him a reassuring scratch behind his ear. His head was practically level with Kit's shoulders, causing her to laugh to herself. After all, Runt was larger than the average dire wolf, yet he was only a puppy – a puppy that was magically enhanced by the old woman in the hut. Kit had considered that the elder may have been the lesser deity, Fenrir, in Berrat form, but she never thought to ask her. Well, truth be told, she had thought about it, but she didn't have the courage to go through with it.

"Don't worry, Runt, I've got this covered," Kit said to him as she continued to scratch his head. "Just stay close and leave it to me to deal with."

From a distance, one could really see just how sprawling Aarall was. Its formidable, gray-green outer walls spread out so wide that it would take the better part of a day to walk around the city. Mount Toka, the tallest and most dangerous mountain in all Arnnor, reared up to the east. The giant ice statue of Titan, reaching thousands of feet into the sky, seemingly carved from the side of the great mountain, stared down at Aarall and the Temple of the Fist.

As they got closer, the riot of colors from the merchants' tents, spreading out on either side of the city's main gates, came into view. It was late afternoon and the marketplace outside the city walls was still doing brisk business. Kit was hoping that the crowds would have died down, allowing them to slip through the gates unnoticed, but that was not to be.

"Look at the big puppy!" The shrill cry of a young Berrat girl startled Kit out of her thoughts. Her long white braids were bouncing haphazardly as she raced toward them as fast as her little feet could carry her. Runt's ears perked up at the sound of her voice. He was practically begging to go see the little girl, but Kit sternly told him to stay. He gave a small whimper before sitting beside her.

Both Kit and Indie did their best to stop the child, but she slipped past them with ease. A moment later, she buried her light bronze face in Runt's chest. "Runt, I'm so happy to see you," she whispered into his thick black fur. She pulled herself away so that she could look at him more closely. "I think you're going to cause a panic if Kit brings you into the city." Lump, who was more than a little put out that he wasn't getting his fair share of loving, pushed his way past Runt and pressed himself against the small girl.

"What?" The child's words completely took Kit by surprise. "How do you know my wolf's name? How do you know *my* name?"

"I may be old," the child replied, her eyes dancing with mischief, "but I don't easily forget the names of people I love." And with that, the small girl wrapped her arms around Kit's waist and gave her a big hug. She pulled away and giggled uncontrollably, thoroughly enjoying the completely baffled look on Kit's face. The sound of the child's laughter was sweet and melodic.

The little girl gave Kit a quick wink as she nuzzled into Lump's ruff. "We've met before, in my house to the north." Runt, who refused to be pushed aside by Lump, quickly gave the girl's face an enthusiastic tongue-bath.

Still seeing that Kit did not know who she was, the child giggled wildly again. "I made the armor you're wearing. I changed Runt here so that he would be big enough to protect you."

"You? You're the old woman in the hut?" Kit blinked at her in disbelief, as nobody else knew how Kit obtained her armor or the fact that Runt was just a puppy.

"You know, people don't like to be called *old woman*," she said with a grin. "But I suppose I never did properly introduce myself. You may call me *Fenrir*."

While Lump and Runt continued to vie for the child's affection, Indie immediately fell to his knees and bowed his head. Kit, unsure of how to react, followed the young man's lead. "Again, you grace me with your presence. How can I be of service to you?"

"I am here to help you," Fenrir offered. "After you left, I was afraid of what might happen if you brought Runt into a city. I came to give you this." Fenrir held out a thick collar, made of black leather and a bright green metal of some sort. As Kit took the collar from her, Fenrir turned to Runt. "This collar is for you to wear. While you have it on, you will appear to be a popular domestic dog."

Runt quietly growled at the prospect of wearing the collar.

"Don't worry," Fenrir assured him. "Kit will always see you as you. As will any friends, as long as she permits it." Fenrir giggled wildly again. "Anybody who is Kit's enemy will also see you in your true form. That way, they'll know better than to mess with her, or you."

This appeared to satisfy Runt. He moved closer to Kit, holding out his head so she could put the collar on him. As the small priest fastened the buckle, Runt shimmered for a moment, but otherwise she saw no change in him. "So, what would he look like to anybody who didn't know he's a dire wolf?"

"He'll appear to be a very large golden retriever, much like Lump here." Fenrir giggled as she spoke. "I'm pretty sure everybody loves goldens, so he'll be welcome almost anywhere." No sooner did she finish, Runt pranced about, holding his head and tail high in the air.

Lump growled, appearing not to appreciate Runt's impersonation of him. Kit smiled and shook her head. "I wish I could see what he looks like as a golden."

No sooner did the words leave Kit's mouth, the dire wolf shimmered again, his wolf form shifting to that of a golden retriever.

"Sweet Titan!" Kit blurted out. "You could be Lump's twin brother!"

Fenrir giggled and danced around the boys, singing a little song.

"Lump and Runt, two peas in a pod. One acts like a wolf, one acts like a dog. They could pass as twins, they could, because I made them both, like a good girl should."

"You made Lump?" Kit's eyes were wide in wonder.

Fenrir gave a coy look. "No, I suppose I didn't *make* him. But I did send him to the Temple to keep an eye on you. He was an orphan, wandering around Old Town. If I hadn't rescued him, he'd likely have not made it through the winter. I knew the Temple would care for him." Fenrir continued to dance and skip around, waving her arms over her head. "Now everybody's happy!"

"Your godliness," Indie said, still staring at the ground. The child groaned.

"Stand up, young warrior. Please, do not bow before me, and for the love of all things, do not ever call me that again."

The young man raised his head, his face a bright red. "What can you tell us of the sickness? The one that afflicted the wolves."

Fenrir gently took Indie's hand and rubbed her face against it. "Even though the wolves have brought you great pain, I feel your compassion for the animals. As much as his death brought me great pain, the sickness died with Amaruq, the Alpha Prime."

"Was he Runt's father?" Kit asked. The wolf pup immediately whined and both Kit and Indie moved close to comfort him. When the priest looked back, Fenrir was gone.

"I guess she finished what she needed to do," Indie said with a nervous chuckle. "I can't believe she was here! I can't believe that she knows you. I mean, she *knows* you."

"Let's get moving." Kit's face was beginning to flush, and she really didn't want Indie to see that. "We need to report back to the captain."

As they arrived in the market district, merchants watched them approach. They began calling out, hawking their wares. Kit smiled politely, waving them off so they could pass by. Nobody reacted to Runt's presence, so the collar must have been working.

Closer to the city gate was the food area of the marketplace. The smells of breads, sweets, and cooking meats filled Kit's nose, making her mouth water. Runt whined at the aromas, and Indie's stomach made an audible rumble.

"We can get some food at the Temple." Kit might have said the words, but her stomach was getting the better of her, too.

"Hail, Kit! Are you buying food for Sister Miyuki?"

Kit's face lit up when she caught sight of the southerner, with his ebony black skin, waving enthusiastically to her. Since the day she arrived in Aarall, the merchant had been exceedingly kind to her, and she had often bought from him when Sister Miyuki needed something special for a meal that she was making. As she approached, the heavy man's bright brown eyes fell on Kit, and his dazzling smile greeted her warmly. The man loved to dress in brightly colored clothing, and today he was wearing an intensely vibrant green shirt with yellow threads running through it.

"No, Comden, not today. I'm on my way to see Captain Harding. We just took care of the wolf problem that's been plaguing the outlying villages." Kit was going to mention the wolf hunters whom she thwarted as well, but that was information that didn't need to be shared.

"You took care of the wolves? Titan preserve us! My sister's family lost so many sheep and goats to those beasts that she thought she'd have to shut down her farm and move in with me. Ooh, my wife would not have been happy with that. My sister's children, my nephews, act like they were born directly in Helja. Little monsters they are! I remember a time..."

Kit gave Comden a smile and held up her hand to cut him off. If she let him continue talking, they wouldn't make it into the city before the sun set.

"Here!" Comden continued. "I know you've got business to attend to, but you have to try my new recipe. I call it *prickle-berry loaf.*" He handed Kit and Indie two small loaves of bread. The smell was absolutely heavenly. As Kit went to take a bite, Runt whined and gently pawed at her leg. "Oh, my apologies Lump. I didn't notice you there."

The actual Lump, who had been a few paces behind the group, came bounding forward at the sound of his name.

"Titan save us!" Comden shouted. "There's two of you?" The boys' tails wagged uncontrollably at the excited voice. The southerner quickly gathered up scraps that were piled on one of the merchant's counters. He tossed large hunks of bread to both Runt and Lump, which they promptly gobbled down.

Kit had barely taken a bite of her own loaf when Indie smacked his lips. She cocked an eyebrow and watched as he licked his fingers clean.

"What?" he said as he managed to swallow the last of his loaf.

"Titan's snowballs, Indie. Did you even take time to taste it?"

"I tasted it," he protested. "It was so delicious I couldn't stop myself from *wolfing* it down." He laughed lightly as he watched Runt and Lump gently taking the bits of bread Comden continued to offer them.

When Kit finally got to try her own loaf, the flavors filled her mouth, causing her to moan unexpectedly. "It tastes just like Sister Miyuki's prickle-berry honey," she managed to say between bites.

Comden laughed and slapped his broad belly. "Where do you think she got the recipe, and the prickle-berries to make that honey?" He gave Runt the last of the food in his hand and pointed his thumbs at himself. "This guy!"

Just like Indie, Kit licked her fingers clean, not wanting to waste a single morsel. "Does she have this recipe? I know the brothers and sisters at the Temple would all enjoy having this on a regular basis."

Comden gave her a coy, thin-lipped smile. "No way, little sister. This one is for me and my customers. Besides, the supply of prickle-berries is coming to an end. We'll need to wait until fall for the next harvest." When Kit pouted, he pulled out three more loaves. "Two of these are for you and your friend here but save the third one for Sister Miyuki. If she likes it, maybe the Temple can buy them up for the Feast of Titan's Bounty?" He wiggled his eyebrows at Kit. Comden did good business from his stall, but if the Temple bought his goods for the Feast, it would make him even more popular among the city's population.

Kit and Indie thanked the merchant for the food he had shared, and they headed off toward the city gate. They had barely gone a dozen paces or so when Indie was smacking his lips again.

CHAPTER FIFTY

REPORTING TO THE CAPTAIN

They made their way to the City Watch barracks, where they expected to find Captain Harding. There was a gatehouse barring entrance into the barracks' outdoor training facility that rivaled the front gate to the city. The members of the City Watch that were guarding the gatehouse greeted Kit as she approached. Since most of the guards were now aware that she was doing work for the captain, they were quick to let them through without incident.

When the stone and iron clad barracks came into view, Indie's eyes went blank, and his mouth dropped open.

"It's almost as big as the Temple of the Fist," Kit said, rousing Indie from whatever daydream he was having.

Four more guards that were passing by nodded to Kit before briskly moving along.

"The guards almost look like they're afraid of you," Indie said as he kept a careful eye on the men and women of the Watch. "That's got to feel good, eh?"

Kit laughed brightly. "They don't fear me, but they do fear the captain. The last time some guards treated me badly... it didn't go well for those involved."

"What are you doing with that beast?" a man yelled from behind.

Kit spun around to see Lieutenant Karr, holding his longsword at the ready. His jaw was set, his teeth barred. Fenrir's words to Runt immediately sprang to mind *'Anybody who is Kit's enemy will also see you in your true form.'* The young priest certainly didn't get along with the lieutenant, but she thought he was nothing more than a blowhard. The magic in Runt's collar said otherwise.

The lieutenant pulled back his sword, ready to strike. Lump immediately stepped between the man and the dire wolf, teeth bared. "Put your sword away." Kit's voice was steely as she joined Lump, shielding the dire wolf. "I swear to Titan, I will end you. Back off!" Indie stepped in beside Kit, tightly gripping the handle of his short sword.

"Move out of my way, or I'll gut you both like summer hogs." Spittle flew from the lieutenant's mouth as he bellowed. The man had completely lost his composure at this point.

"Lieutenant!" The shout was loud enough that everybody in the compound turned towards it, including Karr. Standing just outside the gate was Captain Harding. The enormous man was dressed in gleaming silver ceremonial armor, and he was carrying a bastard sword that was nearly as long as Kit was tall.

"Stand down, Lieutenant! Now!"

"Captain!" Karr yelled, turning his attention back on Kit. "She's brought a monster among us!"

"Stand down, Lieutenant!" The captain bellowed a second time. "Have you lost your mind? Back away and sheath your blade."

The muscles in Karr's neck pressed hard against his skin, and his mouth twisted into a loathsome sneer. "I don't know what game you're playing, street rat, but he won't always be here to protect you."

"Guards!" the captain called, "Detain this man. I want him bound and taken to his quarters. I'll deal with him later."

The look of fury on Karr's face immediately shifted to outrage. "Detain me? Me? She's brought that beast into the barracks and I'm the one being punished?" Two guards grabbed Karr by his upper arms. He fought against their hold for a moment before giving in. "I don't know why you don't see what I see, Captain, but this girl is a menace, even if she is a priest. You and Father Hoarfrost are blind to her, but I see everything."

"I've changed my mind," the captain said, his gaze flitting between Kit and Karr. The detained guard's face relaxed, suddenly turning to a look of vindication. Kit's stomach twisted, fearing that the captain had taken Karr's side. "Don't take him to his quarters. Throw him in the dungeons."

Karr thrashed against the two guards holding his arms, earning himself a punch in the face from the captain, instantly knocking him unconscious.

"Take him away," the captain said, his voice threatening. "He is to receive no visitors, no food, and no drink until I've spoken with him. Have I made myself perfectly clear? Anybody who shows this man kindness will receive the same fate."

The two guards holding Karr nodded and started dragging him away. Two more guards joined in a moment later, helping to carry the comatose man.

"What did you do to start this?" Harding asked, turning to Kit. A large vein in his forehead was throbbing so heavily that it looked like it was about to burst.

"She did nothing," Indie said, putting himself in harm's way. Harding loomed over the young man, his nostrils flaring.

"I didn't," Kit said, putting her hand on Indie's arm, motioning for him to put his sword away. "We were coming to see you and... Karr lost his mind. He saw Runt's true form."

The captain glared at Indie. "True form? What in Helja does that mean."

"Not me," Indie said, glaring at Kit, telling her to not say anything further. "The *dog*. We picked him up along the way."

The captain shook his head. He seemed to notice Lump and Runt for the first time. "You found another stray? This is no place to be bringing Temple mascots."

"The big one's name is Runt," Kit said. "I picked him up while I was looking after the wolf problem you sent me on. And this is Indie. He's from one of the villages I visited. He's offered to help as well. You did say you were short of able bodies, so I thought you'd appreciate the extra hands. He's also rather good in a fight."

"Pleasure to meet you, Captain," Indie offered his hand to Harding, but the big man just ignored it.

"Do you know how to use that short sword you're carrying?" The captain was sizing up Kit's new friend. "If so, defend yourself!"

No sooner had the captain said the words, than he brought his bastard sword around in an arcing overhand strike. Indie smoothly stepped to the side and drew his short sword, smashing it down on the captain's blade. The captain shifted his weight in towards Indie, bringing himself inside the young man's guard. Harding quickly spun around, trying to catch Indie in the face with his elbow. Again, the young man deftly moved, sinking below the attack. With the captain's back now exposed, Indie kicked him behind the knee, knocking the big man off balance. With cat-like reflexes, the captain spun around again, this time sweeping the legs out from Indie, causing him to land hard onto his back.

Runt was just about to step in, but Kit was able to tell him to be still before he did.

The captain nodded his approval. "He'll do, Kit," the captain said as he reached out to take Indie by the arm, offering to hoist him up to his feet.

"You should join the Watch, son. You'd be a welcome addition to my ranks."

Indie's look was somewhere between confusion and outrage, but Kit gave him a knowing smile. "Don't sweat it, Indie. He did the same thing to me when we first met. It's his way of making sure you're up to the task, whatever that task might be."

Indie rubbed his backside, looking bruised and confused. He slammed his blade back into its scabbard. He threw his arms in the air, his chest still heaving from the exertion. "It was a test? What is wrong with you people? You could have killed me!"

The captain twirled his enormous sword like it was an extension of his arm. "I could shave you with this if I wanted to. You were in no danger, other than perhaps dying of embarrassment."

Harding reached out and took the bruised young man's hand in his own. "I'm Captain Harding. I run this post. If you're a friend of Sister Standing Bear, then you're welcome here anytime. If you'd like to join the Watch, I'd take you in a heartbeat."

"Captain," Kit interrupted. "I'm not technically a *sister* yet. I might have completed the *Rite of Abandonment* ritual, but I haven't yet been awarded the title."

The captain slid his great sword into the sheath on his back. "Follow me to my office, both of you. I want to hear about the wolf situation."

Chapter Fifty-One

THE CAPTAIN AND THE WOLF

The group followed Harding into his cramped office. It still smelled of leather, dried blood, and sweat. Either nobody noticed or nobody cared.

Kit and Indie took a seat across from the captain's massive rough-hewn desk. While Lump parked himself at Kit's side, Runt moved into a corner where he could see the entire office and the door. He promptly curled up into a small ball, tucking his nose under his tail. Before the captain took his seat, he methodically removed his pauldrons and breast plate. The highly polished steel clattered as he tossed each piece onto the wooden floor.

"You're all dressed up today, Captain. A nice change from the smelly armor you usually wear."

Indie recoiled and stared at Kit in shock. His gaze darted to the captain, then back to Kit.

"What?" she asked, in mock surprise.

The captain pressed his lips together, trying his best not to let her get under his skin. "Kit, if you weren't of use to me, I'd drag you by your ear back to the High Priest and let him deal with your insolence."

"But I am of use," Kit said with a wide grin. "Besides, you seem to like having me around. There were a number of other people you could have chosen to help, but you picked me."

The captain put his elbows on his desk and his face into his massive hands. He grumbled something incomprehensible before slamming his hands onto the top of his desk.

"Indie, why are you hanging out with this... person? I require her services, so I'm forced to deal with her, but you're doing so of your own free will." He scrubbed his face again and slowly shook his head. The captain was looking more weary than usual. "Like I said, there is a place for you in the Watch. It seems like a win, win. I get a good man, and you get away from... her."

Indie laughed at the captain's joke, looking incredibly uncomfortable as he did. The priest feigned shock and outrage, but when she wasn't getting the intended reaction, she shrugged her shoulders. "If you two are finished having fun at my expense, maybe you want to hear about the wolves we dealt with?"

The captain sighed heavily and leaned back in his chair, the wood groaning under his bulk. "Yes, Kit, that's what we're here for. Please, tell me all about the wolves."

"Do you want to hear about the hunters as well?"

The captain sat up in his chair, his face becoming considerably more serious. "Hunters?"

"Yes, hunters!" Kit scooched up to the front of her chair for dramatic effect. "But first, the wolves."

Kit recounted her story of the animals, how they were poisoned by mushrooms, likely causing them to behave erratically and aggressively. She told him how they were forced to put them down when they found them. She also told him about the dire wolves they had encountered, suffering from the same affliction.

"What about the hunters?" the captain interrupted. He was clearly more interested in that part of Kit's story.

"Just be patient," she replied, holding up her hand to stop him from talking. "I'm getting to that. The story about the wolves is important."

Harding rolled his shoulders and took a deep breath. "Then get on with it," the captain said through clenched teeth. His face was becoming redder by the minute.

"Well, I can't say for certain, but I think it was the hunters who were poisoning the wolves." Kit pushed back into the large wooden chair. Her feet were no longer touching the floor. She swung them back and forth a few times before continuing. Apparently, these chairs were designed with tall people in mind, and at well under five feet, Kit did not meet that criteria.

The two men cleared their throats.

"I think they were poisoning the wolves to make them aggressive. My theory is, if the cities and the outlying villages were being attacked by the animals, then nobody was going to complain about the hunters killing off the wolves in the area." Kit gave the captain a cocky, satisfied smirk, letting him know she was finished.

The captain spoke slowly to her, like she was too dim to understand his words. "And... What. About. The. Hunters?"

"Oh, right!" she rolled her eyes at him, like she was planning on getting to it. Kit wanted to say a voice told her to travel north, but she feared it would make her look like she'd lost her mind. Thankfully, Indie spoke up, saving her from having to make up a lie.

"We wanted to make sure that we had killed all the diseased wolves, so we decided to continue our search. That's when we ran into the hunters."

Kit's eyes glazed over, and her hands shook violently as she recalled the memories. "They killed a dire wolf so that they could take her puppies from her."

Runt whined as Kit recounted the story of his mother's death. He got up from his place in the corner and sat beside her. The girl gently stroked the white star on his forehead. "After we took care of the hunters, we found the dire wolf puppies and made sure they had a good meal."

"You *fed* them? Why didn't you just kill the pups?" The captain's face was grim. He didn't really want to hear the answer to his question. Runt was giving a low growl when Harding asked about killing the puppies.

"Kill them? No way!" Kit said, flinching backwards, her back instantly pencil straight. She gave the wolf an affectionate scratch on his head. "We kept Runt with us, and used the other pups as bait to catch the hunters. I knew he'd would have no trouble following his littermates." The dire wolf pup gave Kit a smile at the compliment.

"Runt was one of the puppies?" the captain chuckled to himself. His body visibly relaxed. "I hate to break it to you, Kit, but he's not a wolf, and he's definitely not a *dire wolf.*"

The captain's chuckles were now a full-on laugh. He was having a lot of fun at Kit's expense. "I hope the wolves you were killing weren't golden retrievers as well." The big man slapped his hand across his knee and laughed all the harder.

Kit laughed along with the captain. Indie stared at the two of them like they had both lost their minds. As quickly as it started, Kit's laughter dropped off. She gave Indie a tiny wink.

"We'll see who's laughing now," she said to the captain with a wide grin. "Runt *is* a dire wolf."

As the words left her mouth, Runt shimmered as his form morphed from dog to dire wolf. For the first time, the captain experienced Runt in his natural form. The spell Fenrir placed on the collar was working perfectly. Kit broke the illusion when she permitted the captain to see Runt as his true self.

"Titan's snowballs!" he cried, scrambling from his chair to grab his sword.

Runt gave the captain a satisfied smile, his thick, red tongue lolling out the side of his mouth.

"You won't need your weapon, Captain. He's on our side," Kit said, while Indie covered his mouth, trying to suppress a laugh.

Runt moved away from Kit, around the desk, towards the captain. When he got within a few feet, he sat down and panted, his immense tongue dangling from his mouth. The captain released his grip on his sword and tentatively held his hand out to the wolf. Runt immediately licked his fingers and rubbed his body against the man. As big as the captain was, the pup's back was nearly even with his waist.

"I thought you said they were puppies," the captain said casually as he gave Runt's thick neck fur a good rub.

"He *is* a puppy. Fenrir turned him into a full-sized wolf so that he could protect me."

The captain's hands immediately stopped petting the wolf. "Fenrir?" he asked, one eyebrow cocked up in disbelief.

"Well, that's a bit of a long story," Kit said as she called Runt back to her side. She recounted how the wolf spirit was talking to her, helping her hunt down the hunters. Kit also went on to tell Harding of the old woman, and the hut in the woods.

"And after we took care of the hunters, the old woman, Fenrir, gave me this fine suit of armor." She stood up and twirled for the captain, giving him a full view of the magnificent creation the wolf-god had made for her.

"How do you know the old woman was Fenrir? She isn't known for visiting us mortals, but when she does, she usually appears to people as a great white wolf." The captain had that skeptical look in his eyes again.

"Well, I know because she told me so. She brought a wolf back from the dead. She helped me communicate with the wild wolves." She pointed to Runt with her hands. "And she made a puppy into a full-sized wolf."

Kit paused for a moment as she considered the things Fenrir had done. "I suppose she might have just been an old mage, or a necromancer of some sort, but I know in my heart that it was the real Fenrir."

"She's telling the truth," Indie offered, his head nodding enthusiastically. "I saw her myself just before we came into the city. She was just a small girl, but she gave Runt the collar he's wearing. It's what makes him look like a dog instead of a wolf, except to Kit's enemies. That's why Karr attacked him. I'm sure of it. He reacted the exact same way you did when he saw the dire wolf."

"Since the first day we met, Karr has hated me," Kit said. "I have no idea why, but with Fenrir's magic on Runt, I know it's true." Runt yipped and smiled. "See? Even Runt knows it was Fenrir's magic."

The captain rolled his eyes. "So, in addition to everything else, now you're suggesting that Runt understands what you're saying?"

Kit smiled back at the captain. "Well, let's see how well he understands." She considered the problem for a moment before coming up with an adequate demonstration. "Runt, close the door and keep the captain from leaving."

Runt immediately closed the door with his muzzle, before moving himself between the captain and the door. He got into a crouch and began to growl. The growl grew into a full snarl, the big wolf's tongue licking through his razor-sharp teeth. Spittle dripped from his lips as his claws dug deeply into the floorboards.

"Okay, Kit, you've made your point. He clearly understands what you're saying."

Runt's snarl immediately turned into a smile, just before he pounced on the captain, knocking him off his feet, flat onto his back. He promptly gave the big man's face a thorough tongue-bath. Perhaps this was the wolf's way of apologizing for being aggressive towards him. Perhaps it was because he was an exuberant puppy that simply loved to lick.

"Okay, Runt, let him be." Kit was laughing so hard she could barely get the words out. Though Runt understood the command, at this moment, he was choosing not to listen. The oversized puppy continued to give his new friend all the kisses he could manage, and then some.

The captain reached around his attacker and grabbed him in a bearhug. With a quick shift of his hips, he rolled the wolf over onto his back. Runt struggled for a moment to get free, but as soon as the captain scratched his belly, he stopped fighting.

"Okay, Runt," Harding said with a broad smile. "I need Kit to finish her story so that I can get back to work."

"That's really all there was, Captain. Well, except for the fact that the hunters might have been working for somebody." Kit shrugged her shoulders with the last comment. "I don't know who, though. I mean, why would somebody hire hunters to kill off the wolves in Arnnor?"

The captain retook his seat. Runt moved in beside him, trying to get Harding to continue scratching him. "Off the top of my head, I have no idea. But I'll ask around."

The captain headed for the door and opened it. "So, Indie, if you do decide to join up, don't hesitate to drop by."

"One more thing, Captain." Kit was not quite ready to end the conversation, even though the man seemed to have heard enough and was ready for them to leave. "What happened to On'nak?"

The captain's face went dark. "He's still in the dungeon. He'll be seeing the Magistrate in a few days. His parents are hoping to plead his case, but he tried to murder you, as well as several children. As far as we can tell, he was the one responsible for all the children's deaths. I expect he'll be executed for his crimes. Truth is, I'm surprised you didn't cast judgment on him yourself."

Kit's bottom lip quivered. "But he's just a boy! He believes he's fighting for a good cause, for the freedom of his people." She thought back to the events at the Cheeserie with Karim's mother. "There is a man, a Berrat man, named Pental, who has been getting the Berrat citizens all fired up. He's the one who brainwashed On'nak into doing what he did."

"The reason for his crime is irrelevant," Harding stated and crossed his heavily muscled arms across his chest. The matter-of-fact tone in his voice told Kit that she was not going to convince him. "He's guilty of murder and attempted murder. Regardless of why, we can't have our citizens killing each other just because someone gets into their head."

"Oh, ya?" Kit challenged him. "What if somebody, a powerful mage for example, cast a spell on you, or made you drink a potion that forced you to kill someone? Should you be executed for that?"

"That's completely different, Kit. The person would no longer have been in control of themselves, so they couldn't be held responsible."

"Words, potions, spells? What's the difference?" she countered. "If somebody can convince you that what you're doing is right and just, then how can you be held accountable?"

Captain Harding's expression didn't change. It was still hard, like it had been carved from a block of granite.

"Thankfully, it's not my decision to make. If you feel this strongly, you can speak on On'nak's behalf before the Magistrate." He opened the door a bit more, as if to make a point. "We're done here for now, Kit. I have things to do, and you need to go see the High Priest. Father Hoarfrost has been looking for you for two days now. We both know he is not a man who likes to be kept waiting."

"Yes, sir." Kit headed for the door with Indie right behind her. Lump yawned, his pink tongue lolling out of his mouth. Slowly, he got to his feet, stretched, and followed along. A moment later, Runt came bursting out the door, practically knocking Kit over as he did.

The massive wooden door closed. From behind it, Kit heard the captain.

"Sweet Titan! What am I going to do with her?" There was a loud crash, like something had been thrown across the room.

Kit chuckled to herself as the group made their way to the barracks' exit.

CHAPTER FIFTY-TWO

HOMECOMING

Kit paused at the base of the imposing sight of the stone stairs leading up to the Temple. Indie's mouth was agape as he gawped at the ominous task before him.

"First time to the Temple?" Kit asked with a small laugh. "Climbing up is much harder than it looks."

"What? Seriously?" Indie's eyes were practically bugging out of his head. "It looks pretty hard, and you're saying it's harder than it looks?"

"Race you to the top!" Kit shouted out as she bolted up the stairs. Runt was already halfway up to the top before she had even climbed three of the steps. A moment later, Indie and Lump caught up, threatening to pass her by.

The girl dug deep, not willing to let Indie beat her to the top. She pushed herself, fighting to keep up. When she found herself lagging, she called upon her priestly magic, summoning a speed spell to aid her in this *battle.*

"Titan, hear me," she whispered with ragged breaths. A sudden burst of energy coursed through her. She bounded up the stairs with ease. By the time she was halfway up, Runt was already at the top. She continued pushing herself, disregarding that her heart was beating so hard that she could feel it in her throat.

When Kit joined Runt, she turned around to see how close Indie was behind her. Shockingly, he still had a long way to go. "Hurry up, you big poke!" She was enjoying this far more than she should.

"How did you do that?" Indie asked when he made it to the top. His face was bright red, and he was sweating profusely. "I was passing you, and then you suddenly started climbing the stairs as fast as Runt."

"I didn't speed up," Kit chided. "You got tired and slowed down. You need more training."

"I'm telling you, I never slowed down. If anything, I climbed faster than I even thought possible, just trying to keep up with you." Indie was still gasping for air, but his skin color was returning to normal. He used the sleeve of his shirt to wipe the sweat from his brow.

Lump finally crested the top step, giving Kit an incredulous look. "Sure, whatever you want to believe," she said with a dismissive wave of her hands. "C'mon, let's take Comden's loaf to Sister Miyuki."

"Aren't you supposed to report to the High Priest? The captain made it sound like you were to waste no time."

"My duties will still be there when I get to him. We don't want the bread to go stale, do we? Besides, I want to show you around the Temple."

Indie shook his head and let Kit lead the way.

They headed through the main hall of the Temple into the Nave's interior, dimly lit by braziers tucked into alcoves along the side walls of the room. Each footfall on the stone floor echoed through the expansive chamber.

There were several priests, acolytes, and visitors going about their business. Nobody seemed to be paying any attention to their arrival, so they continued through to the staircase at the back. They traveled down several flights of stone stairs until they got to the floor where the kitchens were. Kit had been up and down those stairs so many times that she no longer noticed the quality of the workmanship, how every stone fit so neatly with the ones adjacent, that there was barely a visible seam between them.

"Why did they put the kitchens in the basement?" Indie asked as they headed through a set of large double doors. Like the stonework of the stairs, the quality of the workmanship of the kitchen doors, all the doors for that matter, was beyond reproach.

"Heat rises!" Kit replied simply, like it should be obvious. Indie's look said that he needed more of an explanation than that. "Well, the kitchen fires and the clay ovens churn out a lot of heat. Like I said, heat rises, so, that heat travels up through the Temple, warming the dining halls above, as well as the Nave, the private chapels, and the classrooms."

Kit had a bit of a sour look on her face. "About the only things the kitchen doesn't heat are the dormitories, which are perpetually cold. I complained once about how cold our rooms were and I was told, '*You should offer your discomfort as a sacrifice to Titan. Consider what he must endure. Surely you can survive a bit of a chill.*'"

Indie laughed at her comment. "It sounds more like they just don't want to bother having fireplaces built to keep you warm."

Kit gave him a shrug. "The rooms have them, but it's considered weak to ever light a fire in them, unless the temperature dropped so low that not doing so would likely mean death." She was about to continue when she saw her friend. "Hey, there's Sister Miyuki!"

They made their way through the rows of long tables and benches to where Sister Miyuki was delivering a basket of fresh muffins to a table of priests. Kit's mouth watered at the sight. "Sister Miyuki is the best baker in all of Arnnor, but I can't wait to see her face when she tries Comden's prickle-berry loaf."

"I thought you said the dining hall was upstairs. This kitchen looks like it could seat forty or fifty people."

Kit laughed at Indie's comment. "These tables are typically used by kitchen staff for their meals, but we all come down every now and again if we're looking to grab a quick snack. The dining hall upstairs can seat hundreds of people!" She no sooner finished speaking when Sister Miyuki called out a greeting.

"Oh, hello, Kit. Nice to see you," said Sister Miyuki as the round-faced priest waddled over. Even covered in flour and a mixture of stains, the woman exuded warmth and friendship. She promptly gave Kit a warm embrace that was so full of love that it made Kit homesick.

"Have you been to see Father Hoarfrost yet? He's been searching for you for the past two days," the priest asked as she raised her eyebrows, her bright green eyes staring at Kit expectantly.

The young priest couldn't help but roll her eyes. "No, not yet. I just got back from a mission that Captain Harding had sent me on." She pulled out the loaf

Comden gave her and presented it to Sister Miyuki. "I wanted to deliver this to you first. It's Comden's new recipe."

Sister Miyuki gave the loaf a gentle squeeze before putting it to her nose. She drew in a deep breath, savoring the sweet, floral aroma of the bread. She was just about to comment when she seemingly noticed Indie and Runt for the first time.

"Well, hello there," she said to Indie, her eyes dancing between the two young people standing before her.

"And hello to you, too," she said to Runt. "You look just like Lump!" The chubby priest's face turned bright red. "I meant the dog, not you, good sir."

Everyone had a good laugh at her jest.

When they finally stopped laughing, Kit got to her introductions. "Sorry, Sister Miyuki, this is Indie and my furry friend's name is Runt."

"Pleased to meet you, Sister. Kit speaks very highly of you." Indie gave her a small bow as he extended his greeting.

"She does now, does she? Well, I'm glad to hear it." Sister Miyuki gave a chuckle before returning her attention to the loaf handed to her. "Prickle-berry bread," she stated. "It seems like such a waste of a fine fruit, but Comden knows what he's doing." She pulled a piece of the bread off the loaf. With a discerning eye, she squished it between her fingers and gave it another sniff. "Nice texture," she mused before popping it into her mouth. Her eyes went wide as she gave it a thorough chew.

"Oh my," she said with a bit of a gasp. "This is wonderful, truly wonderful." She pulled off another piece, again enjoying its aroma before popping it into her mouth. "Oh, what a masterpiece this is. I take back my earlier comment. This is a marvelous use of the fruit."

"I think he's hoping you're going to buy up what supply he has left for the festival," Kit whispered. It was not like anybody was listening, but it was typically bad form for members of the Temple to be advocating on behalf of vendors.

"Oh my, yes. This bread would make a wonderful addition to the Feast." Kit could see the wheels spinning in her head as Sister Miyuki pondered the treat.

"It's too sweet to be served with dinner, and I've already planned dessert." She threw her arms up and laughed deeply. "Who cares when it gets served, as long as the guests get a chance to try it out."

Sister Miyuki finished off the last of the loaf and licked her fingers clean. Again, her face turned red with embarrassment. "Oh, I'm so sorry. I should have shared this with you." The priest looked mortified with herself.

"We brought it for you," Indie interrupted. "We've already eaten our fill of it." Runt and Lump growled lightly in unison, glaring at him in disagreement.

"Oh, poor puppies. I bet you're starving, aren't you?" Runt spun in a circle, indicating that he would, most certainly, enjoy some food. "Kit, why don't your new friends stay here for a proper meal while you go see the High Priest?" She was giving Kit *that look* that told her it was not a request. Sister Miyuki may have been the Temple baker, but she was also one of the highest-ranking priests there.

"Yes, sister," Kit replied, bowing slightly, acknowledging her rank. "I'll head there right now."

"Good!" she said, bobbing her head as though to punctuate the statement. "Be on your way then. I'll make sure your friends are well cared for."

And with that, Kit turned on her heel and headed off to the High Priest's office.

CHAPTER FIFTY-THREE

REPORTING TO THE HIGH PRIEST

The young priest slowly made her way up the stairs to Father Hoarfrost's office. Her mouth was going dry as she continued to ascend the steps. A feeling of nausea crept up through her stomach. This sudden feeling of nervousness only served to reinforce the fact that inside, deep inside, she knew her recent actions might not be appreciated by the High Priest, her mentor, a man she considered to be her friend. The fact that he even entertained audiences with her said a lot. Most acolytes would never have private meetings with him, nor would he be *personally* giving them duties.

She cringed at the thought of how she had been treating him, all things considered.

When Kit got to the door of his office, it was slightly open, and she could hear people talking inside. Judging by the tone, Father Hoarfrost wasn't happy. As Kit was just about to head off, Brother Powder came out of the room. His normally pale face was now bright red and covered in beads of sweat. When he saw Kit, he quickly averted his gaze and rushed past.

"Come in, Kit!" the High Priest shouted. "I know you're out there!"

Kit blinked in confusion.

How could he possibly have known that?

"Titan's blessings upon you, Father," Kit offered as she walked into the room. "I can come back later if now is not a good time."

"Sit!" the old priest said. His voice was firm, but completely in control.

"I'm here to report on my assignment." Kit tried to sound formal, in an attempt to appear respectful, but the dubious look on the High Priest's face said that he wasn't buying it.

He held up his hand, telling her to stop talking. He then quietly moved behind his desk and took a seat. He slowly gathered up a sheaf of parchments and neatly stacked them. From there, he arranged his quills, placing them in descending order by size. Every second he spent performing these mindless tasks felt like an eternity to Kit. She knew he was going to rip a strip off her, and the waiting was killing her.

Just get it over with.

The priest's face became hard. "I'll get to it in my own time, young lady."

Titan's snowballs! Is he reading my mind?

No sooner did the thought pop into her head, she regretted thinking it, especially if the old priest could read her mind.

Just when it looked like Father Hoarfrost was about to speak, he stood from his chair and walked over to one of the office windows. He gazed out at the statue of Titan, took a deep breath, and slowly let it out. Kit couldn't help but think that whatever he was going to say, it was going to be bad... unbelievably bad.

Still staring out the window, he finally spoke.

"Are you not a member of this Temple?"

Before Kit had a chance to answer, he again held up his hand, cutting her off.

"Am I not the High Priest in this Temple? Did you not address me as *Father* when you came into my office?"

Slowly, he turned from the window to face her. When Kit looked past him, she could see the statue of Titan in the background. As High Priest, he was Titan's representative here on Orth. When he spoke, he spoke for Titan. Her studies had always stressed that.

Again, with the same methodical pace, the priest moved from the window back to his chair. He then slowly, deliberately, lowered himself into it before casting his gaze fully upon Kit.

"*I* sent you on a mission. An important mission. And you, a not-yet-anointed priest, thought that you could go running off on an errand for Captain Harding?"

"But I did complete your mission," Kit blurted out, desperately hoping to quell his anger.

"Silence!" he shouted in reply, waves of cold emanating from him. Frost formed on the edges of his desk and around the window frames.

"I shouldn't have to learn of your *exploits* from other members of the Temple, let alone from *prisoners*!"

Kit's mouth instantly went dry. "You spoke with On'nak? Was he okay? He doesn't deserve to die!" The words were tumbling out of Kit's mouth before she had a chance to check herself.

The High Priest's eyes hardened even more, narrowing to something barely more than a slit. "I will tell you when you can speak. Until then..." he let his words hang. The room's temperature dropped several more degrees.

"The mission I sent you on was simple, but it was important. The *problem* you encountered at the fishing village is not an isolated incident. People are dying, Kit. Do you understand? They're *dying*!" The old priest's face softened, and the room's temperature slowly returned to normal.

"The boy you brought back killed those children just because they were human. Children are without fault, but he killed them anyway. Then, when you saved that child's life, he tried to take yours for doing so. Is that a correct account of the events?"

The old priest paused for a moment, leaving Kit unsure if it was a question meant to be answered, or if he was simply pausing to make his point. Kit nodded slightly, hoping that a non-verbal response wouldn't make the situation any worse.

"The young Berrat tried to kill two people that we know of. It is highly likely that he was also responsible for the other illnesses and deaths in the village. Did you think to ask him that? No. No, you didn't. Instead, you let him spin you a tale of woe and hardship, and now you feel he should be freed, because somehow, it wasn't his fault."

Kit kept her head down, staring at her feet like they might somehow save her. While she did, something deep within her snapped.

"He was brainwashed," the young priest shouted, her hands clenched into tight fists. The words flew from her lips, again coming out before she had a chance to stop them. "His actions were not his own. The words of somebody else had poisoned his mind, turning it into something horrible, something..."

Kit suddenly realized that she was crying. Tears were falling down her cheeks, puddling on the floor beneath her. She struggled to speak and stared back down at her feet. "Surely Titan can understand forgiveness! Justice doesn't always have to mean death."

When she looked up, the old man's face was a mixture of pity and pride.

"Good." He said with a small smile. "Very good."

"But?" This was not the reaction Kit expected.

"But nothing. It's true, we stand for justice, and as priests of Titan, we deliver justice with swift and decisive action. People often view us as harsh, possibly even cruel. But, when the lives of innocents are on the line, we need to temper that justice with compassion. That's what you did. You're barely a full priest, but you are incredibly wise for your age."

"I thought you were angry with me." Kit sniffed, wiping her nose with the sleeve of her tunic.

"Oh, I am. I'm furious with you. But I'm also proud of you." Father Hoarfrost offered up a thin-lipped smile with his last comment.

"How? How can you be both angry and proud?"

"I'm proud of you for looking beyond the obvious. I'm proud of you for seeing the good in people, when all they're showing you is the bad."

Hoarfrost leaned back into his chair and knitted his fingers together, letting his hands rest on his lap in front of him. "But even though you handled the mission well, you should have come to me first, before running off on another quest for Captain Harding. We might have been able to deal with the boy before the Watch processed him, but now, there is no option but to have him stand before the Magistrate. He will most likely be executed for his crimes..."

Kit thought Father Hoarfrost had finished, but he hadn't.

"All of that was bad, but then you dragged Brother Powder into it. You had him give you prohibited potions, dangerous potions that if used inappropriately, could kill. He should have known better, but I know you. I know how you work people. I know how you... *bend them*... to your will. I know because you've done it to me on multiple occasions. I don't know how you do it, but you do."

"I can't help it if I'm charming," Kit said with a small grin and a shrug. She tossed her long black hair over her shoulder, just to emphasize the point.

"Now is not the time for humor, little priest. You're not going to smile your way out of this."

A sudden tightness gripped Kit's chest as terror ripped through her.

"What's to happen to me?"

"What indeed?" Father Hoarfrost leaned forward, now drumming his fingers on his exquisitely crafted dragonwood desk. There was a gleam in the old priest's deep blue eyes as the slightest hint of a smile appeared at the corner of his mouth.

"I promise, Father," Kit stammered. "I'll do better. I won't leave on missions for Captain Harding without your approval. I'll... I'll do better."

"I know," Father Hoarfrost said as he nodded slowly. "It's the responsibility of every anointed priest to put Titan and this Temple before all else."

"Anointed, Father?" Kit blinked rapidly, wondering if she misheard the man.

"We will have the ceremony at first light tomorrow," Father Hoarfrost said, "before you decide to break your word to me and rush off on another mission."

"I wouldn't. Thank you, Father. I promise, I won't do that." Kit's heart raced. Her fingers tingled and her stomach churned. Bile crept up into her throat.

"Get some rest, Sister Kit," Father Hoarfrost said, motioning to the door to his office. "You look like you could use a good night's sleep."

Kit quickly stifled a yawn. She gave the high priest a quick nod and a smile before excusing herself. As she walked down the hall on her way to her cell, butterflies rose up in her stomach. Tomorrow she would be an actual priest of Titan, the first and most important step in freeing her god. She thought back to the dream, the one that started this adventure. It felt like it was a lifetime ago, and yet, it was still crystal clear in her mind.

"I will find a way to free you," she whispered. "I won't fail you."

THE STORY CONTINUES...

The story continues with *Hand of Titan,* the next novel in the Priest of Titan series.

Read on to discover more about Amaruq - The Wolf Spirit. This bonus short story offers some additional insight into the plight of the wolves, as well as Amilta, our tiny Berrat hero.

AMARUQ – THE WOLF SPIRIT
A VEIL OF ENTROPY SHORT STORY

Amaruq sniffed at the wind as it blew through his thick, obsidian-black fur. In the northern reaches of Orth, with little human population, the frost-laden air currents could carry a scent for miles.

The huge wolf reveled in the juxtaposition of the warm spring sunshine and the last of the winter's gripping wind, but the task set before him was grim. A sickness had been afflicting many of the northern wolves, which transformed otherwise peaceful creatures into mindless killing machines.

A small pack of gray wolves had told Amaruq that they had sighted his quarry, a great white wolf named Frost, near a small village outside of Aarall, the largest city in the barony. This information made the huge wolf cringe because, if Frost attacked the humans, they would likely unleash an army of hunters to seek out and destroy all the wolves in the area. There were already reports of hunters killing hundreds of wolves between Aarall and the northern city of Silverhawk.

As the Prime Alpha, the absolute leader of the wolves on the northeastern continent, Amaruq had spent the last five years working to establish a truce between the humans and the wolves. The truce had resulted in the wolves staying clear of human settlements and the humans leaving the wolves in peace.

Padding through the tall grasses north of the Spiderwood Forest, a haven for giant arachnids, Amaruq continued his search. The forest was south of the village where the wolves had spotted Frost. He had yet to pick up Frost's scent, but knew that he would eventually locate the white wolf.

Amaruq's ears perked up and swiveled on his head as he searched for the source of a wolf howling out in pain. Changing his pace from a slow walk to a steady trot, he moved southwest along the forest's edge, breaking into a run when he saw a large, male, gray wolf limping out of the thick undergrowth, a gaping wound on his side.

"Our pups," the gray wolf said as blood poured from the deep gash left by his attacker. "My mate, Accalia, is still within, trying to penetrate their nest."

This close to the forest's edge, Amaruq knew they had to be dealing with wolf spiders, massive hair-covered creatures that were nearly the same size as the gray wolves. Wolf spiders had oversized fangs, capable of rending flesh from bone, but it was their venom that was their primary weapon. If they had bitten this gray wolf, his time on Orth would soon come to an end.

"I will retrieve your pups," Amaruq said, his jade-green eyes filled with intensity. If the spiders had already carted the pups to their nest, there would likely be no way he could get to them, but he would try his best to carry out the rescue.

Heading through an opening in the bramble surrounding the forest, the wolf charged forward. He followed the sounds of Accalia's growls and her pups' yips. The trees were ferrous wood, evergreens with broad, heavy leaves that remained on the branches even through the harshest winters. The bright spring sun barely penetrated the thick canopy, casting the area in dark, forbidding shadows.

With each breath of wind, the tree limbs clacked together, sounding so much like the clicking of spider mandibles that it put the wolf's teeth on edge. *The enemy may well be upon us sooner than we realized,* he thought as he came upon Accalia, waist deep in spiderwebs.

With snapping jaws, she fended off the attacks of two forest crawlers. The shiny black arachnids were about half the size of wolf spiders, but they hunted in groups of two or three. Their venom was less potent than their larger cousins, but their webs could immobilize their victims until they finally succumbed to their bites.

While the female gray wolf was utterly ensnarled, the spiders could easily stride across the webs along thick threads that ran just above the tangled mass. With a single leap, the dire wolf landed in front of the smaller wolf. He grabbed one of the forest crawlers by the thorax and crushed it in his massive maw. He shook his head as he tried to rid his mouth of the creature's thick gray innards.

The second spider, realizing that she no longer had the advantage after witnessing the fate of her comrade, scurried off into the thick mass of silver webbing.

"My pups are within the web," Accalia cried out, biting and pulling at the mass of webs wrapped around her leg. "Lord Amaruq, please don't let them die."

The dire wolf growled and snarled at the webbing that had tangled around his legs. Like the smaller wolf, each movement tightened the web's hold on him.

"Protect your muzzle," Amaruq ordered as he unleashed a blast of frost pellets from his mouth. He began spraying the cone of frozen air until it coated the webbing in a thick layer of ice. He yanked his paw up and the strands binding his body snapped like dry twigs. Accalia bit at her own bonds, each one breaking easily within her teeth.

"Follow," Amaruq said as he broke through the brittle webbing, sending it spraying across the ground like shards of crystal threads. He continued to push through the webs with the smaller female at his heels.

"They're just ahead," Accalia whimpered desperately, "to your left."

Amaruq could hear the pups thrashing, but he maintained his direction.

"Free your pups. There are more spiders up ahead."

While the mother bounded through the webs towards her pups, Amaruq pressed forward toward the sound of clicking mandibles.

"Fenrir, protect me," the dire wolf muttered as a hairy brown wolf spider lunged from a mass of webs. Sick green venom dripped from its fangs as it raised her front legs, preparing to strike.

"Your god is not here, leader of the northern wolves," the great spider said, her voice so high pitched that it hurt Amaruq's ears. "You would risk your life to save this bitch's pups? You are a fool, and the north will be better off without you."

Amaruq sprayed a fresh blast of frost across the webs, freezing them on impact.

"Spider, free the pups and you can have me."

"My name is Szari, not that you will need to remember it. Those pups are my offering from those that seek my protection. It would be rude of me to set them free."

Amaruq's muscles coiled as he readied himself to leap at the spider.

"If you don't release them, it will be the death of you, Szari," he snarled back at her. The dire wolf pulled back his lips, exposing his own formidable blade-like teeth.

With surprising agility, the wolf spider moved her bulk towards Amaruq. She unfolded her fangs, holding them high over the wolf's head. Using her front legs, she grasped out at Amaruq and brought down her deathly fangs to seal his fate.

Amaruq bolted beneath the great spider and grabbed hold of one of her many hair-covered legs. With a twist of his neck and a shake of his head, the wolf snapped a leg off the spider and tossed it aside.

The spider screeched in pain as she tried to pivot herself, bringing down her dagger-tipped legs in rapid succession, hoping to impale the wolf that hid in her shadow.

With each thrust of her legs, Amaruq evaded the attack. He grabbed at a nearby leg and crushed it in his jaws. Again, Szari screeched out in agony.

"Enough," she cried out in desperate surrender. "Enough."

"You will receive no mercy," Amaruq growled before he grabbed another leg and ripped it from the spider's abdomen. Blood and entrails seeped from the gaping hole that it created.

With only five legs still attached, the wolf spider could no longer manage her great bulk. She tried to swing her body around to bring her fangs to bear, but the wolf was too fast. Amaruq ducked to the side before leaping onto the spider's back. Using his long claws to maintain his purchase, he grasped the creature at the back of its head and bit deeply. The spider shuddered as the wolf's teeth pierced through her skull. With each flex of his mouth, his fangs sunk deeper and deeper into the spider's carapace, crushing it with the sheer power of the dire wolf's jaws.

Szari tried one last time to shake the wolf before her spirit left her. Only when he was sure she had passed did he release his iron grip on her.

The yips and barks of tiny voices drew Amaruq's attention away from the dead arachnid. The pups were scampering through the broken remains of the web while their mother finished killing the last of the forest crawlers.

"Come," Amaruq called. "Stay with your children."

She gave the shiny black spider one more shake before dropping its lifeless body to the ground. With a couple of leaps, she took her position in front of her pups and led them back out to the relative safety of the open fields. She cried out at the sight of her mate lying on his side, his lifeblood leaking out of him.

"My Lord Amaruq," the wolf cried out, her pups clinging to her legs as they watched their dying father. "Can you help him?"

The Prime Alpha moved in beside the fallen wolf and sniffed at his wound. He tentatively licked at the edges and pulled his head back. The wolf's saliva had healing properties, but Amaruq doubted it was enough to heal such a grievous wound.

"Will my papa be okay?" asked one of the pups, his gray and brown muzzle matted from his tears.

"I don't know, little one," the dire wolf responded as he carefully watched the wound slowly knit together where he had licked it. "Maybe."

Amaruq continued to lick around the wound while the wolf laid motionless, his chest rising and falling in slow, labored breaths. The wounds continued to knit together and as they did, Amaruq continued to apply his healing powers.

The wound had nearly healed when Amaruq stopped and shook his head.

"Papa," the cub called out as he squirmed past his mother and laid his chin across his father's thick neck fur. "Wake up, papa. You have to wake up."

"Lord Amaruq?" Accalia asked as the rest of her pups scrambled over to their father's side, each of them taking turns licking at the wounds like the Prime Alpha had done.

"Only by Fenrir's grace will he survive," the wolf said. He dipped his head low. "Fortunately, the venom was weak, but he has lost a lot of blood."

"Papa!" one of the pups screeched as he spun about in tight circles.

The big wolf's eyes were open. His breathing was now strong and steady. He was about to stand, but his mate quickly, lovingly, put her paw on his shoulder.

"Be still, my love," she said, her voice thick with emotion. "Our children are safe. Rest now."

"You will live to see your children grow to be strong, healthy wolves," Amaruq said as he bowed beside the big wolf. "Perhaps Fenrir has plans for you yet."

"Thank you, Amaruq," the boisterous pup called out, his eyes wide with wonder.

"Lord Amaruq," his mother corrected. "You will address him as Lord Amaruq, or you will keep your muzzle closed."

"Be at peace," the dire wolf said as a broad smile crossed his black face. "We are family and now is a time of celebration."

Amaruq gave the small cub a forceful lick, knocking the pup off his feet. The small wolf squealed with delight as all the pups ran to the dire wolf, waiting their turn to be given his blessing.

The dire wolf turned and watched Accalia lying next to her mate, carefully cleaning off the remaining blood from his fur. Amaruq bowed respectfully to her and bounded off along the forest's edge. He had a grim task ahead of him, but his heart was now lighter, knowing that life will still go on.

⚜

The morning sun was now high in the sky, its bright yellow rays cutting through the chill and warming the ground. Amaruq raised his head, trying to pick up Frost's scent. He had been the Prime Alpha for nearly five winters now and the wolves thrived under his leadership. The sickness that was spreading through his pack threatened their very existence. The disease afflicted the wolves' minds, turning them into senseless killers.

Amaruq had picked up Frost's trail just south of a large human settlement. Once he had his scent, it took the dire wolf no time to find his pack mate. When the great white wolf finally came into view, bile rose in his throat.

The sickness is spreading.

Amaruq watched Frost, his packmate and close friend, snarling and snapping at the wind.

It makes no sense.

He moved in closer, hoping that Frost's mind wasn't so far gone that he couldn't still speak with him.

"Frost!"

The blue-white wolf continued to snap at an unseen foe. His once glorious coat was a mass of matted fur and bare patches of diseased skin, sure signs of him having been infected. He either could not hear his pack leader, or his mind was too broken to recognize the voice speaking to him.

"Frost, come to me!"

Amaruq put his full authority behind the command, pushing as much magic into his voice as he was able. The big white wolf ceased his attack on the wind and turned his attention to his leader. For a brief moment, there was recognition in the great white wolf's jade-green eyes. He gave Amaruq a devastated whimper, but that moment quickly passed as Frost's eyes glazed over and turned milky white.

"Enemy!" Frost wailed as he pinned back his ears.

He started moving closer to Amaruq, circling him as he became unbridled in his infliction.

"All enemies must die!"

"Frost! Hear me!" Amaruq screamed as he turned towards the white wolf that had moved off to his right. Again, the alpha pushed as much of his magic as he could into his voice, but to no effect.

Amaruq pulled back his lips, exposing his full set of canines. If he could not speak with him, he would need to end his life.

"I do not fear you, old wolf," Frost growled as white and lavender foam dripped from his lips.

The words caused Amaruq to freeze. These were not the words of his pack mate, his friend. Even though Frost was a great white wolf, one of the most fearsome creatures of the northern reaches of Orth, he would never disrespect his Alpha had he been in his right mind.

"I see you, friend," Amaruq said, trying a different tactic. "I see you, but I hear somebody else, somebody speaking through you."

Frost laughed. "You're too clever for your own good," he said through his bared teeth, his tongue sliding out in a grotesque fashion. "Once you have joined my ranks, our numbers will swell across the north."

"Your ranks?" Amaruq asked. "And who exactly are you?"

"Don't you recognize me? It hasn't been so long since you banished me from your pack."

"Shade!" Amaruq snarled, his hackles now raised to their full height. "Or should I call you Omega?" Omega was the lowest form of insult an Alpha could give to a wolf. It marked him as being the lowest of the low, the last in line for ascendency to the leadership.

"Whose pack have you joined? Why would you do this to your kin?"

"My master's plans are his own, but in return for my servitude, he will make me the northern pack leader." While Shade continued speaking through Frost, the white wolf had been closing in on Amaruq in an ever-tightening circle.

"Master? You are a dire wolf, and we serve no master, only the *pack*," Amaruq snarled, unable to mask his disdain for Shade.

"You expected me to serve *you*," Shade said, his voice full of contempt. He shook his great head as lavender spittle flew in every direction. "You expected everyone except your precious mate, Polaris, to serve you."

"Follow! Not serve! I am nobody's master, but I set the rules for the pack. If any member does not like my rules, they are permitted to leave."

Shade laughed in disgust. "To what end, oh glorious leader? If we leave the pack, we have to leave the area. You won't let loners hunt on your lands. When we leave, we enter into another Alpha's territory. If we don't join their pack, we're killed outright."

"Your mind is twisted," Amaruq said as he turned to face the white wolf. "I forced you off my lands because you were killing indiscriminately, like you always have. You attacked the humans and their food, turning them against us."

"And now all the infected wolves will do the same, indiscriminately attacking everything and everyone in sight." Shade barked out a laugh as he lunged for Amaruq's throat. The white wolf sailed past the pack leader as he stepped to the side. Throughout the entire conversation, Amaruq had been waiting for him to make his move, which made it easy to avoid the white wolf's powerful jaws.

"Shade, enough! You don't have to do this."

Amaruq had no desire to kill Frost, especially if he was somehow under the control of this lowly, exiled pack member. As the great white wolf wheeled around for another attack, Amaruq hit him with his magical breath, a steady stream of frost and ice pellets forming as he opened his mouth, using his breath as his weapon. Even though Frost was practically immune to the cold, it created a distraction, allowing Amaruq to move around him.

When the flurry came to an end, Frost's eyes became their natural jade-green color.

"Kill me," he whimpered. "Don't let him take control of my mind again. I can't ..."

Frost's eyes glazed over again and turned the same milky white as they were previously.

"Don't you think it's fitting?" Shade said, once again fully in control of the white wolf's mind. "That your enemy will bring you down using your friend?" Frost's mouth was opened wide in a silent, mocking laugh.

"My friend is, and always will be, my friend. You, Omega, are a blight on this world and I will make it my mission to see that you are wiped off the face of it." Shade cringed at being called Omega.

Shade moved into attack range. He might have been in the body of Frost, but he did not have Frost's fighting skills or instincts. His movements were crude, his actions predictable. Shade's muscles bunched up, announcing his impending leap.

Amaruq dropped to the ground as Frost's body sailed at him. He rolled onto his back while the great white wolf's teeth snapped haphazardly at his face. As soon as the wolf had passed over him, the black wolf scrabbled back to his feet. With one quick lunge, the pack leader was on Frost. He wrapped his massive jaws around the white wolf's throat. Frost fought to free himself, twisting and turning to force the Alpha's jaws open. He raked at the obsidian wolf's belly with his hind paws but was unable to make contact. Amaruq shook his friend's body violently and without mercy. With each shake of the head, his fangs buried deeper into his neck. When the teeth met with the white wolf's arteries, the contest was over. Frost struggled for a brief moment before he succumbed to the attack.

Amaruq released his grip on the wolf and Frost's lifeless body dropped in a heap on the ground.

"May Fenrir guide you to the great Beyond where you will walk with our ancestors."

Amaruq unleashed a mournful howl, announcing the death of his pack member and friend. Along with the echo of his voice off the nearby mountain ranges, dozens of other wolves added their voices to the heartbreaking song.

"I will avenge your death, my friend. I will find Shade and whoever it is that's controlling him. I will end their miserable lives so that you may rest in peace."

Amaruq sniffed the air, trying to pick up any scent that may have been on the wind. If Shade was within range, he'd hunt him down and end this madness once and for all, but there were no scents other than those of Amaruq and Frost.

"Helja!" the big wolf swore. "If I can't smell him, maybe I can follow Frost's trail back to him."

Moving back to where Frost had fallen, Amaruq began to retrace his steps. They were haphazard wanderings, perhaps the result of Frost trying to fight against Shade's mind control. They eventually headed off in a straight line. The dire wolf put his nose into a paw print, trying to determine how old it was. A drip of crimson fell onto the bare ground, followed by several more.

"Sweet Fenrir, no!"

Amaruq swiped at the side of his muzzle with his paw, leaving it covered in blood. He could only assume that Frost had managed to put his teeth on him as he went for the kill. He hadn't felt the bite, but the evidence suggested that it happened all the same. Amaruq recognized immediately that the wound was a death-sentence. The infected wolf's saliva would transmit the disease to him, and within a few days, he too would lose his mind.

Seeing that time was working against him, Amaruq picked up his pace as he continued to retrace Frost's steps. He hoped beyond reason that they would lead him back to wherever Shade was hiding.

Amaruq followed the trail for well over an hour before he spotted the first wolf in the distance. He quickly barked out a greeting to a smaller gray wolf, who replied with a series of high-pitched yelps. The nature of the response was in part a submissive greeting to the Alpha, and part warning.

Amaruq broke into a full run, each stride covering nearly thirty feet.

There were four gray wolves circling a fifth wolf. Like Frost, her eyes were milky white. She was snarling and snapping at the surrounding air, attacking an unseen enemy.

"Back away from her!" Amaruq barked out. The gray wolves immediately distanced themselves from the infected wolf. Since Amaruq was already sick, he had no fear of the smaller wolf's bite.

"Are you going to kill them all?" the infected wolf asked Amaruq. "My disease is spreading faster than even you can run."

"Omega!" Amaruq snarled. "Why? These wolves are of the north. They are your family. How can you torture them like this, all so that you can try to claim dominance?"

"Omega?" questioned one of the wolves, a small female who could not have seen more than one winter. "Her name is Sheba, and she is no *omega*."

Amaruq would have liked to explain it to the pack, but Sheba suddenly decided that she was going to attack. With lightning speed, the smaller wolf moved on Amaruq, trying desperately to put a bite on him. Her strike targeted the dire wolf's legs, and it took Amaruq by surprise. She was not trying to kill him, she was trying to wound him, to infect him.

Amaruq didn't get to be Prime Alpha by allowing an opponent to easily fool him. As Sheba moved in on his legs, the dire wolf leapt out of the way. With one swift motion, he took the back of her neck in his jaws. She flailed about, trying to claw at Amaruq's throat in a futile attempt to force him to release his grip on her.

I'm sorry.

With a single shake, the female's neck snapped. As her lifeless body hit the ground, the milky-white color of her eyes disappeared.

The group of gray wolves immediately began to howl, announcing the death of their sister. The Prime Alpha cut off their mournful song.

"We will mourn our dead when there is time, but for now, we need to find the source of this disease."

The five gray wolves immediately bowed to Amaruq and awaited his command.

"Shade was my pack's Omega. He is involved in this somehow." Amaruq explained. "You will find my mate, Polaris, and have her meet me at our den."

The wolves' eyes became wide with fear. They looked back and forth at each other, waiting for someone to speak up. Finally, a female, so small that she could not have seen more than one winter, stepped forward.

"We cannot do as you command," she whimpered hesitantly. She knew that defying her leader was practically a death sentence, but she confronted him anyway. Her ears were down, and her tail was tucked between her legs. She crawled up to Amaruq, her belly never leaving the ground.

"That was an order!" the wolf snarled. "It was not a request."

The female rolled onto her back, exposing her throat to her leader. If he wanted to kill her, she would make it easy for him.

"Forgive me, my lord, but ..."

"But what?" Amaruq snarled at her, crimson spittle flying from his maw.

The poor little female was petrified, but she found it within herself to speak.

"Your mate has been bitten. Her mind is not her own."

As she spoke the last of her words, the tiny wolf closed her eyes and waited for Amaruq to snuff out her life. After several seconds, she opened them. Amaruq's gaze was vacant, his eyes unfocused.

Who will lead the pack now?

The news of his mate's condition utterly shattered his heart, but as always, the pack came first. When he finally managed to regain control of his emotions, the wolf called out to the young female.

"What is your name?"

The small wolf leapt to her feet and immediately took on a submissive stance.

"I am Amilta, and this is my pack."

Despite the situation, seeing this tiny wolf declare herself a pack leader made Amaruq laugh.

Thinking that he had just insulted her, Amilta snarled under her breath, making the wolf laugh even harder.

"How old are you?" he snarled. His change in tone caused the little wolf to back away. She lowered her head so that her eyes stared at the ground.

"I am eight years old," she responded. At no point did she raise her eyes to meet her leader's.

"Eight?" Amaruq questioned. "You don't look like you've seen more than a single winter." When she did not reply, he barked at Amilta. "Speak when I ask you a question."

This time, the little wolf raised her head and met his gaze, unflinching.

"I am eight years old," she replied with authority. "But I have been a wolf for a little more than a moon."

Amaruq's eyes narrowed at her words. He began pulling back his lips, exposing his ferocious teeth to her.

Once again, Amilta lowered her eyes. As she did, her body shimmered slightly and her wolf form melted away, revealing a young Berrat girl dressed in rough-spun wool, adorned with beads and small shells. She was small, even for a Berrat, barely more than three feet tall. Her long, pointed ears twitched as she waited for her lord's reaction. Beads of sweat began to form on her deep bronze skin.

"You're a Berrat whelp!" the wolf couldn't have hidden his shock if he tried. The other four wolves moved in beside Amilta and bared their teeth at Amaruq. "And your pack is willing to die to protect you."

"Be still," the small girl cooed at her wolves. "If our leader decides I should die, then that's what I will do. If it is Fenrir's will, then it will happen."

"How dare you speak our god's name!" Amaruq snarled. "You and your kind are followers of the old gods, and they have no time for us wolves."

"Gaia, the earth god, has no time for wolves," the Berrat girl laughed and raised her face to the dire wolf. "She has no time because she's busy keeping the whole world safe. She knows the plight of the creatures of the wild, and that's why she has asked Fenrir to care for the wolves." The words seemed to take the wolf aback. His snarls died off as he cocked an eyebrow at the tiny girl.

Amilta's eyes became wide, and her jaw dropped.

"My lord, you've been bitten." She reached out to touch the place on his muzzle where Frost had wounded him.

Before she could lay her hand on him, Amaruq pulled away, putting space between him and the small Berrat girl.

"You can no longer search for Shade, but we will take up the hunt for you." The small girl's cheeks were wet with tears. Even at her young age, she understood the ramifications of the Prime Alpha's death.

"Who are you to hunt a dire wolf, even if he is a lowly omega?" Amaruq snarled, infuriated by the impetuous little girl who stood before him. "You would dare to give *me* commands?"

"Be at peace, Lord Amaruq, leader of the north-eastern realm," said a calm, melodic voice.

The dire wolf spun around to see who might speak to him this way, and as he did, he encountered a great white wolf. She had long beaded braids and painted whorls on her brilliant white fur.

"Fenrir, my god!" he gasped before he dropped his head low. "I am graced by your presence."

"Arise, Amaruq," she commanded, her voice full of compassion. "It is a dark day when my chosen leader has been infected."

The wolf-god changed her form to that of a young Berrat warrior. She looked very much like Amilta, with long white braids and blue whorls painted on her deep bronze skin. She placed her tiny hand on the wolf's head.

"Please," she said as she stroked his thick, black fur. "There is little time, and there is much to do."

"What do you ask of me?" Amaruq questioned, his eyes shifting from his god to the Berrat child. He was surprised that she showed no fear of the god standing before her.

"Let Amilta take up the search for Shade. You need to seek out your mate because, in doing so, you will set this world's destiny into motion."

The big wolf's face was awash with confusion. He blinked slowly at the Berrat warrior.

"I had believed my destiny was to lead the wolves into the *final battle*."

Fenrir buried her face in Amaruq's neck.

"I thought so too, but destinies change. Nothing is written in stone, especially where the *Fates* are concerned." She passed her hand over the dire wolf's muzzle, healing his open wound. "I can heal the wound, but I cannot cure your infection. I am afraid that there is no cure for the affliction. It will only release its hold when death takes you."

"My passing will not keep me from my destiny." Amaruq pulled away from Fenrir, allowing him to look her in the eyes. "I will resist the call of The Great Beyond. I will not yield to its summons. I *will* lead my pack into the final battle."

Tears began to roll down Fenrir's cheeks. Her shoulders heaved as she held back a sob.

"Never before have I witnessed a soul with such resolve. Well, almost never." She took the black wolf's muzzle in her tiny hands and drew his face close to hers. "And you will meet her too, before your time here is done."

Fenrir wiped the tears from her cheeks and turned to Amilta. "Take what's left of your pack north to the city of Cormorant. I cannot say for certain, but I believe that's where Shade's magic is coming from. If you find him, track him down, but do not attack. He is under someone's protection, someone much too powerful for you to engage."

"Yes, my god," Amilta replied before she transformed back into her wolf form. Without another word, she loped off to the north-west, in the direction of Cormorant.

Amaruq watched as Amilta and her small pack of gray wolves disappeared across the fields, the tall yellow grasses swallowing them like a wave over tiny rocks.

"She's only a child," he said before the dire wolf turned his gaze back to Fenrir. "She cannot stand against Shade, even if she had a dozen wolves with her. He will eviscerate them."

"She will not need to stand against him," Fenrir replied. Her eyes had a distant look to them. "But she is far stronger than her tiny body might suggest. She may have been born Berrat, but she has a wolf's spirit."

"Much like you, I'm guessing." Amaruq laughed lightly as he raised his eyebrows at his god. "But you were an accomplished warrior before Titan raised you to divine status. It was the only good thing that *false god* ever did for our world. He seeks only death and destruction for his own personal amusement."

"He is not all bad," Fenrir said with a small shrug. "He is but a wayward child, with nobody to teach him any better, but that is about to change. Everything is about to change." Fenrir gave Amaruq one last big hug. "Run now. Run to your mate. She is near your den." Tears again began to fill the little god's eyes. "Her time on Orth is coming to an end."

Sensing that the wolf was about to bolt away, she grabbed him by the face and stared deeply into his bright jade-green eyes.

"What you will see will drive you mad. Pay no heed to what your eyes are showing you. Instead, listen to what your heart is telling you. I see it clearly now. It is meant to happen, and you are meant to be a part of it. Heed my words, Amaruq. Steel yourself for what is to come."

The big wolf bowed his head, allowing the bright white star on his forehead to touch Fenrir's shoulder.

"I do not understand, my god. But I will try." With that, Amaruq turned and loped off due west towards his den.

Amaruq raced across the countryside, through large open meadows of tall grasses and wildflowers, up and over gentle, rolling forested hills. Two huge mountain ranges rose up on either side, telling him that he was nearing his den and his mate. The wolf could typically run many hours without rest, but after only a few, he was already panting heavily, and he was unable to steady his breathing. His heart was beating much too fast, forcing him to slow to a trot, hoping that he could continue to move forward while regaining some of his strength.

"Now you're mine!" the voice of Shade chimed in his mind.

"Get out of my head!" Amaruq snarled as he spun around, hoping beyond reason that he might catch sight of Shade.

"You might be able to rid yourself of me now, but when the poison fully takes its hold on you ..."

Amaruq finally pushed Shade out of his mind. He was panting even harder, his chest heaving, stinging with every breath.

What magic is this, that he can reach into my mind so easily? It's only been a few hours since I became infected.

The big wolf's skin felt like it was on fire. He dropped to the ground and began scratching at the ruff of his neck with his hind paw as he ripped out chunks of fur. The large black tufts blew away with the wind.

Seeing how fast the infection was progressing, Amaruq pressed on, despite the way his lungs were burning from the exertion. It didn't take long before he felt his mate's presence. Dire wolves were able to communicate with their mates from a short distance, even when they could not see one another.

Amaruq bent his head down and let it sway side to side as he reached out through the *bond*. Finally, he established a connection with his mate, but her mind was a jumble of confusion and fear. Her thoughts were coming fast and incoherently, as though she was trapped in a fever dream. Wading through the chaos, Amaruq pushed deeper into her mind, only stopping when he sensed Shade's presence. Amidst the mayhem and madness, Amaruq could hear his Omega taunting his mate, provoking her, driving her to madness.

"Alpha, where are you?" his mate shrieked, her thoughts cutting through the big wolf's foggy mind.

It was Sable, his Beta! Relief rushed through Amaruq when he discovered the infected wolf was 'a mate,' but it wasn't Polaris. As the alpha male, it was his responsibility to sire all pups within his pack, so he considered all females of breeding age his mate, but Polaris was his true mate, his true love.

He suddenly grasped the dire reality of the situation. As Beta, the second-in-command, Sable had the potential to transmit the disease, unchecked, throughout their immediate pack. Given her status, no member within their ranks would dare defy her. Another wolf wouldn't even attempt to put her down, making her an unstoppable carrier of the contagion.

His position as Alpha Prime made matters worse. Far worse. As the leader of the entire northern realm, there was no wolf to keep him in check. While Sable could spread the infection through her pack, Amaruq could decimate the entire region.

I must put Sable down. Once I do, I will find a way to end my own life. The cycle must be broken.

With renewed purpose, Amaruq dug deep into his magic, hoping to find a way to mask the pain he was enduring. He knew where Sable was, he just needed to get to her and kill her.

Minutes into a hard run, Amaruq's lungs were burning so badly that he was on the verge of passing out. He reduced his speed to a slow trot, but each step still felt like hot steel was being thrust into his chest.

He was panting heavily when his Beta, Sable, came into view, but she was not alone. Amaruq's mate was locked in pitched combat with two humans.

The first was a young, petite nomad girl with long black hair, dressed in studded leather armor, wielding a small wooden shield and an iron battle hammer. The second, a much larger, young nomad male, was with her. Like the girl, he too had long black hair, but his was braided into a single, long ponytail. He moved gracefully in his simple leather armor. Although he carried only a single short sword, he wielded it like it was a natural extension of his arm. Both were young adults, but their movements marked them as skilled warriors.

A blind rage suddenly filled Amaruq's mind. Humans were attacking his Beta. He had to come to his Sable's aid and fight by her side. Even though he was unable to run, the great black wolf pressed forward as fast as his body would let him. Unbidden, Fenrir's words crashed through his anger. *What you will see will drive you mad. Pay no heed to what your eyes are showing you. Instead, listen to what your heart is telling you.*

Amaruq came to a halt and laid down in the tall grass. Through the swaying stocks of green, he watched and waited.

I came to end her life. Maybe they will kill her for me.

As he shook off the idea, fury rose in him again, his breath coming faster.

It is not their task to end her life, it is mine!

Once again, he remembered Fenrir's words. *You need to seek out your mate. In doing so, you will set this world's destiny into motion.*

He could only assume that this was what she meant. Amaruq watched as the young girl drew Sable's to her. She banged her shield, attracting the wolf away from the man.

This young girl has a strong spirit.

The small woman reminded him of the tiny Berrat girl who was off seeking Shade's location. Both girls possessed the heart of a wolf. The small human was worthy.

Sable began to circle around the girl as she worked her way towards the larger male. She kept her head low, and her teeth bared. Even from this distance, Amaruq could see that her eyes were glazed over, the same milky color of Frost's eyes before he killed him.

As Beta padded to the left, the young girl barked out an order to her cohort. As she did, she leapt at Sable, slamming her shield into the dire wolf's shoulder. The impact sent Amaruq's mate rolling across the grass.

Sable quickly sprung back to her feet and turned her attention to the girl, the one she now perceived to be the greatest threat. With a single bound, the wolf closed the distance between her and the adolescent female. The wolf's jaws, covered with foam and drool, snapped wildly at the girl's face.

Again, using her shield as a weapon, the young woman slammed it into Beta's open maw. It didn't appear that the attack did any damage to the wolf, but it clearly enraged Beta even more.

Clever girl. If she can make Beta lose control of her emotions, she'll open herself up to the attacks.

As Amaruq expected, Beta began attacking the girl with reckless abandon, her teeth snapping wildly. The young woman easily avoided every strike. Beta's attacks were cut short. She howled out in pain and dropped to the ground. The young man's sword dripped with her blood. As she was attacking the girl, Beta completely ignored the other opponent, and she paid the price for not being aware of her surroundings.

Gravely wounded, Beta picked herself up off the ground. Her movements were weak, and her footing was unsure. She gathered up what strength she had left and coiled her muscles for one final attack on the young man. Before she could strike, the female human brought her hammer down in an overhand swing, crushing the dire wolf's head on impact. Whatever torture Beta was enduring from the poison, instantly came to an end. Even though Amaruq knew this was what needed to happen, he lowered his head in respect to his second in command.

When Amaruq raised his head, he watched the two humans inspecting each other.

They're checking to see if they're infected. They understand the danger.

A moment later, a large wolfdog sprang from the grasses, racing for the group. Amaruq couldn't be certain, but he sensed a connection to Fenrir in the animal. Were these three somehow associated with the wolf-god? It didn't seem plausible, but the Alpha Prime's instincts on such matters were rarely wrong.

After a brief reunion, the human male ran off with the young woman hot on his trail. Amaruq's breathing was now back to normal, and the searing pain in his chest had abated. He waited a few minutes to make sure the humans had left before he went to check on Beta.

Amaruq cringed when he witnessed Beta's condition. The force the tiny teenager had put into her attack, the one that had sent Beta to the Beyond, was impressive.

"I'm sorry your life had to end like this," Amaruq said as he inspected Beta's broken body. The affliction had badly ravaged her. More than half of her coat had fallen out, and the rest was matted and blood-stained. "I will see that your death is avenged."

Amaruq was about to leave when he felt a compulsion to bring Beta's body back to his cave. As he was deciding what to do, a voice broke through to his mind, the words like poison that twisted his thoughts.

"Bring her to your den. Leave her with the prizes she has collected for me, with the prizes that you will collect for me."

The pull on Amaruq's mind was too strong. It was relentless, merciless, the affliction wearing him down, making it impossible to fight off Shade's magic. The dire wolf flew into a rage and began snapping at the wind, hoping that somehow Shade was nearby, maybe invisible, but with some luck, he would be caught by a random attack.

The voice inside his head called out to him again, this time more forcefully.

"Bring her to your den. Leave her with the prizes she has collected for me, with the prizes that you will collect for me."

Unable to push the voice from his mind, Amaruq took the fallen wolf by the scruff of her neck and started dragging her to his cave.

⚬⚬⚬⚬◈⚬⚬⚬⚬

By the time Amaruq made it to the entrance of his den, a natural cave in an outcropping of rocks, his chest was heaving badly. The burning in his lungs was still there, but it was dulled by the constant bombardment of thoughts that Shade forced into this mind.

As he stepped into the outer tunnel that led into his home, he encountered her, the tiny nomad woman who killed Sable. The surprise of seeing her in his den pushed Shade out of his mind, allowing Amaruq to think clearly.

Salvation! I just need her to kill me!

Amaruq dropped the lifeless body of Beta onto the ground in front of him. He stared briefly at her carcass, fearing that the disease would take his mind again. Slowly, deliberately, he stepped over Beta's corpse. With his head low and his ears pinned, he bared his ferocious teeth at the girl. A low, threatening growl rumbled from deep within his throat.

Kill me! Please, kill me!

At that very moment, the small girl unleashed a frost attack on him. The air glistened as it traveled towards Amaruq, coalescing into a giant ice shard by the time it hit the wolf squarely in the chest. The ice bolt exploded on impact, causing practically no damage to the wolf.

"I'm immune to cold attacks, you foolish girl," he said, projecting his thoughts at her. *"Use your hammer! End my life."*

Amaruq lunged at her, throwing his weight into the girl, knocking her hard against the wall.

Make her angry. Force her to kill me.

He started slowly moving around her in a similar fashion to a lion stalking its prey. Each movement of his huge body blocked her from retreating into his den.

"Kill her!" the voice of Shade shrieked, once again breaking through Amaruq's mental defenses. *"She's down and helpless! Finish her!"* Using as much will as he could muster, Amaruq fought against Shade's voice. For his pack, for all wolves, he could not allow himself to lose control.

In the few seconds that Amaruq fended off Shade, the young female drew her battle hammer.

Good girl. Clever girl.

"Hey wolf!" a voice called from behind Amaruq from within his den. "Hey, over here!" it called out again.

Shade, once again, assailed Amaruq's mind, his voice urging him to kill the girl. As he began to bear down on her, Amaruq felt the bite of steel on his hip. The large dog sprang forward, haranguing Amaruq.

"There are three of them," Shade screeched in his mind as Amaruq spun around to face his new attacker. *"Kill them all! Kill him first, he's the dangerous one!"*

The magic in Shade's voice pushed Amaruq into a berserker's rage. He launched a series of attacks, his teeth and claws working in deadly unison. The human male's defenses broke down immediately, allowing the dire wolf to get in multiple, devastating bites. In mere seconds, the young man was drenched in his own blood. Amaruq opened his jaws, ready to finish him off, when something crashed against him. The force hurled his body through the air, slamming him into the side of the tunnel.

The searing pain of broken bones knocked Shade from his mind, allowing Amaruq to clearly see his attacker. He tried to stand, to meet his end on his feet, but there was no strength left in them. The Alpha Prime gazed at his attacker, desperately wanting her to take his life while was still in control of himself. He stood motionless, begging her to finish him.

His heart swelled as the battle hammer come towards him in a wide-arcing swing. Before the attack snuffed out his being, one last thought passed through his mind ...

Thank you!

There was a sudden, breathtaking burst of warmth that radiated through the wolf's body. Amaruq's mind was free, truly free of the relentless, never-ending battle with Shade.

"It is time for you to pass on to the great Beyond," a sweet, melodic, familiar voice said.

"Fenrir?" Amaruq called out.

"Your time on Orth has come to an end my friend, creature of the wild. Join your brothers and sisters in eternal peace. You've earned it."

"Fenrir?" he called out again. Amaruq couldn't see her, but he knew his god. "My work is not done here. I must stop Shade. He seeks to rule the northern packs. It cannot be allowed to happen."

"It's your time to move on, Amaruq. Others will take up the fight for you. You have broken the cycle of affliction. You were the last. The young girl who brought you peace, her name is Kit Standing Bear. She will take up the quest now so that you may join the Beyond."

"No!" Amaruq growled back. "I will not leave until Shade is finished. If the human girl is to do this, then I will help her."

"Your spirit is as strong in death as it was in life," Fenrir said, her voice full of love and hope. "I will permit this, but first, I need to speak with Kit. Seek me out to the north at my hut in the woods."

The intense warmth that Amaruq was feeling disappeared with Fenrir. As Amaruq's spirit rose from his body, he looked down at the young girl wailing over the fallen male, her mate perhaps.

"Titan, I beg of you," she called out. "I am but your humble servant, once again asking for your assistance. This man does not deserve to lose his life this day, as a result of saving mine!" She pressed her hands against a horrible wound across his side. Blood was gushing between her fingers as she cried out again. "Please, Titan, help me save his life. In his place, I offer up my own."

A blinding white light filled the room.

"You would offer your life to save a stranger, a man you only met hours ago?"

A visage of a human woman appeared next to the girl. She looked over at Amaruq and gave him a small wink. The woman's voice was quiet and smooth, but still, it echoed through the chamber.

"I accept your offer."

The woman reached down and touched her finger to the young man's forehead. A warm, golden aura appeared around his body. It engulfed both him and the small girl. Kit fell to the side and rolled onto her back, revealing her mate, fully healed. When he opened his eyes, he saw Kit's lifeless body lying still on her back next to him.

"Sweet Titan, no!" he cried out as he took the girl in his arms. He placed his ear to her chest, checking for a heartbeat. His eyes became wide, and he called to the female, desperation in his voice.

"Kit! Kit, wake up!"

When Kit's eyes fluttered open, he quickly wiped tears from his cheek and gave her a warm smile.

"I thought I had lost you."

"You're okay!" Kit screamed, practically knocking the man off his feet as she sprung up from the ground. She quickly pulled him into a deep hug and pressed her face against his chest. "I thought you were going to die."

The young man pushed Kit back to look at her.

"Why would I have died? The wolf never got near me. You were like a crazy person, swinging your hammer about like a berserker in a full rage."

"But you were bitten!"

Kit examined his side and his arm. They were completely intact with no sign of injury whatsoever. It was then that she looked down at the body of the wolf, her face showing a profound sense of loss for putting him down.

Kit bent down before Amaruq's body and offered a prayer for his passing.

The wolf's spirit shook his head.

You are a remarkable person, Kit Standing Bear. I have witnessed it, and so has a Fate. In you, I put my trust, my faith. Amaruq's spirit moved next to Kit. Her aura, her life force, was so strong that he could feel it drawing him in. It filled him with hope.

Placing his muzzle next to her ear, Amaruq whispered, his voice full of sorrow and rage, "Avenge!"

AFTERWORD

Thank you for reading my novel. Reviews are critical to the success of every indie author. I would ask that you leave a review on Amazon, GoodReads, and Book-Bub. If you have any thoughts or comments that you'd like to share directly with me, I would love to hear from you. You can email me at paul@paulmouchet.ca.

Do you want more stories? You find links to all my novels on my website. You can also sign up for my newsletter, Marvelous Mondays, which I send out every other week. They're full of fun pics, snippets of what's going on in my life, and book news.

Also, if you'd like to discuss my stories with me and other fans, in a safe, friendly environment, please connect with me on my Facebook group ~ Paul Mouchet's Reader's Group.

You'll find the link to all my social media accounts on my website. I look forward to chatting with you.

Happy Reading!

www.ingramcontent.com/pod-product-compliance
Lightning Source LLC
Chambersburg PA
CBHW032143190726
48290CB00005BB/1379